ISLES OF CORRUPTION

ELYSE THOMSON

TWO LAURELS PRESS

Isles of Corruption

For questions and comments about the quality of this book, please contact us at elysethomson.author@gmail.com

eBook: 978-1-7388426-8-1

Paperback: 978-1-7388426-9-8

Hardcover: 978-1-7383655-0-0

CONTENT WARNINGS

For my readers who prefer not to read the content warnings, please feel free to skip this section and dive right in.

For my readers who would prefer a list of content warnings before proceeding, I've provided what I hope is a fairly substantive list below.

Content Warnings: death, grief over dead sibling, grief over dead spouse, violence, blood and gore, maiming, swearing, sexism, classicism, pregnancy, consensual on-page sex.

Glossary

<u>**Royal Titles in the Empire of Mages**</u>

Emperor/Empress: Supreme rulers of the Empire. Addressed as Your Majesty.

<u>**Noble Titles in the Empire of Mages in Descending Order of Power:**</u>

Magister: Male governor of an imperial province. Addressed as Your Grace. Plural = Magistri

Magistra: Female governor of an imperial province. Addressed as Your Grace. Plural = Magistrae

Dominus: Son of a magister. Addressed as Your Resplendence. Plural = Domini

Domina: Daughter of a magister. Addressed as Your Resplendence. Plural = Dominae

Illustrus: Landowning nobleman with a significant estate and/or distinguished military service. Plural = Illustri

Illustra: Wife of an illustrus. Rarely, a landowning noblewoman with a significant estate and/or distinguished military service. Plural = Illustrae

Nobilissimus: Son of an illustrus or a minor nobleman with a small estate. Plural = Nobilissimi

Nobilissima: Daughter of an illustrus or wife of a nobilissimus. Rarely, a minor noblewoman with a small estate. Plural = Nobilissimae

Governmental Titles in the Empire of Mages in Descending Order of Influence:

Praetor: The head of the imperial bureaucracy. Answers to the imperial family directly. Directs all administrative officials in the Empire.

Logothete: Minister in charge of a large administrative department (Taxes, Public Works, etc), answers to the praetor directly.

Asekretis: Middling minister assigned to tasks or specific projects by a logothete. Answers to a logothete directly.

Notarios: Lowest ranked bureaucrat, assigned humble tasks by an asekretis. Answers to an asekretis directly.

Military Titles in the Empire of Mages:

Strategos: Top general of the Empire's military forces. Answers to the imperial family directly.

Admiral: Top officer of the Empire's naval forces. Answers to the strategos directly.

Slang in the Empire of Mages:

Elementalist: Elemental magic elitists who discriminate against those without elemental magical gifts (control of fire, water, earth, wind, lightning, darkness or light). They believe theirs is the superior form of magic.

Menial: A mage without an elemental magical gift.

Feral: A derogatory term for beast mages.

Royal and Noble Titles in Elmheim and the Riverlands

King: Ruler of a kingdom. Often married to a king/queen, except in a witchlands territory.

Queen: Ruler of a kingdom/queendom. Often married to a king/queen.

Consort: Husband of the queen of a witchlands territory, or alternatively, husband of a noblewoman in a witchlands territory.

Prince/Princess: Child of the king/queen.

Jarl: Ruler of a large territory, often made up of many towns and villages. Gender-neutral term. Title can be hereditary or bestowed by the king/queen.

Fru: A noblewoman or spouse of the Jarl. Ruler of a small territory, often made up of several towns or villages. If married to a Jarl, co-ruler of a large territory, often made up of many towns and villages. Title can be hereditary, or bestowed through marriage to a Jarl.

Drottin: A nobleman or spouse of the Jarl. Ruler of a small territory, often made up of several towns or villages. If married to a Jarl, co-ruler of a large territory, often made up of many towns and villages. Title can be hereditary, or bestowed through marriage to a Jarl.

Governmental and Administrative Titles in Elmheim and the Riverlands

Wise Woman: Administrator of a town or village. Strictly used for witchland territories, and only given to a woman.

Shield-Master: Administrator of a town or village. Used throughout the Riverlands. Gender-neutral term.

Huskarl: The right-hand of the jarl, aiding the jarl in a variety of ways. Often helps administer the jarl's territory.

Slang and General Terms used in Elmheim and the Riverlands

Draugr: The hungry, violent, undead creature that results from someone succumbing to the corruption curse. Not everyone who is cursed becomes a draugr. Plural = **draugar**.

Witchlands: A territory of primarily witches and wizards that is ruled by witches. Fiercely matriarchal.

Witchling: A person of mixed magical heritage whose witch/wizard magic/appearance is most prominent.

Faeling: A person of mixed magical heritage whose fae magic/appearance is most prominent.

Elvish: A person of mixed magical heritage whose elven magic/appearance is most prominent.

LETHE, THE EMPIRE OF MAGES

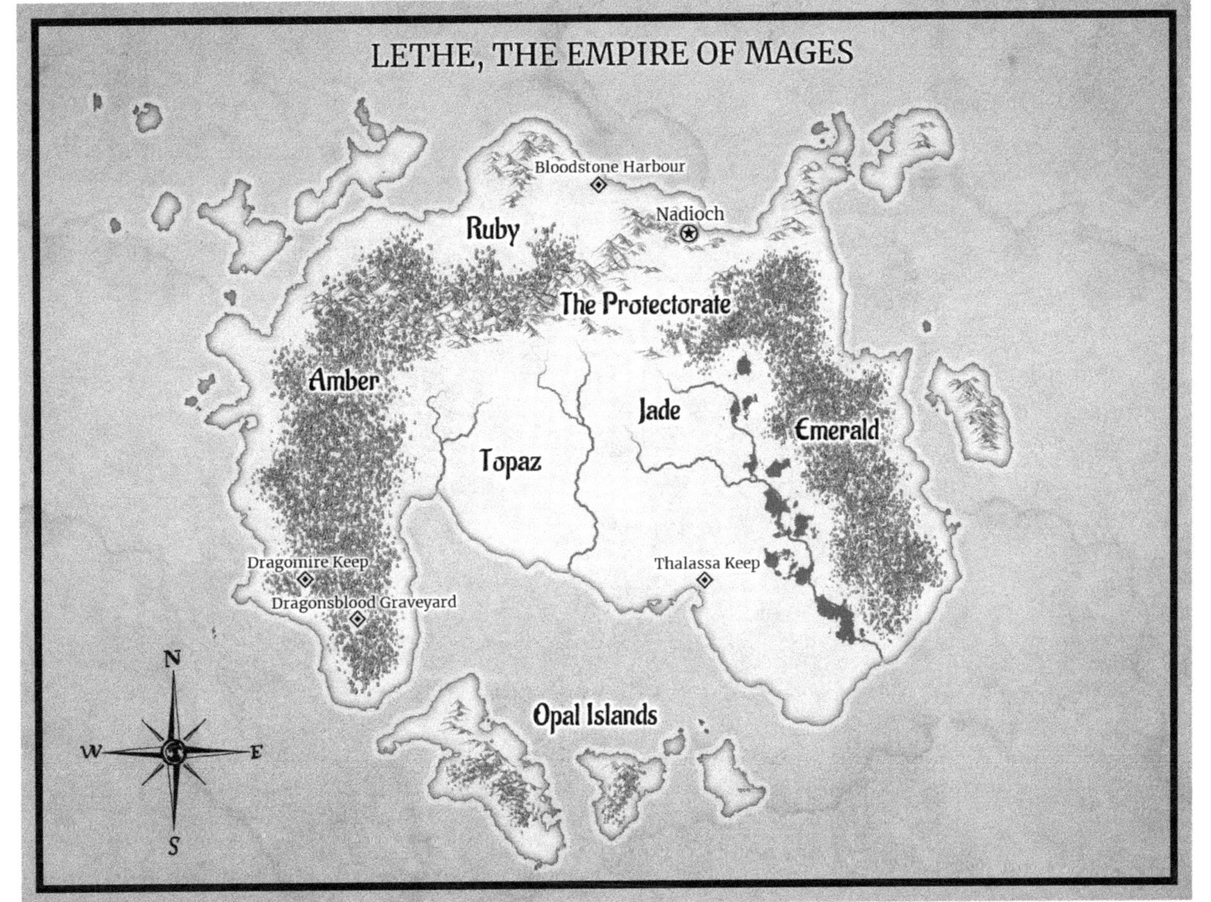

S
E W
N
Ashla
Sigimar's Keep
ASKR
Elmheim
Kingdom of Rei
Nor
Agnetha's Home
Queendom of Isro
Wassa's Village
Otmar's Keep
Kingdom of Gortos
THE RIVERLANDS

For Lisa,
My 'wife'
I miss you.

PROLOGUE

Attaining glory was a harrowing business.

Sigimar stepped closer to his twin brother as the sickly grey forest enveloped them. Through the gloom, tangles of ancient, twisted branches reached out like grasping talons. Footsteps fell as soft as whispers on the hard-packed earth, their silence not out of reverence, but abundant caution. A thick, dark shroud of fog had blocked out all but the barest hint of sunlight since they'd entered the lost, ancient kingdom of Ashla three days past.

Sigimar's brother held his hand aloft, cutting through the fog with the warm, glowing, magical light emanating from the tips of his fingers. Branches dissolved into ashes, flaking away and disappearing before they hit the ground. Dag's light was the only thing keeping them from choking to death on the toxic miasma pervading everything in Ashla. The further into this cursed landscape they ventured, the thicker it became.

A wellspring, the source of the malicious haze, was close at hand. If they could just reach it, Dag could purify it and free the land of this corruption. At least, that was what the ancient tales surmised.

In hindsight, perhaps betting their lives on disreputable sources was a foolish thing to do.

Sigimar gripped his axe. He didn't possess Dag's rare magic, or much magic at all, for that matter. He was there to protect his brother with bronze and brawn from what lurked on this side of the gloom. He hadn't failed them thus far. Sigimar prayed to the forgotten gods that it would remain so.

Dag's gaze rose to meet Sigimar's.

"The corruption has latched onto you," he whispered.

A thin scratch ran along Sigimar's arm, his coat and flesh split in an earlier attack. Normally his wounds would have healed, but black blood oozed out against his muddy-green skin, tiny dark veins forking out. Suppressing a shudder, Sigimar shrugged.

"Don't waste your light on me. I'll be fine for hours yet," Sigimar replied in a hushed voice.

Dag's brows furrowed in brotherly exasperation. He turned so that the light hit Sigimar's scratch head-on. The corruption hissed softly as it dissipated.

"We should turn back. I won't last another three days, not with the miasma this thick, and not going as slowly as we are. I can't even clear more than this small pocket around us, and the smallest breeze covers the trail we've cut."

Exhaustion dragged at his brother. Lines bracketed Dag's amber eyes. His green skin had an ashen cast, sweat dripping from his pale hair down his face despite the early autumn chill. Worry warred with the need to see this task through. They'd never gotten so close to the source of the miasma in all their centuries keeping it at bay along the frontier of Elmheim. They might never get another chance, might not be lucky enough to come so far without being killed. Or worse, someone else would discover what Sigimar had and beat them to the wellspring. Then all their toil, all their hardships, all their dreams, would be for naught. Being brash, being bold, charging in where others hesitated—that was how they would attain glory.

"Half a day more. If we haven't reached the wellspring by then, we'll turn back," Sigimar bargained.

Dag's shoulders sagged as he turned around to inch them forward through the fog. Sigimar hated to push Dag past his limits, but they would never defeat this encroaching corruption if they didn't take risks.

The raids on cattle and the unwary had grown in number these past few seasons. More and more warriors were tempted to try their luck in the miasma. After all, the king of Elmheim was offering extraordinary rewards for anyone who could dispel it, no matter how far-fetched the theory or method. But it meant more people lost to the curse, returning as the very draugar they'd sworn to kill.

Not an hour later, Sigimar caught a foul scent on the breeze. He touched Dag's shoulder and held a finger up to his lips. Dag nodded and gathered strands of magic together. Sigimar's long, pointed ears twitched as he listened for the footsteps of their stalker and readied the battle axe in his hand.

Behind him.

Sigimar turned. His axe was raised and already swinging as the pale grey draugr leapt at him, jagged maw wide, claws extended towards his throat. The axe crunched through the hardened shell of the creature's skin, cleaving it in two.

But the draugr squealed with its final breath before Sigimar could behead it.

"Shit," Sigimar cursed.

The sound echoed out in the fog. The eerie silence died as the forest erupted in clicking and screeches. Sigimar and Dag fought back-to-back, spilling corrupt blood with spell and bronze alike as creatures leapt at them with ravenous ferocity. Sigimar's hands were growing slick with the black ooze as bodies and parts piled up before him. He caught the last of them as it leapt from the branches, mouth wide and breath rank, hacking its head clean off.

Dag's back was pressed to his own, their ragged breaths resounding in his ears. Sigimar did his best to calm his racing heart and slow his breathing, to focus on any threat that might still be lurking. This far into the miasma, the draugar were getting smarter, less predictable.

"Have...have we got the lot of them?" Dag asked between gasps.

Sigimar strained his ears. Save for their panting, the forest was silent once again.

"I think so. Can you continue?" Sigimar asked as he wiped his face with the only relatively clean patch of his cloak left.

"I..." Dag hesitated.

"We should be safe for some time. We've killed all the creatures within screaming distance by now," Sigimar said.

Gods, he needed this to work out. If they could just find the wellspring, even if Dag didn't have the energy to purify it, they could tag it with a beacon spell and then come back better provisioned for it before the snows came. They would celebrate through the winter for having reclaimed long-lost and dearly needed land. Sigimar and Dag would finally be rewarded for their centuries defending the frontier, compensated with lands and titles. It was a crazy dream for orphan castoffs, but one they'd held dear their whole lives, as it was only on Elmheim's frontier that nameless soldiers could attain the same fortunes as princes and jarls.

Dag sighed.

"You're right. We don't have to go so slowly now." He turned around and held his hand aloft, light radiating forth, dissolving the corpses around them. The black ooze coating them hissed and bubbled, purified.

Sigimar clapped his brother on the back and smiled, following behind him. Though Dag was shorter and less brawny, he'd been exceptionally gifted with magic. He possessed the same ambitions that Sigimar did. Together they were the perfect team. Where others had failed, they would succeed.

Several more hours of brisk marching and even Sigimar was having difficulty in the miasma, his breathing laboured, as if the air were thinner here. Dag, however, seemed entranced.

"Can you feel that, Sig?"

"The weight on my chest?" Sigimar quipped as he swiped at the sweat-slicked, burgundy hair plastered to his brow.

"No, the...call of that magic? I think we're close."

Sigimar stretched his limited magic outward, sensing. Ahead, something dark and cold brushed along his mind. Sigimar recoiled and suppressed a shiver. He readied the axe at his side.

Sigimar grunted his assent.

"I hear it," Dag whispered, his voice reverent. "Gods below..."

"Then let's be done with this," Sigimar said.

Sigimar summoned the energy for one last push. If he put his all into reaching the wellspring, he was certain that they could purify Ashla, be rid of this damned miasma and become heroes of legend.

"Should we rest?" Dag asked.

Sigimar shook his head.

"It's not far. Let's purify this cursed thing. We'll use your enchanted stones to get back if we fail."

Every team that went into the miasma carried them as a last resort. The little stones, enchanted with the healing light, glowed weakly but could just manage to ward off the miasma and the draugar within. They were essential if one ventured too deeply and didn't have the strength to return. Naturally, they'd pilfered a few extras.

Without another word, Dag marched onward. Sigimar kept close, desperate for a breath of cleansed air, the vise around his lungs tightening with every step. As they neared the spot, Sigimar, even without using magic, could sense the terrible call of the wellspring.

Without warning, Sigimar and Dag stood in the eye of the storm, a strange, unnaturally calm clearing. It had been days since they'd had such visibility around them. In the centre of it stood a stave with malevolent, glowing symbols and a harsh, piercing blue gem the size of Sigimar's fist nestled atop. It listed to one side, sunk into a bubbling puddle of muck.

As Sigimar scanned the clearing it was evident not a single living thing dwelt within—not a blade of grass, not even a withered branch. Though the miasma wasn't present, his lungs still worked twice as hard to breathe what little air occupied this strange zone.

Dag tried to rush forward. Sigimar caught him by the waist and hauled him back. Dag's brows pinched, his face and body constricted as though in pain.

"Wait here," Sigimar commanded, refusing to budge until Dag had control of himself.

As he approached the stave, he saw no evidence of sigils or symbols on the ground, nor did he spy any traps of a physical nature. Standing at the edge of the filthy pool, he tore the stave from its resting place. It came loose with a wet, sucking slurp. Even touching the thing made Sigimar's flesh crawl and his innards squirm. Every part of him recoiled.

It was why he hesitated to hand it to Dag when his brother rushed up to him and stared at the thing like a man possessed.

"Dag? Use your light."

"Can't you hear it, Sig?"

"This thing is evil. Use your light to purify it."

"Just...let me hold it." Dag reached for the stave.

Sigimar pulled it away, eliciting a snarl from his brother.

"Use the light and it's yours," Sigimar lied.

The damned thing was going to find itself smashed into a thousand pieces the second it was purified.

Dag hesitated but complied. As the stave was bathed in a warm glow, the miasma began dissipating.

"It's working!" Sigimar whooped as he looked around.

The clearing widened as the miasma thinned out. Even breathing became easier. They'd done it. Their dreams would finally come true. Fame and fortune would be theirs.

A deep, groaning wail rang out, one unlike any he'd heard in all their days in Ashla. His heart stopped. The draugr must be massive. Another hellish wail. It was closer. Sigimar dropped the stave and held his axe aloft, scanning the gloom for the approaching threat as the ground beneath him shook. When it charged into the clearing, Sigimar's heart leapt into his throat. He'd long grown accustomed to the twisted, grey forms of the creatures within the miasma, but this one was different. Too many eyes glared, too many sharp-toothed mouths drooled with dark spittle, too many bent, spindly arms and legs kept the corpulent, house-sized draugr lumbering forward.

"Hurry!" Sigimar cried out as he rushed the creature.

He couldn't let it get close to Dag, to the stave. Sigimar hacked and split through shell and flesh but the massive creature was undaunted, pushing forward. He was quickly losing ground, letting the beast get closer to his brother. A bony, clawed hand snaked out from below and grabbed Sigimar by the ankle, tossing him aside like a child's toy. Dazed by his fall, Sigimar lurched to his feet unsteadily, the world spinning. His eyes focused on his brother's entranced expression as Dag bathed the stave in light, heedless of the monster barrelling towards him.

"Dag! The draugr!" Sigimar screamed as he raced forward.

But Sigimar was too slow.

The draugr was too fast.

And Dag had not heard his cries.

Dag didn't look up at the creature, or the first rays of sunlight as they pierced the shroud of the miasma that had blanketed the continent of Ashla for untold millennia. Miracle and nightmare played out in a single frozen moment that would sear itself into Sigimar's very soul. The draugr flaked away in the sun and the nearness to Dag's magic, screaming all the while, yet not slowing—never slowing.

"Dag!"

As if the spell had finally been broken, Dag's head jerked up, his eyes wide as one of the gaping jaws of the draugr snapped shut around his neck.

CHAPTER 1

Truthfully, Hypatia had known for the better part of two years that if her husband ever returned to her, it would be as a corpse. It shouldn't have come as such a shock to her when she was handed a fragment of his skull, his beautiful, conical, seashell-like horn attached. Absently, she ran a finger along it.

"Where did you find...?" she asked.

Should she call this fragment 'him' or 'it'? She pushed down the trickle of hysterical laughter that might have bubbled up at the morbid thought.

"Washed up on the shore. I'm so sorry. He was a good sort."

To her, Kosmas might as well have hung the moon. To everyone else? No, her husband had not been considered a good man. Amiable, driven and easily distracted, certainly; but in Lethe, the Empire of Mages, beast mages were never considered good sorts. Especially those, like Kosmas, whose beastly appendages could not be easily hidden.

Hypatia was immediately on alert.

The man before her, Diocles, shared their trade: ruin explorer and artefact dealer. He was also gifted with control of the element of water, a respectable magic, one which made him socially superior to her deceased beast mage husband. He was dressed in a fine, red linen tunic, his short leather boots shiny with polish, his long dark hair slicked back, and an appropriately solemn look on his olive-toned face. Had he been anyone else, she might have invited him in, but he was a known elemental magic elitist—and a pig.

"Thank you for bringing this piece of Kosmas back to me. I would like to be alone now."

Diocles didn't move from her doorway.

"I haven't seen you at the market for months," he began.

Hypatia refused to show him her desperation. Her noble education had prepared her to show an indifferent mask at all times. That she needed to use it now, after all she'd done to escape her former life, was salt in her wounds.

She hadn't gone to the antique markets because she'd already sold nearly every artefact she and Kosmas had found together. She'd even sold most of her precious research notes and journals, lovingly, painstakingly collected. Since Kosmas' disappearance, selling the things they'd discovered together had felt like bartering her heart away, each object full of happy memories, now gone forever. Only one journal and artefact remained, and she didn't have it in her to look at them, much less sell them.

Hypatia raised her brow, refusing to answer him. She grabbed the door handle. Diocles grabbed the thick, warped wood of the door. He looked around inside her small cottage. Nothing was new or without signs of mending, and nothing matched. Her own attire was no better. The once-saturated hue of her simple, threadbare gown had faded years ago. She knew what it would look like to the more successful Diocles, who boasted a small shop and residence within the town limits.

"You must be short of funds...and I could always use an assistant."

Only her quickly fraying restraint kept her from spitting in his face. Hypatia was no assistant. She and Kosmas had been equal partners in all things, bar one; she had always been the one to sell the objects to their wealthy clients in the Ruby Province. A beast mage labourer would never have been allowed inside the homes of nobles, merchants or rich eccentrics. Just as a woman would never be allowed to call herself a real scholar, no matter her discoveries.

"You may leave now, Diocles."

He held the door open as she tried to force it shut. Sick dread curled in her gut.

"Think about my offer, Hypatia. A woman without funds, alone in the world, it's not safe."

Her flinty, grey-eyed glare had him putting his hands up and backing away.

"I'll check on you in a few days, maybe bring a loaf of bread and some cheese. We can talk then."

Hypatia answered him by slamming her door shut in his face. She waited until she was certain he was truly gone before she sank to the floor cradling the last piece of her husband in her hands, her mousy brown curls falling forward. She had no more tears in her. The well had gone dry months ago. She had only the dull ache of closure to comfort her now.

She ran her finger along his horn, as she had been wont to do in the night when she woke and he lay deep in sleep beside her, huddled close on their small cot. Now that he was well and truly gone, she would have to go back out into the world. But the thought of ruin exploring brought her no comfort, and if there were a market for translating old texts or tutoring, no runaway noblewoman would be considered for the post. Neither could she teach at the newly erected Selenicas, for every teacher required references she dare not provide. Eventually, though, she would run out of the very last of her funds. Hypatia didn't know which was more distasteful: Diocles' offer, or submitting herself to the mercies of her family after having disappeared the night following her father's and brothers' funerals five years ago. Was there no other way?

"What would you have done, my love?" she asked aloud.

It was a bad habit she'd formed in the years alone.

Her husband, ever the determined optimist, would have told her to move forward with every step. But what if every step only felt like backsliding? Hypatia picked herself off the floor and began packing her meagre remaining possessions. Better to run away than deal with the looming, leering Diocles. Being alone in the world wasn't the dangerous part for a woman of Lethe. The danger lay in having a man like him know it.

It didn't take her long to gather everything she wanted to take with her. She padded her husband's remains in an old tunic that had long ago stopped smelling of him. All that was left was the last artefact, nestled under the floorboards.

She pried the wood up and reached down deep, her fingers brushing roots in the cool earth pit. She snagged the leather strap of Kosmas' satchel and pulled it up. Tucked inside and dusted with dark earth was an opaque crystal ball that exuded weak, colourful streamers of light. Touching it left an oddly tart taste in her mouth.

Kosmas had tucked it inside their hiding place the night he'd found it and kissed her goodbye the next morning as he went to survey a potential site in a tidal cave. He'd never returned. She covered the ball in a clean but ragged cloth, muffling the bands of light and erasing the taste on her tongue, placing it safely away in her pack.

At least it hadn't been the oily little Nobilissimus Nicander that had darkened her door, her husband's remains in hand. He'd been pestering her for months to leave her little home. No doubt he would have extorted her into trading her every belonging to return Kosmas to her.

Her door rattled with the sound of a fist beating against it.

"Shit."

Thinking of the bastard seemed to have summoned him.

"Hypatia!" Nobilissimus Nicander bellowed as he pounded on her door. "I know you're in there!"

Would there be no escape from weaselly, obnoxious men today? Why was it that when she was down, someone always showed up to kick her? Nicander had been attempting to get her to sell her home since the moment she and Kosmas had purchased the plot of land and built their small cottage. It was a feat very few commoners had managed in the years since the new Empress Selene had legalised the practice. Except Nicander coveted their small plot for its beautiful view of the sea, and berated them constantly for the eyesore of their home near his countryside estate.

Hypatia stopped herself before ripping open her door, her fist aching to punch Nicander between his nasty red eyes. What better way to vent her misery than ensuring that wretch shared in some of it? But she'd never been in a fight in her life, much less thrown a punch. She had to be smarter than this, no matter how much her heart screamed inside her. Hypatia breathed deeply. If she were to leave this place anyway, she should sell it. And if Nicander wanted it so badly, he could finance her getaway.

She put her pack out of view so as not to give the game away.

"Hypatia! Open this door!" Nicander yelled.

Hypatia allowed the door to creak open, the scent of Nicander's musky perfume clogging up her nostrils. He was as short as she, with tan skin and sun-bleached blonde hair. There was nothing in his features which made him appear anything other than an average nobleman. It was only when he opened his mouth that he became entirely odious. His carriage driver, some distance away, studiously ignored the whole interaction. A wise course of action.

"Nobilissimus, how unexpected."

He sneered at her and held a scented silk scarf to his nose, wafting more of his stench her way.

"Bloody stinking peasants," he muttered.

"If you had not torn down the public bathhouse, perhaps we peasants would not offend your noble senses so," Hypatia replied, her expression free of any of the malice he deserved. In an effort to 'civilise' the area, he had driven all public amenities that catered to the lower classes into ruin through frivolous lawsuits. All but the most stubborn or the most prosperous had been slowly forced out of the area.

"When are you going to leave, hmm? I've just heard your husband is officially dead now. Go back to your family, as any respectable widow would."

Were Diocles and Nicander colluding? No one else should know of Kosmas' remains being found unless the artefact dealer had loose lips. Given what she knew of both men, she wouldn't put it past them to team up against her. It only drove home how quickly she needed to leave. Nicander was an ass, but he was more likely to use his words to hurt her. Diocles, however, had always stared at her with more interest than she'd liked.

"Well, the funeral feast must be held, and a proper mourning period must be observed, Nobilissimus. That is the least a proper widow must see to," she began, stringing him along.

"To hells with that! You've been mourning for years now! And who in the hells would attend a funeral feast for a beast, you silly woman? Your non-existent livestock, perhaps?"

Do not punch the man you're going to fleece.

Do not punch him.

"Perhaps if a generous benefactor made a donation towards the costs, I could host the funeral feast in a timely manner."

"Begging already, Hypatia? You must be nearly out of coin by now." He smiled, having long ago disposed of any manners he might have been taught. Or, if he had them at all, he used them only for his peers.

If only he knew.

"Oh, don't worry yourself on my account. Diocles has offered me a professional partnership. I expect to live comfortably for many years to come. In. This. House," Hypatia enunciated.

Nicander flushed. It was all the proof she needed that they'd been working together.

"But I might be convinced to move. Diocles' store is in town, after all. It is quite the trek to make daily. If only I knew someone willing to pay me handsomely for my land. There is so much to consider. But I am wasting your time, Nobilissimus. Good day to you." Hypatia put her hand on her door and began closing it.

His meaty, bejewelled fingers grasped the door, a crazed light in his red eyes.

"You're selling?"

"Perhaps I shall write to the strategos or empress to allow me to set up a memorial to my husband. They are so generous to the common folk. Just think, where our house stands, I could have a statue erected in Kosmas' likeness." Hypatia sighed, enjoying the sight of Nicander openly squirming. "Though, it depends on the offers I receive. I am attached to this place. It would pain me deeply to leave." The last part was at least true. It almost put a crack in her perfect façade. Later. She could curl up and lick her wounds when she was somewhere safe, away from these predators.

"A hundred gold coins." Nicander pounded his fist on her door.

"A thousand gold coins," Hypatia countered.

"You greedy bitch!"

"*Two* thousand gold coins. One thousand for my land. One thousand for your rudeness."

"What in the hells would you even do with that gold?!"

The last time she'd run off she'd had half that much. Courtesy of the empress' largesse, she'd lived comfortably, if simply, for half a decade. To a man like the nobilissimus, it was the cost of a new wardrobe for the season, maybe a new racehorse for the Hippodrome or a plush carriage. Once, to Hypatia, it had been the cost of a single dress. What a fool she'd been.

What fools they'd all been.

"Ah, I see you're not serious. Do you think Magister Ruby would purchase the land from me? I hear he is quite generous, as well as very officious, in his business dealings."

She hadn't had this much fun in years, watching Nicander sweat as he considered what the attentions of his betters might do to him. After all, the empress had lived as a commoner most of her life and loved nothing so much as finding ways to do away with the nobles she openly despised. Magister Ruby, a cousin of the emperor, had been born with a stick up his ass and worshipped at the altar of the judicial system. No doubt Nicander's many shady dealings would provoke the ire of both. The only reason Hypatia hadn't called attention to Nicander in the past was that she herself had been trying to evade their—and her remaining family's—detection.

"Two thousand if you leave immediately and keep your mouth shut," Nicander growled.

"Done. Once you deliver the gold and an excellent horse, the land is yours."

She'd never seen such an openly gleeful look on Nicander's face, not even when he'd brutally run the last of the beggars out of town.

"As it happens, I had planned to go into town today." He snapped his fingers. An attendant hopped from the back of the carriage and bowed to Nicander. "Two thousand gold coins. Put them in a sack and onto one of the horses."

Within moments one of the three horses pulling the carriage had been detached, the coins counted, bagged, and hefted over the horse's back. At least he'd left her one with reins. Perhaps he hadn't had time to think of depriving her of them in one last petty act. Hypatia grabbed her pack and added it to the gold across the horse's back.

She noticed Nicander's renewed sneer. He probably thought she didn't know how to ride. It wasn't a skill commoners possessed. Horses were for the elite or for pulling the ploughs of wealthy landowners.

Hypatia rucked up her skirts and swung up onto the horse's back, much to the astonishment of her audience. She took the reins in hand and turned the horse so that she could look down on Nicander.

Apparently, she wasn't above some showmanship or pettiness of her own.

"Tell Diocles he is a pig," she said, urging the horse towards the dirt road.

When she dared look back, black smoke billowed up from where her house once stood. Nicander was a fire mage, after all. She was only surprised he hadn't set it alight ages ago. She turned her eyes away. Best get to the nearest port. Ships sailed to distant lands every day, some of them ruled entirely by women if the rumours were to be believed. She would be safe there. Safe to curl up and mourn, freed from the weight of her family name for good.

The humid breeze brought the scent of burning wood with it, stinging her eyes. Kosmas would have thought of this as just another adventure, a hundred new dreams dreamt up in the time it had taken her to ride this far. But he was gone and she was alone, and her only goal was to disappear. Perhaps one day she would have dreams and adventures again. Until then, she would put one foot in front of the other.

She only hoped the destination would be better than what she'd left behind.

CHAPTER 2

"You have a lot of nerve, ignoring my summons."

Sigimar ignored the voice, focusing on the wall of miasma before him. Withered grass peeked out beneath the blanket of disturbed snow, defiant of the threat of death not a few paces away. The bone-crunching clicking of a draugr echoed from within the gloom. Sigimar readied his axe.

"I'm busy," Sigimar growled.

"No jarl is too busy to answer his king. Not even Jarl Ashla."

Sigimar hated his title. He hated his lands. He hated his keep. Presently, he also hated the warriors under his command. Not a single one would agree to light his way through the miasma on the frontiers of his land in Ashla, all because he'd developed the bad habit of ploughing into the toxic fog alone, seeking vengeance for his brother's death. Killing those creatures was the only thing that brought him even a moment's relief from his grief. He'd settled for tempting them into attacking him on cloudy days, when the sun's rays wouldn't dissolve the draugar instantly. It was a pity that, though sunlight could kill the monsters the corruption created, it couldn't heal those who had yet to succumb, or rid Ashla of its curse.

"This one is."

"Is he always this moody?" the king asked.

"No, usually he's worse," Drest, Sigimar's huskarl, replied. "And actually, this is an improvement. There was a long stretch in the beginning where he simply never rose from his bed."

It took an effort of will to push the memory of his lowest point from his mind and focus on the task at hand.

"Is he...covered in blood?"

Face, arms and chest, to be precise. The kitchen staff had been leery of handing over the goat's blood that morning, but they'd done it despite their reservations. At least being jarl was good for something.

"Among other things," Drest sighed. "The better to bait the draugar."

"Ah. Charming."

"Quite."

"Leave, or shut up," Sigimar hissed.

The clicking was getting closer.

"Won't be long now, King Erlendr. The creature is nearly upon us," Drest drawled.

Sigimar pivoted. Blackened claws as long as fingers lunged out of the gloom, proceeded by yellowish-grey arms as thin as twigs and a slavering, toothy maw. He brought down his axe with a vicious swing, severing the head in one crunching blow. It rolled across the snow, painting it black. Sigimar put his axe to rest against the trunk of a sapling, gathered up the body and tossed it atop his growing, macabre mound. The snow had turned into grey slush beneath.

"What on Oblivion do you intend to do with all those, Jarl?" King Erlendr asked, his tone wry.

Sigimar turned to face Erlendr then, or rather, the king's reflection. Drest held half an orb in his hands, angled to face Sigimar. Half a dragon's eye, the other half sitting in King Erlendr's castle fortress in Askr, the capital of Elmheim. Ashla's newly uncovered lands belonged to Elmheim, the kingdom across the narrow channel, as did its only jarl, much to Sigimar's dismay. He supposed he should be grateful Erlendr was infamously friendly with his jarls, but he found it difficult to be grateful for much of anything lately.

"Maybe I'll make some furniture," Sigimar replied dryly.

"How resourceful."

Sigimar grunted in reply, determined to wait out the King. Whatever he wanted, Sigimar would likely want no part of it. He raised his bloodstained chin, heedless of the chill winds dusting him with quickly melting snowflakes.

The elf king, last Sigimar had seen him, stood a full head taller than he, though his build was rangier. Skin ruddy, his braided, white gold hair had nary a strand out of place, and his keen, sky-blue eyes were as piercing as they were cunning. Erlendr sat upon a chair made entirely of mammoth tusk, the ivory gleaming, made comfortable by the pelts of numerous animals. The elmwood desk before him was littered with hide scrolls, parchment, and clay tablets, evidence of the many and varied realms that paid tribute so that Elmheim could afford to protect them from the miasma on its seaward frontier.

"I had no notion you were so enamoured of arts and crafts, nor that you had so much free time on your hands. Do you prefer women, Jarl?"

Sigimar raised a burgundy brow.

"Men? Both? Neither? Doesn't matter?" Erlendr asked.

"Women," Sigimar answered, cautious.

The king was obviously scheming. Was it not enough that Sigimar had unwittingly bound himself to the ancient pact the moment he'd been ennobled? He could never leave Elmheim or Ashla without his king's permission as long as he lived, trapped at the border, staring into the abyss that devoured his brother. Did Erlendr think forcing a woman to journey here would make that fate more bearable?

Sigimar flicked a concerned glance at Drest, who kept his expression carefully neutral. The dragon shapeshifter's dark hair was braided away from his long, tan face, his green eyes giving nothing away. Gold horns curled up atop his head, the only glittering adornment on his person, clothed as he was in a dark, fur-lined cloak. He adjusted his grip on the dragon's eye half-orb. Sigimar briefly wondered if Drest, a dragon himself, was bothered at the use of his kinsmen's bodies in this way, but kept his curiosity to himself. After all, Drest hadn't chosen a life on Elmheim's, or Ashla's, frontier—he'd been banished for devouring the hearts of fallen dragons. It had saved his life from the wing rot slowly killing him, but left him a pariah among his own kind and unable to father children, not that he'd seemed so inclined.

A pity, given Sigimar's rising suspicions.

"Excellent. You're to wed." Sigimar's gut sank. Gods below, it was just as he'd feared. Erlendr continued, ignoring Sigimar's panic. "All of the Riverland realms have paid for their protection in gold, goods and the blood of their kin this generation. All but Otmar of Gortos. He's refused to send his daughter, Princess Farohildis, unless an unwed jarl of suitable renown made himself known in my kingdom. I have given you a decade to settle in, and I can think of no one more renowned than The Hero of the Frontier."

"Don't call me that!" Sigimar snapped, bitterness burning in his veins.

"Still sensitive about it?" Erlendr asked.

Sigimar's nails bit into his fists, his jaw clenched as he held back his fury. There was nothing heroic about getting his brother killed. Erlendr knew exactly how absurd such a title was, and yet he dared utter it. The bastard was lucky he was shielded by distance, and a fortress built into the side of a mountain.

"Shut. Up," Sigimar hissed.

"My king, please stop angering the jarl. At this rate, he's going to demand I spar with him to vent his anger at you," Drest quipped dryly.

Erlendr laughed.

"Have the jarl cleaned up, properly groomed and outfitted for the journey to Gortos. I've taken the liberty of readying the bride gifts.

They'll be waiting for you when you arrive in Askr. And Sigimar? Leave your bronze axe at home. If it's within reach, I guarantee you'll be too tempted to wield it on Otmar to stop yourself. Take the amber and gold axe, like a proper noble. At least if you end up bashing Otmar's skull in with it, the bastard's head is the harder of the two."

Sigimar stifled a groan.

The Riverlands were obligated to send fighters and magic-wielders to Elmheim to keep the miasma at bay. Although anyone who agreed to fight was given free food and lodgings regardless of status or ability. It had been an enticing offer that had tempted two orphans desperate to stay together many years ago.

Since he'd become titled a decade ago, Sigimar hadn't bothered to think about this particularly distasteful aspect of his new duties. It was well known that jarls on the frontier, either elevated due to feats of courage or born into the nobility, married the nobles from the River-lands as part of the ancient pact. He and Dag used to imagine the beautiful Riverland princesses they would wed when their glorious deeds transformed them into jarls. But now, even that boyish fantasy had become a poison pill to swallow. Sigimar hadn't even protected his own brother. He didn't have the right to wed a noblewoman. And the last thing he wanted was to be the jailor of an unwilling bride.

There was enough misery in Ashla already.

"I am unfit for this task. There must be another jarl for the princess to wed," Sigimar replied.

"There are. Several, in fact. But I've chosen you. Are you refusing your king?"

"Would it matter if I were?"

"No."

Stubborn bastard.

"I refuse."

"Your objection is both noted and irrelevant. Do at least *try* not to scare her off. Otmar's line has produced talented healing light wielders in every generation for tens of thousands of years." Erlendr looked Sigimar up and down, his platinum brow raised. "I'm sure a handsome man such as yourself need only smile occasionally and dole out a few compliments to charm the womenfolk."

Sigimar scowled. Sometimes he wondered if he were even capable of another expression anymore. King Erlendr's goading cheer seemed to bring out the worst in him. He probably did it on purpose.

"Drest will teach you the proper etiquette. He is quite well-versed in matters of courtly speech, as well as the wooing of a lady. Speaking of, Drest, a young woman named—"

"My king, the magic is fading, I can't—" Drest cut in before covering the half-orb with cloth and ending the magical connection.

"It's a shame you didn't do that earlier," Sigimar said.

Drest shrugged.

"I put him off as long as I could. I've visited Askr often enough in your stead, and he's become increasingly pushy over the years. He's been demanding to speak with you for two years now. Eventually, he'd have sent a ship and dragged you back by the beard. Or summoned you through the crystal."

An involuntary shiver ran down Sigimar's spine. As a child, trapped in an orphanage without his brother, he'd made a habit of running away, desperate to get to Elmheim where Dag had been scrounging together enough coin to prove himself a suitable guardian. Nausea churned his gut as he remembered the summoning sickness caused by the cheap tokens the orphanage would use to drag him back. Gods, those were dark days.

He shook himself.

Sigimar scratched at his filthy, matted mess of a beard. He was touched that Drest had put Erlendr off for so long. There was blessed little to be thankful for of late. Sitting down in the filthy snow, he put his head in his hands.

"I'm in no fit state to be wed," he groaned.

What would a fae princess gifted with extraordinary magic want with an elvish nobody? He'd been entirely self-educated, really only knew how to swing an axe, and possessed a title and lands he'd never earned. Sigimar didn't want anything to do with himself. How could he expect a refined, educated, powerful princess to?

"No, but I don't see you have much choice in the matter," Drest said.

Sunlight began peeking through the grey sky above. Wherever its undiluted rays touched, the black, corrupted blood bubbled and hissed as it turned to smoke, purified.

"You can bond over your mutual distaste for the arrangement." At Sigimar's frown, Drest grinned. "Well, would *you* want to marry you right now? All you do is growl and mope about or run into the miasma like a damn fool."

"I'm protecting the land," Sigimar protested.

"When the sun doesn't, the amplifier protects the land." Drest rolled his eyes.

The ancient magical amplifier that had risen shortly after the cursed stave had been purified ensured a steady stream of the healing light pulsed over most of the land he'd uncovered. But the borderlands were still dangerous, the wall of miasma prone to encroaching with powerful winds, and nothing was foolproof. Sigimar refused to trust a device he didn't fully understand.

"This..." Drest waved his gloved hand at the stack of beheaded corpses. "Is you moping."

"I'm in mourning," Sigimar grouched.

Drest's expression softened.

"I know," he said, tone gentle. "But as we've discussed many a time, what happened to Dag was not your fault."

"But—"

"No, it wasn't. Do we need to play the blame game today?"

"No," Sigimar groaned.

Drest, who had been with Sigimar since he'd first been named a jarl, was always trying to help him beat back the worst of his inner demons—a valiant attempt to get him to blame something else for Dag's horrifying end. To blame something other than his own reckless greed. Some days it was a hopeless proposition. Others, less so.

"You know, shocking as it might seem, mourning, brushing your hair, and taming your beard are *not* mutually exclusive activities."

"I brush my hair," he protested.

Drest's expression made it clear he was unconvinced.

"I'll clean this up and teach you what I know about wooing a woman of means. Impress her, and half your battle will be won."

Sigimar sighed, resigned.

"Get a ship provisioned. We'll sail before the rivers completely freeze."

The rivers beyond Elmheim were deep, wide and fast, but as Autumn waned, even they would become impassable.

Drest raised a dark brow.

"You plan on taking a boat to pick up a fae princess? Do you want to be laughed at all the way back to Elmheim?"

"What's wrong with a ship?"

"Nothing, if you want to make plain your appalling lack of magic."

Sigimar snarled. If he'd had even a fraction of the magic Dag had possessed, his brother might still be alive. Though he had fae ancestors—he'd certainly inherited the colours of the fae—he'd received none of their magic. Too much magic-deprived elf had asserted itself. Another one of his many failings.

Drest was entirely unfazed by his outburst. Few things scared a man who could become a dragon as big as a castle.

"You're a jarl now, not some backwater grunt. You have talented fae and witches at your command. Tell them to create something spectacular for you to travel on. You don't want your wife sneering at you every day of your shackled lives, do you?"

"No," Sigimar muttered.

Drest nodded.

"I'll handle it. You can thank me by bringing back a pretty witch I've been exchanging letters with. And by grooming yourself. I don't even want to think about what it'll take to brush out the knots in your hair."

Sigimar stared at his bloodied, muddied hands, his filthy tunic and leggings, his boots that still had bits of draugar clinging to them. He hadn't looked at himself in a mirror in an age. He was certain his burgundy hair was as much a mess as his beard. This was how he aught to look—like a failure, an imposter, a villain with the gall to be breathing while his brother's ashes rested in a burial mound fit for a true hero.

Drest took a deep breath, his throat glowing like burning coals, and unleashed a torrent of fire, setting the mound of corpses alight. The sun peeking through the clouds would take care of the rest. There was nothing more to say. Sigimar began trudging back to his castle. He was in no state to welcome a woman into his life, let alone a wife. But ready or not, his king had given him an order. Somehow, he was going to have to find the strength to be the man Dag had always believed him to be. To be the man his brother had raised him to be.

Another bloody farce.

He pitied the princess already.

CHAPTER 3

Hypatia cursed every man in existence. It was just their luck that she hadn't been born with that particular mage gift. Otherwise, the whole male population of Bloodstone Harbour would now be clutching themselves in agony.

Yet another ship's captain had refused to allow her passage, no matter how much gold she'd offered. Passenger ships were a rarity and only sailed to Maat where a mage ruled as queen alongside a fae king... a queen Hypatia knew personally and preferred to give a wide berth to. Gods knew what Queen Taisiya would do to Hypatia if she ever set foot in her realm.

The rest of the seagoing ships were for trade, and the space she would take up was worth twice her weight in gold. A few had made her other, more distasteful, offers in return for passage, to which she hadn't bothered answering politely. Hence, the curses they deserved being heaped upon them.

Hypatia sat in the town centre, clothed in sturdy, respectable clothes, courtesy of her recent gains, her pack by her side as she trained her gaze on the water flowing from the elaborate fountain. The children of merchants raced around it, taunting each other, while those of local nobles kept their noses aloft, led by well-dressed tutors and escorted by guards. Fish, meat and fruit vendors advertised their goods and gossiped amongst themselves.

She hadn't planned on staying in town quite as long as she had. If she didn't leave soon, the cost of her lodgings, food and stabling would eat through her coin in a matter of weeks. She'd already foolishly bought back a few of her beloved research tomes from a local scholar, leaving her shorter of coin than she should have been. Would it be worthwhile to get aboard a ship to Maat after all? From there she could get some-where—anywhere—else. Surely Queen Taisiya didn't have all the ships inspected, or worse, have people looking for her?

All she wanted was to live in peace.

"Hypatia?"

It was a voice Hypatia knew far too well.

And it sent a fearful chill down her spine despite the brutal humidity.

"Stop the palanquin and give me my cane."

"But Illustra—"

"Hush, and do as you're told."

"But the illustrus—"

"Is not here. My cane." A bejewelled, tawny hand pierced the gauzy blue veils floating about the sides of the palanquin. A servant in a fine tunic handed the occupant a gold and wooden cane, assisting the occu-pant from her confines. Airy blue silk flowed out, a whisper above the cobbled stone.

Oh no.

A beauty with tawny skin, eyes glittering like sapphires, and platinum blonde hair coiled atop her head in elaborate braids stood proud, her penetrating gaze pinning Hypatia like a spear.

The former Domina Roxane Sapphire.

Once, her closest friend.

And now, the one person whose hatred Hypatia deserved most.

A smile turned Roxane's severe beauty into breathtaking warmth. It was a kindness Hypatia in no way deserved. Roxane strode forward, her cane clicking in time with her steps.

"I knew it was you. But what in the gods' unknowable names are you doing here?"

"I—"

Hypatia didn't have a chance to respond as Roxane swept her up in an embrace. She barely came up to the statuesque woman's chest and was instantly enveloped in the scent of her friend's perfume and the soft glide of silk. It felt like a lifetime since she'd felt anything so fine. Certainly since she'd been held with genuine warmth.

"I've missed you."

Hypatia's lip trembled as she fought back tears. Roxane had always been like that, spiting the cruelty of her upbringing with boundless love.

"I'm so sorry," she replied, her throat choked with emotion.

"Shhh. None of that. It wasn't your fault."

But it was. In every way, it was. None of Roxane's—or the countless others'—suffering would have happened if not for Hypatia.

"It was my research," Hypatia croaked.

"Your father was the traitor, not you. Is that why you're dressed like this? Did you think you needed to run away?" Roxane's voice was hushed.

"A-among other things," Hypatia answered.

Roxane stood back and tipped Hypatia's chin up, forcing her to meet her eyes.

"Your mother?"

Hypatia nodded.

Roxane cursed in a shockingly unladylike way.

"I don't blame you for any of it. I just wish you'd come to me. I might not have been able to prevent your mother from gambling away her coin and yours, but I could have asked my half-sister for emancipation on your behalf. She has the ear of the empress and has proven to be kinder to us than we deserve. I could still—"

"No! If I'd stayed..."

The empress would have discovered her role in the treason that had changed the face of the imperial court. The only reason she hadn't yet was that their interrogator hadn't asked the right questions—of any of the women victimised by that horrid ritual. If Hypatia had managed to escape justice, her mother would have sold her off in marriage to pay her debts, or kept Hypatia prisoner so that the empress' annual largesse to the victims of the ritual would flow directly into her pockets. At best, Hypatia would be forced, day after day, to face the women victimised by her crime, all the while wondering when the axe would fall. At worst, she would feel it cut clean through her neck. She might be a coward, but she'd rather not be a dead coward, or a trapped one, if she had a choice.

"I couldn't stay. I can't. I don't deserve—"

Roxane pressed a finger to her lips.

"You deserve to be happy, Hypatia. After what our fathers did to us, we all deserve to be happy, in whatever form that takes. You're Illustra Bright, ward of Empress Selene. If you wish to spend your life in scholarly pursuits, you need only ask. If you wish to be free of your family, you need never see nor hear from them again. Much has changed since the empress took the throne. If you let me, I'll show you what a noblewoman in Lethe can accomplish."

It was as if Roxane had cast a spell on her. Hypatia wanted to believe her with every fibre of her being. And as she stared up at her friend, she could see how the years apart had changed her. She'd always had a core of steel, but now she had the confidence her horrid father had always tried to beat out of her as a girl. She walked with a cane after her year in a coma, but she'd never stood taller. Gone were the shadows from her eyes, the stain of bitter resignation. Roxane was happy.

"I...I don't know."

"Well, isn't that a first?" Roxane smiled, hand on hip.

An unexpected snort escaped Hypatia then. It was the closest to laughter she'd managed in years.

"I'm not going to drag you back to Nadioch, or tell anyone who or where you are if you don't wish it. I'll come through this square on my way back from my current appointment. If you're interested in what I have to show you, wait for me or go to my villa. Tell my servants we are old friends, and they'll treat you well." Roxane took hold of her hands, soft bronze on roughened olive. "I have missed you so much. Please say you'll at least let me see you again?"

"I..." She should refuse. Trouble and pain followed her wherever she went. But it had been so long since she'd seen a friendly face. She didn't have to stay anywhere she didn't want to. Her mage gift made running away remarkably easy. What could a day or two hurt? The next passenger ship wouldn't arrive for a few days yet. "Alright."

"Illustra Rivers, your appointment..." her servant prodded.

Hypatia blinked, confused. Rivers had been the name bestowed on the daughters of Magister Sapphire after his treason—and the victimization of those daughters—had come to light. If Roxane had married, she would have taken her husband's noble name.

"You kept your unmarried name?"

Roxane smiled again.

"My husband had none, so I gave him mine." Hypatia reeled at the thought that another former domina had chosen someone outside of the nobility to wed. Such a thing would never have been allowed before. Seeing her dumbfounded look, Roxane nudged Hypatia's open mouth shut, a mischievous look in her eyes. "As I said, much has changed since Empress Selene took the throne. I'll see you soon, Hypatia."

Hypatia stared as Roxane was carried away in her palanquin, her mind failing to comprehend all that she'd learned. She sat back down, clutching her pack to herself as her mind spun. Would she really be free to live as she pleased—to love whom she pleased without censure? Cold comfort for a woman who had done just that until Kosmas had been cruelly taken from her. If she'd known, could she have given him a better life? Would it have prevented his death?

"Hypatia?"

She didn't respond, lost in her thoughts as she was.

If she hadn't run away, would her life have been better? If she'd stayed and fought for her freedom, would she be a proper scholar now? But if she had, she would never have met Kosmas, never known real, soul-searing love. She never would have learned to stand on her own two feet.

"Hypatia?"

And yet without him, she'd been brought to her knees. Had she learned nothing at all? Had loss been her only lesson? Could life really be better? Could she really be free of her family and past, and so easily?

"Hypatia?"

"What?!" she snapped, furious, glaring up at the person who had so rudely interrupted her jumbled, racing thoughts.

Oh no.

Not him.

"I knew it. I knew you were a noblewoman the moment I saw you." Diocles smirked.

What was he doing here? Bloodstone Harbour was a day's ride from the town Diocles lived in. It had to be a coincidence. A terrible, horrid coincidence.

"You're mistaken."

"No, I'm not, *Illustra Bright.*"

Her heart crashed against her ribs as he advanced on her. She gripped her skirts in her bloodless hands, grateful her shoes were more practical than pretty. If she had to run...

No, focus.

"Do you know what your kin are offering as a reward for your safe return? To think that fool Nicander just let you go." His lips twisted into something far uglier than a mere smirk, the gentleman's veneer discarded. "Luck was on my side when I decided to follow you. As they say, one man's loss is another's gain."

"I'll scream," she threatened.

"And I'll tell them you're my addled wife. Who would come to your defence?"

Roxane would, but if she caused a scene and embroiled her friend in scandal, it would get back to the empress, to her family. To free herself from Diocles, she would have to use her real identity. She'd be dragged back to Nadioch. And the capital was the last place a traitor wanted to find herself.

So Hypatia did what she was best at.

She disappeared.

Several people who had been watching their interaction gasped, Diocles included. One of the food vendors muttered about teleportation mages as Diocles cursed a blue streak.

If only.

Wrapped in her magic, in a spell few light mages had ever mastered, Hypatia was invisible but still very much present. She held her breath, praying Diocles would move so that she could sneak away. Though unseen, she could still be heard if she made a sound. A squeak of protest nearly escaped her lips as Diocles reached down, grabbed her pack and slung it across his back.

If Hypatia's freedom cost her all her gold and the last of her possessions, so be it. There would be no returning to Roxane now. Diocles was unlikely to keep his mouth shut about her whereabouts. Yet another thing he'd ruined for her. Still, she had the horse, its stabling paid up for the next few days. She could sell it and her current dress and shoes for the coin to get passage to Maat. She may have to travel wedged up against livestock and wearing threadbare rags, but it would be worth it to be free of Diocles and everything he would do to her.

If only Kosmas were here. He would have...

Kosmas!

His remains were still tucked inside her pack. Hypatia got to her feet, moving without thinking, racing after Diocles, heedless of the people she had to shove bodily out of her way.

Anything but that. The world could take everything else from her, but not that.

When she finally reached the villain, she threw herself at him, knocking him to the ground face-first. Though short, Hypatia was no waif, her curves padded powerful muscles built up over years digging up artefacts. But the impact of the fall was enough to dispel her magic, making her visible once more.

Before Diocles could recover, Hypatia wrestled the pack off him, the top tearing open as Diocles tried to snatch it back. She raced away to shouts of '*thief.*' Just before she disappeared into an alley, she crashed to the ground, losing her grip on her pack and her leg giving out. A sharp, hot burst of pain wrenched a cry from her lips. The artefact popped out of her pack, unwrapping itself from the moth-bitten cloth she'd covered it in, rolling deeper into the alley. Her leg bled profusely, red rivulets running between the cobblestones, her dress torn by a blade of ice lodged into the brick of the nearby wall.

"Hypatia!" Diocles howled.

She made the mistake of looking back at him. Blood trickled down his head and poured from his nose and split lip. Fury twisted his features. He wouldn't stop at just hurting her—not now.

Hypatia scrabbled into the alley, limping, desperate to escape. If he caught her... No, it didn't bear contemplating. He could not be allowed to catch her.

Hypatia braced herself on the wall of the alley, leaning for support. Before she fully got to her feet, Diocles knocked her down again with a kick to the back of her knee. She pitched forward, face and hands scraping the cobblestone. As his hands reached towards her, his intent plain, she let loose her magic. Bright, searing light blinded him. Hypatia reached for the nearby artefact as Diocles crumpled, screaming as he clutched his eyes. She raised the orb high above his head and smashed it into his skull over and over until he stopped moving.

A crowd had gathered in front of the alley, more curious than alarmed. Such violence was not uncommon here.

While the shock still numbed her battered body, Hypatia struggled to her feet, grabbed her things and fled further into the alley. She made it around the corner before her legs gave out.

"Young woman, are you in need of assistance?"

Hypatia jerked her head from side to side, trying to find the source of the query.

"Ah, down here."

A woman's face had appeared in the orb still clutched in her bleeding hands. Her face was as pink as a peony, her long, mossy green hair unbound and her eyes glittered like peridot. If her strange visage hadn't given her away as fae, the pointed ears would have done it.

"I am Farohildis, and you must be a distant relation if you've managed to activate the twin of our orb. But never mind that, you seem to be in distress. Can I offer some assistance?"

"I—"

"She fled back there!" Diocles' voice echoed down the alley, sending Hypatia's panic spiralling.

"Can you get me out of here?" Hypatia asked the fae woman.

Fae magic was supposed to be awe-inspiring in its power and breadth. And Hypatia would need a miracle if she were to get out of this.

"Summon you? Yes, but without time to prepare, the journey would be quite painful. I would also require a favour in return, for the magic to work."

A hysterical laugh bubbled up. A simple favour in return for her freedom? That was nothing. As for pain, what was a little more to her now, beaten, bloody and bruised as she was?

"Please! Do it!" she cried as the shadows of her pursuers loomed large on the wall of the alley.

Hypatia closed her eyes and clutched her belongings to her. Farohildis hadn't lied. Pain had her screaming until blessed unconsciousness took her under.

CHAPTER 4

Sigimar hated his future in-laws with a consuming passion. Like a lightning strike in the dead of night, it jolted him out of his gloomy malaise. Since his very first step into the territory of Gortos, he'd been beset by so much ill luck that only an empty-headed fool would believe it had any resemblance to coincidence. King Otmar wanted Sigimar to leave his kingdom.

First, they'd been raided by pixies in the night, light-fingered little lower-fae who loved nothing more than the feel of enchanted objects. A great number of bride gifts disappeared, never to be recovered. Then, a travelling null had come upon them, dissolving the summoned beasts they'd been riding up to that point merely through proximity. Luckily, they'd already landed for the evening. Had they been mid-flight, they could have plummeted to their doom.

One null was bad luck, but every day his entourage summoned more magical beasts of burden, and another null would inevitably find their caravan, with predictable results.

Infuriated, but not one to give in to such pettiness, Sigimar had ordered horses and beasts of burden to be found and purchased for the rest of the voyage. Except every purveyor of the beasts that could be found charged a king's ransom for every miserable creature. And miserable they were—stunted, sickly, frail and slow. Still, they hobbled onwards.

The caravan's only solace was that the pixies had failed to steal the pocket realms his people had brought with them for shelter, and the nulls had been chased off before they'd managed to destroy them.

Until a null had crept through their camp in the night, destroying even that small comfort, ejecting them from their beds directly into the deep snow as the magical constructs collapsed into nothingness. The null had paid for it in blood, and had at least confirmed the identity of their tormentor. Still, they soldiered on, knowing they could at least recreate their magical lodgings provided they found proper sacrifices.

Just as he was feeling grateful that he might yet have a warm place to bathe and lay his head at the end of the day, game became impossible to find. No birds flitted between trees, no rabbits hopped about, and no foxes leapt at prey unseen in the snow drifts beneath their paws. Without regular, living animal sacrifices to bring the pocket realms into existence and sustain them, warmth, comfort and personal grooming became unattainable luxuries. They were also running low on supplies. No game? No meat. And with the snows this deep, nothing else could be scrounged either.

Sigimar and his company had been sleeping huddled together for warmth around fires and inside their few tents for several days. Shapeshifters took their animal forms when they could. The rest tried to sleep amidst the chattering of teeth, praying the cold wouldn't take any of them in the night. Whatever warmth charms they could create were few and weak. He had summoners aplenty, even a healer, but most had come as an honour guard and protection against banditry. The art of enchantment was not one they'd expected such a need of.

No longer were there any jokes or camaraderie amongst his fellows. Not even gallows humour passed the lips of his people. When at last they reached the market town half a day's ride to the castle, everyone breathed a sigh of relief. Their journey had been extended an extra month because of King Otmar's pettiness. Several clean, comfortable inns dotted the main streets of the picturesque town, and there was sure to be a market with the enchantments they required. Sigimar, on his pitifully small horse for one of his size, nearly wept with relief.

But every innkeeper refused to allow them entry, claiming to be full to bursting with non-existent lodgers. Every merchant smiled ruefully, sweeping their hands across suspiciously bare shelves.

Never had Sigimar wished to have his proper axe in hand more. The small amber axe with its gold haft that he kept by his side was little better than a hammer, and wouldn't do the kind of damage he wished. It was supposed to be a mark of his noble station. It might have been made of offal for all the good it did him and his caravan. King Erlendr was looking more like a prophet by the day. Given the opportunity, Sigimar would happily make an orphan of his future wife. Thus far, his entourage had refused to allow him to carry the bronze weapon, but he suspected all it would take was one more insult before they would hand it over to him as he greeted his future father-in-law.

Sigimar woke the morning of the last day of his journey to Otmar's keep hungry and cold, warmed only by his fury. He'd shared his tent with as many men and women as could fit, all of whom had left the moment dawn arose. Pulling himself out of the tent, he reflecting that Ashla was not, in fact, the worst place in Oblivion to spend his days. At least there he could get a warm bed, a hot bath and something other than jerky for food. Sigimar instantly regretted leaving his tent as the first bit of news met him.

"Jarl, there have been...complications."

Sigimar watched the long, erect, white ears of the hare shifter, Ingi, twitch, despite the neutral expression on the man's pale face. Ingi acted as the lead on this hellish expedition, keeping the whole caravan organized. He also, apparently, had patience in spades.

Funny, Sigimar was fresh out.

"What now?"

"Several of the horses disappeared in the night. We're securing more, but the proprietor is…reluctant."

Bloodshed would be a welcome release. At least he could warm his hands in the proprietor's entrails.

"Give me my axe."

Had Ingi's lip twitched in amusement? He seemed to have a very twisted sense of humour.

"That would be unwise."

"Then lead me to the bastard."

Ingi nodded and led the way. Sigimar followed closely behind.

The green elvish man sneered as Sigimar approached him, small, protruding tusks stretching his lips into a fearsome expression. He was easily as tall as Sigimar and equally muscular. There would be no intimidating this one with brawn or bad temper.

Pity.

"And what excuse do you give to deny my coin?" Sigimar asked.

The proprietor shrugged his broad shoulders, made larger by the thick fur of his cloak.

"I don't like you."

Sigimar's hand flexed at his side, searching for a real weapon that wasn't there. The man watched his twitching hands with amusement, not caring at all despite the ornament at his hip. Anger wouldn't work. Dag had always reminded him to use his head before he resorted to using his fists. Such things seemed easier to remember when one was in a less murderous frame of mind. He took a calming breath, though it escaped as a hiss between his clenched teeth. If the bastard despised him, and indeed, it seemed the whole of Gortos was out to get him, then perhaps he would care for Sigimar's future wife.

"So be it. I'm sure the princess is accustomed to walking through the deep snow. I will be certain to tell her that it was you who denied her a proper mount." The man's dark eyes widened as Sigimar turned his head to the dark-haired, white-eared, hare shifter beside him, "Let's be on our way."

"Wait!" he called as Sigimar strode off.

Sigimar stopped.

"What?"

"I'm willing to sell you one of my horses."

Sigimar turned away.

"I shall need at least six. Two for her personal use, two to pull her carriage and two more to pull the wagon that carries her bride gifts. If you cannot provide at least this many, well…"

"We could always burn the bride gifts, Jarl," Ingi added. "Or better yet, dedicate the lot of them to the forgotten gods, to bless our journey out of Gortos, given our ill-luck thus far. Better to be rid of the extra baggage either way, rather than risk the gifts falling into undeserving hands. I'm sure the princess will understand."

The elvish man's natural spring-green face took on an ashen cast. It seemed that despite their hostility towards him, the princess was beloved by Gortos.

"I have six to sell you, Jarl," he conceded.

Sigimar nodded, holding back his grin. At least one thing was going right this day.

They hitched up the horses and began the half-day march towards King Otmar's stronghold. At this point, Sigimar wouldn't be surprised if the wily prick set hellhounds on them, or even a small army.

The path to the keep made for an intimidating slog through deep, newly fallen snow. Evergreens added the only spot of living colour to an otherwise bleak landscape. The grasping branches of leafless trees curled over their heads on the increasingly steep trail. The final approach squeezed the caravan through a narrow gorge nestled between two tall, rocky outcroppings, as if the landscape had been cleaved by an enormous axe. High above, there could easily be archers lying in wait. Even someone with a few boulders could crush the lot of them below.

"Ingi."

"Jarl?"

"Give me my axe and shield. If we're to be assaulted before we reach the threshold, I mean to survive."

"But King Erlendr—"

"King Erlendr made it clear that King Otmar refused to give up his daughter if there wasn't an unwed jarl to marry her. So he can either marry his daughter to me to satisfy the ancient pact, or he can ensure there are no unwed jarls from the frontier here to marry his daughter. What do you suppose his solution to this problem will be?"

Ingi nodded gravely. He wove through the carts and soldiers and returned with Sigimar's bronze axe and shield. The weight felt comfortable, right. Sigimar, like most of his entourage, had dismounted when they first reached the gorge. Conversation had ceased the moment he'd taken hold of his weapons. In the quiet, he caught the sound of something, or someone, approaching from the cliff on his left.

"It doesn't sound like a scout," Ingi whispered.

It really didn't. It sounded like someone was tumbling down a hill—grunts of pain, the snapping of twigs, the utter lack of stealth. Whoever they were, they'd be in rough shape by the time they reached the caravan. If they didn't smash their head to pieces from the final fall.

"Be on your guard. It may be a diversion," Sigimar said.

Sigimar's ears twitched as he listened to the incoming wretch, picking up distinctly feminine cries of pain. When she finally flew over the lip of the cliff above and fell, Sigimar dropped his axe and shield to catch her. As the battered, freezing creature dared to open her eyes, her shocked, grey gaze met his own.

CHAPTER 5

Hypatia woke in an unfamiliar bed with her body aching. Terror galvanised her into action. She struggled to rip off the tangled sheets—only to find she'd been redressed. Her hands trembled as dark thoughts raced through her mind. Clumsiness overcame her and she fell onto the cold stone floor, bruising her knees and wrist. The only escapes afforded her were the heavy wooden door with its shiny brass fittings or the too-narrow window that looked far, far down onto rolling, snow-covered hills dotted with evergreens and denuded trees. Her pack was nowhere to be seen and neither were her shoes or clothes.

To her dread, the door began to creak open. If only she'd been born a fire mage, or almost anything else, she might have the magic to fend off her captor. Instead, Hypatia turned herself invisible and tried to calm her frantically beating heart and her shuddering, panicky breaths.

A woman with skin as pink as a rose and vibrant green hair stuck her head into the room, her bright green eyes going wide at the sight of the empty bed.

The fae woman posed a question in a strange language.

Hypatia recognised her from inside the crystal ball. Relief slammed into her. She was with her rescuers, not unknown captors. Now that she thought on it, her hurts had mostly been healed, the only bruises the ones she'd just given herself. Still, better to be cautious. Hypatia slipped behind the door and released her magic.

"Hello?" Hypatia replied in the mage tongue.

The fae woman rounded on her, a smile on her face. A string of incomprehensible words tumbled from her full lips, which left Hypatia in complete confusion. Though the woman's tone and expression indicated she was in a good mood, the harshness of the language didn't lend itself to conveying such. Hypatia mused that it probably sounded completely brilliant when shouting commands on a battlefield or cursing up a storm.

The woman wore a dazzling yellow dress embroidered with tiny red roses. The fabric had a heavy, velvety look to it and clung tightly to her upper body before it flared out at her petite waist. A thick, brown woollen cape was clasped at her throat with a golden pin.

Seeing that she wasn't being understood, the pink fae woman touched three fingers to her own lips and nodded with a smile. As Hypatia was about to muddle through a few words of her own, the woman reached out and pulled her head closer. Words and understanding flooded her mind, filling it to the point of agonizing pain. As quickly as it had struck, the spell dissipated, leaving her with a dizzying headache. Hypatia swayed on her feet.

"The pain will fade quickly. Translation spells are like that."

The fae woman had spoken true. In moments the pain was gone, and yet she fully understood the woman before her.

"You speak the mage tongue?" Hypatia asked.

She shook her head, green flowing curls swaying softly.

"Well, yes and no. Have you never performed a translation spell before?"

"No, I haven't."

"As I hear it, you are speaking my language, and as you hear it, I am speaking yours. It is the same spell woven into the crystal, though the one I just performed is permanent rather than temporary. However, if you were to say a word with no comparison in my tongue, I would hear it in your own tongue. If you stand in a room with only my language being spoken, you will hear your language yet speak mine, and vice versa if I were to travel to your realm."

Overcome by her curiosity, Hypatia couldn't help but ask.

"And if someone knew neither of our languages, what would they hear?"

The fae woman shrugged.

"I'm not certain. I learned all the Riverland languages through the spell when I was a child. But allow me to reintroduce myself properly. I'm Farohildis."

"Hypatia." Hypatia curtseyed.

"Good day to you, cousin. I never thought I would have a witchling as a cousin, but Oblivion is a strange world."

"I'm not a witchling though. I'm a mage."

"What's a mage?"

It was a very good question to which Hypatia didn't have a good answer. How could she define herself as a mage, as opposed to a witchling or a fae, in a way that wasn't entirely superficial? Or without relying on a cultural knowledge that she simply didn't possess?

"I'm not certain how to answer that question."

Farohildis laughed, the sound bright and cheerful.

"Never you mind. I'm simply pleased your magic is unlike that of a witch. Such a dreadful feeling whenever they're about." She shivered with disgust. "I've unpacked your belongings into the chest there." She pointed at the carved chest at the foot of the bed which Hypatia had missed in her panic. "But I found some bone, and I wasn't certain what you wished to do with it. Is it a keepsake, or would you like to find a suitable place to bury it in our ancestral plot? Oh, I suppose we could also call a necromancer if it's from someone you wish to speak to one last time."

Farohildis spoke so quickly that Hypatia had to take a few moments to absorb what she'd been told. She could speak to Kosmas again? Her heart leapt at the possibility.

"You can...bring him back?"

"Have you never hired a necromancer?"

Hypatia shook her head.

"He can be brought back for a short time. The spell dissolves the remains though, and afterwards there's no guarantee that the necromancer will call forth the right soul."

The swiftly crushed hope was an arrow to her breast.

"You can't bring him back for good?"

Sympathy shone in Farohildis' green eyes. She placed a comforting hand on Hypatia's shoulder.

"No, not without a body to put him in, and any body readily available is rotting. Summoned creatures are the only option, and they won't appear if a disembodied soul is nearby. Such a coincidence is of the gods' making. I'm sorry, Hypatia."

Hypatia collected herself, banishing the stinging tears. She should be grateful. Who else got to say a proper goodbye in circumstances like hers?

"Why would you do this for me?"

"We're family, aren't we?" Farohildis asked with an elegant shrug, as if such compassion were entirely natural amongst families.

"Then I would like the chance to say goodbye."

Farohildis nodded.

"I'll tell Father immediately. In the meantime, why don't you get dressed and join us for a meal? I can give you a gown of mine if you'd prefer something warmer."

"That is kind of you, but I'll wear my own dress."

Farohildis smiled and gathered Hypatia up in a hug.

"I'm so glad you called to us when you did. I'll return soon to show you the way to the dining hall."

With that Farohildis was out the door, humming a cheery tune. Hypatia held back a sob. When was the last time she'd received such kindness? Seen such a genuine smile? Roxane had bestowed such things on her only the other day, but they'd been the first in so long that receiving them still felt strange and new. Ah gods, she knew she owed these people a favour for rescuing her, but she would sell her soul to see Kosmas again. Hypatia threw her clothes and shoes on, all of which had been neatly tucked into the chest, cleaned and mended. She waited impatiently, her foot tapping with nervous excitement.

What could be taking so long? Hypatia opened the door to peer into the hallway. Her eyes were met with soaring stone covered in tapestries, and stone floors made plush with pelts. She'd expected a chill draft, but it was warm and pleasant. Would her rescuer be upset if she left the room? Would Farohildis know any differently if Hypatia remained invisible while she looked about?

Decided, Hypatia roamed the halls, hidden, following the sounds of voices, eyes taking in the strange style woven into the tapestries. The door to a room much like the one she'd woken in was slightly ajar, giving Hypatia a small glimpse of Farohildis' yellow dress and brown cloak, her back turned as she spoke to two other fae, one silver and blue, the other striped in orange and brown, her hair black.

"You," the blue-skinned, silver-haired fae man kissed Farohildis' forehead, "are the," he kissed her cheeks, "wiliest princess in the whole of Oblivion!"

"I'm free now, right?" Farohildis asked.

"Not yet," the striped fae woman answered. "Why you sent a curse rather than a tracking spell I'll never know. We could have been done with this situation years ago rather than waiting until the eleventh hour."

"You know what to do?" the blue and silver man asked Farohildis. Farohildis nodded.

"She knows to be quiet?" the green-haired fae asked.

The man smiled, his hand on Farohildis' shoulder.

"She has two husbands and five children to feed. She had to agree to keep her mouth shut before I paid her twice her stated price. She'll not betray us."

"So, what now, loves?" the striped woman asked, her brown eyes twinkling. "Do we feast to the occasion?"

The blue and silver man laughed.

"It's only fair. But do not celebrate before it is done. No need to tempt the gods."

When Farohildis turned around to leave after a final hug, Hypatia hurried back to the room, uneasy. What were they discussing? Surely it hadn't been Hypatia herself. The woman they'd mentioned had multiple husbands and children! And they were royalty! No doubt they had all manner of state affairs to discuss. Whatever it had been, it was not her business. Her unease was just punishment for eavesdropping where she shouldn't have.

Hypatia retrieved Kosmas' horn and skull fragment, her stomach a pit of butterflies. When Farohildis returned, it was all Hypatia could do not to leap at her.

"Your realm's fashions are so light, Hypatia. Do you not have a cold season there?" Farohildis' brows pinched in worry as she plucked at the thin material of Hypatia's dress.

It made Hypatia feel even guiltier for the intrusion.

"We do, but it snows very rarely in the parts I've travelled."

Farohildis unbuckled the jewelled clasp at her throat and swung her rich brown cloak about Hypatia's shoulders, its golden embroidery glittering in the light filtering through the narrow windows. It settled about her, unexpectedly heavy, warm and rough.

"You'll catch a chill in such things. Please, wear this for now." She smiled. "The necromancer has already responded to father's summons. She is setting up her ritual as we speak. Would you like to eat first, or..."

As if she'd be able to keep the food down for nerves?

"I would like to see the necromancer first. If that is possible."

"I thought that might be the case," Farohildis said, reaching into a well-hidden pocket in her gown's full skirt. "This is a contract that needs to be signed. My father has, of course, already agreed to pay the necromancer's fee, but you should be the one to sign this here." She pointed to a small blank spot on the heavily lettered scroll.

It was a script she'd never seen before.

"I don't know what this says."

"It's a standard contract," Farohildis replied. "Necromancers prefer to be paid upfront and stipulate that they're not responsible for any emotional damages to either the contractor or the deceased, and always state that the remains must be of the person being called. As you can probably imagine, their business can be a little unpredictable and quite emotional for all involved."

Hypatia nodded. She was no stranger to business contracts—or grief.

"Do you have a bottle of ink and a quill?"

"Ah, this must be signed in blood with a fingerprint. Sorry," Farohildis apologised, sheepish. Farohildis produced a pin from her pocket and held it out for Hypatia. When Hypatia hesitated, Farohildis pulled it away. "If you're uncomfortable, we can always wait on the necromancer," she offered.

Hypatia would think of nothing else until she saw Kosmas again. There was no reason to wait, aside from her own baseless paranoia. Farohildis had been true to her word thus far. She certainly took better care of Hypatia than her own family had.

"No, I don't want to wait," Hypatia replied, taking the pin from Farohildis and pricking her finger, waiting until enough blood welled to coat her finger. That done, she pressed it to the parchment. Satisfied, Farohildis tucked the document under her arm and cast a small healing spell on Hypatia's finger. An unnecessary kindness. It left an oddly tart taste on her tongue.

"Alright, I'll show you the way. Bring the remains."

Hypatia couldn't concentrate on the tidbits of history Farohildis regaled her with as they walked through narrow passages and descended spiral stone staircases. Sculptures, tapestries, pelts and weapons decorated the walls until they descended to a basement level. Though magic warmed and lit it, there was still a distinctly earthy scent and no natural light in the room they entered. Inside, a woman with golden, braided hair and sun-kissed skin swathed in thick, dark robes raised her head at their entrance.

"Necromancer, this is Hypatia. She is the one who requires your services." Farohildis turned to Hypatia. "I'll be waiting outside to give you a bit of privacy and so as not to distract the witch with my magic during the ritual."

"Thank you." Hypatia grabbed her hand and squeezed it.

Farohildis placed her hand over Hypatia's and squeezed back, a smile creasing the corners of her eyes.

"You needn't thank me, Hypatia. I hope you find the closure you seek. I'll see you when you're finished here."

Farohildis nodded her head to the necromancer and closed the door behind her.

"I didn't expect another witch." The necromancer smiled.

"I'm not a witch. I'm a mage."

"Oh?" she asked distractedly as she drew a symbol on the floor. "Have you ever participated in a necromantic ritual?"

"No."

"Place the remains in the centre. It's safe for you to be inside the circle as well, but if you wish to leave it, let me know. What is the name of the one I'll be calling?"

"Kosmas," Hypatia answered, her heart leaping into her throat as she saw the marks on the floor. She shoved down her trepidation, refusing to let old fears rob her of the chance to see Kosmas again. This was not Lethe. It was not the cursed circle she'd reconstructed for her research.

"The ritual will eat away at the remains, and you'll only be able to speak with Kosmas as long as the remains last. After that, no guarantee what gets called up is actually your dearly departed. Are you ready?"

"Yes," Hypatia replied, not entirely sure if she'd spoken the truth.

There had been so much she wished to share with Kosmas, wanted to say, that she didn't know if there would ever be enough time. She'd had two years to think of all the things she would tell him, and now her mind was distressingly blank.

Hypatia placed his precious skull fragment in the centre of the strange patterns, symbols and swirls, twitchy at the knowledge that she would need to give it up to see him. Her gut roiled as the necromancer chanted in low tones and slit her arms, letting the blood flow. Hypatia let out a slow breath, reminding herself this was for Kosmas. The symbols glowed, and a mist enveloped the circle.

Hypatia gasped.

Kosmas stood before her. His crooked grin and mischievous dark eyes brought tears to her own and tugged her lips into an answering smile. She forgot her fears, leapt at him and stumbled, landing in a heap. He was just an illusion in the mist.

"Kosmas?"

"Hello, my love." He smiled wistfully, his scaly tail sweeping from side to side. "I don't think I can touch you like this, but it's so wonderful to see you."

"I've missed you," she croaked, wiping away tears.

"And I you," he laughed. "But don't go getting any ideas. Life is for the living. I expect you to live until you're old and grey and you've collected enough adventures for the two of us. I want you to be happy and loved. Promise?"

Hypatia swallowed passed the lump in her throat and nodded.

"I will. I promise," she lied. She was wholly undeserving of either.

He approached her and knelt, his misty hand cupping her cheek. She wished she could feel his warmth, smell his comforting scent, but it was not to be. There were so many things she'd never been able to tell him, dark secrets that stained her soul. Yet she couldn't make herself say them now that his loving gaze was upon her for the first time in two years. She didn't know if she could survive his scorn.

"Are you safe?" he whispered.

"I...why do you ask?" Her gut sank.

"I found a strange crystal ball. I was going to surprise you with it when you woke. I put it in your arms, but the second it touched your skin, a woman with green hair appeared. I didn't speak with her long, but Hypatia, when I refused to go to her, I think she cursed me, and potentially you. Whatever you do, get rid of the artefact, and don't trust anyone you see in it."

A chill ran down her spine. Her heart tripped into a racing beat, pumping dread into her veins. Green hair. And a curse...*instead of a tracking spell.*

"K-Kosmas...I made a deal with her to save my life. I owe her a favour. She's the reason we're speaking now!"

His eyes reflected her growing panic.

"Hypatia, run!"

CHAPTER 6

Hypatia swiped the last fragment of Kosmas' horn and tore out of the necromancer's circle. Wrapping herself in her magic, erasing herself from sight, she barrelled towards the heavy door as the necromancer collapsed on the stone floor howling in pain. She couldn't stop, refused to, hardening her heart. The necromancer might be in league with her supposed rescuers. Hypatia raced up the stone steps and onto the ground floor of the castle. Sprinting blindly through the tapestry-laden hallways, she reached a door leading to her freedom. Heaving it open cost her precious time, a battle against shin-deep snow blocking the way.

Freezing air made her gasp. Hypatia squinted, eyes tearing up at the harsh daylight reflecting off the blinding white. Pushing her trepidation aside, she ploughed through the deep snow, desperate to be away from Farohildis and her family. A narrow path, partly snowed-over, was marked by the impressions of footprints leading away from the castle. Hypatia followed it. To one side was a rock face, to the other was an icy, steep decline dotted with a few trees clinging on. Anything below that was impossible to make out from her vantage.

Despite hiding herself from sight, anyone possessing eyes or ears would stand a chance at locating her. Her short, soaked boots squeaked and crunched the snow, footprints impossible to miss. Her breath sawed out of her cold-seared lungs. Her feet were like ice stuck through with pins. Wind lashed her faced like a cat's claws. Clutching her borrowed cloak as closely as she could, her fingers burned. She'd never known cold like this, never imagined it would be so painful. Already she was shivering.

One moment of distraction was all it took.

She planted her foot wrong on a slippery patch beneath the snow and slipped. Hypatia tumbled down the slick decline, crashing through snow, snapping the stems of young trees. Jagged rocks and icy bumps cut and bruised her from head to toe. Up and down lost all meaning in the whirl.

Then she was free-falling.

She squeezed her eyes shut, bracing for a landing that would surely shatter bones.

The impact stunned her but not in the way she expected. Strong, warm arms wrapped around her. Her eyes flew open. What she saw had her gasping. A man with brownish-green skin looked down at her with amber eyes brimming with concern. His long burgundy hair tickled her neck with its thick braids as he cradled her close. She noticed his ears were pointed, just like the fae, yet his were quite elongated in comparison.

Would he be a friend or foe?

"That was quite a fall. We heard the whole of it. Do you think you can stand?" he asked, his voice a deep rumble that sent shivers down her spine.

"I'm not sure," she replied.

"Ingi, call Brynja the healer to attend to me."

Hypatia noticed the tips of the man's rabbit ears before she looked down to find the man they were attached to. Just how short was Ingi? Just how tall was the man who held her?

"Is that wise?" Ingi asked.

"Do you hear or scent anyone else on the trails above?"

"No, Jarl."

"Neither do I. Were there others up there when you fell?" the man asked her.

Hypatia shook her head. A mistake. Instant nausea roiled her gut as her head spun.

"I'll be back shortly," Ingi said, bowing before he raced off.

Hypatia only then noticed she was at the head of a long line of encumbered men and women, all dressed in furs and mail. Some appeared as mages did, some with animal appendages and all with varying shades of skin tones she was familiar with. Others appeared fae, as Farohildis had, while some towered over the rest, their ears stretched and even more pointed.

The man holding her looked her over, assessing, his eyes lingering on her sodden, torn, filthy clothes. When his eyes met hers, she felt naked, as if he'd seen through to the foolhardy fear that had driven her poorly planned escape. Would he drag her back or set her free?

"You must be freezing."

"Yes," she answered, uncertain.

He nodded, decided. About what, she didn't know. Striding towards one of the wagons, he edged past the team of woolly oxen that had stopped and were currently digging through the snow. He seated her gently on the vacated driver's seat and winked.

"I brought these as gifts, but I don't think they'll be greatly missed," he said, lifting a crate twice her size off the cart and placing it beneath her dangling feet.

He tore off the lid to reveal snow-white fur garments, all of which looked enviably warm. Hypatia shivered. When he stood tall again, she realised with a dull shock that he must be half a man taller than her, and twice her width. Given how effortlessly he handled the large crates, much of it was muscle.

He could easily snap her in half.

"You'll freeze to death before noon if you run about in clothes like that." He touched her ankle. She flinched. "May I?"

Hypatia nodded, wary. She let him pull off her boot with impossibly gentle fingers and then dry her foot with his cloak. Reaching into the crate, he pulled out a tall boot wrapped in fur. He slid her foot into it but stopped at the torn hem of her skirt.

"I'll look away, but the wet fabric shouldn't go inside the boot. Can you move it out of the way?"

She paused, not knowing if she could trust him. Hypatia searched his compellingly severe face.His eyes were deep-set, his nose long and his strong jaw accentuated by a bushy beard of the same burgundy as his hair. He wasn't smiling, lending him a businesslike seriousness. She searched his eyes for guile or threat, yet found none.

Not that she was a decent judge of such things, if recent events were taken into consideration. A frigid gust made up her mind for her.

"A-alright."

Hypatia pulled her damp, clinging skirts up with some wiggling and effort, all of which reminded her of new injuries. The man softly pulled the boot up over her knee, expertly tying the leather laces. She allowed him to do the same for the other boot. Hypatia quickly shoved her skirts down when Ingi and another woman got close. The woman was tall, broad-shouldered and possessed a full figure and dark brown skin. She looked like she could be a mage, but now Hypatia knew better. This healer was a witch. Her eyes betrayed her as older than her youthful appearance suggested. She clucked at Hypatia.

"Got into a fight with the hillside, I see. I'll get you healed up in no time."

The magic felt warm as it wrapped around her, soothing her hurts and clearing her head.

"Thank you."

"Just following orders. No thanks necessary." The witch smiled.

"Dry her clothes, if you can," the tall man said.

"If I *can?* Gods below, what do you take me for?" she grumbled.

With a flick of the witch's wrist, the wetness clinging to Hypatia's skin, hair and clothes was gone. Before Hypatia could thank her, the woman strode off down the line.

Already the tall man was pulling more items from the crate. He placed a fuzzy hat on her head, tying it under her chin, and wrapped an impossibly soft length of fur around her neck. A pair of thick gloves followed, which she gratefully donned. Finally, he helped her down off the cart, his hands strong and sure on her waist. Unclasping Farohildis' cloak from around her, he quickly swaddled her in a coat, the same bright white as the other garments and equally warm. He knelt to fasten the ties that would keep it closed. When he was done, he stood, looked her over and nodded, satisfied.

Hypatia had to look up and up to see his face. The top of her head just reached his ribs. Despite his size and bulk, he was sweet and gentle. She would not forget this man's compassion.

"If you follow our trail in the snow, you should reach a small market town before dark." He fished a coin from a pouch at his hip and placed it in her hand, closing her gloved fingers around it. "Stay at the inn. With luck, we'll be returning there tomorrow, maybe sooner. If you wish, you may join us on our journey to Elmheim."

"Thank you." Tears stung her eyes. There were good people in the world, and she would hold this fact close to her heart.

He shook his head, a rueful look on his face.

"I know a runaway when I see one. I've been one too many times to count. Do me a favour, and don't get caught."

"I won't," she swore, both to him and to herself.

She patted her hip where, miraculously, the tiny remnant of Kosmas' horn still resided in her skirt pocket. Hypatia would escape the fae and whatever they had in store for her. If life was for the living, then she would live hers as she chose.

Sigimar waited until the woman disappeared into the distance before taking up his axe, shield, and the lead position once more. His caravan soon came upon the imposing façade of King Otmar's keep. Set on a natural rise, several tiers of stone walls followed the natural curves of the hill. At the top sat a bloated stone structure, like a diseased crown. A call went up when his caravan appeared before the entrance to the first wall. The doors slowly creaked open, struggling mightily against the thick snow they were forced to push aside.

"Don't let your guard down. They may just be penning us before the slaughter," Sigimar whispered.

"I don't see the archers nocking their bows," Ingi replied.

Sigimar continued forward, heartened that if he were to die, at least his last act had been to help the pretty runaway with eyes that reminded him of spring storms. He'd wanted to know her name but suspected she wouldn't have been truthful. She'd been fleeing his future in-laws—a ringing endorsement of their characters! It dredged up dark memories. He'd run away from the orphanage and been dragged back so often, he still had to fight a shudder at the thought of the cheap summoning tokens the nannies had hoarded.

"If we die, I want you to know you've been a good travelling companion, Ingi."

The hare shifter snorted.

"And you've been a humourless bear. If we survive, you should take the little witch back as a mistress. I doubt your fae princess will be warming your bed for at least a few centuries, given your welcome."

Sigimar chuckled. He was less worried about how to go about having a relationship with his soon-to-be wife and more concerned that she would slit his throat or transform him into a beast she could sell off or slaughter for dinner.

Though, the more he thought on it, the more tempting the idea of bringing the witch back was. Her magic would naturally repel his bride, and she'd been intriguing in her way; sun-kissed skin, hands callused in unusual places, a slightly hooked nose and full lips, her dark hair swept off her face in intricate braids.

"The little witch was terrified. I doubt she would join us."

"Oh? Then maybe I was watching a different interaction. When was that *other* time you smiled at a woman and she gazed upon you like a hero from a song?" Ingi smirked.

"Where have you been hiding your wit all this time?"

"With my blades, Jarl."

Sigimar noted that Ingi carried no shield, preferring instead two short swords and a number of small daggers. The others of his entourage shared Ingi's readiness for battle.

Good.

The guards at the gates watched his caravan in silence. The only reaction his people seemed to stir in them was the odd lob of spit sent their way. The inner gates continued to open to admit them. Not a single archer nocked their bow. A blessing. Elves and the elvish could be brought low by poison, poisoned arrows posing a particular problem. They often brought elves low enough that someone could truly kill them by taking their head, and given Otmar's scheming thus far, he would put nothing past him.

Every step forward only ratcheted up the tension in Sigimar's gut, though he held his limbs loosely through centuries of battle practice. When at last they reached the doors to the ugly castle, they were opened to admit him.

The guards standing watch crossed their spears in his way.

"No outsider may enter while carrying weapons."

Sigimar reluctantly shed his weapons, handing them to Ingi, taking his ceremonial amber axe only. The guards allowed him entry, but barred the hare shifter's way.

"Only the jarl may enter. Everyone else remains here."

Ingi stepped back, his lips pressed in a grim line.

"I'll return shortly with my bride. Turn the caravan around in preparation," Sigimar said, hoping they weren't his last words.

Ingi nodded.

Sigimar turned and strode through the castle entrance. Inside, the place gave off warmth and cheer, a myriad of tapestries and colourful carvings decorating the walls. Anxiety kept him on alert. The servants, when they did appear, completely ignored him. He was left to follow the well-worn path to the inner hall where Sigimar hoped he would find King Otmar. The guards at the door flicked their eyes over him, their stony expressions giving nothing away as they opened the intricately carved oak doors. No greetings or announcements were made as he entered. Instead, he was met with the cold, mocking gazes of his future in-laws and bride. They sat on thrones of gold-plated bone. The rugs at their feet were the skins of animals. Warriors were present, feasting, but only in small numbers. He noted that *they* had been granted permission to carry weapons.

Sigimar knelt, presenting his amber and gold axe as proof of his identity.

"Greetings to King Otmar. I am Jarl Sigimar Ashla, come on orders of King Erlendr of Elmheim to marry your daughter, Princess Farohildis."

King Otmar sneered, raising his grey-blue chin and flicking a strand of silver hair behind his pointed ear. Queen Asta, her skin striped like a tiger's eye, placed a bejewelled hand on her husband's. Both were dressed in fine fabrics, glossy furs and ceremonial bronze breastplates, gold and silver crowns atop their perfectly plaited hair. By the queen's side sat

Princess Farohildis, radiant in a yellow embroidered gown. Only her equally cruel sneer marred her beauty.

"I am not at all sorry to disappoint you, Jarl. You will not be taking my daughter back to Elmheim with you. The pact only requires one of my blood, and so we have procured the sacrifice required," Otmar announced.

The princess was the last of her line, the only living child of King Otmar. This fact was widely known. Did they believe they would be able to insult Erlendr this way or defy the terms of the ancient pact without consequence?

Sigimar stood up at the affront, keeping an eye on the warriors who watched with interest but not battle intent. The queen tossed something small at him. Sigimar caught it. The object in his palm knocked the breath out of him, leaving his lungs in a painful rush. He wanted to lash out, to scream, to do as he'd done for the past decade when guilt or sorrow or horrifying memories threatened to consume him. Anger would have been easier. But he stood before royalty, their loyal swords not a few paces away. It was all he could do not to let his hands tremble as bile crept up his throat. Did Otmar know? Did they know what heartbreak and horror this small token had dredged up? The desperation and loneliness?

"Father, I don't think the jarl knows how to use the summoning token," the princess cooed, the sly tilt of her smile a vicious mockery as she twirled a strand of green hair around a pink finger.

"His elvish blood has robbed him of the magic to use it, maybe?" the queen mused.

Sigimar had enough magic to activate the dreaded clay token, but he was too busy keeping himself from crumbling to speak. He wouldn't do it. Subjecting someone to that would be monstrously cruel.

"If you can't say the words, you'll never meet your bride, Jarl," Otmar taunted. "She disappeared only an hour past, so if you would prefer to hunt her like the animal you are, you're welcome to put your nose to the ground to catch her scent."

The warriors in the hall chuckled.

It would be better to find the woman connected to the token than use it to summon her. The process was unpleasant, nauseating, and exhausting. It was meant to weaken the person summoned, so that they would be pliant and quiet. Sigimar had been left lying in his own sick often enough as a child after being summoned back to the orphanage he'd fled. The only thing stopping him from crushing the hellish thing was his oath to Erlendr to bring a woman back. Sigimar shoved his memories back down where they couldn't affect him and raised his eyes to Otmar's.

He wished he could plant his axe in the dusty, withered crevice where Otmar's heart supposedly lay. If he used just enough force, would he be able to pierce the blackguard's breastplate with the amber head of his ceremonial axe?

The princess rolled her eyes.

"You overstay your welcome, Jarl. If you won't summon her, I will," she declared. A tendril of her magic reached out to the token. "I summon thee whose blood lies within."

"No!" Sigimar cried, huddling over the token to prevent her magic from reaching it.

But it was too late.

A woman slammed into him, stumbling back. Sigimar steadied her with his hands on her small shoulders. A horrible weight crushed his heart in his chest. He recognised those clothes. He knew those eyes. Sigimar had just wished her well and told her not to get caught. And now, this woman was captive once more, and he her jailor. She gasped for breath and swayed on her feet. He pushed down the screams in his head. Pocketing the token and sheathing his ceremonial axe, he knelt down to her height and spoke so that only she could hear him.

"I'm going to slow your racing heart, alright?"

Her panicked grey eyes began to roll back. Sigimar, through long practice, wove the only spell he'd ever mastered and placed his hand on her chest.

"*Slow*," he whispered.

The woman doubled over in a fit of coughs, her breath sawing in and out, gradually slowing. She looked up at him and then around, eyes lingering with dread on Otmar's family.

"No," she croaked, voice full of terror.

"Congratulations on your marriage, Jarl. If Erlendr wants to contest it, please give him the contract with my regards." Otmar grinned and tossed a scroll of parchment at Sigimar. "Her belongings are at the entrance. Now, be gone."

Sigimar grabbed the parchment and placed it in a pocket of his cloak. The woman was swaying on her feet, no doubt suffering the debilitating vertigo that followed a summoning.

"Put your arms around my neck if you can," he said to the woman in hushed tones.

With shaky hands she complied, moaning as he gathered her up in his arms and stood.

"Close your eyes and breathe slowly. It will pass," he whispered to her.

Her breath fluttered against his neck. He spared one last glare at the smirking king and the sneering royals at his side.

"King Erlendr will hear of your actions. I will petition him so that not a single soul from all of Gortos benefits from the treasures of Ashla."

"Has the miasma addled your brain? Ashla is a toxic wasteland filled with cannibalistic monsters! Only the Hero of the Frontier has made any headway," the queen scoffed.

Sigimar smiled. It felt ugly.

"*I* am the Hero of the Frontier. *I* cleared a territory of miasma half as large as Gortos only a decade ago. *I* am the wealthiest jarl beyond the mountain pass, and when I uncover even more of the lost continent and its treasures, my court will put yours to shame! My wife will live better than any queen!"

News of his feat had travelled to Gortos, but not his description. The slack-jawed shock on their faces made that plain. Sigimar turned and strode away. It was better this way. He had no desire to wed Farohildis with her cruel sneers and crueller magics. While his entrance had been unremarked upon, his exit was closely watched. He reached the castle doors. A single chest sat nearby. Did the woman really have so little?

The guards opened the outer door.

"Ingi!"

Ingi jumped to attention, confused at the sight of him.

"Her belongings are in that chest. Add it to one of the carts, and let's be on our way."

"But...she isn't...is she?"

"Let King Erlendr sort that out. For now, treat her as such."

Ingi bowed and grabbed the chest summarily handed to him by one of the guards.

"What is your name?" Sigimar asked her.

"Hypatia," she whispered. "I'm not your wife. I refuse. You can't...can't decide that for me. You have no right. I have not consented to this marriage."

Not surprising. This wasn't his idea of a proper marriage either.

"And I won't ask anything of you. Whatever trickery Otmar has used, King Erlendr will set it right. Until then, I will protect you." He swore it as much to her as to himself. He could put aside his own misery long enough to do that at least. Then he could go back to rotting on the frontier like the useless, broken man he was.

"What if they...?"

Sigimar transferred her weight from two arms to one. She was light enough that it was no strain. She moaned as she shifted, tightening her shaky grip on his neck. He pulled the token from his pocket and held it up before her.

"Open your eyes, Hypatia."

She squinted at the object between his fingers.

"This is a summoning token, largely used against children who have a tendency to run off. Only one can exist with a person's blood in it at a given time. I have the only one that can drag you back here." He crushed it to dust in his fist and presented her with the evidence. "And now it no longer exists."

"Good."

Sigimar waited until they had left the final wall ringing the keep before he approached Brynja.

"I think I'm going to be sick," Hypatia moaned.

"Not if I can help it. Healer!" he called.

Brynja rushed to his side. He knelt so the woman could work her magic on Hypatia.

"Summoning sickness," Sigimar explained to the bewildered witch.

She nodded in understanding and pressed a gentle hand to Hypatia's forehead to work her magic.

"Poor girl. Not your day, is it?" Brynja smiled sympathetically.

Hypatia let out a dark chuckle.

"Not my year, actually."

"You're in good company now, so rest easy," the healer reassured her.

"Thank you," Hypatia sighed, colour returning to her cheeks.

"Jarl, we have a sleigh prepared. Perhaps it would be better to..." Brynja suggested.

Sigimar nodded and gathered Hypatia back up into his arms, following the witch along the length of the caravan.

"I can walk now," Hypatia announced.

"You'll be asleep in minutes, trust me," Sigimar replied.

"I feel fine," she protested.

"Good. Then my healer has the skills she was hired for."

Hypatia released an exasperated sigh.

"What is your name?" she asked peevishly.

"Sigimar."

"Sigimar, I would prefer to walk on my own. I'm not about to fall asleep amidst a group of strangers, well-intentioned though they may be." She yawned.

"I've had summoning sickness too many times not to know better," he replied, hiding his smirk as he stepped into the sleigh and settled himself. The shifter with the reins nodded at him and set the horses into motion.

"I don't need to be in your arms." She scowled, taking her hands from his neck and crossing her arms.

"How else will you keep from falling off the bench onto the floor? How will you keep warm?" he asked

Despite her frustration her eyelids were drooping.

"Stubborn ass," she hissed.

He couldn't suppress the grin that bloomed on his face.

"Takes one to know one."

As Hypatia drifted off to sleep in his arms, Sigimar wondered how long it had been since he'd smiled so much.

Chapter 7

Angry whispers woke Hypatia. Eyes shut and breathing even, she listened. Sigimar's arms still cradled her, her head resting on his chest, nose tickled by the fur lining of her scarf. Heavy blankets kept her pleasantly warm, even as a chill gust stung the exposed skin of her face. Sigimar carefully shifted her so that even that was blocked out.

"What possessed you to insult King Otmar in his own castle? In the heart of his territory?" Ingi hissed.

"They knew full well what that token would do to her. Does she look like she belongs in Otmar's court? No. They obviously kidnapped her and then treated her like chattel," Sigimar retorted.

Ingi sighed. "We'll be lucky if they don't set all the beasts of Gortos on us in the night. And don't think we'll be staying at any inns on our way. If we thought we had trouble travelling here, just wait until news spreads."

"He won't kill us and risk violating the pact," Sigimar whispered.

Hypatia tensed.

"Otmar might not kill us, but the cold very well could. Either way, we'll find no help in town."

"Set up the camp then. Have some of the fae and witches work on warmth charms, if they're capable. And if anyone on watch spots a null, use them as a sacrifice for a pocket realm."

What on Oblivion had she just gotten herself caught up in? An angry king, cold that killed, and sacrifices? Gods below, maybe Kosmas had been right—maybe Farohildis had cursed them both two years ago. Hypatia strained her hearing but nothing more was said. Had Ingi already left? Would she be sleeping outside? Would she survive the night?

"Good evening, little eavesdropper."

Hypatia's eyes popped open, and she tried—fruitlessly—to put some distance between herself and Sigimar. He hadn't hurt her yet, but at this point, she'd be a fool not to be wary, especially after all that talk of violence. It was difficult to make him out in the dark, but she could've sworn she'd seen his lip twitching up into a smile. Above her, the sky was full of unfamiliar stars. Just where on Oblivion was she?

"That implies I intended it. I did not. And how did you even know?" She kept her voice steady and conversational. Men were about as predictable was wild boars; one did not anger one without paying for it.

"You're in my arms. Of course I would know."

"As to that, you can let me go now."

He sat her on the bench opposite him in the open-air sleigh. She pulled the blankets closer, regretting the loss of his warmth. Hypatia tried, without success, to locate some kind of escape route. The caravan had long since stopped, and everyone seemed busy preparing the camp, setting up tents and adding wood to a blazing fire. The woods beyond were shrouded in the darkest night. She was entirely alone with the man before her.

"How are you feeling?" he asked.

"I'm well, thank you."

He stared at her for a while in silence before sighing and scratching at his beard in irritation. She gripped the blankets, paralyzed by fearful uncertainty.

"I know you're afraid. You have every reason to doubt my intentions. I suspect your time as Otmar's prisoner was…unpleasant. You may run away, if you wish, but the cold will kill you tonight, and I've found the people of Gortos to be collectively indifferent to the fate of outsiders. If you decide to stay, I will treat you with the utmost care and respect." He took a scroll from his pocket and unfurled it for her benefit. She squinted, recognizing the odd contract she'd signed in blood. She shivered, and not with cold. "If your signature on the marriage contract is genuine, you won't be able to deny the magic drawing you towards Elmheim for long. It would be best to journey with me there to have my king dissolve it. Once that's done, you'll be free to go wherever you please."

Hypatia swallowed back bile. Gods below, if he were telling the truth...What had she done? How could she have so foolishly signed a contract without knowing its contents? Why had she trusted Farohildis? Her fervent desire to have some measure of closure with Kosmas had blinded her. She hadn't even gotten the chance to tell him she'd loved him.

"Oh...I see."

"Will you join me on my journey to Elmheim?" he asked, tucking the scroll back into a pocket of his cloak.

What an absolute mess. She'd traded being a traitor in hiding and her mother's pawn for being Farohildis' plaything and an unwilling bride. At least there was a way to be out of this latest quagmire—not that she relished travelling in this cold, or begging royalty for favours.

"I don't suppose I have any other options," Hypatia replied shakily.

"For what it's worth, I'm sorry this happened to you." His bushy brows pinched with pity.

"It was my fault for being so careless." She clutched the blankets tighter, wishing she could just close her eyes, curl up on herself, and sleep it all away. It hadn't worked two years ago when she'd wallowed in the deepest depths of her grief, and it didn't work now.

"Are you a witch?" he asked.

Hypatia shook her head.

"I'm a mage."

"I've never heard of mages before. Can you make warmth charms?"

"I'm afraid not." She smiled ruefully. *Wouldn't that be nice in this frigid hell?*

Sigimar shrugged as if it was no bother. The breeze that cut right through to her bones suggested otherwise.

"And where do you come from?"

"The empire, originally."

"Which empire?"

What an odd question. She'd never really considered it, but she supposed there were probably empires aside from her own.

"Lethe, the Empire of Mages," she answered.

"I've never heard of it."

It was Hypatia's turn to shrug.

"Lethe doesn't know of Gortos, Ashla or Elmheim either."

And unsurprisingly so. Until a few years ago, Lethe had refused to countenance relations with the peoples outside their isolated continent. What she wouldn't give for a proper map.

"Do you have anywhere you wish to go?"

Hypatia nodded.

"I...I was hoping to go to a land ruled by women. I'd heard of such places, and before... everything, I'd been trying to reach it."

He crossed his arms, eyes distant, thinking.

"You mean the Witchlands?" he asked.

"You know of it?" She widened her eyes in hope. *Please, gods, let this nightmare be over soon.*

"There are many such places. The Queendom of Isro is the closest, and it's on the way to Elmheim."

Hypatia almost wept with relief.

"Then, can't you take me there instead and rip up the marriage contract now?"

"No. The contract is enforced through blood magic that has roots in the ancient pact between Elmheim and the Riverland realms. Only the King of Elmheim has the power to free you."

"The Riverlands?"

"Ah, right, these names mean nothing to you. Come." Sigimar leapt from the sleigh in one agile movement that was at odds with his size and bulk.

He held up a hand to help her down the steps, which she needed in the deep dark. How was everyone seeing anything when the only light came from the stars and campfire that quickly lost its brilliance in the night? She misjudged the distance to the ground and stumbled, only to be saved from planting her face into the snow when Sigimar steadied her. She caught the scent of his fur cloak, her eyes riveted on his enormous hand swallowing up hers. He was just so overwhelmingly *big*. She cleared her throat and stepped away.

"What did you want to show me?" she asked.

"Wait here."

He walked off towards a tree and snapped a twig from it, easily reaching a high branch. When he returned, he knelt at her feet, smoothed out the trampled snow and began drawing lines. Even if she squinted, she would never make it out. Hypatia created a light in her hand, holding it over Sigimar's sketch in the snow.

He froze, slowly looking up at her, utter shock in his expression.

"You wield the healing light?" he asked, his voice tight with some strange emotion.

"Just light. There's nothing medicinal about it," Hypatia replied, unsure how to interpret the awe and concern in his amber eyes. Her magic was common and rather unremarkable in Lethe. Were lights and appearance charms rare in this part of Oblivion?

"Are you certain?"

"Well, yes. I've never healed anything with my light."

If she'd been born with healing as her mage gift, not only would she have been able to solve her family's financial woes single-handedly, but none of the worst parts of her life would have happened. If she'd had such a gift, a scholar's life would have unfolded for her without a single obstacle, even as a woman.

"Can you enchant light into objects?"

"No, I'm afraid my enchantment skills are rather limited. I can create little prisms, like mirrors which can reflect light and attach them to objects, but I'm afraid it's more pretty than practical in its effect. And they disappear the moment I stop concentrating."

That only seemed to baffle him more.

"Is there no corruption in your realm?"

It was such an odd question. She wasn't sure what it had to do with anything. Wherever there were people, inevitably there was corruption at all levels of society. Greed and ambition were omnipresent. In Lethe, it had felt like everyone's loyalty had come at a price... even hers.

"Of course there is," she replied.

"Apologies. It's just that those born with the healing light are highly sought after on the frontier—in Elmheim. They often have scores of men and women vying for a chance to have children with them. It is the only power on Oblivion capable of keeping the miasma on our borders at bay. If you had such power, King Erlendr would not, on principle, grant you freedom."

A chill ran down her spine. Thank the gods she was only a light mage, talented, but in no way one of those poor souls kept like prize stallions by Sigimar's king. Perhaps not having been born a healer was a small blessing after all. Sigimar stared another moment at her light before turning back to his drawing.

"This here," he pointed to a large circle, "is Ashla, blanketed by a thick miasma as tall as mountains, toxic to nearly everyone. Occasionally a strong wind pushes the miasma across the narrow channel into Elmheim here. In our corner of Oblivion, an ancient pact was signed by the ancestors of Elmheim and the Riverland realms beyond, binding their rulers to send provisions, warriors, and one of their kin each generation to keep the miasma at bay. Elmheim is everything beyond this mountain range," he swept a hand across a huge swath of land shaped vaguely like a sausage, "and is only accessible to the Riverlands through this narrow pass by boat," he pointed to a natural choke point in the middle. He had drawn several other lands and lettered them with unfamiliar symbols. He pointed to one only a couple of shapes away from the narrow pass. "This is Gortos, where we are now. This area beyond the mountain pass is what we call the Riverlands. Our journey will take us up through friendlier territory, places like Isro and Rei, before reaching the lake here," he pointed to an irregular shape in the centre of everything and below the pass, "where we can board a ship and travel to Elmheim. My land is here, in Ashla," he drew a circle in the southernmost corner of the Ashla-circle, "where a patch of the miasma was recently cleared."

"It seems far."

"It is. But with luck, we'll reach Elmheim before winter takes hold."

"This isn't winter?" Shock and despair laced every word. She didn't even want to imagine a place that got colder. If Isro was this miserable, perhaps there were Witchlands somewhere warmer that she could go.

Sigimar laughed.

"No, this is late autumn. If it were winter, we would not be travelling by foot."

Such an odd thing to say. Curiosity piqued, she couldn't help her next question.

"How else would you travel?"

"Through the skies. The ground routes would be entirely impassable."

"You can fly?" Her mouth dropped open in shock. What weren't the strange people outside the Empire capable of? Light that healed, dastardly objects that could teleport a person against their will, and now flight?

"Not me. But summoned beasts certainly can, as long as their summoners can expend the magic to keep them in this plane." He grinned. "What kind of peoples live in Lethe that flight surprises you?"

She blushed, feeling like some ignorant rube.

"I've only seen winged beast mages and wind mages fly before," she admitted. She'd not been in Nadioch when the fae had first come to Lethe's shores, flying through the skies on magical beasts and boats. In truth, the tales had seemed almost too fantastical to believe. More the fool her.

"What of fae, shapeshifters, nymphs or witches?"

Hypatia shook her head.

"There are only mages within Lethe."

From her experience of the fae, that was probably a blessing in disguise. Though Sigimar seemed nice enough.

"Your realm sounds very strange," he remarked.

"Not my realm. Not anymore," she replied, heart aching.

That life was over for her now. If she ever returned, her family's bounty on her would ensure she would never be able to know peace. And if her sins were revealed, she'd be made to rest in peace—after losing her head.

"No family, friends or lovers waiting for you?" he asked, not unsympathetically.

Roxane, her only true friend, deserved a better friend than Hypatia had been to her. Inside her cloak, her fingers found the tiny remnant of Kosmas' horn. Kosmas had been her only family worth remembering—loving. She blinked back tears, hoping she hadn't been too obvious. She snatched away her light, leaving them in darkness.

"I would only bring scandal to those I care about. The rest would use me cruelly or were lost to the void. And the only one I ever loved in that place is dead." To her horror, her voice was not only brittle but caught on the last word.

Sigimar stood, folding her into his arms, a comfort she hadn't experienced since Roxane had done so. Gods below, had that only been over a day ago? In the last two days she'd been embraced a handful of times, more than she could remember receiving in the past two years. And yet within the span of two days, a lifetime of emotions had shaken her to her bedrock. Seeing Kosmas again after two long years had only made the emptiness of her life painfully noticeable. The cruelty of Diocles and Farohildis had been salt in her long-standing wounds. How starved for kindness and affection must she be to find comfort in this stranger's embrace? Even now, she didn't know if she could trust her judgement, given her spectacular lapse with the princess. But she wanted this sympathy so badly. She wrapped her arms around his big body.

"I won't ask again. I'm sorry," his voice rumbled in his chest.

She gripped him tighter. He ran a soothing hand across her back.

Until the sound of polite coughing interrupted the moment.

Hypatia let go, scalded by more than just her embarrassment. She pushed back her tears, quelling the emotions tightening her throat.

"Your tent has been prepared, Jarl, Fru." Ingi bowed.

"Fru?" Hypatia asked, her voice strained.

"It means wife of the jarl," Ingi replied.

"But I'm—"

"Married to the jarl, are you not?" Ingi interrupted. "If someone doesn't use your title, they not only diminish you, they diminish Jarl Sigimar Ashla, Hero of the Frontier."

"Don't call me that!" Sigimar snapped, his voice like a crack of thunder. Hypatia flinched, yet Ingi remained unfazed, save for a twitch of his tall, white, rabbit ears.

"As you wish, Jarl. If you'll follow me?"

Sigimar turned to her then, his hands fisted as he tried and failed to meet her eyes.

"I apologise for my outburst. You've had enough to fear today. I shouldn't have added to it."

Hypatia snagged a hand on Sigimar's cloak, praying she wasn't making a grave error. He looked down at her glove, but with what expression, she couldn't read in the darkness.

"Are you alright, Sigimar?"

His dark chuckle held no hint of mirth.

"No."

Just a single word, and yet it contained a world of pain. Maybe there was something alike in them after all.

"Come down here, then."

He knelt, and she could see the bitter, tired look in his eyes. *As if staring into a mirror*, she thought. She wondered what loss he'd suffered, and did what she'd wished someone had done for her long before now. Wrapping her arms around him, she pulled him close for a hug. He froze. Had he not expected to receive kindness, even after giving his own? Had he been as alone as she? Tentatively, he wrapped his arms around her. He let her hold him for a short time. When she shivered, he sighed.

"Let's get to the tent before you freeze."

Sigimar took her hand and led her to the centre of the caravan where a roaring fire gave off a semblance of heat. People were stretching out gloved hands towards the blaze, huddled closer than was perhaps wise. A few transformed from people into smoke and then into animals she couldn't name, most with thick, furry pelts and shaggy coats before they settled before the flames. Some of the witches booed at them and called such magic unfair. Ingi waited by the fire for their arrival. The healer, seated by the blaze, turned around and spotted them, a salacious grin on her face. She held up a skin of liquid. Alcohol, if her cheery countenance was anything to go by.

"To the jarl and his fru! Try to keep it down tonight, eh?" She winked.

A congratulatory cry and a few happy laughs went up amongst the people at the fire.

"Keep your thoughts to yourself, and try to take your own advice," Sigimar intoned, which led to some good-natured teasing about the healer's noisy nightly activities.

Hypatia hoped no one could see her blush at the crude joke. Or her mortification that they thought she would do such a thing with a man she'd only met today. They turned away from the fire while another round of loud congratulations chased them to the nearest tent. Ingi held open the thick, felt flap. Hypatia stopped in her tracks. Were they to spend the night...together? Alone? Had the witch not been joking?

"It's probably not what you're used to, but the bed is made of furs, and there are warm blankets," Sigimar said.

"There is also a warmth charm keeping the temperature above freezing," Ingi added.

"But it's for both of us?" Hypatia asked, keeping her voice quiet.

Ingi shrugged.

"The few other tents are full to bursting, hence why many of the shapeshifters took their animal forms tonight," Ingi explained.

"I'm not...comfortable sleeping next to a man," Hypatia hedged.

Ingi's lips twitched.

"Of course. If the fru prefers the company of women, I'm certain Brynja, our healer, would keep you warm tonight."

Hypatia looked back at Brynja, who was already seducing three others at the fire, all women. She turned away, her cheeks heating. They were most certainly not jesting about nightly activities. Surely in this cold, that was unwise?

"Ingi," Sigimar said in a warning tone.

Ingi bowed his head and sauntered off.

"Would you prefer to sleep alone or in the company of women? There will be several who will happily huddle up with you tonight," Sigimar offered.

"But where will you sleep?" Hypatia asked, shivering already.

"By the fire with the shapeshifters," he nodded.

He would freeze to death out here. She felt like ten kinds of fool. Everyone else was either sleeping outside in animal form or huddled for warmth with multiple other people. He'd been kind so far, even though she'd been a complete stranger to him. One night huddled close wouldn't kill her, but the cold certainly would. Even clothed as she was, she might not be able to stay warm enough throughout the night. And yet, fears lingered.

"You vow not to...to force me?"

"Force you to what?" he asked, confusion plain before horrified understanding widened his eyes and twisted his expression. "Gods below, never! Wait here, and I'll gather some of the women to bunk with you."

Hypatia sighed, catching hold of his cloak before he charged off.

"No, let's share the tent."

"There's no need. If you're uncomfortable—"

"If I find that it is uncomfortable, I'll tell you."

Sigimar assessed her, hesitant. At least he seemed an honourable sort. Eventually he relented, lifted the flap and ushered her inside where the temperature was balmy in comparison. Sigimar came in after, taking up altogether too much room. He settled on the furs and patted the place beside him.

"Best sleep while you can. We'll be up at dawn and travelling quickly until we're free of Gortos."

"Because of the king?" she asked, recalling Ingi's dire warnings.

"Because my temper got the better of me, but yes, also Otmar."

Hypatia settled in, keeping as much space between her and Sigimar as she could. Despite her clothes and the blankets, she was too cold to sleep.

She remembered how warm it had been in his arms, but embarrassment and trepidation kept her from sliding closer.

"I won't bite," he remarked.

Was even he feeling the uncomfortable chill that pervaded the tent? No wonder each one was full to bursting with people.

"I'm not worried about your teeth," she intoned, her brow arched.

Sigimar snickered.

"Only fools risk losing their parts to the cold. I simply want whatever warmth you can share. Aren't you cold?"

Hypatia shivered, swallowed her pride, and closed the distance between them. He snaked an arm around her, drawing her flush against him. As she was about to protest, the unmistakable sounds of lovemaking penetrated the tent.

"Are they really...?"

"Yes. Every damn night," he grouched.

"But you just said—"

"And they're fools. But they're making warmth charms. Old magic. Try to block it out, if you can."

Making warmth charms? Old magic? She flushed, not certain she wished to know more. It seemed like the whole of the camp could hear the lovers, and not everyone was content to politely ignore it.

"If you can't make her scream in under a minute, you're doing it wrong!" someone around the fire called.

"Has your tongue frozen off yet?" another queried.

The sounds only intensified.

"How can they, when they know everyone can hear them?" Hypatia asked, her face flaming. She hid it in Sigimar's chest, which rumbled from his quiet laughter.

"I think that's the point."

The sounds dragged on until embarrassment became annoyance.

"How long?" Hypatia asked, not bothering to hide the acid in her tone. There was something to be said for stamina and quite another thing to be said for gratuitous obnoxiousness.

"Long," he answered, shifting so that a hand hovered over her ear. "I'll block out some of the noise. Try to get some sleep."

His large hand covered her ear under the fur of her hat, his fingers threading through her loosely braided hair, thumb resting against her cheekbone, branding her skin with his warmth, even through his gloves. Most of the noise was replaced by the dull hum of his pulse as she rested her head against his chest. She closed her eyes and, miraculously, slept.

Chapter 8

Sleep had been elusive for Sigimar. It gave him far too much time for his least favourite activity—brooding. Or, according to his huskarl Drest, his only activity. He'd spent much of the night mentally cursing his healer. Once quiet took hold of the camp and the warmth charms dispersed to his people, anxiety tormented him until the early hours. He was nothing more than a fraud. He wasn't a hero, a gentleman, or a leader. He was just the loathsome creature that had profited from his brother's death.

He didn't deserve Hypatia's companionship and certainly not her unexpected kindness. She should have sent him to sleep outside like the scum he was. Because it was obvious from everything about her that Hypatia was noble-born. The grace with which she carried herself was the kind he'd only witnessed at Erlendr's court, her words too refined for his ears, her manners impeccable. He'd grown up amongst hardened warriors and outcasts of all kinds, more at home swinging an axe and singing a bawdy tune than turning a pretty phrase or donning a polite mask. In every way, she was his better.

No longer could he resort to anger in the face of guilt, pain or grief as he had while wallowing in Ashla. Not with Hypatia expecting him to be a protector. She'd been through enough. That fiery temper had protected him, shielded the parts of him that were cracked or shattered. It was always easier to reach for anger than to accept the nakedness of vulnerability. But as he watched her sleeping beside him, trusting him to keep her warm and unharmed, he knew the man he needed to be.

Though no matter what he did, he would never be the protector she deserved, that Dag had thought him to be, that the whole of Elmheim believed he was. Every accolade was poison in his veins. Every fancy mark of his station was a dagger to his heart. Every act of obeisance a screaming condemnation of his failure. Every draugr he slew, a vicious reminder of Dag's last moments. And now Hypatia, summoned like a runaway prisoner to be wife to a person wholly unworthy of her, was another reminder of it all.

At least he could take her to Erlendr and help her regain her freedom. It would be a relief to send her on her way to the life she deserved. One good deed wouldn't undo all the carnage in his wake, but it would be something.

As the sun dawned, Hypatia began moaning and tensing in her sleep. She jolted awake, a desperate, fearful gasp escaping her lips. She struggled, tangling herself in her cloak and blankets.

"Shh, you're alright, Hypatia."

Eyes the grey of a spring storm stared up at him with more trust than he deserved. She looked away, took a shaky breath and placed her hands against his chest, not to push him away, but as if she were anchoring herself. He put his on top and squeezed. The fear cleared from her eyes. For the first time in too long, he wanted to deserve that trust, to be worthy of something, to be more than a miserable fraud freezing his balls off on the frontier.

"Sorry, I thought... I couldn't remember where I'd fallen asleep, and I was dreaming of, well, running."

"I promise you're no longer Otmar's prisoner."

Her laugh was shaky. There was an awkward pause as she collected herself, pulling away from him as he did the same.

"That's a relief."

"Nightmare aside, how did you sleep?" he asked.

"Like the dead, despite our neighbours." Her grin was irresistible. He grinned back.

"Good."

She searched his face, her dark brows pinching with concern. Hypatia reached a gloved hand towards his face.

"Did you sleep at all, Sigimar?"

He blinked at her gesture, surprised by the intimacy. It was a kindness he didn't deserve. Hypatia snatched her hand back before she'd even reached the tangle of his beard, as if only now realizing it, pink suffusing her cheeks.

"I'll survive," he answered. "Are you hungry?"

"Starving."

"Then we'd best feed you."

"Yes, I'm told I'm rather irritable without food."

"Funny you should say that. I was told something similar just the other day," he said as he levered himself up and away from her warmth.

She stared at him thoughtfully, pondering the comparison. He scowled.

"I can see it." She nodded.

"Smart ass."

She chuckled. It was a lovely sound.

"I want to know everything about the realms of Oblivion," she said as she sat up, shivering.

"Just 'everything'? Not too difficult, then." He grinned, holding the flap of the tent open for her.

Hypatia ducked out of the tent, stretched, and then hugged herself, grimacing at the cold. As Sigimar followed suit, she watched him, thoughtful.

"I assume you can read?"

"I can."

"How many languages?"

"A few," he answered, ushering her towards the roaring fire.

"Then I want you to teach me. My ignorance already cost me dearly. It's not a mistake that bears repeating. What a pity this translation spell doesn't also pass on that knowledge."

"It's old magic. The spell was created long before languages were written."

"Old magic? You used that term last night. What other kinds of things are accomplished through old magic?" she asked.

It seemed her mind had a scholarly bent. He liked her better already. Sigimar sat on a dry log by the fire, patting the space next to him. He was handed a piece of tough jerky and a skin of warm mead by a member of the caravan with apologies for the meagre fare. He shrugged it off. It wasn't as though they could buy or hunt for better, given no town in Gortos was willing to sell to them and Otmar had cursed the wildlife to flee their presence. Hypatia accepted hers with grace. She began a valiant effort to chew through the jerky, expectant eyes trained on him.

"Well?"

"Did someone say 'old magic'?" Brynja asked, cutting in.

Sigimar kept his expression neutral. Brynja the healer stepped from her tent and stretched, a sly grin on her face. She was an integral part of his entourage and had already proved her worth ten times over. After all, her nightly activities powered the warmth charms they relied on. He wouldn't scowl at her, no matter how much he wanted to because of his lost sleep.

"Yes," Hypatia answered. "I don't think we've been properly introduced. I'm Hypatia."

"Brynja," the healer answered. "At your service, Fru Hypatia." She bowed.

"Oh, there's no need for that. You may call me Hypatia."

"As you wish. If you're interested in old magic, I'm a bit of a scholar myself, as is the jarl, I'm told." She winked at Sigimar. "Old magic is the first tamed magic. Long ago, all magic was wild and unpredictable, until the first of us were given the rituals to harness it, straight from the gods and goddesses themselves. But just like a wild animal, it'll bite you if you don't approach it correctly."

"No, *wild magic* will bite you. *Old magic* is far too ritualistic to bite. It's more likely not to work at all than to fight you." Sigimar frowned.

"Aha! You passed my test. I knew you were scholarly, Jarl." She turned her merry gaze to Hypatia. "In any case, the most fun kind of old magic is, of course, sex magic."

Hypatia coughed on a piece of jerky. Sigimar patted her back and raised his brow at Brynja. The meddling witch winked. Was she flirting with Hypatia? If the little mage's blush was anything to go by, it was working.

"I...see," Hypatia wheezed, her face flaming red as she stared at the healer.

"Your Jarl can tell you all about it. Elves and elvish folk often make use of old magic since it doesn't require magical aptitude to perform."

"Thank you for the lesson, Brynja," Sigimar's tone made it clear she was dismissed. He shouldn't have been so peevish. Of course, Brynja was the better catch with her sunny disposition and effortless charm.

"You're most welcome, Jarl, Fru." Brynja smiled and sauntered off to find her own rations.

Hypatia recovered, clearing her throat.

"What did she mean about magical aptitude? And what is an elf?"

Sigimar blinked at her, surprised she didn't know such basic facts of life. But if her Empire of Mages was as isolated as she'd implied, she could be wholly ignorant of such things.

"Elves possess the least magical aptitude of all the races, barring humans. If we have magic at all, it is often wild magic, the kind you must tame."

"What's a human?"

Sigimar laughed.

"The bane of the gods and the reason the forgotten gods exist at all. Who do you think forgot them in the first place, before the magical races were created? They look much like you or Brynja. There are a few of them in King Erlendr's court if you would like to meet them."

"Ah, perhaps in this instance, discretion is the better part of valour."

Sigimar grinned.

"Scared?"

"Cautious." She rolled her eyes, chewing thoughtfully as she watched people come and go, packing up the camp. "Brynja called you an elf, but you look fae, and you performed a spell when my heart was racing so fast I thought it would burst. Was that old magic or wild magic?"

Sigimar shook his head.

"Elves tend to be quite tall, and our ears are much longer than a fae's. I have a fae ancestor somewhere, hence my colouring, but that is where our similarities end. I am considered elvish, since I take mostly after my elven parentage. The magic I used after you were summoned back to Otmar's keep was wild magic, tamed through words. It is one of the few spells I know."

"Oh." She swallowed, realizing something. "When you said you had experience with summoning spells, you really meant it." She shivered, though the fire was blazing, "Was there someone there for you, to slow your racing heart?"

His heart contracted painfully.

"No. Being summoned was punishment for running away. The orphanages were full to bursting, and they couldn't keep track of all of us," he said, instantly regretting the slip. Stupid fool, to reveal his lowborn origins to a noblewoman. She'd lured him into letting his guard down with all her curiosity.

"You must have been a very determined child." She smiled sadly.

It was not the reaction he'd expected. Maybe she was just being polite?

"A stupid one. I never learned the lesson."

Hypatia shook her head.

"A brave one. You ran, knowing what failure meant, and did it any-way."

She might as well have reached into his chest and embraced that aching, broken part of him.

"And how do you know I wasn't just a coward, running from some-thing worse?"

"Were you? Running from something worse?" she asked, without the barest hint of judgement.

No. He'd been running towards his brother, who had become an adult at the rate of a fae man, full grown at one hundred years. Whereas Sigimar had grown up as an elf did, taking three times as long to reach the same milestones. It hadn't mattered to the orphanage that they were brothers or that the separation had broken their hearts. Until Dag had come back to them with proof of a stable income and a roof over his head on the frontier, Sigimar had stayed prisoner in that orphanage.

"No," he answered.

"I didn't think so. It was love, wasn't it?"

"Why do you say that?"

"What else would be worth chasing, or enduring for, if not love?" she asked wistfully.

"And is that what keeps you going?"

She paused, her eyes far away.

"It did. Once."

Hypatia's hand rested on her hip. Was there some talisman inside her coat? Sigimar chewed his jerky, wondering at the woman beside him.

"And now?" he asked cautiously. Had this small woman discovered how to move forward? How to be whole?

She stared at the fire, pensive, sipping her mead.

"Hope that I might be loved and happy again, I suppose. Hope that I will find the home my heart is seeking."

"Hope," he echoed.

She nodded.

Did he have any of that left within him? Did he believe, with even the smallest part of his heart, that he could be happy again? As they ate, quiet, contemplative companions in loss, he wondered if, on their journey to Elmheim, she would show him what hope looked like.

CHAPTER 9

Hypatia wanted to curl up on herself, hide under a rock and simply perish. The moment the words had left her lips, she regretted them. Waxing on about love and hope? To a complete stranger? One she was in an awkward, contractual situation with? What better way to announce to all and sundry that she was desperately lonely and that her mind was composed of feathers, candy and children's tales. She might as well have bared her breasts for his perusal and asked him to comment on the colour of her areolas. That, at least, might have been a shade less mortifying.

Sigimar hadn't said more than a few words to her since the camp had been packed up. No doubt because he thought her a silly, dreamy-eyed girl. As the caravan trudged through the deep snow, Hypatia was seated across from Sigimar in the sleigh, blankets and warmth charm piled atop her. Even so, she was cold—though no amount of torture would ever make her admit it. No one else was so pampered, Sigimar included. Without even a hat, his long burgundy hair flew in the breeze, snowflakes melting on contact with his head and long, pointed ears. His bright amber eyes scanned the forest, always watching. She did her best not to stare at him overmuch for fear of compounding the awkwardness of their impasse.

Eventually, though, she would have to speak. There was only so much interest she could take in the wintry landscape, trees bowing under the weight of the snow and ice, the sky a brilliant blue. Sigimar, for his part, kept his counsel. As the silence stretched on between them, she searched her mind for something—anything—to converse about. But would he welcome endless questions, or would he then consider her both pathetic *and* a pest?

"When I was summoned...you mentioned the 'treasures of Ashla.' What did you mean by that?"

Everyone liked treasure, right?

Sigimar blinked as if surprised by her voice. He unfolded his thick arms and relaxed in his seat.

"Ashla has been impenetrable for many millennia. With some of the miasma gone, we've uncovered ancient artefacts that are still very useful. And clever. King Erlendr believes they will benefit both Elmheim and the Riverlands, provided they're safe to use and their internal workings can be duplicated."

Hypatia leaned forward, heart fluttering at the very thought of ancient, mysterious artefacts.

"What have you found so far?"

"Many things. The majority of which we don't understand. The most useful is a magical amplifier. We're using it to ensure the miasma doesn't roll back into the cleared territory."

"What does it look like?" she asked, on the edge of her seat.

"Are you a scholar of some sort?" he asked, his mouth quirking up at the corners.

What a perfectly dreadful question. No woman in Lethe would ever be considered a scholar. The best she could hope for was recognition as an amateur enthusiast, never to be taken seriously. But here? Would it be different?

"Of a sort. I was a ruin explorer and artefact dealer before," she replied, sitting back, her hands in her lap. No need to appear over-eager, or mention what else she'd done. Some knowledge should stay buried.

"Really?"

"Yes. It was rather thrilling. Though it's been some time since I..."

Not since Kosmas was alive. She'd not picked up a single trowel or brush in the two years he'd been gone. If only she hadn't been sick that day, she might have saved him. Without him, or the desire to explore, she'd been forced to sell the lot of her tools and most of her notes this past Spring to feed herself. Just another piece of herself—her heart—gone. Too bad she hadn't sold that loathsome crystal ball first. Or smashed it.

"...since I had the inclination," she finished.

"Are you still inclined? Because Elmheim has very few who've made a study of the ancient past. Warriors, enchanters and healing light users are thick on the ground, but scholars are sadly rare."

"Are you...trying to recruit me?" she asked, raising a brow.

"Would you sign on if I were?" He smiled, leaning forward, a hand on his thigh.

The urge to explore and uncover had withered inside her after Kosmas' death. Would it even hold the same thrill alone, or would it be a constant reminder of what she'd lost? Would she be able to lose herself as she'd done before, hours passing her by as she delicately freed one mystery after another? It did sound rather tempting, like a cool ember had unexpectedly sparked to life in her heart. It'd been so long since something had interested her. Since getting out of bed had held any promise. Then again, she'd be a fool to leap headlong into danger when she could scarcely protect herself.

"I'm not sure. I also recall tell of cannibalistic monsters. Personally, I like all the parts of me attached as they are and in their current configuration," she quipped.

"I can't fault you for that." He grimaced, scratching at his beard. "Ashla is dangerous."

Another silence descended. She'd obviously stepped in something, if the grim, faraway look on Sigimar's face was any indication. He must have lost loved ones to the dangers of his homeland. Given his hatred for the title of 'Hero' Ingi had spoken of the other night, those losses must have cut deep. Heroes rarely became so titled through unassuming deeds or enjoyable journeys.

"I'm sorry. I should not have made light of it."

Her voice seemed to have snapped him from another reverie.

"Don't apologise, Hypatia. The jokes on the frontier tend towards the dark and twisted." He forced a grin. "If my conversational skills are lacking, it's because I've neglected them for some time." Sigimar threaded his fingers together in his lap and looked down, not meeting her eyes.

"You're not alone in that." She smiled.

When he looked up, his amber eyes had softened.

A sudden chill breeze cut through her then. She shivered.

"Would you like to sit next to me?" he asked, opening his cloak in invitation.

"Would that bother you?" She hesitated.

"If it did, I wouldn't have offered."

"Oh, alright then." She picked up all the blankets and snuggled into Sigimar's side, delighted to find he was a veritable forge beneath his cloak. He curled his arm around her and pulled the cloak around them both. Suddenly, the world was nearly sweltering. "How are you so warm?" she gasped.

He chuckled.

"I'm elvish. The elements rarely bother us."

Then why had he asked for her warmth the night before? She stared up at him, brow raised. Had it all been an act because he'd known *she* was cold? If so, it was rather gentlemanly of him.

"And what thoughts are buzzing through your mind now?" he asked, a small grin lighting up his face.

Hypatia flushed.

"Will you tell me what else you've found?"

"It would be my pleasure."

Sigimar had become so accustomed to living almost entirely inside his own head, he'd forgotten to make conversation with Hypatia as they'd travelled. Luckily, Hypatia seemed to be a talkative sort, dragging him out of his morose inner musings more than once. In truth, he was grateful for her company. They spent the ride in pleasant conversation about the artefacts his people had uncovered, and a failed attempt to teach her some of their alphabet. Given she'd been unwillingly bound to him and Elmheim, he would not have faulted her for trying to kill him, flee, or, at the very least, making the journey miserable.

What in the hells had he been thinking, trying to get her to come with him to Ashla? Elmheim's shortage of scholars notwithstanding, Hypatia was an educated noblewoman. She had options. Many of those were infinitely better than what he or any on the frontier could give her. It was also becoming apparent that she had nothing in the way of martial skill. Elmheim was no place for her, let alone Ashla.

Once she was freed from the contract, he would see about sending her somewhere safe. Somewhere warm. Away from the miasma. Away from the draugar. Away from him. It would be for the best.

He would just have to savour his time with her while it lasted. In truth, it reminded him of the days before he'd become jarl, before all the expectations he could never live up to, before his title and legend grew so weighty they crushed him. Instead, he could just discuss the things he used to enjoy—history, relics and languages.

Once he'd left the orphanage for good, he'd spent his long childhood devouring every text, learning to read and write every language, spoken and dead, in the Riverlands. He'd been almost grateful he'd had no aptitude for magic because it allowed him more time to read. Had there been no need for it, had he not been so taken with tales of heroism and glory, he might never have picked up an axe and shield. Maybe in another world, without the miasma, meddling princesses and unearned titles, they would have met as fellow scholars.

Cerulean skies bled into brilliant fuchsia, and that in turn to the deepest indigo. Stars winked against obsidian, and yet their conversation continued. Even though her yawns had become more numerous than her questions—truly a feat—she still buzzed with curiosity. Curled up once more in their tent, the camp gone quiet save for the boots of the patrol sinking through the deep snows and the pop and crackle of the bonfire, she whispered her queries.

"How often must you use the amplifier device to keep the miasma at bay?"

"It's tied to the phases of the moon, so every new, first-quarter, full and third-quarter moon, it requires another infusion of magic, but it can only amplify a single spell," he replied, his voice as quiet as hers.

But would it always work so well? Would it continue to save what little they'd uncovered and brought back to life? Or would the miasma roll back over the whole of the territory, swallowing the people and turning the lot of them into food or a hoard of monsters, a plague of untold magnitude upon Elmheim?

The past few decades had already seen such a plague, as people plunged into the gloom, looking as much for a way to end it as for the glory and riches offered by King Erlendr, rewards that had grown beyond counting. It was why he and Dag had first hatched their crazy scheme, tempted by those same rewards. But how much worse would the plague of new draugar be if the amplifier failed? So much rested on something they barely understood. And many recklessly crossed the narrow sea between Elmheim and Ashla even now, spurred to greater folly by tales of him and his deeds. His actions had sewn seeds of foolhardy success, and now Elmheim reaped a harvest of horrors. Would he be responsible for more death in the end?

Hypatia yawned, covering her mouth with an ungloved hand, observing social niceties no matter how exhausted.

"Was Ashla always covered in miasma?"

Dark circles had formed under her eyes, only visible in the night by his keen sight.

"No, not always, not according to the legends."

Legends that had convinced him to find the source of it. Theories in dusty, crumbling tomes had convinced him that it could be dispelled. He in turn had convinced Dag.

Not all knowledge was a blessing.

"What do you think they used the device for back then? Maybe they used it to build roads or cities, or even to grow crops," she postulated, her eyes closed now.

"And maybe they used it for conquest," he teased.

"Such a pessimist," she mumbled. This time, her eyes stayed shut as she snuggled closer to him.

She wasn't wrong.

"Sleep, Hypatia. You can scold me tomorrow."

Unintelligible grumblings were all she could muster before sleep finally took her.

He brushed aside a lock of hair that had fallen across her cheek without thinking. Sigimar froze. Hypatia was not his to touch, she never would have spoken to him without the damn contract, and she would be leaving shortly. It was for the best, and he knew it. The time they spent together would be a pleasant diversion, but no more. He settled himself as best he could and prayed fatigue would take him, too. Pessimist that he was, the last thing he needed was another sleepless night spent in his own company.

And yet, he hoped for another day like the one he'd had.

CHAPTER 10

Wind like ice battered Hypatia's face and body, screaming past her ears, searing her skin. Whenever she chanced to look down instead of forward, her stomach dropped to her toes. The summoned beast's reins in her hands were her tether to the land of the living. She clasped them with a death-grip.

Flying was glorious.

"Alright, little mage, any longer outside the bubble and you'll freeze to death," Sigimar shouted to be heard above the howling wind.

It was true that the only warm parts of her were those in direct contact with Sigimar, a band across her belly where his arm held her secure, and her back flush against his front. It was also true that being inside the bubble prevented her from experiencing the sheer, elemental power of flight.

"Fine," she shouted back.

Sigimar handed the reins to the driver as he pulled her back into the bubble, a pocket of air that kept out the wind and cold. The bubble encompassed most of the harness and the house-sized saddle that had been summoned along with the enormous dragon on which they rode through the skies. The saddle, shaped and decorated like a pleasure barge, had tall oval windows out of which the passengers could watch as the world outside zipped by. Goods had been tied down at the back, while fae, shapeshifters and elves milled about or lounged on the sumptuous furniture.

The whole of their caravan had fit on two summoned dragons, one containing those with fae magic, the other with witch magic.

Hypatia had learned that fae and witch magic repulsed one another, and no one wanted to risk falling out of the sky because of it. The fae of the caravan had approached her with wariness, until that caution had turned to wonder. Her magic, they explained, was like nothing they'd ever experienced. Sigimar had glared them into retreat before she'd needed to say such scrutiny made her uncomfortable.

They'd taken to the skies after breakfast, as they had for the past week, concerned that if they didn't leave Gortos soon, they would either starve or face armed conflict. It hadn't been possible earlier in their journey, fearful as they'd been of Otmar's retaliation. But a few days of safe travels convinced them to risk summoning transportation now that their rations were low and the people of Gortos unusually hostile. Hypatia had been only too glad to discover she wouldn't have to spend more days in the cold. At least, not if she so chose. Flying had been worth the stinging pain. She was happy she'd finally worked up the courage to do it.

Sigimar chuckled when she turned to face him, her teeth chattering as warmth returned to her extremities in a rush of painful prickling. He knelt down, a boyish grin on his face.

"Your hair is covered in little icicles."

She didn't doubt it. Ice clung to her eyelashes and had formed a thin casing on strands of her windswept hair. His fingers went to work snapping them off as he tried and failed to suppress irreverent grins. Yet he treated the wild strands with the utmost care. It never ceased to surprise her how a man who easily lifted crates that horses struggled to pull could at the same time be so gentle.

"You're n-not much b-better." She retorted as her teeth chattered from the cold. Her shaking hands brushed frost from his beard and thick eyebrows.

"I think this one is the most impressive." He held up an icicle the length and thickness of a porcupine quill.

Hypatia laughed, pulling one of his thick, burgundy braids forward so that he could see it for himself. Encased entirely in a thin sheet of ice, she gripped two places along it and snapped it, scattering tiny plates of ice between them. Sigimar's roar of laughter had every head turning. He took her hand in his.

"Let's get you warm."

She let him tug her to the staircase leading to the second floor of the structure. As it had in the past week, it had been created entirely for their personal use, complete with an enormous bed scattered with rose petals. The hints of the caravan were getting rather more heavy-handed of late. They'd elected to stay outside of it, Hypatia out of embarrassment and Sigimar because the implications angered him. But as cold as she was, she would be happy to curl up in something warm and dry.

"Jarl, Fru, a moment of your time?" Ingi interrupted.

Sigimar stopped and nodded, pulling Hypatia close to warm her inside his cloak, covered save her head poking out through the thick, fur-lined garment.

"The queen of Isro wishes to extend her hospitality. She is engaged elsewhere but has said that anywhere we land within her territory will welcome us with a feast and appropriate lodging."

Hypatia wondered briefly how the queen had communicated with Ingi but held back her questions. She would ask Sigimar another time.

Sigimar snorted.

"It sounds like she's heard about Otmar's behaviour."

Ingi shrugged.

"If she wishes to contrast herself favourably with him, let her. The rations will only last another day as it is. We'll reach one of the larger towns of Isro before dusk. Permission to land, Jarl?"

"You have it."

Ingi nodded.

"A bath has been drawn and new clothes laid out in your apartment." Hypatia could feel Sigimar tensing to protest. "You're not a lowly warrior like the rest of us, Jarl, not anymore. The both of you need to greet our hosts properly attired and smelling of something other than sweat, wood smoke and horse."

A bath sounded heavenly. A few days without bathing or being able to change her clothes was more than enough, and she hadn't exactly expected to be able to do either as they travelled through the freezing snow and camped outside hostile towns. She'd managed a quick and perfunctory scrub only once since they'd begun flying during the day and camping at night, and even then, she'd required Brynja's help to melt the snow into something warm enough not to freeze her skin off. Hypatia shivered at the memory, willing it away.

"Thank you, Ingi." Hypatia smiled.

Hypatia took the stairs two at a time as Sigimar followed. Flinging open the door to their apartments she gasped, approaching what Ingi had modestly referred to as a bath.

"Sigimar, this could fit a whole army! What was he even thinking? Didn't he just say that rations were low?"

"It was conjured, just as the rest of this apartment was."

Hypatia pulled off her glove and ran a finger through the hot water, sighing despite the sting of it.

"Then why can't they conjure food? Or for that matter, more baths?"

"Magic can't fill your belly or provide nourishment, and those with the magic to conjure are already straining themselves every day just to summon and sustain our transportation."

"So if I drank this, it wouldn't be like drinking water?"

"Yes and no. It would taste and feel like water, but it wouldn't quench your thirst."

"How odd."

Sigimar laughed as he unclasped his cloak and tugged off his gloves and hat. He sat down on a chair and set to unlacing his boots.

"I've been told fae magic is like that."

Hypatia swallowed hard as Sigimar continued to remove his clothes without a care. Something she'd thought long dead unfurled in her core, as unexpected as it was ferocious. She...*wanted*. It hit her like a body blow. The force of the attraction scared her as much as it held her captive.

When he stripped out of his tunic, she was certain not an inch of her felt the least bit chilled. The whole of her head might as well be giving off steam as the remaining ice melted in the flush of her embarrassment. She'd known Sigimar was large and possessed an uncommon strength, but she wasn't prepared for the sight of him beneath his bulky clothes. Or for what that sight would do to her. Burgundy hair dusted thick arms of corded muscle, a barrel chest, and shot down in a line leading directly to his pants. And those pants beneath his outer layers hugged him like a second skin, outlining muscled thighs in loving detail. She looked back up, trying to remember her manners. A hint of gold glinted from both his nipples. Her inner muscles clenched. Gods below.

Shame scalded her. She'd spoken to Kosmas barely more than a week ago. The last remnant of his horn lay in her pocket. It might have been two years since she'd been with a man, not since before Kosmas had gone missing, but it was no excuse. Kosmas might have told her to be happy, but the jarl and she were in a contractual marriage, one about to be dissolved so she could go freely on her way. This was not the place to start looking for a relationship or a dalliance... even if she were so inclined.

Sigimar noticed her silence and looked up, taking note of her expression, her heated complexion. His attention only made her burn hotter.

"I'm sorry. I'm making you uneasy again, aren't I? I'll wait outside. Let me know when you're done bathing."

"It's not...I'm not...uneasy."

He raised a quizzical brow.

"But men scare you, don't they? I assumed you prefer women."

"I—wait, what? Why do you think that?"

"There's no shame in it, Hypatia. In Elmheim such things are normal. I saw you blush whenever Brynja spoke to you, so I assumed."

Hypatia choked on her next mortified breath. She'd blushed because Brynja had so openly discussed intimate matters, and how, precisely, she created warmth charms at night. How on Oblivion was she supposed to look at the woman and not blush afterwards?

Sigimar slung his tunic back on, convinced he'd discovered the truth. If she were loyal to the memory of Kosmas, she would let Sigimar believe he had the right of it. It would be the right thing—the proper thing—to do. She was a widow, with a memento of her late husband in her pocket. But she was also a woman who hadn't felt lust in far too long. Two years of grief and loneliness had convinced her she was dead inside. Yet it roared back to life, a flame devouring dry kindling. She should let him leave, keep this side of herself locked away.

But she didn't.

"I don't prefer women! I prefer men, and you don't scare me," she blurted out, shame, exhilaration, and fear tearing her apart, her heart pounding madly.

Sigimar stopped, his spine ramrod straight, but didn't turn around. When he spoke, his already deep voice was rougher, which, of course, only made matters worse.

"The offer still stands. I can wait outside if you prefer."

The moment he'd disrobed, the questions had pummeled her. What would he be like, this hulking man with his impossible gentleness? How would it feel to be desired by him? To have all his sweetness and passion directed at her alone? Would the awful, yawning loneliness in her finally abate? After so long, would his touch incinerate her? In the battle within her, curiosity was king, yet doubts plagued her.

"I...wouldn't prefer that." Hypatia swallowed. "But...don't look." She took a strip of fabric—a belt?—laid out on the bed and approached him. "Crouch down?"

He turned, his eyes closed, and knelt before her. She tied the thin fabric around his eyes. Her finger grazed his ear and he tensed, his fists bunching.

"I'm not sure what this changes."

She wasn't entirely certain either, except that the idea of him both naked and being able to see her reaction to his body was more than she could handle.

"It's for modesty," she lied, the most unconvincing falsehood to cross her lips in some time.

"Whose?" he asked, bewildered.

"We don't have long until we land," she replied, refusing to answer the unanswerable.

"In case you can't see it, you should know I'm rolling my eyes."

She flicked his forehead.

"Y-you can use the bath now," she muttered.

"Can I? I think if you wanted my eyes covered, you should help me to the tub."

Hypatia chewed her lip, wondering if he were teasing her. Yet there was no sly quirk of his lips. She took his hand and led him to the lip of the tub, backing away. He slipped off his tunic again, revealing a broad-shouldered back of perfectly sculpted muscle. Hypatia held back a groan as she tore her eyes from the sight and began stripping out of her own layers. When she pulled off and folded her simple gown, she looked up to find Sigimar's pants had followed his shirt. He'd turned, giving her the perfect view as he gripped the side of the tub. Her eyes wandered down his body, alighting on an alarming sight.

Gods below, had his father been a horse?

How did such a thing even...fit?

Unable to see her open-mouthed stares, Sigimar stepped over the lip of the tub and sat himself down in the bath, relaxing into the heat of the water with an audible sigh. He unbraided his hair and then slipped beneath the surface, only to re-emerge entirely too wet for Hypatia's comfort.

"If you're coming in, will you hand me the soap?"

Torture, that's what this was. Well-deserved, absolute, self-induced *torture*. She swallowed, gathering her courage. He couldn't see her. It was just a bath. A much-needed bath, and Sigimar was being his usual unflappable self. No nonsense.

Hypatia perused the soaps and bottles arrayed on the stand beside the tub. She selected one with a scent she approved of before handing it to Sigimar. Then she looked to the high sides of the tub, deciding how she would make it inside. Jump? Maybe kick herself over, like seating a horse? Thankfully Sigimar was blindfolded and preoccupied. She hoisted herself up to gauge the distance to the water below and then, misjudging her balance on the wet, rounded metal lip, fell in face first.

"Hypatia!"

Sigimar hauled her up as she coughed the water out of her throat and nose. He set her back into the tub.

Mortification.

It was the only word which perfectly described embarrassment so bone-deep she thought it might undo her. Better to cling to something—anything—else. Like the admittedly unfair anger that he'd been able to see her the whole while. How else had he so unerringly assisted her? She scowled as she sank below the sloshing water, her face flushing painfully.

"You can see me. Well? What do you have to say for yourself?"

He tugged the sodden fabric from his eyes and tossed it onto the floor. Sigimar's amber-orange eyes devoured the sight of her. Her pulse thrummed against her skin.

"You're beautiful," he murmured.

Hypatia's heart skipped. She'd heard it often in her former life as the daughter of a magister. Merchants, nobles and servants alike had paid her every pretty compliment, and every last one had left her feeling cold. But it had been so long since anyone had really meant it, or even said it to her. And none of them had said it in this way, not with such raw and open honesty. Did he suspect what he was doing to her?

"Are mages so uncomfortable with nudity?" he asked.

"T-turn around," she muttered.

"Why? *You* certainly had your fun looking."

An indignant squeak emerged from her lips. Sigimar laughed. She splashed him. He covered his eyes with his arm, smirk still visible as water dripped from his beard.

"I thought for a moment you might unhinge your jaw," he teased.

An outraged shriek of pure humiliation was all she was capable of in that moment. And still the giant laughed, despite another wave of water aimed directly at his smug face. Still covering his eyes, he taunted her.

"If you splash hard enough, you *might* cover the traces of drool on the floor."

There had been no drool, no matter his crude jokes! She may have looked her fill, but he'd disrobed in front of her and bared himself in all his masculine glory. He'd had no shame, just an enviable comfort in his own skin. Not everyone could share his nonchalance, and certainly not Hypatia, who had not cared for her appearance in years. As he laughed, a fire burned in her breast. She would put an end to his horrid teasing!

Too busy laughing at his own crude jokes, and shielding his eyes from the water she was dashing at him, he didn't see her stand up in the tub, nor did he resist when she yanked his arm away from his face. She grabbed his face in her hands and planted her lips on his, shocking him into silence. His hands flailed before gripping the sides of the tub, his eyes widening. Sigimar froze. The metal of the tub groaned and bent under his grip.

"What? Nothing to say?" she taunted, enjoying the sight of his wide-eyed surprise. "And here I—"

Sigimar's mouth captured hers. Hypatia was the one shocked into silence as his tongue swept across her bottom lip. She dragged in a shaky breath. That was all it took for his tongue to slip in, tasting hers. Anger? What anger? Hypatia wrapped her arms around his neck as Sigimar's hands pulled her flush against him, holding her in place as she lost her balance. The crisp hair of his chest grazed her nipples, bringing her back from the brink. She pulled away, her eyes locked on Sigimar's lips as her own tingled from the scrape of his beard.

"I...I'm sorry. I shouldn't have..." She couldn't finish the thought. His kisses had unleashed a starving, maddened animal inside her, and she wasn't even certain she wanted to corral it. It took an effort to drag her eyes up to meet his. He stared at her as if he were under the same spell as she.

"Yes, you should have," he growled, claiming her lips for another searing kiss.

She wrapped her arms around him, slanting her mouth over his, claiming his tongue with her own. One of his hands roamed lower, a shivery thrill of need making her moan. The moment they came up for air, he pressed feverish kisses to her neck. She sank her nails into the skin of his shoulders as one of his hands squeezed her bottom.

"Should I let you go?" he asked in a raspy rumble.

His hands were hot brands on her skin. She liked the feel of his calluses as his thumbs made lazy sweeps across her back and hip. Aching and slick, she wasn't certain why he'd stopped.

"I don't know," she answered, her head spinning.

She liked his kisses, the wet slide of his chest against hers, his hands caressing and possessive. She wanted, but she shouldn't.

"Choose. Please," he pleaded, shifting beneath her.

Her thigh grazed something firm beneath the surface of the water. It left her in no doubt as to the source of his discomfort. There was no denying the answering, coiling tightness in her core, but her heart protested. She didn't think she was built for the casual dalliances that so many others seemed to enjoy. The last thing she needed now was more heartbreak. She needed to be rational. Damn it all.

"I think you should let me go." She made herself say it.

Hypatia hated every word.

His breath came out as a hiss between his teeth. Setting her away from him, Sigimar turned to give her his back, the tips of his ears taking on a reddish hue.

Hypatia's own face flamed as she followed his lead, turning away, undoing her braids and washing her hair. Gods, but that had been intense. Her heart was still racing, her body screaming its need. Then she caught sight of her folded gown, the one with a piece of Kosmas inside the pocket. Shame assailed her anew, yet it wasn't enough to snuff out the spark of lust. She took the nearest bar of soap and scrubbed herself raw. If only the ugliness inside her could be washed away as easily as the layer of grime.

"I'm not a good woman," she whispered.

"Why would you think that?" he asked, his tone soft and chiding.

Tears blurred her vision. She didn't deserve kindness—she deserved scorn. As a noblewoman, she would have been expected to remarry soon after her husband's death with little thought to her feelings. But for five years she'd lived as just Hypatia, and, for three of those, happier than she'd ever thought possible. She'd loved and been truly loved in return. What she'd shared with Kosmas had been special—precious. Was it an insult to that love to seek comfort in another? Would it ever feel uncomplicated or right to burn for someone else?

"Because I'm staring at the last fragment of my husband. I know I should never have wanted that kiss, but I did, which only makes me feel like I'm the worst sort of person."

"You're already married?" he asked, alarmed.

"I was. I thought the contract I signed was for the necromancer who let me speak to him one last time." She choked back a sob, entirely blinded by tears. Except she hadn't even done that right, had she? She'd never even told him she'd loved him or even given him a heartfelt goodbye. "I didn't think I would ever feel anything again, not like this," she croaked.

Hypatia hadn't realised how cold she'd become inside until she'd burned for Sigimar's kiss. Still burned for it, the memory of his tongue, his skin on hers, imprinted on her. She should never have given in to these desires. The torment she felt now was what she deserved.

Hypatia heard Sigimar leave the tub and buried her face in her hands. No doubt he was as disgusted with her as she was with herself. It would be fitting that she bathed in her own foolish tears.

"Hypatia."

She sniffed and wiped at her bleary eyes. Sigimar was kneeling before her outside the tub.

"Give me your hand."

She complied. He placed the fragment of Kosmas' horn in her palm and closed her fingers around it.

"I'm relieved you don't regret our kiss. And I don't think you're a bad person for feeling that way. You told me you were loved and happy once, that love was worth chasing. So chase it. Chase it as you hold the memory of it close, so you don't lose your way." His solemn expression turned into a lopsided smile. "And if you decide to chase it with me in mind, know that you can and should do better."

Hypatia choked on a laugh, gripping Kosmas' horn in her palm. As she met Sigimar's concerned eyes, she realised he was being entirely unfair in his evaluation of himself. After everything she'd been through, she knew a good man when she saw one.

Chapter 11

Sigimar kept an eye on Hypatia as she plaited her hair, her grey eyes fixed on a point outside the window as they descended from the sky. There'd been no tears since he'd helped her from the overlarge tub, but he could see they weren't far from the surface. He'd known she was dealing with her own grief, but he hadn't expected her to be a widow. She seemed too young for that.

He grimaced at his reflection. What in the hells did she see in him? How could he possibly meet her expectations, when she'd known true love and happiness with another, better man? He touched his lips. *Never should have kissed her back.* He'd opened a door inside himself. Now he was too tempted by what lay on the other side to ignore the whispers leaking through the cracks, trying in vain to shut them out.

Sitting in a chair facing a small mirror, he hacked away at his bushy beard, eyes wandering back to Hypatia in the reflection. He hadn't lied when he'd called her a beauty. She was shorter than the average witch, with lightly tanned, olive-toned skin, full curves and a graceful, confident stride that commanded attention. Ashen brown, wavy hair framed intelligent grey eyes, a hooked nose and soft lips. Lips he prayed he would have another chance to kiss.

"Shit," he grunted, glaring at the finger he'd nicked with his blade. His wound was already closing up, courtesy of elven healing, but his beard was only looking worse the more he tried to trim. He'd stopped bothering to do more than hack at it for the past decade in Ashla. How had Drest fashioned it over a month ago?

"Do you need help?" She looked up from her braid.

"Yes. Else I'm going to have to shave everything and look like a boy rather than risk looking like a fool." He sighed as she padded over to him.

Sigimar handed her the blade, which she put aside, taking a small pair of scissors instead. He sat still as she worked away.

"Thank you for being considerate of me," she said, her eyes focused on his chin.

"You don't have to thank me," he replied, his fists squeezing the fabric of his tunic. It was the least she deserved.

"Yes, I do. I don't think you realise how uncommon it is in others. You're not what I expected," she admitted.

"A man with no finesse in his grooming habits?" He smiled, but with little mirth.

"I didn't mean that." She flicked her grey eyes at him, one brow arched. "And I suspect you know it."

"What did you expect?"

She snipped away, lost either in thought or concentration. When she spoke, it was halting.

"Not kindness. Nothing...real? I'm phrasing it poorly," Hypatia sighed. "In Lethe, nearly everyone wears a false face, smiling politely as they hunt for weakness. It's almost preferable when someone is openly vile. Trusting anyone is usually a mistake. It was...very lonely." She paused and looked him in the eyes. "All of that is to say, I'm glad it was you I was tied to, even if it was a trick, and even if it's temporary. Farohildis and her ilk were fools not to see your worth."

Sigimar swallowed past the lump in his throat. Praise he didn't deserve. He hated and craved it from her, then hated himself for wanting it.

"I'm not an honourable man," he confessed.

"I've seen no evidence to support that conclusion," she retorted light-ly.

"I could be putting on a false face right now," he insisted.

She paused in her ministrations to look at him with a softness that nearly undid him.

"I know you are. But it's not the kind I'm worried about."

"You can't know that."

Placing her hands on his shoulders, her eyes, deadly serious, ensnared him.

"Are you cruel, Sigimar? Violent when you don't need to be to survive, or against those who can't defend themselves? Do you think yourself better than everyone else?"

"No."

Hypatia nodded, satisfied. She pressed a kiss to his forehead.

"Why don't we make a deal? I'll show you the kindness I think you deserve, and you show me the kindness you think I deserve. Maybe by the time we reach our destination, we'll both believe we deserve it from ourselves."

Sigimar smiled, though he knew it wouldn't reach his eyes. If she knew what kind of man he truly was—unworthy, wretched, greedy—she wouldn't offer such tempting sweetness. And yet, the sincerity in her gaze made him want to try to be the man she thought him.

"Deal."

She stepped back and showed him his reflection. He'd never kept his beard so closely cropped, but he had to admit it did look good—more like a nobleman than a wild man.

"Do you like it?"

He watched her as she pushed the scissors around on the dresser, her eyes downcast, soaking in the sight of her in the fashions he was accustomed to. She wore a gold-embroidered, deep crimson dress, thick straps with ornate golden clasps atop a fitted cream tunic with long decorative sleeves. She looked like a princess, the kind he used to dream of as a boy.

"Yes, very much."

Sigimar stood, shaking the whiskers from his clothes.

"Ready?" he asked.

"I think so."

Grabbing her new cloak, he buckled it at her throat. Hypatia touched her hand to his. He caught her look of determination. With her other hand, she cupped his cheek and guided his head down.

"If I kiss you, will it upset you?" Sigimar asked as they were nose to nose, greedy bastard that he was.

"I hope not," she said, her breath fanning across his lips.

The whispers calling through the cracks in that door urged him forward. And if there were one thing he'd come to believe over the years since Dag's death, it was that he was, at heart, a weak man.

He pressed his lips to hers, softly this time, so as not to scare her off. But when her tongue swept across his, he could swear he felt it all the way to his bones. The jolt of need it stirred in him was a crack of thunder that reverberated through him. Gathering her close, he deepened their kiss, drinking her passion deep. She wrapped her arms around his neck and head, as if she could pull him even closer than she already had. The fabric of her sleeve grazed his ear. He gasped as pleasure-pain nearly brought him to his knees.

"Mercy, Hypatia."

"Did I hurt you?" she asked, eyes wide.

"My ears are sensitive."

"I'm sorry. I didn't know. Will they be okay?" She pulled her hands away, brows pinched.

He released a shaky laugh as he tried to calm his galloping heart. Okay wasn't the problem—being more than okay was.

"Yes. But I wouldn't go touching anyone else's pointed ears."

"I won't. It would hardly be polite to do the equivalent of poking people in their eyes."

"Ah, I wouldn't quite say that," he hedged.

"Then what would you compare it to?"

He could feel his face heat and hoped she wasn't watching his ears go red. He cleared his suddenly parched throat.

"Like caressing a man's cock," he muttered.

"Oh! Is that...so?" She turned her curious stare to his ears, the wanderings of her buzzing mind clear.

Sigimar stood straight and smoothed his clothes, ostensibly fighting non-existent wrinkles. Distance, he needed distance. The quizzical little mage was adding kindling to a flame. A knock on their door brought him back to the night ahead.

"Ready for a feast?" he asked.

"Yes. What do you think there will be to eat? I quite enjoyed the drink we had these past few mornings. What is it called?"

A little grin pulled up the corners of his mouth as he watched her eyes sparkle with enthusiasm.

"The drink is called mead. As for the food, we'll have to wait and see."

Sigimar and Hypatia joined the fae portion of his caravan in the main compartment of the summoned beast's saddle. Ingi looked them over and nodded, his ears twitching as he did a surreptitious double-take of Sigimar's trimmed beard and Hypatia's kiss-darkened lips. Sigimar gave him a warning glare.

"We'll land in a matter of minutes. The Wise Woman of the town will come to greet you and welcome you into her hall. What do you know of witches, Fru?" Ingi asked.

"Nothing pertinent, I suspect." She smiled ruefully.

"Witches are firmly matriarchal, as a general rule. The queendom of Isro is no exception. The Wise Woman will defer to you, rather than the jarl. You will need to present yourself as the leader in his stead. It would be best to treat the jarl as more akin to a favoured servant, rather than an equal."

Sigimar held back his snort. The farce wouldn't be all that unbelievable. He was, in truth, barely fit to be Hypatia's servant.

"I'll do my best," Hypatia said.

"Jarl, you should follow behind Fru Hypatia, speak to a woman only when spoken to, and eat only after she has allocated your portion of the feast to you." Ingi turned back to Hypatia. "Brynja will act as your attendant, Fru, so rely on her while the Wise Woman entertains you."

Hypatia merely nodded along, not looking the least bit flustered, which was more than Sigimar could say about himself. Drest had tried to drill noble etiquette into him before he'd set off for Gortos, but he'd retained very little of it. Now he wished he'd paid more mind, if only so that he could be a help rather than a liability to Hypatia.

The dragon landed, shaking and shifting the occupants inside the main room. When he steadied Hypatia, their eyes met. Her gaze darted to his ears and back, the slight blush on her cheeks heating his blood.

"You should exit first, Fru."

Hypatia started, looking away and clearing her throat.

"And here I thought I'd never have to do this again."

She released a breath and adjusted her posture and expression. Tilting her chin up and sharpening her gaze, her grey eyes swept out before her with barely repressed dissatisfaction. She raised her hand and then her brow at him. Despite her much shorter height, she managed to look down on him.

"Attend me."

Gods below, she really was noble-born. She was like an entirely different person. Hypatia hadn't been turning a fanciful phrase when she'd said that people wore masks in her empire of mages. He placed his hand under hers and followed a half-step behind as she exited the dragon's saddle, stepping down a flight of conjured stairs to the snowy ground. Brynja was already waiting, an appraising eye taking in them both.

"So Ingi has already warned you. Good. If you don't understand something, remember to look to me, rather than the jarl, and I'll explain it."

Hypatia nodded and took the lead towards the largest structure in the town. An enormous wooden hall in the town's centre, its sloped roof bearing a thick layer of snow, stood twice as tall as the rest. Light shone through the windows, the scent of cooked meat drifting on the breeze as the sounds of merriment leaked out into the dusk. At the door, a witch with greying hair, pale blue eyes, tanned, lined features and a plump figure waited with several younger witches flanking her. By the looks of their similar features, they were the Wise Woman's daughters. Hypatia inclined her head to the woman as they reached the front step.

"Greetings, Wise Woman. I am Domina Hypatia Diamond of Lethe, the Empire of Mages. This is my husband, Jarl Sigimar Ashla. We have been invited to accept your hospitality."

"Greetings, Domina Hypatia Diamond. I am Wise Woman Wassa. I am pleased to offer you and your consort my hospitality. Though I must admit, I had expected a fae princess."

"Please, call me Hypatia. I recently learned that King Otmar is kin, and thus I took the fae princess' place in the marriage contract."

Wassa considered her before laughing uproariously. She wiped tears from her eyes and smiled.

"It's just as well. I doubt that hothouse flower would have been much use on the frontier, or anywhere else, for that matter. As for consorts," Wassa gave Sigimar an appreciative once-over, "well, let's just say that little Farohildis is probably kicking herself for her maidenly terrors. Please, call me Wassa. Come inside, and enjoy the feast. It is my honour to welcome you to the Queendom of Isro."

Sigimar followed the women into the hall, ducking to avoid hitting the top of the doorway. He was shown to a table close to yet separate from Hypatia's, who was seated in a place of honour beside the Wise Woman. With Brynja beside her, Sigimar was confident the mage was in good hands. Hypatia selected his portions and had a servant place them before him. After that, he was but an afterthought. Just as he preferred it.

Maybe it wasn't so bad to be a man in the Witchlands after all. No one expected anything from him. No one asked him to recount the horrors of the frontier, or praised him for his despicable failures either. Sigimar dug into his meal with relish as wizards of the Wise Woman's household came and went, chatting amiably amongst themselves and paying him no heed. At least, until a familiar wizard sat across from him with a grin on his face.

"Sig! You ugly giant, I thought it was you!"

"Haimo." Sigimar nodded at the stocky, pale, blond wizard with green eyes and an easy smile. "What are you doing in Isro? I thought you said you were going to take your wages from Elmheim and become a merchant?"

Haimo laughed and nodded his head at a tusked, elvish woman seated at another table having a drinking contest with a pair of rowdy witches.

"After serving a tenth of my life up there like a good little recruit I decided to see the world. Got married along the way! Now we're travelling merchants with a route from Elmheim to Maat and back."

"Congratulations."

If only Sigimar had been so clear-eyed, rather than thirsting for the rewards Erlendr had promised. Perhaps he could have become a tutor or scholar. Dag could have settled down, as he'd dreamed of. Such fools they'd been.

"My thanks! So, who is the insane frontiersperson who uncovered Ashla? I've been hearing about them since I crossed into the Riverlands.

Hero of the Frontier, granted titles, lands, and the hand of a princess. Lucky dog. Bet you're just a little jealous, eh? Bastard got all you ever wanted."

"Who knows?" Sigimar shrugged. The last thing he wanted was to ruin his dinner by claiming that tainted title in public. Already the mead soured on his tongue, and his meal turned to rocks in his gut.

"So, if you're here, where's Dag? Where there's Zig, there's Zag," Haimo joked.

The question slipped through Sigimar's defences, a sword between his ribs. He hadn't heard those nicknames in a decade. Unprepared for what the sound of them would do to him, he wavered on a precipice. He couldn't reach for anger, not in front of Hypatia, not here, not anymore. But without it, something worse was dragging him under. It must have shown on his face, because Haimo's eyes widened.

"Ah, gods, Sig, I'm so sorry. How did he...?"

Bile surged up his throat. Sigimar wasn't going to be able to keep his food down. He crashed out of his seat and rushed for the door to the hall, heedless of who he shoved out of the way. He made it as far as the treeline and emptied his stomach into an ugly bush. Sigimar sank to his knees in the snow, one hand braced on the rough bark of a tree. He tried to slow his breathing, to tamp down his roiling gut as Dag's last moments played in his head over and over. Dag's terror-filled eyes as the jaws of the creature snapped shut around his neck. The gush of blood as his corpse slumped onto the ground. The screams of the draugr drowning out Sigimar's own as the sunlight dissolved the monster into nothing, leaving Sigimar's life nothing but an empty, meaningless husk.

"Sigimar? What happened?"

Hypatia had run out of the hall without donning her cloak, concern furrowing her brow. Her hand stroked his back in slow, calming circles.

"Go back inside. It's too cold out here for you without your cloak."

"I'm not leaving you out here alone. Will you tell me what's wrong?"

Tears stung his eyes. Everything was wrong. It should have been him, not Dag, who'd died. It should've been Dag by Hypatia's side. It should've been Dag with the glory and rewards while Sigimar's body had burned on a pyre.

She should know what kind of man he was. She should look at him not with kindness but hatred. It would be no less than he deserved, a failure resting on the laurels of a better man.

"I should be dead. I got my brother... the one who loved and raised me, who risked his life so I could have the childhood he never had—I got him killed! I was greedy, obsessed with glory. It was he who was gifted with the healing light. He was the one who purified the wellspring and freed Ashla from the miasma. Dag should have been the one to get the damned title and lands! My only job was to protect him! Instead, I pushed him too far. He died in terror, eaten by one of those fucking creatures! It was my fault! Mine! I should have been the one that died, not Dag!"

He couldn't make out her expression through the tears. Hypatia didn't say a word. She just reached out and held him close, his head resting against her shoulder as she stroked his hair. He fisted the material of her dress in his hands and crushed her to him, burying his face in the fabric as the tears fell. He would take what solace she offered him. Now that she knew what kind of man he was, it was certain to be the last.

CHAPTER 12

A fist had gripped Hypatia's heart at the sight of Sigimar's shocking exit from the hall. She'd kept a neutral mask in place and made a few unflattering remarks about emotional men before excusing herself to see to her husband. Wassa had waved her off without any obvious affront and told her where her rooms in town were located. A woman with blonde hair and striking green eyes tried to speak with her, but Hypatia swiftly brushed her off, her sole focus getting out the doors. The second she'd left the hall, she'd sprinted to Sigimar, crumpled in the snow.

Then he'd told her.

Hypatia had held her broken giant until the sting of the freezing night was too much to bear. Brynja was waiting by the door of the hall with Hypatia's cloak, which she gratefully donned as Sigimar followed silently behind her. Arranging for simple food and drink to be sent to their room for the evening, she led Sigimar there to warm up. He hadn't spoken for the rest of the night, but had partaken of the simple fare and readied himself for bed when she'd urged him. She held him until he fell asleep.

The room was dark with weak strands of light filtering through the narrow windows. A small table and chairs were arranged before a fireplace heated without the use of wood or flame, and the floors were covered in plush carpets that muffled sound. Luckily their bed was large and soft, made of gleaming, carved wood. The carvings were rather indecent in nature, depicting a number of scintillating feminine fantasies.

Sometime in the night, she'd ended up draped across Sigimar's chest. She'd woken to the glint of sunlight on his nipple piercing, which only brought a silly smile to her face. Pushing her hair from her face, she found surprisingly vulnerable amber eyes staring at her. Propped up on a few pillows, Sigimar looked at her as if he expected her to reach into his chest and tear his heart from his breast. She kissed his chest, and he released a shuddering breath.

"I don't deserve—"

She pressed her fingers to his lips.

"We made a deal, didn't we? I decide this right now, not you." When it looked like he wouldn't protest again, she cupped his cheek, stroking with her thumb. "I'm so sorry, Sigimar. You must have loved your brother very much."

He pressed his lips into a tense line and nodded, his eyes shut tight.

"If your brother loved you even half as much as Kosmas loved me, then I know he wouldn't want you to suffer like this. Somewhere in here..." She laid her hand above his wildly beating heart as hers broke for him. "...you know that too."

"I'm not sure I do," he said, despair creeping into his voice. "You don't understand."

"No, I can't. What happened was awful, but did you become the creature that devoured him?"

"No," he replied, reluctant.

"Then place the blame where it belongs. On the creature."

"I should have saved him!"

She shook her head.

"It wasn't your fault."

His breath caught, and he wavered, covering his face in his hands.

"Why can't you just hate me? I could handle your scorn."

"But you can't handle compassion?"

He removed his hands and scowled.

"I can't handle *your* compassion. You make me want what I shouldn't."

Her heart fluttered in her chest. It was the same for her. That she wanted at all still felt like a kind of betrayal, but for good or ill, her desire was slowly consuming any sense of shame inside her. She'd been strong in so many ways for so long. If she were to break now, better to be shattered by lust than hollowed out by grief.

"And what shouldn't you want?" she asked.

He looked away, refusing to answer. Raising her brow in challenge, she grazed his nipple piercing with the tip of her finger. It was hot to the touch. His head snapped back to her, eyes wide.

"Was it something like that?" she asked, kissing his chest again. Her kisses trailed up and stopped just before the glint of gold. If she weren't resting on his chest, she would have sworn he'd stopped breathing. He swallowed.

"Among other things," he replied, his voice husky.

"You make me want things I shouldn't, too. But perhaps self-recrimination ought to be ignored in favour of kinder sentiments. Perhaps, instead, we should be bad influences on each other."

He nodded slowly. Her eyes turned back to the gold, and her mind buzzed with questions. Curiosity got the better of her, as it usually did.

"Why the piercings? It couldn't have been comfortable."

He seemed almost relieved for the change of topic.

"Elves heal too quickly for most forms of enchanted tattoos. I didn't want anything a draugr could rip off my face, and these were less painful than the other options."

"They're charms? What for?"

"Deflection of magical attacks and sensing magic."

"How does it know if the magic is an attack or not?"

"Spells have the same intent as their caster."

"Fascinating! Where does one purchase charms like these?"

"Thinking of getting piercings of your own?" he asked, a sly grin on his face.

She smiled back, glad that the shadows had been banished, even if only temporarily.

"Well, mages can only use one form of magic. It would be prudent to have some sort of protection."

"You can only use one spell?" he asked, alarmed.

"I'm not really sure that *spell* is the right word. I can manipulate one element—light. Some mages can manipulate fire or water, but never more than that one thing. What a mage does with it is only limited by their imaginations and the extent of their training, I suppose."

He stilled again, dread suffusing his features.

"Please tell me you can regrow a limb if it's severed, or that you can sense the magic of others."

"I can't do either of those things," Hypatia replied, bemused.

"Gods below, I didn't realise..." He tucked strands of escaped hair behind her ears and stared at them as if calculating. "Your ears would be as heavy as boulders if you had a piercing for every protection you would need."

His brows furrowed in concern and sympathetic pain, his thumbs stroking her earlobes. Little twinges of pleasure coursed through her at his light touch. What had they been discussing? For a man who claimed caressing his ears was an innately sexual act, did he know what he was doing to her? Her eyes lit on his nipple piercing. The strangest urge to taste it took hold of her. She gave in, running her tongue along it. His gasp jostled her on his chest. She chuckled.

"Hypatia!"

"Hmm?"

"What are you thinking?" He tried to make his tone censorious, but it came out pleading.

"About what you might do if I ran my tongue along the shell of your ear," she answered honestly.

"I would fuck you until you begged me to stop."

His crude language only heightened her desire. Tempting. She contemplated how best to go about it. Sigimar was a large man in every aspect.

"Neither of us is ready for that," Sigimar groaned.

"Yet," she whispered.

Sigimar swallowed, his eyes on her lips.

"Yet," he agreed.

A knock on their door interrupted them.

"Jarl, Fru, we've restocked our supplies and summoned transportation. The weather witches are warning of an incoming storm, so it would be best to leave before flight becomes dangerous," Ingi said.

"Wait a moment, Ingi," Sigimar called back. He levered himself up in bed. Hypatia slid down his chest, landing in his lap.

"How long should you tell him to wait?" She grinned up at him.

"Don't tempt me," Sigimar growled playfully.

"Why not?" She sulked, sliding a hand along his thigh.

"Reasons," he grunted as he swung his legs over the bed, dislodging her onto the covers.

Hypatia sighed as Sigimar trudged to the door, hiking up his pants, speaking in whispers to the shapeshifter. She drank in the sight of him. When she touched him, her thoughts were focused solely on the desire rising to a fever pitch within her, or the little mysteries he presented. It was in the moments apart, when her mind wandered, that the self-recrimination stung.

But there was no one left alive aside from her to point fingers at her behaviour, at least, no one in these strange lands. No one here knew her as Hypatia, daughter of the two-time traitor, noblewoman expected to wed and breed and nothing more. No one knew her as Hypatia, wife of

Kosmas, two years a widow, lonely and desperate for warmth. No one except Sigimar, and he wasn't holding that against her.

As he spoke with Ingi, she wondered what it would be like to be with Sigimar. Would the pleasure be worth the pain of separation later, when she left to go her own way? She didn't know, and with the potent drugs of lust and curiosity circulating in her veins, she wasn't sure she would let the consequences stop her.

Ingi bowed and left. Sigimar closed the door and turned to face her.

"Get dressed, little mage. Some merchants will be here soon."

"Oh? For what reason?"

"You'll find out soon."

She huffed, inquisitiveness thwarted by Sigimar's brick wall of an expression. They dressed without speaking, Hypatia sneaking peeks at Sigimar all the while. By the time there was another knock on the door, they were both fully dressed. A pity.

Sigimar opened the door, stepped aside and allowed three witches to enter the room with several wooden cases in hand.

"Domina Hypatia Diamond, we've come with our best selection of protection charms. Please choose however many you like."

She flicked her eyes to Sigimar, who smiled.

"Please, accept this gift from me to you. It would gladden me if you were to choose one of every charm."

Warmth bloomed in her chest as the merchants opened their cases to display an array of amber beads and golden animal figures, none of which were any bigger than her smallest fingernail. She picked out one from every sectioned tray with a smile. Once that was done, the merchant placed them all in a velvet bag and tied it shut, handing them to Hypatia.

When they were alone again, she looked up to Sigimar.

"Thank you."

"You need the protection. Keep them somewhere safe on your person."

Hypatia nodded, slipping the bag into the pocket of her cloak, and followed Sigimar to the summoned dragon and the strange barge strapped to its enormous back. The longer she spent at his side, the less she questioned her attraction to him. The kinder he was, the easier it was to forget that niggling sense of shame and the easier it was to let this heady feeling rule her. After so long, she finally felt warm inside—hopeful instead of wearily defiant. Maybe by the time they reached Elmheim, she could show him he deserved that same warmth, and to look forward to what the future could bring.

Chapter 13

Sigimar had begun feeling... lighter, of late. He'd never spoken of his journey with Dag into the miasma like that before. To King Erlendr, he'd given the important details, as if he'd been reporting on a task completed rather than the painful end of a precious life. But now that his horrid shame had been recited aloud, its roots in his heart and mind didn't feel quite so grasping. He was by no means free of it, he didn't think he ever would be, nor should he be, but he'd begun to realise that not every memory of Dag made his heart hurt. Dag's name on Sigimar's lips no longer made his throat close up with grief.

No doubt the woman beside him had something to do with it. Bent over her work, quill absently twirling in her graceful fingers, the tips stained by ink, she was more than he deserved. But how much more? Curiosity overwhelmed him.

"I meant to ask, what is a domina?" Sigimar asked.

He was seated close beside her in their apartment, the clouds speeding by the windows as the summoned dragon soared through the skies. This time they rode with the witches, wizards and shapeshifters. Not wanting to be outdone by the fae in the caravan, the witches had conjured quarters that were even more luxurious. The contrived, erotic atmosphere had left subtlety behind several phallic-shaped columns ago, veering straight into the obscene. Sigimar and Hypatia had simply decided not to comment on it and get on with their day as best as possible.

Hypatia lifted her quill from the parchment lying between them. It was covered in letters from both their languages as they tried to find commonalities. The goal had been to create a document that could aid her in future translations. Sigimar admired her single-minded pursuit of knowledge.

"It's a title," she answered.

"I gathered that."

She pursed her lips, thinking. Her grey eyes warily appraised him.

"Do you promise not to treat me differently if I tell you?"

"I already know you're a noblewoman of some sort, if that is what worried you."

"How?" she asked, horrified. He tried not to smile.

"The way you speak and carry yourself. The questions you ask, or don't ask. To someone who grew up among warriors, the difference is obvious."

Hypatia sighed.

"My tutors would be proud, knowing they'd beaten their lessons in so well that even when I tried, I couldn't shake them." She paused, worrying her bottom lip. "Domina is the title given to the female children of the magister. In the hierarchy of Lethe, the only people with a higher rank are the emperor and empress as well as their children, the princes or princesses. Domina was once my title."

Of course she was a mere step removed from royalty. She really was like the princesses he and Dag used to dream of.

"So why did you leave?"

"Because titles like those are chains. I didn't want to be *just* my title, or *just* a noblewoman, for that matter. I would have been expected to forget my interests, to set aside my ambitions and to live under someone else's thumb. All in order to marry and produce children with a lofty pedigree, like a damned racehorse. I wanted to spend my life learning and exploring and making my own choices. Being a noblewoman would have made that...difficult. Though I admit that, given the manner of my leaving, I seem to have replaced one set of issues with another."

Sigimar tried to imagine a society like she described. Erlendr would be torn apart if he tried to force the noblewomen of Elmheim to limit themselves in such a way. Not all noblewomen fought on the frontier's bleeding edges—neither did all the noblemen—but everyone was expected to contribute in ways great and small to keeping the miasma at bay. What she described seemed to mirror the conditions of wizards in matriarchal witch societies like Isro.

"Then I am glad you left, even if the outcome was not ideal."

She blushed.

"Oh...thank you. And I didn't mean that about you. I have enjoyed getting to know you and your world."

"Just not the snow," he teased.

"Yes, well, it's all a bit too cold for my liking." She grinned.

Who in the hells thought preventing this woman from chasing intellectual pursuits was a sound strategy? It was a tragic waste of her talents. Already she could write all the letters of his language and had memorised several small words. The injustice of it all was infuriating, and he was not the one wronged.

"Did no one think that you should be able to do all those things—researching, learning and making your own choices?" he asked.

"A few, but most didn't." She shook her head.

"Elmheim would never allow such restrictions. If you visit for a time, you'll be able to see that not all realms are so closed-minded."

It would do her good to see how life could be, how no one need be restricted on account of their gender. The wizards of Isro never seemed to return once they managed to leave. Like Haimo, they didn't long after places that failed to treat them as equals. Sigimar liked to believe he would have had the courage to leave such a place were he in Hypatia's shoes, but perhaps not. He'd had no strong ties to his homeland, wherever that had been, only to his brother. Perhaps he should count himself lucky not to have grown up with such strange practices.

Hypatia grinned, setting her quill aside and cocking her head playfully. "Are you trying to ask me to stay in Elmheim?"

Hope exploded in his chest until it consumed him. Thoughts he should not have allowed took root in his mind. A library of their own, filled with too many books to ever read in a lifetime, shelves as far as the eye could see and taller than he. A little girl like her perched on his shoulders, gripping his hair in chubby fists as he retrieved a book shelved too high for Hypatia to reach. An apron covering her rounded belly, smudged with the dust of an artefact she'd unearthed, a trace of grey on her nose from peering too closely at it. The image of them together, happy, with children of their own, pouring over old texts and researching the ancient artefacts of Ashla, seared itself into his brain.

He wanted it with a ferocity that frightened him.

"Sigimar?"

He shook himself from his stupor. No, that was the one thing he couldn't have. Hypatia wanted freedom from all the things he and his life represented. Freedom from titles holding her down. Freedom from fearsome monsters. She deserved better. She deserved to explore the whole of Oblivion. He would not become the same chains she'd desperately tried to escape.

"I...I couldn't ask you to do that. Not for my sake." He swallowed.

"Then I'll do it for my own sake. There's no reason I can't explore Elmheim before I go my way."

Sigimar nodded, praying he didn't appear too eager. He should tell her not to linger. It wasn't safe. If that horrid fantasy had proved anything, it was that he was the last person she should spend her time with. Instead, he found himself saying something altogether more like an invitation than a warning.

"If it's exploration you're after, then you may enjoy looking over the ancient artefacts of Ashla. Some are located in Askr, the capital of Elmheim. Legends say the people who created them lived in harmony with each other, had eradicated disease, built monuments that reached the sky, and were so wealthy they had roads made of gold."

"And have you found any artefacts to corroborate the legends?"

"No, sadly not, though many are searching for the golden roads." He winked.

She waved it off, as if a road made of gold were of little interest.

"Well? What happened to them?" she asked. "According to the legends, that is."

"It's said they became so impressed with themselves that they rejected the primacy of the gods, considering themselves equal to the divine."

Her face echoed his disbelief in the claim.

"Who would be foolish enough to become a heretic?"

Who indeed? Gods did not abide heretics, and the forgotten gods of Oblivion were no different.

"The people of Ashla, apparently. Legend says that is why the miasma first arose, as divine punishment. As a result, all heretics are immediately sacrificed to the forgotten gods in Elmheim. If they are innocent, then the gods won't take them below. If they're guilty..." He shrugged. He'd only seen one such person swallowed up by the earth. It was one too many.

Hypatia shook her head.

"You would think that all it would take is one of their number getting swallowed up by Oblivion for them to realise that the gods, do, in fact, make a special exception for living sacrifices when it comes to heretics. But it seems very strange to me, a whole realm becoming heretical and holding stubbornly to such ideas in the face of divine punishment."

Sigimar shrugged again. Legends rarely bothered themselves about being inherently logical. Then again, neither did most people.

"Maybe the forgotten gods made an example of the whole of Ashla, so no one would be so foolish again. Deities are not beyond punishing entire races for the hubris of an individual. Just consider the fae."

"What of the fae?" she asked.

"You don't know the tale?" His brows rose.

"No."

Of course she didn't. There had been no fae in her empire. She hadn't even known what an elf was before he'd told her.

"Ah, the tale goes that fae were the most beautiful of the races, especially blessed by the gods in that regard. The elves were granted strength, the shapeshifters their two natures, the nymphs their connection to the elements, the witches and wizards their enormous amounts of magic. But a single fae believed himself more beautiful than the gods, and even more foolishly, boasted of it. So the gods cursed all fae, and even now, they can only regain their former beauty if they rip out their feeling hearts."

Hypatia's eyes were wide, her attention fixed on his every word. He felt almost silly telling the tale. No one knew if it were true, but it was a good story—simple. Perhaps that is why it had survived the ages. Or perhaps the witches and wizards simply loved a story that proved their rivals in magical prowess had such blighted origins. Who could really say?

"Hold on a moment. I want to write this down. I love collecting these kinds of stories." Hypatia hopped out of her seat and rummaged around in the chest that contained her few personal possessions. She returned to their little desk with a scroll. She unrolled it to an unmarked section and began writing in her script. She paused, furrowing her brow. "You said that *legends* stated the miasma arose due to divine punishment. Do you believe something else is at the root of it?"

Sigimar nodded.

"I do."

He'd spent his childhood learning his letters, and the letters of ancient Elmheim's elves, so that he could pour over the oldest chronicles and theories about the corruption cloaking Ashla. By the time he'd become an adult and his martial training was complete, he'd convinced himself and Dag that the miasma could not only be contained, it could be dispelled. They'd been called deranged fools for believing the scribblings of long-dead, disgraced scholars, but that had stopped when they'd found the wellspring. Only Erlendr knew the full truth of it, and he hadn't made the wellsprings publicly known. The king feared that untold numbers would plough headlong into the miasma, only to return as legions of hungry, corruption-tainted creatures on the frontier. Enough already had when Erlendr set up his rewards, and more had followed in the wake of Sigimar's actions, proving his caution to be wisdom.

"What then?"

"You must swear never to write a word of it, nor speak of it to anyone else."

Reluctantly, she put aside her quill and placed her hands in her lap, an expectant look on her face.

"I'm quite good at keeping secrets."

"I...I told you about Dag. About how it was he who freed Ashla from a portion of the miasma." Sigimar took a breath.

Hypatia put a hand over his.

"You don't have to continue if you aren't ready."

"No. No, I want to tell you," he said, surprised that he meant it. Dag's memory was safe with Hypatia. "I spent my long childhood researching old texts. Some of them spoke of wellsprings of miasma, where the fog became thicker the closer you got. We trekked deep into Ashla and managed to find a wellspring, but it wasn't what we expected. There was a clearing, like the eye of a storm, and a stave in the centre. Dag was eerily drawn to it. He lost sight of his surroundings, saying it called to him. He used his healing light on the artefact and purified a huge swath of land of the miasma shrouding it. Afterwards I...I smashed the stave until only splinters remained."

"So it's not a divine curse," she surmised.

Sigimar shook his head. A divine curse would never have been so easily undone.

"Has anyone figured out what that stave was?"

"Not to my knowledge. But then, I haven't really asked."

"That's understandable."

"Is it?"

Hypatia smiled sadly.

"Yes. Is it so strange that you would avoid things that might bring you pain? I haven't gone artefact hunting since Kosmas died. I couldn't bring myself to."

"And now?"

"I think I could do it again and enjoy it. I think I could do it remembering the good times instead of just the bad."

Sigimar wondered at her strength. Her smaller hand covered his, her warmth seeping into his heart. If she knew how he wished to cage her with his selfish desires, she would run screaming. She might not possess the healing light, but everything about her was a balm on his soul. Was it any wonder after all the grief and pain that he craved the relief of her presence? He was just Sigimar to her, not a hero, not a legend—just himself.

He shook himself from his morose thoughts.

"Tell me about the artefacts of your empire. What things did you uncover there?" he asked.

She grinned, standing from her seat and crooking her finger.

"Come and I'll show you."

Sigimar followed her to her chest of valuables. She handed him a scroll and a few bound books. She was about to shut the lid when he reached down to pick up the last bound book.

"You forgot one," he said.

Hypatia paled, slamming the chest shut before he could get too close.

"Not...not that one."

"Is it some sort of diary?" he asked.

"No. Please don't ask to see it."

Her fingers were curled protectively over the lid of the chest, her shoulders hunched, bracing for a confrontation that would never come. He put her research on the desk and returned to her side.

"I won't ask. But if you want to tell me about it, I will listen."

The tension left her shoulders.

"I'm sorry. After all you've trusted me with...it's just..."

"It's a secret."

Hypatia's grey eyes searched his. She pursed her lips and nodded.

"And you're very good at keeping secrets," he added.

"Yes."

He kissed her forehead and helped her stand.

"Then I've trusted the right person. Now, show me the treasures of Lethe."

It was some time before she finally relaxed. Whatever was within the small book obviously haunted her. At least in one thing, they were perfectly matched. Just as she had been a safe harbour for him, he would be that for her... for as long as she let him.

CHAPTER 14

Hypatia spent the next week working on her written translation guide and moved on from the alphabet to common words and grammatical structure. Sigimar hadn't spoken a word about her notebook, the one that held her deepest shame. It should have been burned long ago, but she hadn't been able to. Just as the knowledge within had been used for nefarious purposes, it could also be used to save someone, and so she'd held onto it as penance. She put it from her mind as she concentrated on the task before her.

As she wrote out a simple sentence, Sigimar nodded with pride at her side. As happy as it made her, she had so very far to go before she could read a proper sentence, to say nothing of the special language of contracts. Even Sigimar had admitted that though he could read the marriage contract, not everything made sense to him. As she stared at the scrap parchment before her and contemplated her sheer ignorance, a headache bloomed behind her eyes.

"What's wrong, Hypatia?"

Groaning and leaning her forehead against the cool wood of the desk, she wondered if the wood was real or conjured, or if the distinction was actually a useless binary. She was, after all, sailing through the skies on the back of a dragon that disappeared into the ether after they landed in a town for the night. The more she learned about fae magic, or any magic outside of Lethe, the less sense it made.

"I'll never understand all this in time."

"In time for what? Why do you need to rush?"

The question caught her off guard.

"I...don't know."

In time for the annulment of their marriage contract. In time for when she said her goodbyes to Sigimar. In time for when she walked away from the spark he'd ignited in her.

"What's waiting for you?" Sigimar asked, his expression closed and carefully neutral.

"Freedom, I guess? When I planned my escape from Lethe, I decided to go to the Witchlands because it seemed like a good place for a woman who wanted to start her life over. A good place for a woman who didn't want to be forced to marry a man if she chose not to."

Sigimar nodded, though he couldn't hide the tightening at the corners of his eyes or the slight slumping of his broad shoulders.

"You should speak more with Brynja about witch societies. She didn't come from Isro, but she came from a very similar realm. I don't want you to be unprepared for the kinds of challenges you'll face if you decide to settle there."

The thought of leaving him felt so melancholy, so bitter. She was genuinely enjoying her time in his company; the pleasure of it had become addictive. He was intelligent and thoughtful, passionate and humble. Part of her wished to assure him that she wouldn't leave, but what was the alternative? Undoubtedly, as a noble, he would marry again once they divorced, and eventually have a family of his own. A man of integrity like him would never hurt his wife by keeping a mistress. In the grand scheme of things, Hypatia would just be a quickly forgotten woman of no importance or consequence.

"*If* I decide to settle in the Witchlands," she said, her heart pounding dangerously in her chest. Gods, what was she thinking? She didn't want the life of a noblewoman. She wanted to dedicate her life to study. But as she caught a glimpse of hope in Sigimar's eyes, one quickly snuffed out as he coughed and looked away, what she wanted didn't seem as clear-cut. Hypatia began to wonder why she couldn't have everything.

"Yes. If," Sigimar murmured. "Oblivion is vast. There are many suitable realms."

"Quite. And you promised to show me the sights of Elmheim first. To immerse me in its culture," Hypatia said, pushing her quill back and forth on the table, edging her hand closer to his. She should not skimp on her education.

"I did. And there are many sights. Many things to experience," he agreed, tapping his finger on the table, turning his body to face hers.

"It will take some time to see them all, won't it? To learn all I should know before I think to strike out on my own?" She sat up and turned to him, tucking an errant curl behind her ear.

"Yes. Many months, at least. And you wouldn't want to travel in the depths of winter," Sigimar noted, stroking his short beard in contemplation.

"No, that would be a fool's errand." She touched his knee.

"Without question." He took her hand in his, as if contemplating its capabilities, smudging the ink on her fingertips, not meeting her eyes. "Summer would be better."

"I think I would like to experience Elmheim in the summer, at least once." Hypatia leaned forward.

"It's...a beautiful sight." His eyes met hers.

She felt that look of desire to the tips of her toes. Forgetting all hesitation, Hypatia pressed her lips to his. Sigimar gathered her up into his lap, tongue eagerly meeting hers. She deepened their kiss, wringing a groan of pleasure from him. Unprepared for what the sound would do to her, a shivery thrill rolled down her spine. She wrapped her arms around his neck and slid a finger along the tip of his ear. His grip on her thigh tightened and he pulled away, nipping her bottom lip and resting his head on her shoulder.

"That...I wouldn't do that," he groaned.

"I did it purposefully."

Sigimar looked up, pained eyes capturing hers and holding her still. It was not pleasure or yearning there in the amber depths. No, it was sadness.

"I'm not worthy of you, Hypatia. I was born an unwanted bastard, grew up a lowly warrior on the frontier and in no way earned my current position. You tempt me sorely, but you also deserve better. I'm not good enough for you."

Hypatia narrowed her eyes and poked him in the chest.

"If you think I'm one to hold the circumstances of your birth or occupation against you, then you can't think very highly of me. I decide who I find worthy, Sigimar. Me. Not you. If I invite you into my bed, it's because I've already made up my mind."

He blinked in surprise.

"I...see..."

Hypatia sighed in affectionate frustration.

"I know you don't. Not yet. But the day you do, you'll be breaking hearts from here to Lethe."

"I don't want to break anyone's heart."

That would be entirely unavoidable. Because hers would break when either he left or she did, when his duty compelled him to find a real wife, or when her need to chart her own course drove her onwards. Until then, though, she planned on making that pain so *very* worthwhile.

"And that's precisely the reason you will," she teased him.

His face remained serious.

"How do you feel about...this? I don't want to upset you again."

How did he not see that he was better than what she deserved, and not the other way around? How did he not know that she was already dangerously attached to his warmth?

"This doesn't upset me. When we're together, I'm happy."

As soon as the words left her lips, the inadequacy of the sentiment hit her. She wasn't simply happy, she was doing the things she loved again, feeling engaged and alive and herself. Curiosity made her world sparkle anew. Joviality lightened her step. Lust fizzled through her veins. She craved life again, instead of passively existing, ghost-like. There were possibilities instead of just miserable choices.

"Truly?" he asked, doubtful.

"Yes."

Hesitantly, he kissed her, sweet and soft. Just as she rested her hand on the scorching place above his heart, the chamber rumbled. They broke apart.

"Get your outdoor clothes on. Now," Sigimar said.

Galvanised by the deadly calm in his voice, she tore off his lap and quickly donned everything that would keep her warm in the bitter cold. The light inside the room dimmed as the clouds they passed through turned dark. Sigimar swiftly packed up their papers and ink in her chest before pulling on his own clothes in a fraction of the time. The chamber rumbled again—harder.

Someone banged on the door.

"Jarl, Fru, you must hurry! We're coming up on a violent storm and need to land immediately," Ingi called.

The next shudder nearly sent Hypatia to her knees. She might have twisted an ankle but for Sigimar's steadying arm. In his other, he gripped her wooden chest.

"Hold onto my arm and the railing as we descend the stairs."

They quickly made their way into the main hall. Sigimar handed her chest to Ingi with instructions to keep its contents safe. Today they rode with the fae, who were all seated on the floor with ropes protruding from the lower wall tied around their waists. Extraneous furniture had disappeared, and all the baggage was tied down with extra care. Sigimar guided her over to an open spot and sat beside her.

"Tie yourself tight. I'll keep you steady with my free arm."

She did as she was told, heart pounding in her chest.

"What's happening?"

"The storm is too strong for magic to calm. We're passing through a rough patch as we descend," Sigimar explained.

"Is it dangerous?"

"You have your protection charms on your person?"

"Yes, but...oh."

Sigimar nodded, his arm snaking around her upper shoulders, holding her firmly as the hall shook with increasing violence. Hypatia closed her eyes and did her best to curl into Sigimar's body, her hands gripping the fabric of his warm tunic. Visions of falling out of the sky raced through her mind. The next forceful jolt tore a small scream from her.

"We're almost to the ground. You'll be alright, Hypatia," Sigimar murmured as his grip tightened.

How could he be so calm when they could fall out of the sky to become gory splatters on the ground below? Didn't he know what falling from a great height would do? Hypatia had been raised on stories of an uncle who died during the Great War, a teleportation mage who dealt with his enemies by dragging them to a spot in the clouds. He would then teleport back to the ground to watch them as they fell. As children, her brothers, Phillip and Kosta, liked to embellish the tale by describing his victims' grisly remains.

Despite Sigimar's reassurances, everything shook and jolted until Hypatia's clenched jaw was sore. She thought her heart might leap out of her chest. Tears streamed from her eyes, and she fought to drag in enough air with her panicked gasps. Both of Sigimar's arms encircled her, though she couldn't make out his words through the pounding in her ears.

"Out. Everyone, get out!" he commanded, his voice strong and sure, no hint of fear.

Only then did she realise the shaking had stopped. He pushed aside the folds of her cloak and rested his hand on her chest.

"I can slow your racing heart if you want me to. But first, open your eyes."

She did, but her vision was clouded by tears. Still, she knew Sigimar was all around her.

"There, that's better. We're on the ground. You're safe. All is well. Take a deep, slow, breath."

She failed on her first few attempts, but eventually she drew a slow, shaky breath.

"Good. Take another. Does anything hurt? Start at your toes and work your way up."

Her hip was sore and possibly bruised, but the real issue was her hands.

"My hands," she answered, her voice tight.

Carefully, he unclenched her hand from around the folds of his tunic. He massaged her palms through her gloves until she could feel the tension drain away. She looked around, realizing they were alone. Shame had her flushing.

"I'm sorry. I was scared."

Sigimar kissed her brow and pulled her into his lap.

"As was I."

"You don't have to lie."

"I'm not."

"You were calm and collected. I was the only one who lost their head." She scowled. She'd never been good in an emergency. Her mind always raced, and she either froze or fled or screamed uselessly. Or begged the assistance of malefactors posing as saviours. Pathetic.

"I've had more practice, and having someone else who needs you to have that veneer of calm helps."

Hypatia sighed and rested her head on his chest.

"I must have looked like a coward." How galling for others to see her true self.

"I think you underestimate just how terrified everyone else was."

She let his warmth sink into her and the sound of his heartbeat calm her.

"Where are we?"

"I'm not certain. Close to the lake though, probably in the Kingdom of Rei. Would you like to go outside and see?"

"Yes. I suppose it would be better to deal with everyone's stares now rather than putting it off."

"You can hide in my cloak if you wish." Sigimar grinned, his eyes alight with mischief.

Hypatia refused to respond to that. Half because of his teasing, the other half because she didn't want to tell him how much she wished to do just that. He helped her up, and they left the hall, descending the staircase someone had conjured. Snow was coming down at an angle in the fierce squall. The members of the caravan were hugging each other, or leaning on the trunks of toppled trees for support, snapped by the body and legs of the summoned dragons. When Ingi approached, even he seemed strained in his posture and expression, his usually ruddy cheeks bloodless.

"Please accept my apologies. We should have been watching the weather more closely."

"Are you certain it was natural?" Sigimar asked.

"No, Jarl. Brynja is of the opinion it was either brought on or greatly enhanced with magic. We're close to the harbour town of Nor, by my estimates. I've sent a scout to look for a nearby town, and others to search for game and sacrifices for food and the pocket realms."

An owl called overhead. Ingi looked up, his eyes going blank.

"We're in luck. The town of Nor is only a short walk from here. Should I let them know we're coming?" Ingi asked.

"Just tell them we're looking for lodging for the night. Don't tell them who we are."

Ingi's stare went blank a moment longer. The owl flew off and Ingi's eyes focused again.

"As you wish, Jarl, Fru. I'll have the sleighs ready shortly."

When Ingi was gone, Hypatia looked up to Sigimar.

"What was that?"

"Hmm?"

"Ingi looked like he was here and then…not?"

"He was speaking to another shapeshifter, the owl. Mind to mind."

"They can do that?" she gasped.

"Yes. He could speak directly into your mind as well, if he needed to. And no, before you ask, he cannot read your mind."

"How did you know I was going to ask that?" She frowned.

"Give me some credit. I've spent the past week or so entertaining your scholarly mind." He chuckled.

"You think I'm a scholar?" she asked, her heart tightening in her chest. Only noblemen could be proper scholars in Lethe. They'd all seen her efforts as unserious hobbies, like she was a child playacting the part rather than a person with something valuable to offer. They were more than happy to buy her artefacts and notes and accept her assertions about their provenance, but no one considered her to be their academic equal.

"How could I not?" he asked, bewildered. "Is there a different term for a person with an impressive intelligence and a curious mind in the empire of mages?"

"No, there isn't." She hid her smile and laced her fingers through his.

He didn't know it, but Sigimar had just slid the key into the last lock protecting her heart. Tonight, she was going to make him hers.

CHAPTER 15

"Respectfully, it would be safer to spend the night in a pocket realm, Jarl." Ingi's ear twitched while his expression remained unreadable.

Sigimar looked at the simple, small lodge and shrugged. It was well-maintained, warm, dry, and most importantly, not made of magic. He'd had enough of things that both were and were not real for one day. A pocket realm, created and sustained by the life of an unwilling sacrifice, was infinitely malleable by the fae who created it. It was also unstable and prone to collapsing in the face magical cancellation, or iron, which was poison to fae magic. Given his experiences in Gortos and the day's inauspicious freak weather event, he was looking forward to sleeping in something that was inherently physical.

He supposed Ingi's distaste for the cottage stemmed from thinking that it wasn't good enough for a jarl. Without being able to use Sigimar's rank, the pickings were slim for lodging in the popular harbour town of Nor. The gale had ended, leaving the wooded area the caravan now found themselves in with a pristine layer of snow and a look of serene, wintry quaintness.

"Rei is a peaceful kingdom on good terms with the rest of the River-lands. King Harald is a good man who takes the orderliness of Rei seriously. Even on the margins of town, we're safer here than we were in any part of Gortos."

Ingi bowed.

"As you say, Jarl. Many of the fae will be sleeping in their pocket realms surrounding the...hut here. I will mark the trees they'll be attached to so that if you require assistance, you need only walk into them. The rest of the caravan will be staying in the nearby lodgings. I've had your belongings and gifts placed in your rooms should you have need of them. I believe the proprietor also stocked some necessities."

"Thank you, Ingi."

As the shifter stood straight and turned to walk away, a snowball smacked right into the side of Ingi's head. His eyes widened with shock—then narrowed in anger. He whipped his head around.

"Brynja!"

The witch cackled with glee. Another snowball flew at Ingi. Ingi dodged, allowing the snowball to hit Hypatia square in the face.

"Oh!" Hypatia gasped.

The caravan was shocked into silence. Sigimar held back a grin as he helped wipe the snow from her face. Her lips were trembling. All traces of humour fled. He was going to pummel that witch within an inch of her—

And then she burst out laughing.

"S-Sigimar," Hypatia said, wiping tears from her eyes.

"Yes?"

"You must defend my honour."

"Oh?"

"Hunt down the one who got me. Avenge me." She grinned.

"It would be my pleasure." He kissed her gloved hand and then bent down to form his own snowball. "Step forward, cur!" he called out.

Snowballs began flying in earnest then, shrieks and playful swearing echoing out in the dusk. Even Ingi had gotten in on the fun, hunting down Brynja with single-mindedness. When Sigimar lobbed his own at the nearest person, he found that Hypatia had run off. He spotted her forming her own snowball. She aimed it at his face. It hit his chest instead, the heavy, wet snow sliding down his tunic.

"Run, little mage," he warned her.

She dutifully sprinted, shrieking with delight as she was pelted with stray snowballs. Sigimar made several of his own and dashed after her, hitting anyone who aimed at her. With his last one left and the tempting target of the little mage racing away, he let it fly, smacking her on her bottom. Her little squeak was well worth the thorough beating he received when he found himself in the centre of a maelstrom. He grabbed a nearby branch, cracked off a portion and began batting incoming missiles back at the gathered crowd. The sky overhead suddenly darkened. Every set of eyes shot upward.

"I win!" Brynja shouted from afar.

Formerly suspended by magic, a thick sheet of snow tumbled out of the sky, hitting the entirety of the caravan when it fell. Sigimar dove for Hypatia, shielding her from the worst of it, listening to her gleeful snorts the whole while. Cold, soaked and full of good cheer, the snowball fight ended, and everyone drifted off to their places of rest for the night. The tension that had ridden the caravan since the uncertain landing had finally dissipated.

"You know, I was wrong."

"About what?" Sigimar asked.

"I didn't think there was anything fun about the snow."

"There's plenty of fun to be had, but only until you get wet. Come, let's dry off."

Sigimar opened the door to the cabin, its triangular roof sloping to the ground on either side. Inside, a central stone fire pit, sunk into the ground, hosted a flame fed by magic rather than wood, keeping the air inside free from smoke. In the back, an impressive bed made for someone the size of an elf had him sighing in relief. Along one side were their trunks of belongings. The other boasted a large tub full of water as well as a small table with chairs. Ingi must have already been inside, because food and drink were prepared. Little lights hovered along the support pillars, bathing the room in a warm, dim glow.

They stripped out of their wet outerwear and clothes, setting them aside to dry. But that left Hypatia wearing a nearly transparent wisp of a dress. Sigimar shifted uncomfortably in his pants at the sight. Like an electric current in the air, the atmosphere between them had changed, charged and thick with anticipation. She grabbed the food and settled in front of the fire, undoing her braids so her hair could dry. Sigimar followed her lead, snatching one of the blankets from the bed to settle around them. They ate in silence as the fire warmed and dried them.

He knew he should say something, but every time he convinced himself he'd found the right words, they scattered from his mind. All he knew was that he liked this woman too much for his own good. What he truly desired, she wasn't willing to give. Sigimar almost caught himself wishing, cruelly, that she possessed the healing light, for then there would be no divorce, no way for her to leave the frontier, and him, forever. And then he would realise he was a monstrous person for even entertaining the twisted fantasy. In the end, he would let her go, as she wished. The alternative, causing her misery and grief, was unbearable to contemplate.

"Is there something on your mind?" she asked.

"No," he lied.

"You've had a strange look on your face since we sat down," she said, inching closer, her bare shoulder brushing his side.

"Have I?"

"Yes."

He dared look at her then. Determination radiated from her. Not being a total fool, he knew what she wanted. An answering hunger curled inside him. From his angle above her, her pale brown nipples were visible, hard points against the thin fabric of her gown. It took an effort of will to drag his eyes and mind away from the temptation. Moving closer without realizing it, one arm slid behind her, propping him up as he leaned over her. He swallowed, paralyzed by the push-pull of wanting and foreboding. There would be no going back—not for him. She would brand herself on a part of him that would never be free of her.

Always the bravest between them, she moved first.

"I'm very fond of you, Sigimar. You feel the same way, don't you?"

"Yes. Very much. Too much," he replied as if compelled, the words flying out of him.

Her smile caught him unprepared. The little mage held his heart in her hands. A bead of sweat rolled down his back as nerves assailed him. He was not unfamiliar with lust and longing, but this was different—more. He shied away from naming the thing that consumed him where she was concerned.

"Do you want me?" Hypatia asked, pushing herself closer, the soft swell of her breast brushing his arm.

"Yes," he said, his free hand pushing up the hem of her gown, fingers skimming the silky skin of her calf.

"Then kiss me. And this time, don't let that be the end of it."

"Is that wise?" he asked, desire quickly eroding sense.

"No. But I find I don't care anymore." Her breath fanned across his lips as she leaned up in invitation.

Gods help him, neither did Sigimar.

Hypatia's heart thundered in her chest as she looked up into his eyes. The starved beast in her approved of the hunger she saw there. It rejoiced when that last tether of his reserve snapped, inaudible. She felt it in the shift of his body, the covetous lust of his hand on her.

Sigimar bent his head down and touched his lips to hers, tentative and gentle. She pulled him close, impatient for more. His arm snaked out to lift her into his lap while his free hand tangled in her hair, cradling her head, tongue sliding against her bottom lip, asking for entrance. She moaned into his mouth, gliding her tongue against his, tasting him.

"Wrap your legs around me," he growled.

She complied, her dress climbing up around her thighs as her arms circled his neck. Without mercy, she ground herself against the quickly growing bulge in his pants. He slanted his mouth over hers, dominating their play of tongues. Both of his hands went to grip her bottom, pulling her gown away. A single finger played along her slick folds before breaching her. She broke off their kiss with a startled cry.

"You're so fucking tight," he groaned, his forehead resting against her collarbone, hot breaths fanning against her chest.

"You have big fingers," she accused, clinging to him as his finger teased her mercilessly.

"What I want to put inside you is bigger than my fingers."

Hypatia giggled.

With her in his arms, he stood with fluid grace and headed for the bed. Lowering her down, he knelt over her, making her feel like the daintiest of creatures. As he freed her from her dress, her hands greedily sought his leggings. She wanted—needed—to see him fully. With some difficulty, she tugged them down, her eyes riveted on his semi-hard member. She sucked in a breath. It was even larger than she'd remembered.

"That's not going to fit," she blurted out. Hypatia slapped her hands across her mouth, wishing she could take it back.

Unconcerned, Sigimar chuckled, backing up as he bared himself fully.

"Yes, it will. I'll get you ready," he said as he tied his burgundy hair back with a strip of leather.

He joined her once more, eyes drinking his fill. Her hands explored the muscles of his chest, dusted with dark red hair, finding his intriguing piercings with ease. Leaning on one arm, he trailed his free hand down her belly to her curls below. Pulling his lips down to hers, their tongues met as he slipped his finger into her once more, his thumb tracing lazy, maddening circles on her clit. Hypatia rode his finger when he added another, stretching her tight. He latched onto her nipple, licking and nibbling. She mewled in pleasure, shifting her hips to take his fingers deeper.

"Slow down. You're not ready yet," he purred in her ear.

"Hurry. Please," she begged him.

Gods, she wanted this—wanted him. She was ravenous, and he was her feast.

"If I rush, I'll hurt you."

"I'm aching right *now*."

Kissing her again, he silenced her pleas. He removed his cruel, glorious fingers and pulled away from the bed.

"Don't stop!" she cried.

Had she been too needy?

"I'm not leaving," he cooed, rummaging around the bottles near the bath before taking one back to the bed. Pouring it on his fingers, he lay down alongside her. He slipped two fingers inside her and carefully fit a third. "I want you more than my next breath. But I want this to be good for you."

Hypatia gripped the sheets and moaned, her legs falling open in invitation. He could barely fit three inside her, yet she was greedy for more. As if sensing her restlessness, Sigimar increased the pressure of his thumb, wringing unexpected, stunning pleasure from her in an instant. She cried out, her back arching, her grip twisting the sheets.

When she came back to her senses, she was panting and he was still inside her, stroking lazily, his eyes full of satisfaction.

"Please."

He shook his head.

"Not yet."

"H-how can you stand it?"

"I'm a patient man. And you're a beautiful sight."

She groaned and reached down for him, hoping to urge him into impatience. When she wrapped her fingers around him, her eyes flew open, wide with shock. She looked down at the hard length in her hand. It was bigger than she'd thought. Bigger than even a few moments ago.

"Gods below."

Sigimar rasped out a pained laugh as her palm slid up and down his length.

"As I said, not yet."

He shifted his fingers, stretching her and slipping them in farther. Pressing his thumb against her hard, he circled, building the pleasure until it was too much. She clenched around him, screaming his name as his lips trailed kisses across her breasts.

Hypatia wasn't certain she would survive his preparations. If he kept doing as he pleased, she would combust long before he ever tried to fit himself inside her. Another shift of his fingers brought her to the point of pain. He withdrew them instantly.

"Wait!"

"No. If I hurt you now, it will only take longer to get you comfortable. We have time, Hypatia."

"I don't care."

"I care."

"But I want more," she pleaded.

A wicked grin broke out across his stern features. It promised exactly what she desired, in the most punishing of ways.

"Then I'll give you more until you beg me to stop."

Anticipation had her trembling. He trailed kisses down her chest and belly, teasing her inner thighs before his tongue found that aching point of need. Sigimar was a man of his word. Over the next span of time, minutes or hours, she didn't know, she lost count of the times he'd brought her to the pinnacle of pleasure and sent her over. Like a master musician, he knew exactly which chords to strike and when, as if he'd known her body his whole life. Slicked with sweat, gasping for air, trembling and weak, Hypatia finally begged for mercy. Only then did he coat his cock with slippery liquid and pull her close.

"Are you certain?" he asked, his expression a blend of need and vulnerability.

"*Yes.*"

He pressed himself against her entrance and slid in by slow degrees. Hypatia must not have been able to hide her shock at the feat, because Sigimar chuckled.

"I can't believe I'm saying this, but it's not *that* big, Hypatia."

He buried himself to the hilt and released a hissed breath. Hypatia moaned. She was at her limit. Even without moving, he hit every pleasurable part of her. Crouched over her, his hands clenched, Sigimar looked like he was in pain, breathing unsteadily.

"Are you uncomfortable?" he asked between clenched teeth.

She moved on him in answer, marvelling at the feel of him inside her, heart pounding as pleasure gripped her.

"Please," she begged him.

This time he granted her wish, withdrawing slowly before plunging back into her. Torturously slow at first. Then faster. Every thrust stunned her, making her think nothing would ever feel more divine. But every time, he proved her wrong. He gradually increased his pace until all that was left of her was need—need for him, for this, for more and faster.

She gloried in the play of emotions on his face, his desire mirroring hers, the trepidation giving way to consuming ecstasy, leaving only the intensity of raw lust. His amber eyes, focused and fierce, did strange things to her. With his eyes on her, there was nowhere for her mind to wander, not a single thought but of her heart thundering in her chest and the feel of them intertwined. She was imprisoned in amber, and she yearned for her shackles.

He flipped her on her side and raised her leg, hooking it over his hip. She held herself up on a shaky arm, her hands fisting the sheets and screamed his name as he slid home. Turning her head to the side, his mouth captured hers, drinking down her incoherent moans. Sigimar was going to kill her with passion and his endless stamina.

"S-Sigimar... I can't—" she gasped.

He bit down at the juncture of her neck and shoulder, sending lightning down her spine. Shifting again, his fingers found her overstimulated bud. With a single light slide she saw stars. His hips moved with breathtaking power, sending him deeper as he cried out with his own release.

Destroyed. He'd destroyed her utterly. Hypatia was no more. She was merely the mindless remnants of the woman his lovemaking had made of her. He laid her onto her back, fluttering kisses down her body and whispering endearments. As she caught her breath, he took a warm, wet towel and cleaned her tender skin with soothing gentleness.

She must have nodded off then. When Hypatia briefly woke, she was curled up next to him, cradling his head next to her chest, his arm wrapped around her in sleep. Hypatia kissed his hair and closed her eyes.

Tomorrow she would figure out how to extricate her heart from this bliss. Tonight, she would luxuriate in sweet entanglement.

Chapter 16

Sigimar hadn't slept so deeply since he'd been a child under Dag's care. It was why, when the dulled clicks first began, and then scrabbling on the roof above echoed through the quiet of the night, he wasn't alarmed.

He woke slowly, convinced that the sounds were only the last remnants of an unpleasant dream, forgotten as soon as his eyes opened. Breathing in Hypatia's scent, his grin was irrepressible. Cradled by her lush, bare breasts, everything was perfect, save for one matter. Her head rested on a pillow atop his arm. He flexed his hand, numbed from the weight of her. Regretting the necessity, he slowly shifted to a more comfortable position, careful not to jostle her into wakefulness.

She'd fallen asleep, exhausted by their lovemaking. He watched her then, content, letting his mind wander through impossible fantasies as he nodded off beside her. Visions of hearth, home, Hypatia, and a happiness that could never be danced through his mind once again as he began to close his eyes.

The wood of the roof groaned. Nightmarish clicking followed. Sigimar shot up, heart hammering. He reached for an axe that wasn't there. Grabbing Hypatia's shoulder, he shook her awake, a hand covering her mouth to prevent alerting the draugr. She came awake in a panic and flailed.

"Shh. You must stay quiet," he whispered in her ear.

She stilled, her hands on his, and nodded. Slowly removing his hand from her lips, he held up his hand to stop her as she began to rise. She froze. The creature clicked above them, shifting to locate prey. Silent and barefoot, Sigimar padded to the long chest which held his weapons. Thank the gods the hinges were well-oiled and the wood beneath him hadn't creaked. He opened the chest, extracting his two-handed axe and shield. He crept back to the bed and handed the shield to Hypatia. It was heavy, sturdy, and probably too much for her to wield effectively, but it was better than nothing.

Sigimar strained his ears, listening for the faintest hint of movement above. A shriek in the distance raised the hair on his neck. Screams rang out in the night. The draugr on the roof skittered off, following the promise of violence. Sigimar rushed to don his leggings and boots.

"Sigimar?" Hypatia asked, her voice trembling.

"Stay inside and bar the door." He grabbed his smallest axe and handed it to her. She clutched it in shaking hands, her eyes wide. "Don't let anyone inside unless I tell you it's safe. Push all the chests in front of the door when I leave, understood?"

"No! I don't understand! What's out there?" she cried, tears rolling down her cheeks.

"I'll tell you when I return. Stay here and stay as quiet as you can."

He pulled on his tunic and set out into the pre-dawn darkness. He closed the door to the cabin behind him, refusing to leave until he heard the first dull scrape of wood on wood. Hypatia was shoving the crates to bar the door.

The camp was already roused. Fae were stepping out of their pocket realms, half-dressed but weaving magic like colourful auroras in their hands. Witches and shapeshifters emerged from their lodgings with weapons in hand. Sigimar trudged through the chill night, slowed by the deep snow, following the noise of the creatures. He passed several cabins before he came upon the one he was looking for. The door was some distance off, sunk into the snow, torn off its hinges. Inside, blood-splattered magical lights flickered, dripping crimson over dark smears on the floor. The draugar shrieked within.

But the screams of the living had gone silent.

Behind him, soft footfalls pressed into the snow. With his excellent night vision, he caught the sight of Brynja and another witch approaching, weapons and spells in hand.

He had no idea how much experience any of his caravan had with what became of people devoured by the corruption curse. Nodding to the witches, he took the lead. The interior of the cabin would make a terrible battleground; cramped, a low roof making it impossible to swing his axe, the walls and ceilings acting as perfect places for a draugr to latch onto and lunge from.

He whistled.

The creatures stopped fighting over whichever poor soul they'd been in the process of eating. A short series of clicks later and they leapt from the house shrieking. Already, whoever had succumbed to the corruption curse had been completely transformed by it. The draugr's eyes were no more than oozing black sockets, the skin stretched tight over bone, now as tough as armour. Its jaw was split wide open, row upon row of jagged, mismatched teeth on display as spittle flew. Claws as long as daggers were outstretched towards whatever warm body they could lock on to, more claws on its feet giving it extra grip in the snow. Its posture shifted between man, lizard and beast, its joints clicking as it adjusted them endlessly.

Sigimar sidestepped the first draugr and brought down his axe on the juncture of its neck and shoulders, where its carapace was thinnest. The second attacked at the same time, gouging the flesh along his back as he ducked to avoid its maw. The witch beside Brynja froze the creature where it landed, her magic securing it. Sigimar swung his axe again and decapitated the second. Brynja raced inside the cabin.

"Gods below—he's still alive! Dragon blood! Now!" she called out.

The other witch raced inside the cabin, vial in hand. Sigimar joined them. If Brynja could piece the victim back together, the dragon blood would cure the corruption infused in their flesh. They would need another person to hold the patient down. Brynja worked quickly, reattaching a severed arm, rebuilding flesh and muscle that had been torn away, stuffing guts back inside, stopping the blood flow from a myriad of deep puncture wounds and gashes. Though the victim was whole now, every healed wound bore the oily black mark of corrupted flesh, inky tendrils reaching towards the heart. Once it reached the heart, no healing light or dragon blood could prevent death or transformation.

"Hold him down," Brynja ordered as she took the vial from her companion.

Sigimar held the wizard's legs, while Brynja and the other witch held an arm each. A single drop of the blood hit the first corruption-tainted mark, and the man's eyes flashed open, a scream of agony tearing from his throat. With sure and steady purpose, Brynja administered the cure over every mark. They flipped him onto his front so she could do the same again, his screams muffled by the floorboards. That done, they carefully returned him to his back and forced a drop down his throat, his agonised gurgle confirmation he'd swallowed it. The wizard's breath came out in ragged gasps, his eyes unfocused.

"Thank you," he wheezed.

"We got them both," Sigimar assured him.

The wizard muttered something, his eyelids drooping.

"Hmm?" Sigimar leaned forward, his ear close to the man's lips.

"*Three.*"

Sigimar's blood turned to ice in his veins.

Hypatia crouched in the centre of the cabin nearest the fire, hoping that, like most creatures, whatever was slaughtering people outside feared it. Dressed in Sigimar's oversized leather armour and clutching the shield and axe Sigimar had given her, Hypatia's insides were jelly. The shield was so heavy it required both arms to raise it. The axe was similarly unwieldy. If it came down to a confrontation, weapons would be of little use in her hands. Hypatia was no warrior. Save for her confrontation with Diocles, from which she'd barely escaped with her life, Hypatia had never fought, never mind won, a physical fight in all her life. She'd always had her rank, her family, or Kosmas to rely on to keep her from harm. How utterly asinine she'd been to assume it would always be like that.

Shrieks and screams echoing in the night left her trembling like the coward she was. Some adventurer she'd become. She'd been so confident that better things awaited her outside Lethe, that she would live for the thrill of strange lands and new knowledge. How foolish. Hypatia hadn't known what she was stepping into. In the empire, the only monsters were the ones she met on the streets and in ballrooms. Or the ones that came knocking with tales of woe and promises of power.

There were *real* monsters here.

Insistent pounding on her door made her nearly jump out of her skin.

"Fru Hypatia!"

"Ingi?"

"Are you secure?" he asked.

"Yes. I've blocked the door," she called.

"Good! Stay inside. There is still one last draugr on the loose. We're hunting it as we speak."

"Is Sigimar safe?"

"The Jarl is part of the hunt, despite my efforts to dissuade him. He has plenty of experience."

Which was no answer to her question, and well Ingi knew it. Dread gnawed at her.

"Please find him, and protect him. I won't leave the cabin."

"I'll go now, Fru. I'll send someone back to guard you. Keep your charms close."

The silence and stillness that followed were their own kind of torture. Hypatia didn't know how long she waited, but eventually she heard footsteps crunching through the snow outside.

"Hello?" Hypatia asked, her voice hushed.

Clicking.

It was her only reply.

"No, no, no, no," she gasped, gripping the shield she could barely lift and the too-heavy axe.

The draugr outside shrieked. The crack of splintering wood was the only warning Hypatia had before the door to the cabin was unceremoniously torn off. A pathetic barricade of crates was all that stood between her and the creature. As it tore through the crates and tossed them aside, she backed up, tears streaming from her eyes, a scream trapped in her throat.

In the firelight, the draugr was a nightmarish vision. Too-long, bony limbs with horrifying claws and a face she would never forget. Its eyes, eyelids and nose were all missing, leaving pitch-black, oozing holes instead. One ear hung by a sinewy thread, slightly pointed at the tip, while wet, stringy hair whipped to and fro with its frantic movements. Its jaw was split wide open, displaying too many needle-like teeth.

And it was blocking the only exit.

It leapt over the mess of crates still littering the doorway and shrieked in triumph. Hypatia did the only thing she could think of: she turned invisible and held her breath. Bone-crunching clicking ensued as the creature adjusted its stance from that of a man to that of a beast. Wet hair slapped on the floor, leaving dark, thick smears. It raised its head high and snuffled at the air. Rushing past her, it flung itself on the bed, tearing into the sheets with teeth and claws.

Hypatia kept her eyes on the draugr and backed away slowly. She needed to get to the door. Her heart raced, threatening to leap from her chest. It took all her strength to keep the shield and axe aloft so that they wouldn't scrape across the floorboards. She was nearly to the haphazard pile of crates when the floorboards creaked under her weight. The creature stopped, as if it were as frozen with fear as she. The click, click, click of the draugr turning its head around to face her held her immobile. Its long black tongue curled around the furry clump of animal pelt in its mouth and tossed it aside.

Between one blink and the next, the creature was on her, clawing away at the shield. She dropped it. The draugr hadn't seemed to register that the shield was now visible, intent only on slashing through it. If it reacted to sound, this might be her only chance to escape. She tossed the axe as far as she could, and it clattered loudly near the bed. Without hesitation, the creature leapt at it. That was when she dared to take her eyes off it and made a run for the door.

"Hypatia!" Sigimar howled.

She saw him sprinting for the cabin. Then she saw the floor, dazed by the impact. The air rushed from her lungs in a painful burst. Visible once more, she couldn't draw in a breath. A clawed hand pressed into the floor near her head, sharp edge a mere hair's breadth from her eye. Wet, clumpy hair fell over her like limp seaweed, coating her in slimy, crimson filth as blood rushed from her nose.

The monster was on top of her.

"Hypatia!"

Ribs cracked as the draugr used her as a spring board. Try as she might, every gasp, every movement, was cut short by agonizing pain.

The creature shrieked once, twice, and then a wet crunching silenced it, clicking and all. Sigimar kept calling her name, scrabbling over crates.

"Hypatia! No! No, please gods, no!"

His shaking hand touched her neck. She wanted to speak, but she couldn't. Sigimar sobbed.

"Jarl! Jarl!" Ingi shouted.

"In here! Get Brynja, now!" he snapped, his voice thick with emotion.

"I'm here! Is she still alive? Don't move her!" Brynja shouted.

"She's alive," Sigimar croaked. "There's blood."

"Step aside, Jarl," Brynja said, her voice calm but commanding. The floor creaked under his weight as he left her side. "Lucky girl," Brynja murmured.

Warmth replaced the agony, and Hypatia dragged in a full breath of air, her broken nose and battered cheek no longer bringing tears to her eyes. Brynja turned her over.

"Get me a wet washcloth. I can't tell if she's been scratched or bitten."

Sigimar handed Brynja the washcloth, his haunted amber eyes searching Hypatia desperately for injuries. They removed the oversized leather armour. Hypatia's eyes widened at the sight of the claw marks nearly shredding the back. The healer wiped away the blood from her skin and pulled the collar of her tunic this way and that, inspecting her back, looking for wounds. Both Brynja and Sigimar sighed in relief.

"Thank the gods," Brynja said.

"Sigimar," Hypatia croaked, her arms outstretched, her hands trembling. She needed his warmth, the feel of him surrounding her. She needed to feel safe. Nothing felt safe.

Sigimar sank to his knees, as desperate for reassurance as she.

"Don't!" Brynja's order was like the crack of a whip. Hypatia flinched. "You've got befouled blood all over yourself, Jarl. Everything it touches will need to be cleansed or burned. If even a drop gets into her, she'll have to swallow dragon blood, just to be safe. As it is, I need you both to strip. Your clothes need to be burned."

His eyes widened, and he recoiled from her. He stripped out of his soiled clothes as Hypatia did the same. Brynja manipulated the water in the tub, cascading it over Hypatia, then Sigimar, sluicing every drop of dark blood from their skin and hair before she gathered up the water and placed it back in the tub.

"Now kneel down, turn around and brace yourself as best you can," Brynja said to Sigimar as she uncorked a vial.

Hypatia gasped at the sight of his back. Dark, crisscrossed marks with malignant, forked veins stretched out, marring the brownish-green of his skin.

"Sigimar…"

"It's alright. Brynja will heal it. I'll be there in a moment," he said, his voice calm.

Brynja clucked her tongue, though her voice was sympathetic.

"Damn fool."

The second the contents of the vial hit Sigimar's skin, he screamed.

Chapter 17

Sigimar woke in an unfamiliar room, fully dressed, with Hypatia leaning over him, her eyes full of tears. He must have blacked out from the dragon blood. Reaching up a hand, he wiped away her tears with a thumb. It was not the first time he'd subjected himself to dragon's blood. Drest, his huskarl and a dragon shapeshifter, had made it a habit to be the first to treat him for corruption-related injuries in Ashla. All the better to teach him sense, or so he'd been told.

"Shhh. It's alright now," he whispered.

It was the exact wrong thing to say, apparently. Hypatia's bottom lip trembled before she choked on a sob. The dam had broken. She crumpled over him, weeping into his tunic. Sigimar wrapped her in his arms and stared at the ceiling. In silent prayer, he thanked the forgotten gods for sparing Hypatia's life.

Dread had compelled him to race along the draugr tracks, all thought of cautiously stalking it thrown to the winds. In his heart he knew—Hypatia was in danger. When he'd seen the wreckage inside the cabin spilling out into the snow, he'd thought he might lose his mind.

"It's not alright. I thought I would die. I'm too weak to raise a shield. I have no idea how to swing an axe. My magic can't protect me. And you faced that thing and killed it in seconds! I'm only alive because of you and luck! And you were so terribly wounded..."

Sigimar closed his eyes and took a deep breath, pushing away his own horror. Every word was an indictment against keeping her at his side—for any length of time. How could he subject her to the dangers of the frontier? That there were any draugar on this side of the mountain pass was the dose of reality he'd needed to snap himself out of his delusions. Hypatia could never be his. He lived in the most dangerous part of Oblivion, doing the least safe work, alongside a motley crew of trained warriors, exiled criminals and the desperate, lured by the promise of a roof and food in exchange for risking their lives. Ashla, Elmheim, the whole of the frontier, none of it would ever be safe enough for her.

She deserved better.

"I'm so sorry Hypatia. I never should have left you alone."

He'd almost allowed someone else to die for his terrible decisions. Again. Another reason he was the wrong person to stand at her side. Someone worthy of her would have put her first. The one she truly deserved would never have left her side. He never should have delegated guarding her to someone else. After swearing to protect her, he'd broken his oath.

He felt Hypatia push off his chest, no doubt sick at the thought of being near him. He almost didn't open his eyes, afraid of the condemnation he would see there. She sniffed. Her palm on his cheek surprised him. It wasn't disgust he saw reflected in her grey eyes.

"Please don't do that, Sigimar. I'm upset because I'm a coward. I've spent my entire life relying on the protection of others, and in the moments no one is around to do that, I can barely do more than run. I hate that you were hurt protecting me, that my weakness meant someone I care about had to put himself in harm's way for my sake." She sighed, wiping tears with her sleeve, her eyes averted. "I'll go back to Lethe. I was deluded to think I could handle life outside my coddled little nest."

Back to Lethe? Where she would languish, her talents never appreciated or recognised? Where someone else would force her to be wed? The idea of her being wed to a man who would never give her the respect and love she deserved was not to be borne! It propelled a fiery poison through his veins. He would never allow it. Not this woman who was stronger than he, who stood tall and smiled despite her sorrows. To see her reduced to such doubt was more than he could bear. If she couldn't see her own courage and strength, then he would teach her to see it, to believe in it.

"*No.*"

She startled, surprised by his vehemence.

"No?"

"No. I won't let you do that to yourself. You'll go to Isro, or somewhere else you can be free and happy, but not Lethe. I'll hire the best combat instructors. I'll teach you myself until we get to Elmheim. But I won't let you give up. Not because of this."

"But you were hurt. And then when Brynja..." She looked away, tormented, her hands trembling as they clutched the material of her dress.

He gripped her shoulders and forced her to meet his gaze.

"I *chose* this life and the dangers that go along with it. Everyone on this side of the mountain pass? They live as you do, relying on Elmheim to protect them from the miasma." He tucked a strand of hair behind her little ear. "There is no shame in not being a foolhardy warrior. There is no shame in relying on others. And I was injured because I ran out without a stitch of armour—not because of you."

She paused, as if she might accept his argument. But doubt reined in whatever hope he'd stoked.

"I'm still a coward at heart. No amount of instruction will change that."

"Hypatia..." he sighed, pulling her close. "I've had centuries of training and centuries more of experience on the frontier. You never stop being afraid. You learn how to continue *despite* it. The people who aren't wise enough to fear... they don't last."

She pushed away from him, searching his face, a strange look on her own.

"C-centuries? Gods below...I never considered..."

Sigimar laughed at her shock.

"Did you think I was older?"

She shook her head.

"Younger?"

"Much."

"How much?"

"I thought you were...in your sixties, perhaps."

"If you add an extra zero and a couple decades..." Sigimar shrugged. "Those with elven ancestors tend to live a very long time. Is it not so for mages?"

"No. Not at all."

He swallowed down new dread. He almost didn't want to ask what he knew he needed to, for fear of what she might say.

"How long do mages typically live?"

"More than a century if they're lucky, but never more than two."

A fist squeezed his heart. So little time. Like a butterfly—there for a season and gone before the next frost. Everything about her was too fleeting. His heart couldn't accept that.

"And you are...?" Sigimar asked.

What if she had but a few decades more? There were ways to extend her life, to let her live more than her pathetically short lifespan, but they required magic he didn't possess. The elven king Erlendr was surely employing just such a means to extend his wizard husband's life. Wizards only lived into their third century, after all. Sigimar needed to find out what his options were.

"Thirty-five."

Gods below! She was young, even by witch standards!

Her scowl was impressive. Another worry must have shown on his face.

"I'm not a child, Sigimar. I was an adult at twenty and legally allowed to inherit property by thirty."

"Thirty-five is very young," he replied, his voice tight.

How was she *thirty-five?!* That was the first bloom of adulthood for witches.

"Six centuries makes you a dusty, ancient relic!" she retorted, poking him in the chest, equally baffled by him.

"Ancient is at least twenty thousand years!" he countered.

"Your scale of time is just...it's just wrong!" She threw up her hands.

"Is not!"

"Is too!"

"Well, I feel childish *now*." Sigimar smirked.

Hypatia's face broke out in a smile as she unsuccessfully suppressed giggles.

"Ah gods, now that I think of it, it's no wonder your skills in the bedroom are so... Six centuries of practice cannot be underestimated."

"Three centuries. I didn't come of age until I was three hundred." Her open-mouthed stare brought out a sense of mischief he'd long thought he'd lost. Sigimar touched her chin, gently nudging her mouth closed. "You'll catch flies if you're not careful."

"I think I need to lie down and get my head around this," she said, draping herself across his chest.

They lay in silence for a time, her fingers tracing patterns on his chest while he kept his arm around her, his thumb rubbing her upper arm. The room they shared was unusually luxurious. Tall ceilings, gleaming, carved wood, bright sunlight filtering through picturesque windows, a large, plush bed big enough to accommodate him and then some. But was it a pocket realm or a real dwelling? He shifted slightly on the bed, noticing a lump in the mattress. Real. Nothing in a pocket realm was ever the least bit uncomfortable unless the fae who created it willed it so. Then again, maybe Ingi had instructed the fae to add just a hint of discomfort for his recklessness.

Propping his head up, Sigimar stared down at Hypatia. Everything about her was so ephemeral. Even this time with her would come to an end far too soon. He held her tighter.

"I'm so glad you're alive, Hypatia."

If she'd perished, he would have broken irreparably. So much so, that he would have gone and done something he knew for certain would get him killed, like storming Otmar's ugly stone keep. Knowing how important she'd become frightened him. Would he be forever destined to lose the people he cared for most?

"And I you, Sigimar. You're a good man. I hope one day you can see yourself as I do."

That was unlikely, but he appreciated the sentiment. Gods, he was going to be a miserable bastard when she left. He pushed the thought away, though the pain of it lingered.

"Do you know where we are?" he asked.

"The harbour of Nor. The local governor, the shield-master? He heard about what you did and who you are from Ingi."

Sigimar groaned. Damn that hare-eared bastard. Never had a shifter been so unlike his inner animal. Ingi was as determined to fête Sigimar's unearned status as a wolf was on the trail of blood.

"Don't be too angry. People began asking questions when they saw the cabins being burned."

It was the only logical response to places tainted by corrupted blood or flesh. No doubt the earth had been salted, too.

"Did your scrolls and notes survive at least?" he asked.

"I...I'm not sure. I didn't ask."

"Didn't ask? But they're your most prized possessions!" He gaped at her.

"I had more important matters on my mind!" She scowled.

More important than the reason she left her empire? More important than her key to living independently? More important than the knowledge she'd accrued? More important than her secrets?

"Such as?" he asked.

She gave him an inscrutable look.

"You, Sigimar. I was more worried about *you*."

He forgot to breathe.

It was a strange thing, to realise the woman before him held his heart in her hands. Stranger still, to comprehend just how much she'd mended it in so short a time. Did he hold her heart, even a piece of it? Greed overwhelmed him. Only earning the whole of her heart would satisfy him now.

As if only then realizing what she'd said, her cheeks heated as the silence dragged on. Every time he tried to tell her that he wasn't worth such concern, the words caught in his throat, like a lie on the lips of a truth-tasting fae. Instead, he simply stared at her like a stupefied fool.

"I...I'll go let Ingi and the shield-master know you're awake." Hypatia turned and hopped off the bed, hurrying for the door.

Sigimar launched out of bed and caught her forearm to stop her, careful not to harm her delicate wrist. She stilled. Turning her around, he searched her face, her own shocked realization mixed up with fear and fondness, desire and something more. He didn't have the right words for the messy jumble of his own thoughts and emotions. So he bent down and kissed her. A kiss of thanks and longing, of panic at the hope eating him alive, of a need so bone-deep he was convinced it had roots in his soul. A kiss she returned, perhaps unwisely, with passion.

That door in his mind, the one holding back his selfish desires, had been ripped off its hinges when that creature had done the same to their cabin. He'd bludgeoned any wisdom he'd had, much like the draugr, to a bloody death. The only reason he knew this was because in its place was a singular, insidious, and ultimately futile thought. *How can I convince her to stay forever?*

CHAPTER 18

Hypatia was doing a terrible job of separating her heart from the matter of Sigimar. Though she was half-listening as Sigimar spoke to the shield-master about the source of the previous night's horrors, her thoughts were as tangled as her emotions. Did it mean anything that she cared more about Sigimar than her prized scrolls and research? It was only common sense that he mattered more. He was alive, a person! Her research, while precious, wouldn't be utterly lost so long as her mind and memory were still sharp. But in the moment, when she'd said it out loud, she'd seen shock and so much more playing across his face. She'd tried to flee from the answering pull of her own heart. It was a doomed courtship—a doomed relationship. But the clever, cruel man, at a loss for words, had told her everything with a kiss. One she would not soon forget.

The words unspoken twisted her in knots.

The truth of the matter was that she was beginning to want things which were mutually exclusive. Hypatia wanted Sigimar fiercely. She wanted his gentle soul and his warrior's body, she wanted his smiles and his too-honest eyes in equal measure. Being with him felt like coming home. Yet she wanted nothing to do with Ashla, Elmheim, the frontier and the terrors tied up with life there. If such attacks were a common occurrence, she had no doubt her time there would be short and her death bloody and brutal. Could she convince him to run away from it all?

She watched him pensively. Sigimar's lips were pursed in a grim line as he pushed back his burgundy hair with his brownish-green hand, amber eyes narrowed in thought. She might be able to convince him, but at what cost? Would he live his long life ashamed of himself for letting her cowardice lead him away from his duty? Would he make the calculation that one century with her wasn't worth throwing away six centuries' worth of honour?

As the daughter of a traitor twice over, she'd always considered honour more philosophical than practical. But Sigimar was different—it clearly meant something to him. Could she forgive herself for asking him to discard it? Could he? Hypatia knew well how much he cared about her. She knew what that look in his eyes meant. Her heart had craved it for years. It seemed she'd found what she'd sought after all, and yet an insurmountable wall separated her from it. A monstrous thing to do, to make him choose, knowing the power she had over him.

"How many casualties?" Sigimar asked, bringing Hypatia's attention back to the conversation.

"Two, not including the crew of the vessel that delivered the draugar and cursed weapons. I only regret, having been long retired from the frontier, that I didn't notice the ones that got away. Please, Jarl, Fru, accept my apologies."

"We accept your apologies," Hypatia said, her hand on Sigimar's.

"Did you recognise the ship that brought them to your harbour?" Sigimar asked.

"I'm not familiar with the vessel, though it was elven-made, western in design. And someone had spelled it to bring on a wicked storm when it neared land. We had to drag it ashore and burn it."

"Slavers." Sigimar's face contorted with disgust.

The shield-master, an elf himself and easily a head taller than even Sigimar, nodded grimly. His long black hair was tied back, only a hint of grey at his temple, his bronzed skin lightly lined at the corners of his eyes and bracketing his mouth. Hypatia briefly wondered at his age.

"King Erlendr has been relentless at stamping out their ilk from our part of Oblivion, but it seems one slipped through the narrow pass, carrying poorly contained, cursed weapons. Whatever crew or victims were onboard were either eaten or transformed. We don't know how many there were to begin with though, so I can't say for certain if the ship was even carrying more than the crew."

"Have you had the curse on the weapons lifted?" Sigimar asked.

"Yes. We're lucky that not all those with the healing light have been lured across to Elmheim." The shield-master grinned. "And don't even think of trying to bribe mine to journey with you. King Harald would have my head if another one ran off for the rewards and glory on offer at the frontier."

"I've no intention of poaching. But may we take the weapons back to Elmheim? I suspect King Erlendr will want to investigate where they came from and how the crew was able to slip through the narrow pass."

The shield-master nodded.

"Best tell him to send reparations to my king. I doubt King Harald will be happy that a piece of the frontier made its way to his kingdom, given he's paid in kin, gold and goods to keep that from happening."

"I'll be sure to do so."

"Then our business is concluded. Your man Ingi has already hired a ship to take you home. A nice one, too! All the rooms are pocket realms. Good luck on the frontier and congratulations on your wedding. You're welcome to return to Nor anytime."

Sigimar and the shield-master clasped arms when they stood. Unsure of the protocol, or the relative importance of their respective ranks, Hypatia curtsied.

"An interesting custom. Where did you say you were from?" the shield-master asked.

"I didn't, but I am from Lethe, the Empire of Mages," Hypatia answered.

"Not Gortos?"

"No," she and Sigimar answered.

"Ah, then you should know the rumours flitting about Nor's harbour. Word of Otmar's mistreatment of you travelled faster than your caravan." The shield-master smiled. "King Otmar has been finding his rivers harassed by pirates, his trade shipments delayed, their prices increasing. And Isro's latest delegation apparently sent silver-plated iron goods. King Otmar sent Isro's queen an urn full of the delegation's blood and cursed the lid to spark if opened. There's talk of Riverland-wide retribution for your treatment at his hands, Jarl Ashla."

"I can't say I pity the man," Sigimar replied coolly.

Neither could Hypatia. And yet petty retributions between realms could spark war, and nothing good ever came of that kind of chaos and destruction.

"Why the blood?" Hypatia asked.

"Witch blood is highly flammable. If opened, the urn could have exploded, just like the iron hiding beneath the silver plating could have killed any fae who touched it."

Gods below, how awful. Hypatia tightened her grip on Sigimar.

The shield-master nodded and said little else, leading them out of his home and along the blustery boardwalk to their ship. Hypatia was glad of her thick furs then. The skies were bright and clear, the rolling waves of the lake glittering in the light, the waters frozen nearest the shore but not at all in the depths of the bustling harbour.

Hypatia felt her innards quiver at the thought of sailing closer to the kinds of creatures that had attacked her the other night. Though soaring through the skies towards them was even less appealing. Given the summoners didn't have the magical reserves to cross the mountains, and with yesterday's terrifying descent still fresh in her mind, perhaps it was a small blessing.

Now that she thought on it, her adventures had all been frightening in one way or another, yet here she stood. She'd survived fleeing from her family, the loss of her late husband, being tricked by a fae princess, biting cold and now a monster attack.

With her gloved hand securely clasped in Sigimar's, she boarded the ship, her nerves settling as they pushed away from the pier. Sigimar began pointing out landmarks across the lake. As he told her about how all the realms on this side of the mountain range were connected by navigable rivers to the lake, she placed her hand on his.

"Have you ever thought of leaving Elmheim, leaving Ashla?" she asked.

If Elmheim were the home he cherished, she would press no further, ask nothing more of him than what he willingly gave her. But if he had no attachments? Then she would propose running away together. Once the contract was dissolved, the magic that Sigimar said would pull her towards Elmheim would be nullified. She and Sigimar would be free to leave. If she could eliminate the danger from the equation, then she could have everything she wanted, and Hypatia was not too proud to admit to being selfish when it suited her.

"Because of the draugar?" he asked, wrapping an arm around her shoulder, a gentle look in his eyes. "Yes, once, shortly after Dag died."

"What made you stay?"

Sigimar snorted.

"King Erlendr. He convinced me to take a title and lands. I didn't know at the time that accepting them would bind me as they do—as they do every titled person in Elmheim. I thought, like anyone else, that once I'd served one-tenth of my natural life on the frontier, I would be free to go my way. Now I can only leave Elmheim at his pleasure, just like every other jarl on the frontier."

"By binding you, you mean magically?" Hypatia asked.

"Yes, much as the marriage contract binds and draws you to Elmheim. I don't fully understand it myself, but it's tied to the old pact of protection. There had to be some guarantee that there would be people to beat back the miasma, and a reason for every Riverland realm to have a personal stake in ensuring that remained the case. So don't let him persuade you into swearing any oaths or taking any titles."

"Or into signing any new contracts," Hypatia added sourly.

"Or that," Sigimar grunted.

A shaky breath escaped her as her chest hollowed out, hope dying a swift death. Hypatia wouldn't be able to keep the man she wanted, not if she didn't want to spend the rest of her short life in constant fear. She should be accustomed to not getting what she desired most by now, but the deprivation still hurt. Except this hurt in new and unexpected ways. When she'd hardened herself and deadened her heart, surviving the trials of her grasping family as a domina, and wallowing in her grief without Kosmas had been torturous but survivable. But she was truly alive now. A spark of happiness had become a conflagration, brightening her life as she'd foolishly believed that, this time, things could be better. Living with that hope made the crushing of it all the more brutal. Perhaps she should have been less afraid of monsters and more afraid of opening her heart. After all, a monster could only kill her, but a broken heart would leave her lingering, limping through days of agony and nights of bitter tears.

Sigimar stood behind her and folded her in his cloak, drawing her close against his chest. She settled against him, letting his warmth seep into her bones. Gods, she would miss this. He made her feel safe and cherished and warm and alive. As they stared out at the disappearing harbour of Nor, he rested his chin atop her head.

"I can hear the buzzing of your thoughts," he said.

"No, you can't."

"Hmm, I think I can," he teased her. "But I already checked, and your research is safe."

"That's not it."

"Will you tell me?"

Emotion choked her. She couldn't. Not all of it. Some wounds were best tended to in the quiet dark of the night when no one could see you weep.

"I don't know how you live, surrounded by those things."

"We take what precautions we can, the same as any herder who knows there are wolves watching his cattle."

He made it sound so reasonable. But it was simple, horrid chaos. Though she supposed his metaphor was apt. Just the thought of staying in Elmheim made her picture herself in the role of a sheep with a leg in a trap, ripe for the slaughter. She'd never wished to lead the life of a warrior, but she wished it now: to be free of her crippling cowardice, to lust for battle, to have an elemental gift worth having. But nothing and no one could make her that, for she was Hypatia, pathetic light mage, whose greatest skills were reading, turning invisible, and running away.

Tears stung her eyes then. She tried and failed to convince herself it was merely the bite of the wind gusting across the lake, filling the sails and pushing them closer to Elmheim. Nearer to the end of her time with Sigimar.

"I'm going to miss you terribly," Hypatia whispered.

His arms tightened around her, and he bent down to kiss her cheek.

"We're not parted yet."

No, they weren't. Not yet. So she'd better make the best of their time together and fill her heart to bursting with precious moments by his side. She would need them when she left.

"Show me our cabin," she said.

When he'd closed the door behind them and swept her up in a kiss, a terrible thought occurred to her. Her heart might never be filled, because every moment with Sigimar only made her ache for more.

CHAPTER 19

Sigimar lay awake in the early morning, snug in the dark confines of his ship cabin, Hypatia sleeping peacefully beside him. His eyes roamed the features of her face, branding them into his memory. He'd never dared call her his wife, but the knowledge that in a few short hours the only thing that bound them would be dissolved by King Erlendr, at Sigimar's own urging, was a bitter pill to swallow. The hope, the fervent prayer, that she might change her mind as they sailed to Elmheim had kept him sane.

Every day he would teach her how to hold a shield or knife, every evening they would work on her written language skills, and every night they would spend in each other's arms. They were the very best days of his life since Dag had died. And yet, despite his hopes, he knew she would not change her mind. Nor should she.

The frontier was no place for her, and well he knew it. Not even Erlendr's castle in the capital, the most fortified in all of Elmheim, was entirely safe. Banks of toxic miasma sometimes drifted across the narrow channel between Elmheim and Ashla, bringing starving creatures with them. Askr was fortified, but the draugar were always adapting to their defences. And so, when the time came, Sigimar would let her go, no matter how much his selfish heart screamed at him to hold her close.

She woke, looking up at him with a sleepy smile.

"My serious Sigimar." She traced his beard with a finger.

She wasn't wrong. He was hers. His heart belonged entirely to her. Catching her finger between his teeth, he growled playfully. Her laughter had him smiling.

"If you want to see something special, get dressed quickly," he said.

"Isn't it usually the other way around?" she teased.

He pinched her bottom, delighting in her squeal of indignation before rolling out of bed. When they were fully dressed, he brought her up on the deck of the ship where a chill wind cut through him. Her wide-eyed gasp made it worthwhile.

The tops of the snowy mountains disappeared into the dove-grey clouds, their sides dotted with towering evergreens. Rough waves battered narrow, rocky shores. Yet this was not what held Hypatia awestruck. As if cleaved in two by the will of gods, a narrow river divided the two mountain ranges. Yet instead of clear sky between them, a glacier of ice arched between the mountains, covering the river in a dark, protective embrace. As they passed under the icy archway, the splendour of the thing made itself apparent. Deep in the gloom, lights winked and sparkled all around.

"What are they?" Hypatia asked, gripping the railing and leaning out as far as she could to get a better look.

"Plants and insects specially bred to emit the healing light and thrive on the glacier."

The ship raced through the tunnel at unnatural speed, pushed onward by the magic of the crew. They would arrive all too soon at the speeds the ship reached. It might have been dangerous, if all the traffic in both directions wasn't monitored, scheduled and cleared before coming or going. Another precaution which made the errant vessel with the corruption cursed goods and crew a shocking occurrence.

"They're beautiful."

And necessary, he thought. They kept the occasional corruption-cursed creatures from crossing through Elmheim into the Riverlands beyond when strong winds pushed a cloud of miasma as far as the capital, Askr. Even light as weak as this was enough to kill what came crawling out of the miasma. Most of the time. Provided it wasn't hiding below the deck of a ship, shielded. But he didn't want to spoil the wonder he saw reflected in her eyes.

"Not as beautiful as you," he said instead.

If he could have stopped time then, and existed in that moment alone for eternity, he would have counted himself lucky that it would be her saucy grin imprinted in his mind until the end of days. As they passed out from under the ice and into the weak light of day, the moment was gone.

They emerged out onto a large, half-moon-shaped lake, ringed by gaily decorated wooden houses on stubby stilts, all as close to the water's edge as could be got without letting the tide in the front door. Some, furthest from the busier shipping docks, appeared as if perched on the water itself, though closer inspection would demonstrate that they were connected to land by a wooden walkway, all suspended by timber driven deep into the muddy banks. Though unlike the myths of ancient Ashla's golden equivalent, the streets of Elmheim's capital, Askr, were paved in well-worn stone, all hewn from the mountain. There had been a surfeit, Sigimar had read, after the castle had been carved into the mountain, as safe a haven as there could be on this side of the pass for Elmheim's ruler and the people who lived nearby. The rest of the stone went to build the wall that protected the city.

"Gods below," Hypatia gasped.

Her eyes were not on the city or its structures, though. No, her eyes were riveted on the abomination in the distance. Askr was walled and fortified for a reason. It sat in a place of extreme strategic importance: closest to the mountain pass—and to the border of Ashla.

Rising up like a dark cloud from the distant shimmering waves was an ominous, toxic curtain that stretched up into the clouds. The miasma, and Ashla's curse. Corruption in its purest, most concentrated form.

"That's..." Hypatia trailed off, horror robbing her of her words.

"The frontier," Sigimar answered. "The toxic miasma of the corruption curse blanketing the lands of Ashla."

She looked at him then, a strange expression turning her features.

"Corruption...curse?"

"Yes, it's the same one that turned a person into the draugr that attacked in Nor."

"Oh..."

He wasn't certain what to make of her reaction. No doubt she was in shock if she'd never seen the miasma before. After all, the corruption curse wasn't usually visible to those without spell-sight. It was only here on the frontier, where every rock and gnarled branch in Ashla was affected by it, that the raw, foul magic was visible to the untrained eye.

"We'll go to King Erlendr's court to plead your case. But first, open your bag of charms." He smiled.

It took her a moment to recover, but when she noted his expression, she raised a curious brow. Pulling it from her cloak pocket, she frowned, no doubt feeling a different shape than she was used to. He'd worked by the dim light of a single candle every night while she slept soundly nearby, freezing at every groan or turn, fearing discovery before he'd finished. She loosened the cord sealing the bag and peered inside.

"Sigimar..." Hypatia pulled the amber and gold necklace of charms from the bag. It was a necklace with three strands, each a little longer than the last, hand-knotted between every charm. She gasped.

"If you want it restrung, I'll see to it," Sigimar offered sheepishly.

"No, I love it. You have a keen eye for colours." She clutched it to her chest.

Sigimar nodded, the tips of his ears heating at her compliment.

"Best wear it under your tunic. Protection charms are always most effective the closer they are to your skin."

It also wouldn't do for her to openly flaunt being the owner of so many valuable charms, but that warning could come another day. Sigimar helped her put it on. Though hidden beneath cloak, dress and tunic, she held her hand to her chest and grinned up at him.

The ship docked at the nearest pier, and he swung over the side of the ship onto the plank, helping her down, his hands on her waist. He briefly recalled the first time they'd met. The first time he'd put his hands around her waist to help her off a cart laden with gifts for a spoiled princess. Thank the gods he'd been tied to Hypatia. It all seemed like a lifetime ago now. And yet, it also felt like he'd blinked, and all his time with her had disappeared—water rushing through his fingers and back into the sea. He would be lying if he'd said he wasn't desperate for more.

Ingi was off the ship next.

"I'll head straight to King Erlendr to request an audience on your behalf. Should I give him the details of our journey, or would you prefer to, Jarl?"

"Tell him. I'm sure you can make a better accounting of it than I can."

"Jarl, Fru." Ingi bowed before racing off.

As others disembarked, they said their goodbyes and paid their respects, filtering out onto the bustling streets and weaving through the markets. Sigimar drank in the sights and scents of home; the fur-lined and heavy wool cloaks, the gleaming snow on rooftops turning darker and thinner the closer it got to the oft-travelled paths, the scents of fish and cattle, the wood smoke of magicless cooking fires, the comforting pale grey of a cloudy sky protecting sensitive eyes from a potentially blinding sun. He wondered what Hypatia saw as they walked through the streets at a leisurely pace.

"Everyone is so calm," Hypatia remarked. She looked up then, no doubt seeing his confusion. "They wake every day to that...that *wall* across the water, and yet everyone goes about their day."

"It's a fact of life for those who live in Elmheim, and especially for those who live here in the capital, Askr. It's unnerving at first, but eventually it just becomes scenery."

"Most scenery doesn't turn people into monsters."

"Point taken."

A prickling sensation raised the hair on the back of his neck. He was being watched. People were beginning to whisper that hated title. Anger and grief rose in a tide within him.

"Sigimar?" Hypatia asked, concerned.

"Is that him? The Hero of the Frontier?" someone whispered to their companion, loudly enough that even Hypatia could hear it.

She saw too much. Her grip on his arm tightened as his own lips thinned in disgust. Tugging him away from the main thoroughfare, she led him to a narrow lane behind the houses.

"Can they see us?" Hypatia asked.

Sigimar shook his head, trying to breathe through the weight on his chest. There was a reason he never came to Askr unless ordered. At least no one in his lonely corner of Ashla made the mistake of calling him that hated name more than once.

"We can't hide here forever," he sighed, weary.

"But what if we could hide in plain sight?" she asked.

"I fear I'm too well-known for that."

"Not for this." Hypatia smiled. "I'm considered a very talented light mage. Do you know why?"

Sigimar shook his head.

"Because I learned that the trick to light magic isn't about raw power, it's about finesse. Try not to be too shocked, and don't let go of my hand."

He blinked, and she was gone. Whipping his head from side to side, failing to catch sight of her, he found that he himself was no more. She laughed as a strangled sound of shock escaped his lips. He felt her then, her hands wrapped around his arm.

"It takes some getting used to, walking about when you can see everything around you but not yourself. Once you do, it can be rather freeing."

"Invisibility is a complex spell," he said, his voice strained as he struggled with the disorientation.

"Yes, it took me many years to figure out how to do it. As far as I know, there are very few light mages who ever attain this level of skill."

"Many years?" Sigimar asked, incredulous.

"Yes. Six, in fact."

Did she know that such mastery made her a prodigy by any reasonable standard? Six years was nothing. He was glad she couldn't see his mixture of shock, awe and envy.

"Now we can be on our way without anyone bothering us."

Without anyone bothering *him*. Still, he was grateful for her polite fiction, and even more so for this freedom. He only wished he could see her and kiss her for it. Instead, they rejoined the main street. It took some doing, walking in a crowded place attached to one another while weaving out of the way of oblivious on-comers. They eventually fell into an easy rhythm, Hypatia directing their nimble footwork while Sigimar told her about the town.

The castle and the road leading up to its slick barricades were impossible to miss. Unfortunately, so were the hanging cages swinging in the freezing gusts, creaking and moaning as loudly as their occupants.

"Gods below," Hypatia gasped.

"Best make us visible," Sigimar said. No need to get a suspicious guard with excellent hearing poking about with the business end of a spear. A moment later, Hypatia dispelled her magic.

"What crimes have these people committed? They'll freeze to death out here."

"Save your pity, Hypatia. They're elven. So long as their heads remain attached and their hearts intact, they'll recover. They're only up there because they're slavers, bold and foolish enough to sail near Elmheim. Erlendr will let them down when he's satisfied, and their victims will decide their fates."

"Ah," she replied, clearly uncomfortable.

As they reached the wooden gates, the doors creaked open. Inside the first layer of defence, welcoming halls housed soldiers and royal crafts-people. They also doubled as safe houses for townspeople who needed protection from the odd bank of miasma rolling across from Ashla. The next layer of defence consisted of the homes of administrators and lodgings for foreign dignitaries. The last layer of defence was the castle itself, dug deep into the mountain. In the deep, permanently frozen basement levels were huge stocks of food, gold and artefacts. It was where he'd delivered the stave Dag had purified and Sigimar had smashed to pieces.

They walked through the slushy, trammelled snow of the first courtyard unquestioned. Ingi had clearly prepared them all for his arrival.

The door of the nearest guest hall burst open. A wave of heat, thick with the scents of cooked meat and mead, blasted out. A man stumbled into the snow, a scowl on his face, accosted by accusations of cheating. Sigimar tried to steer Hypatia away, but she stood frozen to the spot.

"Kosta?"

The man turned, his grey eyes wide. Messy, dark hair framed a gaunt, tanned face with a scraggly beard and a prominent, hooked nose. He was lean in an underfed way and stood a head taller than Hypatia. She broke away from Sigimar's grasp, though he kept a hand on his ceremonial amber and gold axe in case the man turned out to be a malefactor.

"Hypatia?" the man asked, his voice thick.

She raised her hand to his face and choked on a sob. Then, with remarkable speed and power, she slapped him.

CHAPTER 20

Kosta fell to the ground before her, knocked over by the force of her blow. Hypatia leapt on top of him, pounding on him with fists as tears clouded her vision. The wet snow soaked through her skirt where her knees hit the ground. Rage, grief and elation overwhelmed her.

"I—"

"Stop!"

"Thought—"

"Ow!"

"You—"

"Ah!"

"Were—"

"Not there!"

"*Dead!*"

Sigimar hauled her off.

"Is...is that your husband?" Sigimar asked, his voice strained.

Hypatia choked on half-laugh, half-sob.

"My brother," she answered.

Kosta recovered quickly, pulling himself up and brushing off his now-wet clothes as best he could.

"What in the hells are you doing at the ass end of nowhere, Tia?" Kosta asked, rubbing his shoulder with a wince.

Hypatia saw red. Sigimar held her back from lunging at Kosta.

"*Me?!* What am *I* doing here? Where have *you* been?! I thought you were dragged into the void with father by that darkness mage! I went to your gods-damned funeral!"

"*You* try having a giant beast mage with a bloody mace charging at you! I did what any sensible person would and *ran!*"

Sigimar's grip on her loosened, his gloved hands radiating comforting warmth as he rubbed her back in slow circles. As she calmed, she wiped the tears from her eyes. Only then did she see the ire fade from Kosta's stance, swiftly replaced by unabashed guilt and tears of his own.

"I missed you," he confessed, his hands knotting in a tunic too big for his emaciated frame. "A lot." She'd never seen him so frail or unkempt. Opening her arms, he stepped into them and held her in return. He was all sharp angles.

"Where did you go? What happened to you?" she asked.

"I went to the temple."

"That ridiculous mystery cult with an undying flame no one is allowed to see?" Hypatia asked, pushing away to study her brother's face.

At least he had the sense to blush.

"The very same. No one can touch the priests there, no matter their crimes." He shivered, but not from cold. His expression was haunted. "I left when I saw it, or rather, *heard* it. There's a good reason no one is allowed near the eternal flame."

"What are you—"

"No, I'm not talking about it. Suffice to say, I left Lethe after that. I won't bore you with the details." He looked askance. Kosta was always losing in games of bluffing because he could never hide his expressions. No doubt he'd gotten into trouble, and all of it unsavoury. "I ended up being captured by elves and dragged here. Bloody negation cuff. Luckily, they don't condone slavery here, and I was set free." He rubbed his wrist, where a raised, pale scar encircled it. He noticed Sigimar then. Kosta clutched her arm, suspicion and fear in his eyes as he pulled her away. "What are you doing here?"

Hypatia sighed. The one time her brother had decided to be protective, and it was completely uncalled for.

"It's fine. I'm no prisoner. You don't need to whisk me away."

"As if he could," Sigimar muttered.

Kosta's brows furrowed, and he puffed out his meagre, bony chest.

"I'll have you know I'm a talented teleportation mage! The emperor himself often called upon my services," Kosta retorted, his hooked nose raised high.

"He had you teleport courtesans directly into his bedchambers, Kosta," Hypatia said, her brow arched and her voice acidic.

"How did you—"

"*Everyone* knew! Why do you think none of the other domini or dominae ever treated us with any respect?"

"But Father ended the war!"

"Father opened the gates to the invading armies at the eleventh hour to save his own skin. The war was long over."

"Have you no pride? You're a Diamond!"

"There are no Diamonds left, Kosta." Hypatia shook her head.

Kosta fumed, still the proud nobleman he'd always been. The years away hadn't changed him. She didn't know whether to be comforted or worried by that fact.

"So who is he?" Kosta nodded to Sigimar. "And where is your beast mage? The one with the horns and tail?"

Hypatia recoiled as though struck. Kosta's offhanded question ripped the scab off the wound in her heart. Sigimar placed a hand on her shoulder and squeezed with reassurance.

"Kosmas died two years ago," she answered, her voice level.

"Oh. I'm sorry, Tia. When I left the temple, I looked for you. I stayed away; didn't think you would need the kind of trouble I'd bring. Saw you with him then. You looked happy."

"I was."

Hypatia moved to hold the fragment of Kosmas' horn and panicked when she found it wasn't in her dress pocket. When had she last felt it? Seen it? The realization dawned on her then, that she'd left his horn fragment with her scrolls, all safely tucked away in a chest. That it had been there since before her terrifying arrival in Nor. Her relief was swift, but she braced herself for the rush of shame that would surely come. It didn't. Somewhere along the way she'd shed it like an old snakeskin. The grief of losing Kosmas was still there, a wound tender around the edges, but it didn't occupy the whole of her heart anymore. And she was at peace with that.

"This is Jarl Sigimar Ashla. We've come to see King Erlendr," Hypatia added.

"Wait, isn't that the name of the famous warrior everyone is talking about? The Her-"

"Don't finish that sentence!" Sigimar snapped.

Kosta teleported back a few paces in his surprise before blushing sheepishly. He cleared his throat.

"I meant no offence." Kosta eyed Sigimar then, taking note of his nearness and the hand he'd placed on Hypatia's shoulder. "It seems you've found another worthy suitor, Hypatia. Are congratulations in order?"

So talented, her brother. Always able to ask the exact question which would twist her heart.

"No," Sigimar answered succinctly. "And on that note, shall we take our leave?" he asked her.

"Yes, I suppose it would be for the best," she answered. Catching the wistful loneliness in Kosta's eyes, she reassured him. "We've some business to attend to. Will you be here when I return?"

Kosta nodded.

"Yes. I'd...like to catch up with you. If you're not too busy."

Hypatia squeezed his hand and smiled. Maybe when she left Elmheim, she wouldn't be wholly alone.

Their short trek into the castle proper was one walked in silence. This would be the end of the ties that bound her to Sigimar. At least, the legal and magical ones. The threads that bound her heart were too numerous and twisted to cut through.

With every step she took, Hypatia contemplated begging Sigimar not to ask his king to sever their union. Every second step, she reminded herself of the draugr which had nearly eaten her alive, and of the menacing curse which had created it, lying in wait across the narrow channel. And every moment between steps, her mind circled around the fact that the corruption Sigimar had once told her about was not what she'd once assumed.

She'd thought, when they first met, that the corruption he referred to was political, something rampant in Lethe, not the visible curse lingering outside. What if, by some strange twist of fate, her magic was exactly the type that Elmheim sought? Sigimar had once warned her that those with this so-called *healing light* were so valued by Elmheim that they were not permitted to leave.

Love and death.

Life and heartbreak.

She could not have one without the other.

By the time they stood outside King Erlendr's chamber, Hypatia couldn't remember what she'd even seen or passed by on the way there. So lost in her thoughts, hopes and fears, she didn't even hear Sigimar calling her name or notice that her cloak, gloves and hat had already been taken from her.

"Hypatia!"

"Oh! Yes?"

"Are you alright? You look like you might be ill."

"I..." She didn't know how to finish that sentence. How could she describe her inner turmoil to the only man who shared it? How could she debate with him about his own merits versus the dangers she would surely face, dangers she feared would end her life? It wouldn't be fair or kind, and Sigimar deserved both. He deserved someone who could look at the land of Ashla, look at him, and choose both without hesitation. Though she'd told Kosta there were no Diamonds left, that wasn't to say the cowardly and disgraceful parts of their bloodline weren't alive and well. "I'm fine. Just nervous," she lied.

Sigimar frowned. No doubt he knew her deceit when he saw it. Yet he let it pass without comment. He nodded at the elven guards outside the towering wooden door, both of whom stood a head taller than Sigimar, decked in leather and mail and standing in front of wide, painted pillars. They opened the door, and Hypatia tried to swallow down her wildly conflicting emotions.

Inside stood another elf, this one with ruddy skin, hair of white gold and bright blue eyes, a thick circlet of gold sitting upon his brow—Erlendr, by Sigimar's descriptions. Beside him stood a wizard as tall as she but twice as wide, with broad shoulders, chestnut hair and keen hazel eyes, a matching gold band round his head. That would be Erlendr's husband, King Alfric. Ingi was there, too, his white ears twitching. The shifter didn't turn to look at her.

The apartment was disarmingly cosy, like a great, wide cabin with high, wooden beams, two magic fires along opposite walls, each with its own sitting area, a desk and a hideous chair in place of a throne. The floors were covered in furs, the walls in mounted weapons, while benches covered in furs and cushions were placed down the length of the room. Though there wasn't a single window, magic lights hung around the room made it as bright as if lit by the afternoon sun. The only thing which struck her as wrong about it all, aside from the incongruity of a wooden structure inside a mountain, was the distressing lack of reading material in evidence.

"Come in, Jarl. Ingi has just been regaling us with tales of your fraught journey."

"King Erlendr, King Alfric, this is Domina Hypatia Diamond, recently of Lethe, the Empire of Mages."

Hypatia curtsied low and deep with as much elegance as she could in the thick fabrics of Elmheim.

"Greetings, King Erlendr, King Alfric," Hypatia said.

When she looked up, both monarchs raked her with assessing glances, though their final assessments they kept hidden beneath polite smiles. She noticed the wedding contract displayed on the king's desk.

"Greetings, Fru Hypatia. Though unexpected, you are not unwelcome," Erlendr replied.

"Exactly how distant a relative of Otmar are you?" Alfric asked.

Sigimar tensed beside her.

"Very. So much so that he spits on the ancient pact by making her his daughter's substitute. I've come today to petition for a divorce on her behalf. She's not here willingly. She was tricked into signing the marriage contract, and she doesn't possess the healing light," Sigimar said.

"That's rather direct of you." Erlendr grimaced. "But I don't see why I should grant you your request."

Hypatia's heart leapt into her throat. The miasma loomed large in her mind.

"And why not? Anyone else in Elmheim has the right to divorce." Sigimar bristled.

"And do both parties wish it? Truly?" Alfric asked, a knowing look on his face.

A tense silence held the lot of them immobile until Erlendr threw his hands up and clicked his tongue.

"Ingi has already given you away, Jarl. Why in the hells would I grant two people in love a divorce? I don't give a damn if she doesn't have an ounce of magic in her blood, and, despite how she ended up your wife, from the sounds of it she is very much willing."

Though Hypatia stood ramrod straight, she inwardly curled in on herself, panic threatening to overwhelm her as any thought of safety flew out the door. She would spend her every waking moment fearing an attack. Eventually she would be devoured, it would only be a matter of time. She didn't want to die.

"The contract was signed through trickery!" Sigimar argued, stepping forward, shielding her from view.

Erlendr picked up the parchment from his desk and held it out, his brows furrowing with anger.

"*This* contract? *This* can't even be signed by someone not of Otmar's line! That her blood is there at all means she fulfils Otmar's obligations! Don't expect me to go to war with Gortos over a technicality! Otmar's dishonourable behaviour is already riling up the Riverlands. I refuse to add more kindling to that fire."

Sigimar rounded on Erlendr then, gripping him by his fine, powder-blue tunic and glaring hatefully up at the king. Hypatia watched it all, nearly outside herself as the face of the draugr haunted her, its clicks sounding in her ears.

"I'll not make her a prisoner in this land! It's not safe for her here! She has no magic to protect herself!"

Alfric shoved the two much taller men apart with shocking ease. Perhaps that was why, despite the shouting, no guard had bothered entering.

"Then let her prove it. Let her prove she has no attachment to you and none of the healing light. If she can do that, then we'll consider the divorce and discuss what to do about Gortos later," Alfric said, his tone suspiciously reasonable. "A truth-taster was among those brought here by the slavers, and I can easily curse an object with corruption to test her magic." He turned his canny hazel eyes on her then. "Would this be acceptable to you, Hypatia?"

"Yes, King Alfric," Hypatia replied woodenly, shrinking away from him. Anyone who could create the corruption curse must be as dangerous as the draugar themselves.

He strode by her and spoke to the guard at the door. Alfric returned with a small knife in hand. He pushed papers aside on a gleaming elm desk and placed the knife down, his hand hovering over it. He murmured a few words and then stepped aside, beckoning her forward.

"Ingi says you can create light with your magic. Shine it over this blade, if you please."

"How will I know if...?" Hypatia was too afraid to say it. Her heart thundered in her chest as nausea threatened. If she didn't tamp it down, she was going to throw up on royalty.

"All four of us can sense the magic," Erlendr answered.

"I see."

She tried to step closer, she really did, but her feet were frozen to the spot. Frozen because she might have been wrong. her mind raced with the question—what if? What if she possessed the magic they sought? She'd spent these weeks believing she didn't possess the healing light. Had it been a delusion? Had she been so catastrophically wrong, thinking she had a choice in her fate? What if she were made a prisoner of this land? Would they make her face the hordes of draugar? But what if she spent all the rest of her years with Sigimar? Would it be so bad if they lived out the rest of their lives as scholars, lovers, husband and wife? And if she didn't? What if she failed this test? What if she regretted leaving? In leaving, Sigimar would undoubtedly move on.

What if her heart broke beyond repair without him?

"It's alright, Hypatia. The curse is attached to the object. It won't infect you or anyone else here," Sigimar said, his voice and eyes softening at the sight of her hesitancy.

The courage to tell him that such an event was not what she feared deserted her. She took his hand and allowed him to tug her forward. Raising her hand over the blade, she swallowed, her throat dry. She shone a weak light over the blade, not knowing which result she prayed for.

Sigimar went stiff beside her.

She looked around at the men surrounding her, feeling like a wild animal in a hunter's snare. Her anxiety was a living thing, eating her alive.

"Well?" she asked.

"I'll grant you the divorce, Hypatia," Erlendr said.

Bitter relief coursed through her. So her lot would be that of heartbreak rather than a bloody death. At the very least she would be alive to mourn, to regret.

"But as of this moment, you belong to Elmheim. We cannot afford to let a single wielder of the healing light slip through our grasp. Whatever you wish for, I will grant it, but you may not leave."

CHAPTER 21

Every step closer to Erlendr had been like the drum beat of a dirge for Sigimar's heart. He could already feel the fissures forming, the gaping hole of her absence threatening to ruin him. Erlendr's stubbornness had only fuelled his foul mood, until Alfric, cunning bastard that he was, proposed his tests. Except when he'd cursed the blade, he'd also cursed the desk.

Sigimar disliked the subterfuge, but it was a standard test to determine the strength of one's magic. If a person could dispel the curse on the blade, they were strong enough to face the monsters *outside* the miasma. If they could do the same with the other objects infected on the desk, they could enter the miasma without fear, like Dag. Anyone who could dispel the curse on everything including the desk was instantly given a title and lands and encouraged to leave as many descendants as possible.

Sigimar sent out his limited sensing magic, mostly to ensure Hypatia didn't brush too closely to the curse. Though those with the healing light were comparatively thick on the ground in Askr, the thought of corruption latching onto her made him physically ill. But as she shone a dim light over the blade and the cursed desk it stood upon, a tidal wave of emotions caught him in their grip and left him flailing.

Hypatia possessed the healing light.

Too much of it.

And she was entirely unaware.

Joy so overwhelming he nearly wept caught him first. Hypatia would stay. They could be happy together. He would ensure it. Visions of family danced through his mind as he raced to think how to make his keep to her liking.

Then Erlendr had said he would grant the divorce, and his happiness had turned to ash. Even if she were forced to stay, she needn't choose him. With her power, she could have any man she chose, or any number of men if she were of a mind to take multiple. Sigimar was nothing more than a warm body with an axe. A lowly grunt. No precious magic flowed through his veins.

But as he turned to see Hypatia's horror at Erlendr's pronouncement of her captivity, he threw his self-pity aside like the dead weight it was. He would move mountains to spare her from the terror filling her up. He would slay anyone and anything that made her tremble as she did now. He would defy kings, pacts and ancient magic.

Sigimar had always wished to be the man Dag thought him: strong, courageous, just and kind. In the moments that had mattered, he hadn't lived up to that ideal. In fact, he'd failed most of his life to be such a man. Today would be different. *He* had to be different. For Hypatia, he had to become that man.

Shock held Hypatia in its grip, her hands trembling as they covered her mouth. Sigimar pushed Erlendr and Alfric away and stood before her. He waited until she raised her beautiful, storm-grey eyes to his. He knelt down and whispered in her ear.

"Go find your brother. And don't get caught."

Realization dawned, her lips parting in surprise. She pressed them together as her lower lip trembled, eyes misting with tears.

"I won't," she promised, her lips brushing his in a farewell kiss.

Then Hypatia disappeared.

◆◇◆

"Where in the hells is she?" Erlendr shouted, shoving Sigimar aside.

Hypatia crept towards the door.

"She's still here. I can smell her," Ingi offered.

Sigimar rounded on Ingi then, punching the shapeshifter so hard he didn't get up after he hit the floor.

"Bar the door!" Erlendr ordered.

"Don't make me bind you, Sigimar," Alfric threatened. "It doesn't have to be this way."

Sigimar backed slowly towards the door as Erlendr and Alfric closed in on them both. With blinding speed, Sigimar gripped his amber axe and bashed Alfric in the head with the flat of it, cracking the precious stone. Then he turned, ramming the golden handle of it into Erlendr's gut. Without a second backward glance, he charged the door once, twice, and then burst through on the third heave.

"Hypatia, run! I'll keep them off you!" he cried as he fell on the guards at the door, knocking heads against walls until they were incapacitated.

Hypatia ran in earnest then. She cursed herself for not paying better attention to her route on the way inside. But the path was not hard to find. She burst through door after door, shocking guards and any poor soul unlucky enough to bump into her. Sigimar was never far behind, drawing the attention of all as he fought his way through ever-increasing throngs of guards, Erlendr's commands echoing through the interconnected halls.

"No! Don't shoot a gods damned arrow! Do not start firing off spells! A woman with the healing light is running about invisible! Just pin him down and bar the damned doors!"

Hypatia's heart raced as she threw herself at the last set of doors barring her from the outside. She might as well have been an insect bouncing off a window for all the good she did, earning a bruised shoulder for her efforts. Behind her, Sigimar was throwing guards aside like ragdolls. Ah, gods, he was going to get himself killed at this point, and she would be no closer to freedom. She cried in shock when a guard slipped a spear under Sigimar's defences, stabbing him in the side.

"By the doors!" Erlendr called out, sounding out her location in an instant.

She was ready to surrender, fearful that the circle of guards closing in would cut her to ribbons with their spears and axes. When their blades were no more than a single pace from her flesh, a low, sonorous horn wailed outside.

The doors behind her were pulled open from the other side, the guards stepping aside as people pushed past her. She struggled to force her way through the increasingly frantic crowds of people streaming into the castle. The horn blasted again. Armed soldiers called out commands. Hypatia ran through the defensive rings, the doors open to admit towns-folk. She finally reached the outer ring and began searching for Kosta.

"Kosta!" she called. "Kosta!"

He would never be able to hear her in the din. What in the hells was happening?

"Draugar sighted! Shelter with charms!" the soldiers on the wall shouted.

"Kosta!" Hypatia screamed.

"Hypatia!"

Kosta had teleported onto the roof of the mead hall. He scanned the crowd, looking for her. She dropped the magic concealing her and rushed towards him.

"Here Kosta!" she cried.

Hypatia fought against the onslaught of bodies pouring through the front gates. Kosta would never be able to teleport to her in such a volatile, swirling crowd. The risk of appearing inside a person or limb was too high. She fought her way to the hall, Kosta having spotted her and calling encouragements.

Then the shrieking pierced through the clamour. A new surge of fear infected the crowd, sweeping Hypatia away from the quickly closing gates of the first ring of defences—and the mead hall. She might have been dragged back into the mountain castle itself if Sigimar hadn't appeared then and tossed her over his shoulder.

"Kosta is on top of the mead hall!"

"I'll get you there," he growled, shoving people aside.

That was when she noticed the blood stains on his tunic, her hands quickly soaked in red.

"Sigimar, you're hurt!"

"I'll recover," he said as he shoved a guard from his path, jolting her with his swift, brutal movements.

"I'm sorry," her voice hitched.

He bowled through the last of the crowd and pulled her off his shoulder and into his arms.

"Apologise by being happy." His smile was twisted by sadness.

He hefted her up and she grabbed one of the roof slats, scrabbling to get purchase with her feet. Kosta was at the peak of the slightly rounded roof, his hand stretched down towards her.

"You're almost there!" Kosta called to her, his teeth chattering in the cold.

Her freedom was so close she could almost taste it. Hands already numb from the chill weather, she forced herself to hold onto the snowy slats. Her pace was painfully slow, especially with the sounds of dreaded shrieks in the distance and battle just below her, urging her upward. She was nearly to Kosta. He'd manoeuvred to awkwardly hang with half his body over the apex, his hand out, sweat dripping down his face, tongue pressed to a tooth as he tried to edge further towards her.

An arrow whistled through the air. It struck Kosta, pinning his hand to the wooden roof slats. Kosta screeched. Hypatia turned her head to the side, spotting King Erlendr with a bow in hand, his eyes locked on her as he shouted orders. As Kosta continued to wail, the first ring of defences was breached. Creatures overwhelmed the guards on the wall and spilled into the courtyard, a sickly grey wave of hardened flesh and gaping maws. At their back, a bank of dense, dark fog. She hadn't been paying attention when she'd finally made it outside. The miasma now shrouded much of Askr.

Sigimar was below her, fending off creatures now that the guards had turned their attention to their own survival. He was bleeding profusely, made worse every time one of the draugar lunged at him, raking him with their razor-sharp claws. He was armed with only a stolen hand axe, his reach outmatched by the gangly arms of the creatures themselves.

"Hypatia," Kosta wheezed.

The fog had wrapped around them then, sending both her and Kosta into coughing fits. The wound on his hand turned black around the edges, the first inky tendrils appearing moments later. She reached up her hand and shone a light, evaporating the fog around them in an instant, and banishing the infection.

"Oh gods," Kosta whimpered, his free hand gripping the arrow shaft that pinned him. He looked like he was about to be sick. "When I break this, climb as fast as you can. I've only got one good jump left in me."

Sigimar's roar of pain brought her attention back to him. The draugar were toying with him now, taking turns to tear strips off him as they dove past, easily dodging his sluggish axe swings. Erlendr's forces were slowly, methodically, pushing the miasma and the creatures back, but they hadn't even cleared the inner ring. They wouldn't reach Sigimar in time.

The crack of wood accompanied Kosta's muffled scream.

"Hypatia, now!" he pleaded.

She realised then that the price of her freedom would be Sigimar's life. He would be consumed by draugar, all so she could tuck her tail between her legs and run like the coward she'd always been. And he wouldn't be the only one. Even now, guards battled for their lives, screaming as they fell. In the distance, children screamed. She looked back up at her brother's bloody hand. It would be so easy to shuffle up that last small distance between them and grasp his hand, to breed true to her family's shameful legacy. Betrayal was like that—easy. She, like her father before her, could save her own skin by letting someone else bleed and die for her benefit. It would be the safer choice, the wiser one. But she couldn't make herself raise her hand to Kosta's.

Below, Sigimar's cries of pain and foul curses dug into her heart as sure as a draugr's claws. There was only one fear inside her bigger and more insistent than the one that urged her to run. In that moment, a feeling stronger than self-preservation took hold of her, a desperation that tore wisdom to shreds between its teeth. It roared at her not to run, but to protect.

"Kosta, close your eyes," she said, her lips curling up into an openly hysterical smile. Hypatia turned her head and raised her voice as loud as she could. "Sigimar!" The second he looked up, she jumped off the roof and into his arms, her magic coating her in a bright glow. The draugar shrieked as they flaked away in the radiance of her magic. "Close your eyes!"

Light magic, as it was meant to be used, was all about finesse. This time, she would need to marry her finesse to every fibre of raw power she had in her. Hypatia lifted her hands high, stretching her magic further and further, creating little reflective prisms around physical objects all over the city. She pushed until she was certain they covered the entirety of Askr like stars in the night sky. Her head was surely splitting open, yet she pulled on more magic. Something warm and coppery flowed from her nose. She ignored it. Now that her prisms were in place, she just needed to give them something to reflect—her.

"Hold me as high as you can," she told Sigimar through gritted teeth.

He lifted her up, his hands on her hips. She pushed her magic past its limits, burning as brightly as the sun. Hypatia squeezed her eyes shut against the searing glare. She dragged magic from every last inch of her body, pushing it up and out. Ears ringing and arms shaking, she didn't dare stop until she was certain her light reflected off every prism across Askr.

Something was wrong.

Her lungs were gripped in a vise, every breath a sharp pain.

"Stop! Tell her to stop!" Alfric shouted, his voice edged with panic.

He sounded far away. It didn't matter. Hypatia was certain she'd drained every last drop of magic within her and then dug the well deeper, just to squeeze the last bit of moisture from the bedrock.

She opened her eyes to find the dark shroud had vanished, and with it, all the creatures. Hypatia crumpled in Sigimar's arms. He caught her when she swayed, laying her gently on the bloody snow. It felt almost warm against her skin.

"Hypatia! Ah, gods, you're bleeding. What have you done? You could have been free. You could have been safe! Why did you stay?" Sigimar asked, his burning hot hands cradling her face, a wild, desperate look in his amber eyes. There was only one answer she could give him as her vision darkened around the edges.

"Because you let me go."

Chapter 22

Agony was her whole world. Hypatia's skin burned as though it were covered in a thousand salted cuts. Her fingers and toes throbbed as if the nails had been torn off. Every hair on her body was a needle twisting in her flesh, and every breath a lesson in torture. A strangled cry was the only sound she could force from her scorched throat.

"I'm going to take the pain away, Hypatia, but not until you understand why you're in it." Alfric was beside her, his voice that of a stern tutor.

She managed to open her eyes, though it felt like ripping off a scab. The sight that greeted her had her mewling in panic—utter darkness. Where was Sigimar?

Unconcerned, Alfric continued his lesson.

"You recklessly used every last ounce of your magic and then ripped out even more, all for a completely unnecessary light show. One so bright our healers are busy treating the unlucky of Askr for temporary blindness. You wounded your own damn soul! Do you understand? We had to bring in a soul weaver to assess the damage." He sighed. "You'll recover on your own in a few days, provided you don't cast a single spell in that time. Now, will you do that again, or have you learned your lesson?"

Hypatia choked on a wretched sob.

"Well? Answer me, and the pain goes away."

"I won't," she croaked.

"Good."

Alfric laid a hand over her forehead, washing her in a relief so profound she felt like she was floating on top of gentle waves. Sleep might have taken her again, but for the alarming sound of raised voices, crashing, and thudding somewhere nearby.

"Sigimar?" she whispered.

"He and Erlendr are getting things out of their systems," Alfric answered, nonchalant.

"Kosta?"

"The one who can teleport? Making a nuisance of himself. I'll give credit where it's due, he's flinging himself against my wards with reckless abandon in his attempt to take you away. Which, I should add, is rather rude of him considering we had him healed and fed. Twice."

Why hadn't Kosta fled? Where had this brotherly protectiveness come from? She was left to ponder this strange turn of events as the silence between them dragged on.

"When we brought in the soul weaver, she noticed...older scars. She said it looked brutal. Coercive. I understand if you don't want to discuss it, but as you're a citizen of Elmheim now, I would be remiss if I didn't ask. Who hurt you, and are they still alive?"

Hypatia pressed her lips in a firm line. She didn't want to discuss the ritual. Ever. She didn't want to think of her shameful part in it either, of all the lives her blasted curiosity had tainted.

"Does Sigimar know?" Hypatia asked.

"He knows what the soul weaver saw, yes."

She would need to tell him eventually, then. There would be no going to the grave with that foul secret. It scalded her to know that even if she'd burned her notes, it wouldn't have kept her dirty secret hidden. Now she could only hope he wouldn't despise her for it. She prayed Kosta would keep his big mouth shut until she had the chance to explain. But as for Alfric, she owed him nothing. Instead of answering him, she changed the subject.

"I'm trapped here now, aren't I?"

"Well and truly."

Hypatia sighed. She needn't have asked. She'd known her fate the moment she'd chosen Sigimar over her own freedom.

"It's not so bad," Alfric said.

"No, what could be bad about a frozen land surrounded by monsters?" she scoffed.

Alfric chuckled.

"I can tell you what isn't bad." Alfric hooked a finger around her necklace of amber and gold charms. "Being the wife of a man eager to spend a fortune to keep you safe. From what I've heard, you know very little of our lands and people, so let me tell you plainly. These charms around your neck? If Erlendr had been kidnapped by pirates or slavers and I offered them this? Not only would they send him back to me with all due haste and apologies for his shabby accommodations, but they would be inclined to invite us for a feast and make themselves our bosom allies. And Sigimar's humble enough not to boast of it, if your shock is anything to go by."

Damn him, being able to see her expression while she remained prone and blind.

"You're lying," she accused him.

Sigimar would never spend so much on a woman he'd intended to say farewell to. And Ingi, little traitor that he was, wouldn't have authorised dispensing so lavishly with the caravan's funds. She almost asked about the shapeshifter but held her tongue. Anger simmered over his tattling. The intimacies she and Sigimar had shared were not his to speak of.

"Not about this. And what do you have to fear from monsters that dissolve in the radiance of your light?"

"They're faster!" she protested weakly, her limbs immobile.

"Sigimar is faster still. And speed can be taught."

"I'm not a warrior."

"No one is asking you to be."

A fine thing to say, when Alfric walked through life with a warrior's confidence. What did he know of being weak, slow and inherently vulnerable?

"But we'll be living in Ashla itself!"

"That is a fair point, though there is some news on that front which may sway you. We can wait on that until Sigimar and Erlendr are done being...elvish."

"What do you mean? And when will I be able to see again?"

"Your sight should return soon. Notice that your limbs feel like lead weights? When you can start moving your fingers and toes, your sight will start returning. As for our husbands...well, has no one told you yet how most elves live?"

"No?"

"Like violent barbarians," Alfric pronounced. "Tavern brawling is a cherished tradition, and its almost a rite of passage to regrow a maimed or missing limb."

"Sigimar is nothing of the sort! He's kind and gentle to a fault!"

Alfric laughed then.

"With you perhaps, but to a fellow elf?" he asked. "Or my head when it suits him?" Alfric grumbled. "It's easier to let your fists do the talking when the possibility of being permanently injured is removed from the equation."

A particularly loud crash had her flinching. Her fingers twitched. She experimented with curling her fingers and toes. She blinked a few times. Light and dark outlines became apparent.

"I wish to see him."

"Not yet. Rest for now."

"I'm not at all tired," she argued. How dare he treat her like a child!

"Because the pain woke you, pain my magic is subduing. Sleep. I'll make sure our husbands don't get carried away and mar their pretty faces."

The sensation of gently rolling waves returned, rocking her in their cool embrace. Her eyelids felt heavy and her cares drifted from her mind.

"Is this magic?" she asked.

"Yes. Witch and wizard magic is accompanied by a tactile sensation. I'm told mine is rather soothing."

She tried to think of a pithy remark about where he could shove his patronizing magic, but the calm waves dragged her under.

"Come on, pup, are you getting tired? Need someone to tuck you in and sing you a song?" Erlendr taunted, spitting out his most recently loosened tooth with a gob of bloody spittle.

Sigimar was far from done. He didn't know if this consuming anger and guilt would ever end. It ate at his heart, pouring acid into his veins. He was the lowest of the low. Viler than the worst criminal on Oblivion. If he'd been stronger, faster, a better protector, Hypatia wouldn't have tossed her life away to save his. The shame of his failing was not to be borne. If Erlendr and his broken-nosed sneer had volunteered to be his punching bag, Sigimar was determined not to question it too closely. He needed the outlet, and anyway, Erlendr was being an ass.

"You have no damn right to keep her prisoner!"

Erlendr caught Sigimar's fists, a feral grin on his bruised, bloody face. Those bruises and cuts healed before his eyes.

"How thick is that skull of yours, eh? I'm the gods-damned king. Everyone who steps into my realm belongs to me!"

"Not! Her!" Sigimar roared, using that thick skull of his to bash Erlendr's face. The satisfying sound of crunching cartilage met his ears.

Erlendr reared back, loosening his hold. Sigimar tackled him to the floor, the wood slippery with blood. The impact of their bodies shook the room. The king only laughed, barely winded.

"Especially her!" Erlendr said.

Erlendr flipped them with a manoeuvre too fast for Sigimar to catch, the king's meaty arm across his throat, pinning him.

"Fuck you!" Sigimar growled as he tried to dislodge Erlendr's arm.

"You wish," Erlendr scoffed. "Her fate was sealed the second she stepped into Elmheim and fulfilled the contract. It's done, Sigimar."

"She doesn't want this!"

Erlendr rolled his eyes.

"Few do. She'll get over it like everyone else."

"Only if the frontier doesn't kill her first!" Sigimar shoved Erlendr off and scrambled to his feet. Erlendr was already waiting, a smirk on his face.

"Do you plan on sending her out as bait?"

Sigimar charged, landing a solid blow to Erlendr's gut as the king landed one squarely on his jaw, knocking a few of his own teeth loose. He spat them out. New teeth were already rising up to take their places.

"We both know even the wary end up dead out here," Sigimar hissed.

"Is your fear about her or about Dag?" he asked, cutting Sigimar to the quick.

"I'll kill you!" Sigimar screamed, launching himself at Erlendr, who ducked, dodged and wove around all his blows, enraging him further. It was no use. He'd become sloppy in his fury. Erlendr tripped and pinned him in seconds, Sigimar's face mashed to the bloody floor.

"Your brother is dead because he was as wild as you. Who in the hells marches out deep into Ashla poorly provisioned and in a party of two? I'll tell you who—suicidal fools! Dag was reckless. He always was. And the only reason you didn't see it was because you worshipped the ground he walked on. If either of you had a lick of sense between you, you'd have petitioned me for an exploratory mission. Instead, you both ran off without telling anyone where you'd gone!"

Hearing Dag slandered only fuelled his rage. He bucked under Erlendr's hold but to no avail.

"Hypatia, at least, seems smart enough to run when she should and fight only if she has to."

"She can't defend herself!"

"Have you lost your mind? She might as well have summoned the bloody sun! Half of Askr is already convinced her ancestor is a demi-goddess."

And just like that, his anger left him. He stopped struggling, overcome by a horrible hollowness.

"She should never have had to do that."

He would never be able to erase the sight of her after she'd collapsed. Blood had streamed from her nose and ears, her skin nearly grey, as if she'd bled out her own life. Every part of her had been as cold as the snow. And she'd done it for him-for his worthless self. She'd injured her own soul. And this hadn't even been the only time.

He hoped that the ones who had hurt her in the past were still alive, just so he could squeeze the life out of them. No one who hurt her in that way deserved to live.

"But she did. And now we're here." Erlendr pushed off him and leaned against the upturned bench. Or half of it. It had splintered during their fight.

Sigimar rolled over and stared at the ceiling. One of the beams had been cracked when Erlendr had swung him bodily into the air. Sigimar set his own nose straight and wiped away the gush of blood that followed.

"I'll leave for Ashla," he sighed.

There was nothing to be done. Hypatia was under the protection of the kings, sleeping behind unbreakable wards. She might as well have been a continent away.

"With your wife," Erlendr added.

Sigimar turned his head to scowl at the king.

"You granted the divorce. She can have anyone she wants now."

"Gods below, are you truly that dim?" Erlendr asked with equal parts bafflement and derision.

Sigimar looked away, his heart aching. She'd chosen to help him in the heat of the moment, a decision which had doomed her. Now, when passions had cooled, she would regret her choice and mourn the life of safety and comfort she could have had. He didn't think he could bear the weight of being her jailor. For surely that would be what he would become to her—a dreaded chain.

"She deserves better. Someone who can protect her and give her everything she wants and needs. Someone who won't fail her."

Sigimar already hated whoever that would be.

"Fine. Then I'm un-granting the divorce."

"Don't be petty," Sigimar grunted.

"There's nothing petty about trying to save you from self-inflicted folly. And before you start arguing with me, swear you'll ask the woman her opinion before you decide to play the miserable divorcé locked in his keep. Gods know there are enough of those in Elmheim already."

That meant he would have to face her, see her regret and watch her realise he'd been the worst of her options. It would crush him, but he deserved it after he'd failed to set her free.

"Fine."

"Good. Now get the hells out of here, and take a bath. And pick up some teeth on your way out. Alfric hates it when—"

The doors to the bedchamber creaked open. Sigimar sat up and chuckled.

"Too late," Sigimar taunted.

It was the only time he'd seen a look of trepidation on Erlendr's face.

"There are *teeth!* On my *floor!* Damn you Erlendr, you know I hate it when you do that! I'm going to make you mop up this mess with your damned hair." Alfric stepped around the bloody boot prints as best he could and surveyed the damage, grumbling the whole while. Sigimar watched as Alfric approached the chair made of enormous bones, one of the few pieces of furniture to survive the melee, and only because Erlendr had defended it with life and limb. The wizard pressed a finger to it, fracturing it into a hundred pieces with a spell. "Oh, what a pity."

Erlendr gasped.

"Alfric! That was an antique! My grandmother hunted the mammoths herself!"

Alfric raised his chestnut brow.

"And now you can finally commission a chair that isn't hideous." He ignored Erlendr's groans and turned his hazel eyes on Sigimar. "She needs her rest. Go clean up. You look like you've bathed in blood." His eyes scanned the room again, though this time they were unfocused. A second later, his hand shot out to grip a man by the throat. Kosta. "And as for you," Alfric began, pressing a palm over Kosta's forehead, "I'm sick of having you bounce off my wards all day long." He shoved Kosta away with a glowing rune on his head. Kosta gasped, his hands flying to his forehead, a look of panic in his eyes.

"W-what have you done?"

"Sealed your magic. Temporarily. Go back to the mead hall. You can come back—*through the front door*—when you've had something more to eat."

Alfric nodded at the front door. Shocked and confused, Kosta left, his hand still pressed to his forehead. The wizard's eyes burned a trail of displeasure back to Sigimar.

"Well? What are you waiting for?"

"I want to see her."

Alfric sighed.

"Come back when you're not dripping blood and spitting teeth all over my floors."

Sigimar got to his feet and trudged to the door, pausing to look back at the bedchamber doors behind which Hypatia slept. He wanted to see her face one last time before resentment tinged the storm-grey in her eyes. He wanted to caress her cheek and tuck a curl behind her ear before she was inclined to swat his hand away. He wanted to see her smile and hold her close and tell her about the feelings trying to claw their way free from his chest. Convinced that now such things were beyond his reach, Sigimar turned and left.

Chapter 23

The maids that had tended to Hypatia that morning were almost reverential in their care of her. Even as the daughter of a magister, she'd never been treated with such delicate pampering. They bathed her in scented waters heated to the perfect temperature, clucked over every chipped nail and split end, dressed her in fabrics that slid against her skin like velvet and fed her strange delicacies. As much as she appreciated their help when her legs trembled with even minor exertions, the attention was unnerving. It was not friendliness in their gaze, but something akin to worship. No wonder Sigimar detested coming to Askr. It only made her anxious as to what they were preparing her for. Worse, every time she asked, they only tittered and fussed over her more.

That was how she found herself propped up in a giant bed with a thick blanket tucked up to her waist, watching as those same maids cleared up the room, her anxiety gnawing away at her. She almost begged them not to go when they bade farewell and left her alone to wonder at her fate. She didn't wait long.

The door opened slowly. Sigimar stepped inside, his face a closed mask. It seemed he'd received the same treatment, if his impeccably groomed person was any indication. His tunic was finer than any she'd seen him in, embroidered with gold thread at the hem and neckline. His belt sported multiple gems, and his hair had been brushed to a shine with artful braids snaking through it. Even his boots were a work of art, the leather embossed with intricate designs. She waited for him to rush towards her, as she wished to rush towards him. But he didn't move a single muscle once the door shut behind him. Insecurity replaced her anxiety.

"Sigimar?"

"I'm going back to Ashla."

I. Singular. Not we. Gods below, had she been catastrophically wrong about his intentions with her? Had she been fooled once more? Had bringing her like a tribute to his kings been his intent all along? Her heart splintered in her chest. Tears welled up, and her hands began to tremble. Sigimar noticed.

"I'm sorry. I never should have brought you here. But Erlendr has already granted the divorce, and the potency of your magic means you'll have your pick of suitors. I believe you'll also be granted the title of jarl, so if you choose to remain unwed, you may do so with confidence."

Her eyes stung. It was hard to breathe through the hurt.

"You...Is that all you have to say to me?" she asked, reeling from his pronouncement.

He looked away, his mouth set in a hard line, his hands balled into fists at his sides.

"I'm sorry. You deserved better. I made promises I couldn't keep."

He wouldn't even deign to look at her as he set her aside. After all they'd shared, he was going to pat her on the head and send her on her way, job done, with a mere half-hearted apology for tearing out her heart and tramping on it. Hot and angry, a beast roared within her. Hypatia ripped off the blanket and raged over to him, willing her knees not to buckle. She grabbed a thick burgundy braid and yanked him down so they were nose to nose.

"Was I a joke to you, Sigimar? The ignorant, naïve foreigner?" she hissed, full of venom.

He blinked in surprise. Did he think she wouldn't confront him? Did he think her passions were always so amorous? That she was capable of love but not wrath?

"I—no, I never thought—"

"Did you have a good laugh at my expense? Hmm? Did it amuse you to watch me fall in love while playing at the same? Answer me!" she shouted, no longer able to deny the sting in her eyes was anything but gathering tears.

"You love me?"

"Yes, damn you! What other reason could I have for throwing myself off a roof into a pit of vicious monsters?! What do you think you're do—"

Sigimar pulled her close and pressed his lips to hers. She pounded her fists on his chest in protest. Damn the man and his clever tongue. Her body betrayed her. A shiver of pleasure rolled down her spine. Worse, he knew it, taking full advantage to deepen the kiss. Today was the day of betrayals, then, because her body melted against his, her nails sinking into his scalp, desperate to have him closer. Fury still heated her blood, but now its focus shifted from Sigimar to the clothes that separated them. It was only when he broke off their kiss to bury his face in her neck and tease the sensitive spot just behind her ear that some modicum of sense returned to her.

"I love you too, Hypatia," he purred in her ear.

"Then why on Oblivion are you leaving me?" she sobbed.

Sigimar stiffened, seating her on the bed with care. He knelt before her, his big hands wiping her tears as horror filled his amber eyes.

"I don't want to leave you! *Ever.* I thought...I thought you would hate me. Instead of giving you freedom, I chained you to Elmheim...to me. I never wanted to become your jailor. I wanted us to be together, I won't deny it, but not like this. You deserve to have everything you ever wanted."

He turned his gaze, shamed.

Oh, gods, he thought she despised him. After everything, how could he think that?

"You could never be a chain, Sigimar."

"You don't regret your choice?"

Hypatia sighed, getting a hold over her own wildly vacillating emotions. He clung so stubbornly to this terrible image of himself.

"Am I thrilled my neighbours are a toxic shroud and hungry monsters? No. It terrifies me." He began looking away again, so she turned his face back to hers. "But a life lived without you is intolerable. I would make the same choice again. So don't leave me. Please."

"I never thought you would allow me to keep you..."

She pulled him close, her arms circling his head as he pressed it to her belly.

"I didn't think it was possible for someone to make me feel so deeply, not again. I'm only sorry that I have so few years to give you in comparison to your long life," she said, running her fingers through his hair, contemplating the day when hers would be brittle and grey in comparison. Her life would be like a single season over the course of centuries. He deserved more time than she could ever give him.

His eyes met hers, determined.

"I can fix that."

"What is there to fix?"

"I can give you a longer life. I don't know the magic, but Erlendr will. I want you by my side for as long as I live. I have so many things to show you, and there is much to discover in Ashla. It would take a lifetime just to scratch the surface." His ears reddened then. "And...if...if we have children...you will need those years to watch them grow."

It was almost too much to take in, her mind stuttering to a halt at the thought of living centuries. And children! She hadn't even considered it. Mages were only fertile two to four months in a year, and timing such things could be difficult. Though she supposed with so many years before them, eventually the stars would align. In the meantime, they could spend their days learning and discovering.

And then she realised what she had just contemplated.

A life.

A long one.

With all the things she'd once hoped for, and all with a man she loved, whose very presence felt like the home her heart had wanted. Her bottom lip trembled as her eyes grew misty. When was the last time she'd been so full of hope?

"I promise I will make you happy," he murmured, tightening his hold on her.

"I'm already happy, Sigimar."

And for the first time in a long time, it was true.

Erlendr had asked Sigimar and Hypatia to attend him and Alfric for talk of business. If that weren't enough to set Sigimar's teeth on edge, Erlendr and Alfric, seated across from Sigimar on a couch covered in fabrics and furs, shared a look he couldn't quite interpret. Sigimar had Hypatia seated on his lap, his arm cradling her back as she leaned against him. She was still recovering from her overuse of magic a few days before and hadn't the strength to stand. He wanted nothing more than to hold her close until she nodded off in his arms, but they'd decided to get this business out of the way rather than wait.

"There is news from Ashla. Drest sends his regards," Erlendr began.

It felt like a lifetime ago that Sigimar had spoken to the dragon shapeshifter in charge of his lands in Ashla. He would have to thank him for assembling the caravan, among other things. Had he ever thanked the dragon for all he'd done? Shame scalded him when he realised he'd probably said only a handful of kind things to the man in the decade Drest had kept his castle and lands running smoothly. In the decade he'd spent taking care of Sigimar when he couldn't do it himself. Gods, that would have to change.

"I'm not sure how to tell you this Sigimar, but it seems your keep was destroyed," Erlendr said.

"Gods below." Sigimar tensed.

They'd always feared the castle might one day be overtaken by the miasma, the land reclaimed by the foul fog long enough to choke the life from everything that had sprouted in its absence. Had the magical amplifier failed in the end?

"On the bright side, it seems you have a new castle, and no one was seriously injured," Alfric added.

Sigimar's bewilderment must have shown because there was a wry grin on Erlendr's face.

"The humans that were in residence here begged to be allowed to cross into Ashla. I allowed it, given how well the defences have held up over the past few years. It seems in their inquisitiveness, and with the help of an earth nymph, they woke something up that had long been buried. When it rose from the ground, it demolished a sizable portion of the castle," Erlendr recounted.

It seemed the humans were the bane of the gods and now his bane as well. What in the hells had they been thinking? Sigimar knew they were a strange, inquisitive lot, but apparently they possessed little sense. And now they were traipsing all over his lands. Gods help them all.

"Jarl Sigimar, Jarl Hypatia, you are now the owners of one of Ashla's ancient towers. If Drest's descriptions are to be believed, it is quite impressive. The spire has enough living space to accommodate three times the number who lived in your castle previously. And some magical contraption lifts people and goods up and down the whole length of it. As such, I will be sending another team of household staff and warriors as well as plenty of food to last the lot of you through the winter. Consider it my gift to you, Jarl Hypatia."

"Thank you," she replied, her face a polite mask. He would have to wait until later to discover her true thoughts.

"Speaking of Ashla, if we don't leave soon, we'll be here until Spring," Sigimar added.

Soon the dark, icy, narrow sea would become unsafe for sailing. If he had been going alone, he wouldn't have been overly concerned. But now that Hypatia was here, he wouldn't dare risk it. She was risking enough simply living in Elmheim. He would protect her more fiercely than a dragon with their hoard.

"As to that..." Erlendr and Alfric shared another odd look. Whatever conversation they were having with their eyes, it was tense. "The ancient tower contained a portal, and I've long considered getting one for Askr in case of the worst. I have managed to acquire one, and an experienced guide, at great cost. We've already tested it. Drest and the humans were able to safely cross from Ashla to here and back."

Dread clawed at Sigimar. Portals were not easy to come by. Whatever convenience they offered was overshadowed by the strategic risks. So long as few knew of it, the only travellers would be those approved by Erlendr. It would, in theory, allow those in Ashla and Askr to evacuate in case of a dire emergency. But if word spread? How easy it would be to march troops through an open door. Or worse, accidentally spread the miasma and the creatures to unsuspecting places all over Oblivion and beyond. A catastrophe like that could violate the ancient pact, if not in letter, then in spirit. No one truly knew what would occur if that ever came to pass.

By Alfric's cross-armed scowl, he felt the same way.

"We should bury it," Sigimar said.

"No," Erlendr replied, uncompromising.

"It's on my lands. It could threaten the whole of Oblivion!" Sigimar argued. It could threaten Hypatia. Unacceptable.

"Thank you," Alfric muttered.

"Could someone please explain?" Hypatia asked.

"Anyone who has the magic or skill to open the portal could show up in our tower, or wherever Erlendr has placed his portal here in Askr. Anyone. It's a threat so long as it's functional." Erlendr opened his mouth to protest, but Sigimar glared him into silence and continued. "Even if it's only used with the best of intentions, or only in the direst need to retreat, that still risks letting the miasma and the creatures through it, potentially infecting some distant land and peoples without warning."

"Then we should bury it." Hypatia nodded.

They were of a mind on this. Good.

"Exactly!" Alfric added.

As if he hadn't heard any of them, Erlendr spoke.

"Come Spring, I'm sending select groups into Ashla to look for more wellsprings. I cannot be seen sending shiploads of people into the miasma, or I'll have thousands more, people just like you and your brother, running into it, dying or getting infected, and returning as a wave of starved creatures. With the portals now in place, I can send those groups in relative secrecy and keep them provisioned without potentially fatal delays. If we rid Ashla of the miasma, even if it takes a century, it would mean no one else on Oblivion must face this threat. The ancient pact would finally be fulfilled. Your children would know a world free of the corruption curse."

Not just them, Hypatia would be safe. No one would ever have to die like Dag had. But many more would suffer his fate if Erlendr openly sent people to Ashla. Too many would surreptitiously follow, driven partly by Sigimar's own supposed success. He was ashamed to admit it, but had someone else cleared the miasma, and he and Dag had got wind of the king sending more into Ashla for that purpose, they would have been the first to rush into the gloom.

"Please spare us the political platitudes," Alfric groaned, putting his head in his hands. "We could just as easily send ships and say they're full of extra staff for Jarl Hypatia."

"Hypatia's display of power has given Elmheim greater hope, and with it, a new surge in people eager to end the curse. If we do not begin in secret and soon, it'll be too late to stop the ambitious warriors of Elmheim from charging into Ashla on their own. We both know I could make any decree I like about who may or may not venture into the miasma, and we'll still have every hot-headed fool in the kingdom thinking it's better to ask for forgiveness than permission," Erlendr countered before turning to Sigimar. "You haven't lived in Askr for the past decade, Jarl Sigimar, but there are many here eager to reproduce your achievements. Either we take the initiative and do it strategically, or we'll be fuelling the miasma with the foolhardy. Inaction could cost us more in the long term."

"Those portals will cost us more, whether this venture is successful or not, mark my words," King Alfric retorted.

Hypatia looked up to Sigimar, concern swirling in her grey eyes. Sigimar sighed. He could see why the kings were in disagreement. Truthfully, he could see the sense in both sides of the argument. But the portal was on his lands. Whatever came and went through it would be his responsibility. Ultimately though, he suspected Erlendr would not be moved, even if everyone else disagreed. Sigimar groaned.

"You will send me enough warriors to watch the portal every moment of every day. If I receive an unexpected visitor, or even a hint of the miasma gets near it, I'll destroy it. Every arrival will be preceded by a request. Use the crystal to contact Drest directly. Those are my terms. Also, her brother is coming with us."

At Hypatia's raised brow, Sigimar explained.

"If I have to destroy the portal, I'm making sure you have a way out first."

"He can teleport us both, in that case," Hypatia replied, her furrowed brow and pursed lips inviting no argument.

"I can agree to those terms," Erlendr replied, only a hint of a smile teasing the corners of his lips.

Alfric sighed, defeated. "Until you've recovered, Jarl Hypatia, we hope you will remain in Askr," Alfric added.

"Ah, yes, and can we assume the two of you have decided to remain wed?" Erlendr asked.

"You can," Sigimar said.

Both kings seemed relieved to hear it.

"Then we would like to celebrate the union publicly," Alfric said.

Hypatia blushed and raised her brows in question. She looked to be caught between imploring and holding herself back. She wanted the wedding. It struck him then that she would refuse a proper wedding because she knew how much he hated being celebrated. But now his life was no longer about him alone, and that *was* worth celebrating.

"I'll agree, but only if my wife does," Sigimar replied, the tips of his ears heating to say the word. Wife. They were truly married now.

"I...I would be amenable," Hypatia said, doing her best to hide a smile. She laced her fingers through his and gave a squeeze.

She might as well have squeezed his heart. He could think of no better woman to hold his heart in her hands.

CHAPTER 24

"Hypatia?"

Snuggled close to Sigimar and propped up in a bed too large by half, she looked up at her husband. Her heart warmed at the thought. *Husband*. Such a strange and wonderful thing to have found love again, to have found *home* again. She smiled up at him, enjoying the play of flickering firelight over his solemn, handsome face.

"Yes?"

It had been a long and exhausting day, discussing plans for the wedding celebration and then catching up with her brother, Kosta. Though he'd finally cleaned up, his emaciated frame had only become more apparent. At least Kosta planned on sticking around for a time. Hypatia vowed to fatten him up as best she could. But by the look of Sigimar, it was not wedding preparations or his new brother-in-law that concerned him.

He was unsettled, his jaw flexing, eyes full of concern. Whatever it was, he was tensing, waiting for backlash. When he spoke, his speech was gentle but halting.

"If...if you never want to tell me, I won't pry. But if you do want to talk about what happened to your soul, I will listen without judgement. You don't need to carry that alone. Not anymore. Not if you don't want to."

Her heart kicked in her chest and then dropped to her toes. Gods, she would never be free of that taint.

"Oh."

She searched his amber eyes, unsure how to proceed. It wasn't every day a lady divulged her darkest secret to her husband. He said he would listen without judgement, but how could he? Everything had been her fault. So much pain and suffering. So much death and chaos. No good man would want to stand by her side knowing what she'd done. But she couldn't run from it forever, or at least, she shouldn't. How could she truly love him if she couldn't trust him with all the good *and* all the bad? Hypatia took a deep breath.

"It was my fault. Or, at least, I had a hand in it, though at the time I didn't know what I was really doing. No, I had some inclination, but as is usually the case when my curiosity is piqued, I didn't care enough about consequences to question it. I..." She stopped, seeing Sigimar's confusion. Hypatia blew out a breath. He tucked an errant strand of hair behind her ear and simply...waited.

She needed to start at the beginning.

"My father and mother were very highly ranked nobles in Lethe, below only the imperial family, as I've told you. Though we held lofty titles, in truth, we had significantly less power than other similarly titled nobles. Instead of having control of our province, we were more like land managers for the imperial family. After all, our province was where the imperial palace is located. As a consequence, my father always had a bit of an inferiority complex with the other nobles. My mother...often dealt with her troubles by playing games of chance, wagering and losing large sums of money. When a contender to the throne showed up with promises of great wealth and power in exchange for help, my father agreed."

"He needed the money to pay your mother's debts?" Sigimar asked.

Amongst other things. Her father had been as profligate as her mother. Horses, carriages, jewels, the latest fashions—he was determined to have it all, to compete with the other magistri in every way he could. The more they treated him as a jumped-up nobody, the grander everything around her family became. The other magistri were the last descendants of the old kings, allowed to live because they alone of their bloodlines had bent the knee to the emperor. Her father had barely been a noble, and had snuck the future emperor and his army inside the gates of the palace in return for his title. Of course they looked down on him. His second act of treason promised him the power to turn his sneering fellow noblemen into supplicants. For her father, there could be no greater reward.

"Yes, but he wasn't a very good judge of character. That contender...I doubt he would have kept us alive once we'd served his purposes."

In truth, Hypatia was lucky her father had failed in his second act of treason.

"What happened?" Sigimar asked.

"At the time, I didn't pay attention to politics, or much of anything outside my studies. All I wanted was to be a scholar. I didn't care for parties, plays, chariot races, fashion or marriage. I had a few good friends, but most of my peers had no interest in ancient studies. I regularly begged my father to allow me to remain unwed, but for a noblewoman of my rank, it would have been absurd. Then one day, he said yes. He told me if I could complete a recently discovered ancient inscription, given to him by a respectable but secretive scholar, he would grant my wish. I...I was obsessed. For months, it was all I thought about. I was giddy with the thought of finally being a real scholar."

Sigimar was silent, though his thumb stroked her upper arm.

"And then?" he asked.

And then she'd single-handedly blighted the face of Lethe, sealing the fates of everyone she'd ever known—everyone she'd ever loved. Hypatia had brought death, chaos and suffering to countless families.

"I figured it out. At least, I did in a sense. I completed the inscription. It was an old spell to combine the magic of many to benefit a chosen individual."

"Co-operative magic?"

She nodded.

"Yes, I suppose that is a good word for it. I'd never seen the like. Mages can only manipulate one element, but in theory it would allow the chosen individual unspeakable levels of power over that element. The only hitch was that everyone who helped combine their magic had to possess the same kind of mage gift, like light... or fire. It was a thrilling discovery. I told my father immediately. He asked me to draw out the symbols exactly. I should have known then that something was wrong. My father had never been interested in the esoteric."

Her gut twisted. She couldn't bear to face Sigimar just then. Not when she was too busy trying to swallow down the bile as the memories of that terrible night assailed her.

"I did as he asked and drew the symbols on a piece of parchment. Later, a stranger in a mask came—the contender. He told my father to use it. A few weeks later, Father drew the symbols on the floor, within a circle large enough for several people to stand inside. Then, he encouraged my sisters and me to step into the circle and activated the magic ritual."

She released a shaky breath. Sigimar remained silent by her side. Courage failed her. She didn't want to know what she might see in his eyes.

At first, it had been wonderful. The symbols had glowed, lighting up the room, filled with her father's magic. She'd gasped with delight, tracing the symbols with her eyes, nearly weeping at the magnitude of her success. All her hopes and dreams were about to come true. It had been the happiest moment of her life. All was well until Father's light had traced the outline of the last of the symbols.

Until she'd been sundered.

"It was...painful. And when it was done, I felt nothing. I *was* nothing. My father had taken all of my magic and my soul. I spoke only when I was prompted to, thought about only what I was told to, acted only when I was instructed. I'm not even certain I would have eaten if I hadn't been seated at a dining table, presented with food, and commanded to eat. My memories of that year are imprecise and vague, but I know that two other noblemen used the ritual on their daughters, stealing their magic for themselves and leaving at least two in comas. One of the women harmed was my best friend." Hypatia choked on the guilt. She'd done that to Roxane. She would never be able to make that right, no matter how long she lived.

"The contender for the throne, he used the ritual I helped complete to kill people while taking their magic, including his own father, the emperor. He was killed eventually, as were the other noblemen involved, my father and eldest brother included. Their names and likenesses were removed from all public record, their remaining families made wards of the emperor and empress. I helped destroy three of the most prominent families in Lethe, including my own. I helped that contender kill the emperor. No one now living knows my full part in it all. Not even Kosta. I... I'm sorry to burden you with this knowledge."

He touched a finger to her chin and turned her face to meet his. She focused her eyes on the burgundy beard covering his chin, not daring to look further up. What if he were disgusted? What if he thought her weak? Or worse, a monster? Her actions had caused so much suffering, so many deaths. Roxane's coma and the damage to her body had been Hypatia's fault. Intellectually, she understood *she* hadn't taken lives, or made Roxane bedridden herself, but there was no denying her complicity.

"Has no one ever told you it wasn't your fault?" he asked.

Roxane had, but she was compassion personified. Hypatia knew her guilt.

"It *was* my fault. I cared more about the pursuit of knowledge than how it might be used. I cared about my own ambitions more than the consequences. What I did hurt people. Even now, I carry the notes I made about the ritual with me to remind me of that."

"No, you cared about making your dreams come true. Your father and that contender used that against you. You don't need to atone for this. You were betrayed," Sigimar retorted.

"I know I was betrayed," she replied, her voice a whisper. She looked away, tears stinging her eyes. It was no excuse. Not really.

"Look at me, Hypatia," Sigimar's softly rumbling voice drawing her back. His features were pinched with concern. "You don't blame someone for getting stabbed if they're not wearing armour, do you?"

"It's not the same."

"It is. A sharp edge can be used to cut a man down, or it can be used to carve a boat that rescues a drowning victim. You're not responsible for the bad things other people do with knowledge. Your ritual could have helped put out a forest fire, calmed a violent storm, or brought fertility to barren land, as co-operative magic has been used since ancient times. The blame is on the people who used it to harm instead of help."

Tears fell in earnest then. She, too, had hoped her father would see the ritual's potential for good. She wanted so badly to accept Sigimar's words into her heart of hearts. He kissed her forehead.

"You're brave, Hypatia. You kept pursuing your dreams, and you're still doing it. You haven't let anyone or anything take what you love from you."

Hypatia choked, caught between a sob and a laugh.

"I don't think that kind of single-mindedness is necessarily an admirable trait. It has gotten me into a fair bit of trouble."

"Tenacity is a good trait. You can't change my mind."

She sighed and wrapped her arms around him, resting her head against his chest, willing the tears away. He stroked her hair. Now that he knew, she felt some of the weight of it ease off the part of her that had been crushed by it. She'd shown him vulnerability, and he had opened his heart, becoming a safe place for her to be fragile and ugly and weak. If possible, she loved him more.

"It must run in the family. Farohildis was nothing if not wholly dedicated to her misdeeds."

Sigimar's chuckle was partly a groan.

"Gods, don't remind me. Did I tell you about everything her father did to try to get my caravan to turn around?"

"No, I don't think you did."

"Brace yourself for a tale of true misery."

"I was there for part of it, you know." She pinched him.

"Trust me, that's when things turned around for the better, but until that point..."

Hypatia drifted off to what could only be embellished tales of Sigimar's slog through the territory of Gortos.

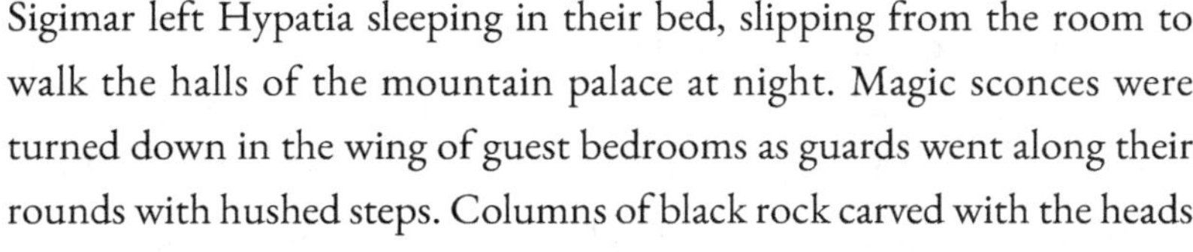

Sigimar left Hypatia sleeping in their bed, slipping from the room to walk the halls of the mountain palace at night. Magic sconces were turned down in the wing of guest bedrooms as guards went along their rounds with hushed steps. Columns of black rock carved with the heads of dragons bore the load of a whole mountain. Precisely how the magic and engineering synthesised was not something he knew much about. Likely for good reason.

He should have remained at Hypatia's side, but he was too angry and restless to remain abed. His wife had been betrayed in the ugliest of ways, by her father, a man who was supposed to love, cherish and protect her. And instead of placing the blame where it belonged, she'd taken the burden of guilt upon herself. For years she'd suffered under the lie that the tragedies in her past were of her own making. Nothing could've been further from the truth. He would spend the rest of his days convincing her of it.

Increasing his pace, he wished he could vent his frustrations. Shout, rend, pulverise and destroy. But the perpetrators of her pain were long since dead. He was left with no one to wreak vengeance upon. He was left to battle ghosts.

As he passed the king's receiving chambers, he paused. Guards still stood watch outside the grand doors. If they eyed him with less warmth than they had before he'd bashed their heads in, he was wise enough not to complain.

If he were to spend all his days with Hypatia, he would need to know of the magic to do it. Erlendr would know.

"Are either of the kings still awake at this hour?"

The guards nodded.

"May I see them?"

One guard knocked on the door.

"Your Majesty, Jarl Sigimar comes to see you."

"Let him enter," Erlendr called back from behind the door, inaudible to any without the keen senses of those present.

Sigimar strode inside to find Erlendr seated on the floor, leaning against one of the benches as he stretched his feet towards one of the magic fires. On the bench by his head was a jug of alcohol. Strong, by the smell of it.

"What brings your morose countenance to my hall at this hour?" His smile didn't reach his eyes.

Sigimar shrugged, found a spot beside the king and sat down, staring into the fire.

"What takes you from your husband's side at this hour?"

"What makes you think I would leave it willingly?" Erlendr scowled, swallowing a great gulp from his drinking cup. "He hates the portals. As much as you do, I suspect."

"He has good reason to. As do I."

"I'm well aware," he scoffed.

Best avoid that topic then.

"Speaking of spouses, I want to know how it is you're extending Alfric's life. I want to share my remaining years with Hypatia."

The silence that met his query was as harrowing as the look of utter devastation on Erlendr's face. Gods below, was there no way for him to do so? Would he really be forced to watch her die in a matter of decades?

"I...I am not extending his lifespan. I can't."

"But there must be some magic that can—"

Erlendr held up his hand, grimacing.

"There is." Erlendr sighed. "Wait here."

When the king returned, face solemn, it was with a length of cloth as red as fresh blood and neatly folded.

"Wrap it around your wrists. Half of your remaining years will be given to her, so long as she consents."

Erlendr held it out for him, but Sigimar hesitated.

"Why can't you use this yourself? Does Alfric object or—"

Erlendr shook his head, looking every last year of his more than two millennia log life.

"You think only Elmheim's jarls and the nobles of the Riverlands suffer from the effects of the ancient pact? If the ancient pact tethers the lot of you, then it chains the very soul of Elmheim's king. The day I accepted this crown, I was bound to Elmheim. No matter how much I wish otherwise, the ancient pact prevents me from shortening my own lifespan. Only my death, or a unanimous vote by every jarl in Elmheim for my removal can set me free." He held the fabric out again. This time, Sigimar took it.

"It feels wrong to profit from your misery."

Erlendr's chuckle was dark as he resumed sitting in his former seat.

"Oblivion profited from yours, Sigimar. Take the damn cloth."

Sigimar clutched it close. But he couldn't leave the king, not now. Erlendr looked after his people like a friend and a father. He never gave up hope that he could make their lives better, even if he had to help them fight their inner demons. He was a man Sigimar had long looked upon as someone worth emulating. They sat in silence a little while longer, sharing the potent liquor.

"When you and Dag dispelled the miasma, I thought I would finally be free of the ancient pact. That I wouldn't have to outlive another spouse. But now we know it was only the first step. The gods can be cruel, Sigimar. Elf or elvish, our lives feel too long, and the ones we love are always gone in the blink of an eye. I know no one likes my plan, the portals, any of it. Alfric and I fought just like this when I put up those rewards to dispel the miasma a few decades ago. He was convinced we would be plagued by more damn draugar as a result, and he was right...but so was I. I pray to the gods, forgotten and otherwise, that I am right once more. Because if I'm not..."

"More draugar, and the curse never ends," Sigimar answered.

And Erlendr would watch yet another person he loved with all his heart grow old, die, and leave him bereft once more. Sigimar thanked the gods he was not a king. Though he still didn't like Erlendr's plan, he understood now what drove him. In his place, with Hypatia's short lifespan on the line, he knew he would have done the same thing.

"I, too, pray you are right."

For his own sake, for Hypatia's, and for whatever future they had together.

Chapter 25

"Jarl Hypatia, you have a guest."

Sigimar groaned and pulled the blanket over his head, effectively trapping his wife with him as he tightened his hold on her. She lay spooned in front of him, naked, her long dark hair unbound and perfuming the sheets. His wife. The words sent a thrill of pleasure through him. The light of early morning streamed through windows made of rock, an illusion as fanciful as the scenery of snowy hills dotted by evergreens beyond it. They'd talked late into the night, and that was before he'd gone to Erlendr. He was in no mood to be deprived of her company at this hour. Damn Askr and Erlendr's bloody court, always busy and bustling.

"I'll be out in a moment!" Hypatia called back.

"Not if I can help it," Sigimar purred in her ear, gently biting the juncture of her neck and shoulder. He revelled in the shiver it sent down her spine.

"We'll have plenty of time for that later," she replied, the sternness of her words lost in the breathy tone of her voice.

"Later won't be soon enough." He trailed a possessive hand down her stomach.

Her breath caught when he stopped just above her dark curls.

"Sigimar…"

"I want to hear you call me husband."

"Then behave."

"Didn't anyone ever tell you that elves are uncivilised brutes?"

"I have heard such nonsense, and I refuse to believe it."

He slid his fingers lower, teasing her with touches too light to bring her release. She tried to grind herself against his hand, but he refused to give her what she sought. As she wriggled and begged, he took satisfaction in how slick she became, in how her struggles brought a flush to her cheeks, in how it made him want her all the more.

"One word," he rumbled in her ear, bringing her close.

"Ah!"

His fingers retreated. Feather-light caresses had her writhing in his embrace, torturing him in turn as her plump backside ground against his cock.

"Husband!"

He gave her what she wanted, swallowing her crescendo of cries with a kiss. As she lay panting beside him, her eyes darkened with desire, he smiled. This was perfection. He wanted a hundred mornings just like this. A thousand. A million. But he knew himself better by now. Sigimar would always want more of her, no matter how many mornings he had with her.

"See? I may be a brute, but I'm very easy to please."

She laughed, slightly winded, her cheeks flushed.

"I can't believe you did that with a guest in the next room. What if they heard?"

"There's no question. They heard. You're not a quiet woman."

"Oh! If you're not careful, I'll—"

"What?" He grinned.

She pulled off the blanket, gifting him the dazzling view of her lush, naked curves bathed in the light of day. She made to straddle him. His grin deepened.

"If this is punishment, I'm happy to take it. In fact, you should punish me every day. Multiple times. Else I'll become rowdy and unmanageable."

"Really?" she asked, all sweetness.

Her hand went to his cock, already erect. He nodded vigorously as she tortured him in turn. She explored his length, studying his every expression with an intensity that had his heart galloping. But his wife was a quick learner, and she soon discovered just how bring him to the brink. He hissed out a breath.

"And now?" She smiled.

He blinked. And blinked again. Then swore. She'd turned his cock invisible. If not for the throbbing ache, he might have believed it gone.

Hypatia fell over in a fit of laughter.

"Ah! The look on your face!"

"Hypatia!" he pleaded.

"Will you behave?"

"I will," he grumbled.

"Then call me your wife."

His heart stuttered in his chest. He cradled her face in his hands. So precious, this woman. He would capture the moon for her if she asked.

"Hypatia, my wife," he said solemnly.

She kissed him and pulled away, her prank undone.

"And don't you forget it, husband."

"Are you certain you should have done that? What about your soul?" Sigimar asked.

"I received permission for small uses of magic just the other day," she replied.

She hopped out of bed before he could snatch her back up into his arms. He would have to content himself with watching the swaying of her full hips and the sight of her hair cascading down her bare back. He grunted his disapproval when she padded across the rugs and pulled on a loose, informal gown.

"I'll be back..." She eyed him appreciatively and winked.

Something warm bubbled up in his chest. He felt light. The smile on his face was making his cheeks ache. He sat up, stunned. Sigimar was...happy. He'd almost forgotten what it felt like.

As Sigimar contemplated that fact, the sound of Hypatia's voice carried. It didn't take much straining of his sensitive ears to make out the conversation, and, when he did, simmering anger replaced his bliss. He was about to storm into the other room but stopped. The fierceness of Hypatia's tone assured him she had this well in hand.

"Why on Oblivion would you think, after what you did, that I would take you on as part of my household?" Hypatia asked.

"I only wanted—" Ingi began.

"What? To have the freshest gossip for the kings? What I did with Sigimar was no one's business but our own!"

"Except it wasn't! You come from far away, a place free of the corruption curse. You have no idea what it means to everyone in Elmheim, in the whole of the Riverlands, for Sigimar to have done what he did."

Gods below, would he never be free of what he'd done? Why was it that no one remembered he'd lost his brother that day? That he could never be proud of it? The grief and anger threatened to overwhelm him, his clenched fists shaking at his sides. And for Ingi to use that as an excuse to trap Hypatia? Unacceptable.

"No one here or anywhere in the Riverlands dared to dream that we could ever be free of the miasma, of the soul-crushing fear of being swallowed up by a divine curse!" Ingi continued. "When he was made jarl, the whole of Elmheim fought tooth and nail to win the prize of serving him for the rest of his days. In the end, the kings hand-picked every single one of his people. I begged to be allowed to serve him on the way to Gortos, as did everyone else who joined him. Sigimar gave a hopeless people a reason to hope again."

That stopped the wave of tumultuous emotions from swallowing him whole. He'd never known that about the people who served him in

Ashla, or about those who had been part of his caravan. What else had he been ignorant of all this time? What hadn't he bothered to find out?

"That still doesn't explain or excuse betraying our trust. If anything, it makes your actions all the more reprehensible," Hypatia retorted.

"Don't you understand? He was miserable, trapped by his own darkness. He deserved to be treated with dignity, respect and care after what he'd done and who he'd lost. And instead, the whole of Gortos treated him with contempt! But the second he laid eyes on you, every single person in the caravan could see a part of that darkness lift. And with every passing day, more of that darkness retreated. No one wanted to see you go, or see what would become of him if you left. The two of you were so determined, and the kings owe him so much, I was afraid they would grant you permission to leave. I did what I thought was right. I know my methods were self-serving, and I apologise for that. I know what I'm asking is selfish in the extreme, but I beg of you to allow me to atone for the wrong I did you. Please, allow me to serve you as your huskarl."

Gods, they'd all known he'd been a shell of a man. And still they'd begged to go with him. He'd been exactly as Ingi had once described him—a humourless bear. He'd been so ungrateful to them, so consumed by his own pain that he'd been incapable of seeing that they had cared. Had he even once thanked them for keeping him company, for keeping good cheer despite his foul moods? For ensuring there was warm mead and as good a meal as could be had? For guaranteeing he had the best of everything, even when they'd been reduced to miserable conditions?

Shame replaced his anger. They all deserved better than how he'd treated them. But instead of the familiar weight of guilt crushing him, he felt the first spark of determination. He wanted to do better by them, to prove they hadn't wasted their time and efforts on him. At the very least, he could thank them now.

He heard Hypatia's frustrated sigh.

"I can forgive you for speaking of my relationship with Sigimar. I can even appreciate that you acted out of love for him. But it is not up to you to decide what is best for me, or for Sigimar. If you wish to serve me, you will need to regain my trust and his. I don't have an answer for your request today, but I promise to discuss it with my husband."

"Thank you, Jarl."

He listened as Hypatia approached the door to the bedroom. There was so much to make up for, so many people to do right by. Instead of wanting to retreat into himself at the thought, he wanted to prove he could be a better man. When Hypatia opened the door to the bedroom and looked up at him, concern in her grey eyes, he leaned down to kiss her forehead.

"You heard everything?" she asked.

"Yes."

"Are you alright?"

He nodded. If he could be the man she'd needed, he could be the man the rest of his people needed, too. Maybe now, he had the strength to do more than just pretend to be that man.

"I didn't...see before... just how many people I had to support me," he confessed.

A small smile had her lips quirking.

"I must admit, while I am grateful to them for it, I envy you that. You are lucky to be loved by so many, even if they don't love you in the way I think they should."

"And what way is that?"

"As a man, and not as their symbol. A symbol is placed on a pedestal, revered and untouchable. But a man needs to know he deserves warmth in spite of his flaws. You should be seen as the man that you are—loved for being the man that you are." Her small smile bloomed then, into a full grin. "But I suppose that is what your wife is for."

He returned her smile then. He had much to be grateful for. Maybe in time they would come to know him as who he was rather than what he represented. But to do that, he would need to be jarl in more than just name. The challenge was daunting, but with Hypatia at his side, he knew he wouldn't be doing it alone.

"You make me feel lucky," he said.

Her grin turned sultry.

"Then prove it."

So he did.

Chapter 26

Never had Hypatia been so ready to fling herself into the toxic miasma of Ashla's frontier. Had she known what the kings of Elmheim had in store for her, she might have volunteered to swim the dark, icy channel with weights around her ankles. She had expected a proper ceremony, maybe a feast and dancing to celebrate her union with Sigimar, perhaps even a pretty, if not exactly practical, new dress.

She got everything she thought she might.

Except the inhabitants of Elmheim took celebration very, very seriously.

Which meant they celebrated as if the world were about to end, and any time spent not joining in mad revelry was not to be countenanced. Days of dancing, games, contests, and feasts ensued, music and laughter filling the city at all hours of the day and night. Erlendr and Alfric gave lavish gifts to every guest in their honour, an expense Hypatia could only dream of tallying. There hadn't been a single sober adult in all of Askr for a whole week. Now, the lot of them were nursing hangovers, among other things. She expected a great number of children would be born out of that unhinged bacchanalia.

Every part of her ached, and only a few were in the delicious way she preferred.

"I shall never accept another drink offered by the kings ever again," she groaned, rubbing her temples.

"I had no idea the aphrodisiac would affect you so strongly." Sigimar chuckled beside her. "I should have explained, but it's such a common drink at wedding celebrations, it didn't occur to me that you wouldn't know."

She turned her head to face him in their bed. They were both dressed for the day, but given her near-inability to walk, she'd decided to lie down until it was time to leave for Ashla. Being a jarl, she was afforded the luxury of indulging in self-pity. Sigimar, on the other hand, seemed to be in perfectly fine spirits and not one bit worn out by the last few days. His smile was all mischief, damn him.

"I'm never coming back here. How can I show my face in polite company?" She covered her face with her hands at the very thought. Sigimar took her hands in his and pulled them away, a gentle smile on his face.

"We don't frown on passion, Hypatia."

Passion was not the word for what she'd done. *Animalistic* came close. *Frenzied* was more accurate.

"I *launched* myself at you! I tore your tunic in two! I nearly tore my skirts in two! And that was all *before* you managed to pull us from the banquet hall!" Hypatia covered her flaming cheeks. She would never live down the embarrassment. For that matter, Kosta may never look at her again. It was a miracle he'd agreed to join her in Ashla after her scandalous display.

Sigimar sighed contentedly and laced his fingers behind his head.

"I will never forget it," he sighed blissfully.

"You're not helping!" She swatted at him. He chuckled, the rogue. Turning to face him, she pursed her lips in displeasure.

"And what came afterwards. Multiple times. I was certain you'd kill me. I could barely move my hips by the end." He waggled his thick burgundy brows as he turned on his side, propping his head up and grinning like a fool.

"Parts of me may never forget. I'm so sore I can barely sit!" She pouted.

"I could have taken you to a healer." He pointed out, his face instantly fierce. "I still can."

"No, you could not. And you will not," she huffed. She'd refused it then, and she would refuse it now. No one else needed to know her shame, or, at least, no more of it than they already did.

"You will see one in Ashla." His tone brooked no argument.

"Fine. But they must be sworn to secrecy," Hypatia warned.

"Is this a bad time to show you our wedding presents from the kings?"

Hypatia sighed. There was a veritable mountain of them. What on Oblivion was she supposed to do with it all?

"Go on then, you cruel man."

He sat up, gazing gently down at her as she lay on their bed. She may never grow accustomed to his looming size. Just the thought of his wide shoulders brought back memories of sinking her nails into them, their sweat-slicked bodies grinding against each other, the pull of his intense attentions. Her cheeks heated again.

Sigimar smiled and kissed her forehead. She wished he could kiss her elsewhere, but that would not be wise. There was no controlling herself where he was involved. He began rustling about, a deep rumble of barely suppressed laughter coming from him in the next moment.

"What?"

"You won't appreciate this now, but you might in future."

"Show me," she grumbled. What prank had the kings played now?

He placed a jar in her hands. She opened it up and smelled. It had no fragrance she could detect. Hypatia dipped a finger in and rolled the slippery liquid around on her fingertips.

"What...?" she asked, then looked up at Sigimar's badly stifled grin. He took the jar from her and sealed it as realization dawned. "I will kill them," she announced.

"You'd have to remain in Askr for that," he teased.

"It sounds like someone wants to sleep on the floor tonight," she growled.

"I don't think that would be good for your aching muscles," he replied, all sweetness and charm.

"Sigimar!"

"Hypatia?" he asked amiably.

"I won't forgive your merciless teasing."

"Really?"

"Really."

"Truly?" he asked, leaning over her, a smile on his handsome face, his amber eyes sparkling with mirth.

Devastating. He was utterly devastating like this. Though she was too sore to take him now, she ached for him. Her lips felt chafed, yet her eyes drifted to his smirk. Maybe it would be worth the humiliation of seeing a healer. He leaned down.

"Be gentle," she whispered.

His brows furrowed.

"Promise me that this time you'll say something if you're hurting instead of demanding more."

It hadn't hurt at the time. It was only after her lust had cooled that she'd felt the twinges of pain. And it had been her own shamed stubbornness that had stopped Sigimar from getting a healer, as he'd insisted. She nodded. Given all she'd demanded of him, it was a wonder she could walk straight.

His lips met hers, feather light and as gentle as a breeze. Her sweet and gentle giant, as tender-hearted as he was passionate. And now he was hers in every way, and she his. As they lay there, learning how softly they could touch one another, a knock on their door interrupted them.

"Jarls, the guide is waiting for you."

"Are you ready for your next adventure?" Sigimar asked.

Was she? Ashla and the monsters within the miasma still frightened her, but the prospect of having her own ancient, enchanted castle to explore was a tailor-made temptation too perfect to ignore. She steeled her nerves, nodding.

Sigimar swept her up in his arms. She rested her head against his chest, listening to his heartbeat. This was where she belonged. The home her heart had longed for. What strange fate to find it so far from the land of her birth.

They descended staircase after staircase, until the air was bitingly cold. The steps were narrow—treacherous. How had so many already gone below, laden with wedding gifts and supplies? Perhaps she would ask Ingi about it, now that he was her huskarl.

The portal was disarmingly plain-looking from afar, a simple post and lintel construction made of large grey stone. It was the lone thing of interest, standing in an empty, sunken chamber deep within the mountain palace. As they neared it, a cloaked figure pressed a gloved hand to the stone. Sapphire ripples winked and rolled in the once-hollow space between stones, moving like water. Armed soldiers stood guard around the room, and archers had their arrows nocked, half-hidden in an upper gallery. Despite the tension and the thrum of her own anxiety, she reached out a cautious hand to the startling blue of the portal.

Perhaps foolishly, she'd expected it to feel like water. Yet it was like air. Thicker, ticklish almost, as if gossamer threads hung within. She shivered. How strange.

"You'll be in my arms the whole time," Sigimar whispered.

With that he stepped through. She shut her eyes, waiting until the strange sensation passed. When it had and she opened them, magic greeted her.

Blinding daylight lit a cavernous room painted in cream, gold and silver. Crates, luggage and other supplies littered a pearlescent floor. High, arched, glass windows veined with silver floral patterns promised views once the purview of birds alone. On the ceiling, white clouds rolled across a pale blue sky, and yet as she stared, she noticed the shape of the clouds began to repeat itself. Was the ceiling itself magical?

So taken with the strange beauty of the place, Hypatia almost missed the man standing before them, hands clasped before him. He was of average height, clothed in a dark tunic and leggings, his lengthy black hair tied back from his long, tan face. Golden horns curled up from his brow, glinting along with his mischievous green eyes. The look he gave her was pure, masculine lust.

Hypatia disliked him instantly.

"You brought my pretty witch after all. You shouldn't have," the stranger purred.

"I didn't," Sigimar growled, tightening his grip on her.

Confusion quirked the man's brow.

"I suppose I will forgive your pettiness. Where is your wife, Jarl? I'm sure the princess is tired from her long journey," he asked, looking around Sigimar.

Had the stranger not heard that the fae princess had sent a substitute?

"In my arms," Sigimar answered. "Jarl Hypatia, this is Drest, my huskarl. Though if he doesn't stop looking at you like a tasty treat, he won't be managing Ashla much longer...Or breathing."

Drest swept into a deep bow.

"Forgive my rudeness, Jarl Hypatia. I was mistaken. Welcome to your new home."

"It is a magnificent home. I just hope the people within it know when not to make unwelcome advances." She raised her brow.

If he had a habit of doing this to the women here, she would ensure he was dismissed. No one liked a handsy man with power.

"Ah, yes, I suppose I deserve that. Rest assured, I quite enjoy breathing. Would you like to settle in, or would you two prefer a tour of the tower? Much remains unexplored, but what has been cleared and sorted is magnificent."

Ah, maybe she didn't despise Drest after all. A whole magic tower to explore! She caught sight of Sigimar's indulgent smile.

"A tour," Sigimar announced.

Drest pulled a scroll from the pocket of his robe with a flourish, unrolling it to a picture of an elegant tower. He pointed to the middle.

"This is where we are now. There's a staircase that runs the whole height of the tower, but there are also three separate magical apparatuses that go up and down to every floor. For everyone's safety, no one has been allowed into the topmost portion of the tower. Several of the floors were trapped when we began exploring, including this one, and I'd rather not lose another limb if it's all the same to you."

She was so caught up with wonder that she nearly missed his last, cheeky pronouncement.

"You...lost a limb?" Hypatia asked.

She looked him over, and yet all his limbs appeared intact. He was remarkably sanguine for a man who had recently been maimed. Had someone crafted him a prosthetic?

"Yes, messy business that. Not to worry though, I shifted it back into being, cleaned up after myself and disposed of the appendage." Drest smiled.

Sigimar must have noticed her shock.

"Drest is a dragon shapeshifter. If he moves between forms quickly enough, he can reverse any potentially life-threatening injuries," Sigimar explained.

"I see," Hypatia squeaked out.

Gods below! How could they be so nonchalant? Drest was smiling and nodding as if a lethal maiming were no more noteworthy than a sprained ankle. She was saved from dwelling on her shock by the arrival of Ingi. The hare-shifter bowed deeply, taking note of her position in Sigimar's arms.

"Jarl Hypatia, thank you for allowing me the great honour of serving you. Your rooms are ready, and Brynja is here should you require her."

"Perhaps later, after the tour," Hypatia replied, fighting a losing battle against a blush. Ingi must know the state of her, if his polite mask was any indication. Gods, she was certain the healer would tease her. Brynja always had a merry look to her and loved a bawdy joke. Hopefully she could be bribed into silence.

"Then perhaps I could accompany you? I would appreciate a chance to better familiarise myself with the structure," Ingi added.

Hypatia nodded her assent and the four of them were on their way. Aside from the portal room, this level of the tower had little more than storerooms, though even those were filled with fantastical apparatuses glittering with gold and faceted jewels. Their tour included several more floors stocked full of treasures. The effort to resist the child-like impulse to reach out and touch each strange and wonderful artefact was wearing on her. Many an unkind thought darted through her mind as yet another refrain of '*Not until it's safe*' passed Ingi's lips, his ears twitching as often as the corners of his lips.

"I believe this will be of great interest, Jarl Hypatia, and most of the contents should be safe for your personal perusal. Though I would recommend having either Jarl Sigimar or Ingi open them first, should any curses still linger."

"Your concern for me is touching, Drest," Sigimar grumbled.

A strangled noise escaped her lips.

It was a library.

Bigger than she'd ever seen, it put the imperial palace's to shame. Walls that seemed to reach the very sky were lined with books or played host to carefully placed scrolls, tablets and rolls of animal skin. How had they all survived the passage of time? How had the tower? Questions for another day. Staircases ringed the walls, leading up to level after level of shelves. Tall windows were the only feature to break up this temple to knowledge. It was more than she could read in a lifetime. Hypatia breathed in that wondrous, earthy fragrance, a part of her scholarly soul coming home for the first time in years.

"These are..." Sigimar couldn't finish his sentence.

"Ancient texts, perfectly preserved. It seems the magic keeping the outer tower in pristine condition did the same for the inner chambers. Your personal library fit very neatly into one of the corners, but the rest came with the tower. Only a handful of people are allowed inside right now. King Erlendr doesn't want potentially harmful knowledge getting out. All that assumes anyone can read the texts," Drest answered.

"Are they untranslated?" Hypatia asked.

"Some of the humans are working on it, but as of yet, very little is intelligible," Drest replied.

"Please tell me our bedroom is on the same floor as this." Hypatia laughed, tears in her eyes.

A whole library of ancient texts, hers to discover. A whole new language to learn. She could hardly contain her excitement. If Sigimar didn't put her down and soon, she might combust from curiosity.

"I will make it so. Give me a day to clear out one of the storerooms on this level, and I'll have your rooms moved." Ingi bowed.

The second Sigimar set her on her feet, she rushed for the nearest shelf, running her hands reverentially along the spines. She could happily spend days, weeks, years here, never leaving. In fact, it was some time before Hypatia could be persuaded to walk away. Even though she winced or wobbled with every other step, she was determined to open every book, unfurl all the scrolls and do her best not to gasp more than strictly necessary. Only when her stomach began audibly grumbling did anyone suggest making their way down to the lower levels.

Once there, a woman approached them. Heavily pregnant, with freckled, ruddy skin and blonde curls fighting for freedom from a tie at the nape of her neck, she kissed Drest on the cheek, a look of carnal familiarity burning in her eyes.

"Hello my delicious beast. How has work been?" she purred.

Drest's wide eyes and faint blush made it obvious he was not used to such public displays. Sigimar burst out laughing, much to Drest's obvious chagrin. Hypatia's consternation only grew. Was this woman aware Drest had been making eyes at her earlier?

"Jarls Hypatia and Sigimar, please meet Sara, my partner and the mother of by soon-to-be-born child. She is human, so please be gentle."

A human? The bane of the gods? Was Drest mad? What if his behaviour upset her?

"How, Drest? I thought your condition made that impossible. And where on Oblivion have you been hiding her?" Sigimar asked.

Condition? Was Drest unable to father children normally? Just what strange powers did these humans have that allowed for such a miracle? She supposed she would have to ask Sigimar about it all later. If such beings had caused the downfall of the forgotten gods, it might be best not to spend too much time in their company.

"The usual way, turns out we're surprisingly fertile as a species, and Askr. Erlendr agreed to send me and the others once I told him who the father was." Sara shrugged.

"A pleasure," Hypatia replied with a polite nod, hoping it would remain true. She was not keen to see the powers humans wielded that so confounded the gods.

"I thought he was supposed to bring back the witch who wanted to be part of our triad?" Sara frowned as she looked Sigimar and Hypatia up and down.

"No such luck, darling. It seems Astrid's arrival has been delayed." Drest shook his head.

"What's a triad?" Hypatia asked.

"Like a couple, but made of three people," Sara explained, nonchalant.

Hypatia's eyes widened as her cheeks heated.

Drest clasped his hands, took a breath and smiled in a way that most certainly telegraphed his discomfort. "Moving on! If you would like to dine in your quarters, I'll have the meal sent there. Ingi can direct you from here," Drest replied, turning on his heel and ushering the human away. "Darling, not everyone is comfortable discussing intimate matters openly," the dragon whispered as he fussed over Sara, pulling her cloak closer about her shoulders.

"Says the man who fucked me on every level surface for a week straight." The woman rolled her eyes.

Drest's strangled note of distress was the last they heard from the would-be triad before he hurried her out of sight.

"Yes, I'm certain you have other matters to attend to," Ingi called after him, grinning.

Sigimar shook from barely restrained laughter. Hypatia did her best not to stare overlong. Did all humans speak in such a strange, uninhibited manner?

Ingi led them to their private chambers, a series of several rooms breathtaking in size, well-furnished and decorated in the same stark hues with intricate gold and silver ornamentation. The ceilings, doorways and windows seemed fit for giants. How on Oblivion did one go about keeping such things clean? She pitied whoever had been assigned such a task.

"Jarl Hypatia, how good to see you again." Brynja surprised her out of her thoughts with a sincere smile and a gentle hug. "I can't thank you enough for allowing me to serve as healer here in Ashla." The witch held her hands, a knowing smile on her face accompanying the warmth of the magic easing Hypatia's aches and pains. Gods bless the woman. Perhaps she'd been too sensitive about going to a healer. She felt much refreshed now.

"I'm just pleased you agreed," Hypatia replied.

They had travelled together for some time. It was good to see another familiar face in this strange, wondrous new place.

"Come, sit, enjoy yourselves. I only wanted to see that you were well. Seek me out whenever you need me, or send Ingi to find me." Brynja winked as she left.

"Do you require anything else, Jarls?" Ingi asked.

"No, thank you," Sigimar replied.

Ingi closed their doors, affording them their privacy.

"Sigimar?"

"Hm?"

"What did you mean by Drest's 'condition'?"

If he were Sigimar's closest friend in these parts, it would be best to know so she could avoid delicate topics.

"As a child, he had wing rot. Incurable, except by devouring the heart of another dragon. He... got what he needed and was banished to Elmheim for it, but even so, I'd heard such a thing made him unable to father children."

Best she not bring it up then. Though he seemed jovial enough, eating the heart of another to survive must have been a terrible, desperate thing for a child to do. She resolved to be kinder to Drest in future.

Sigimar stood at the window, hand on the glass as he surveyed Ashla.

Hypatia plucked a warm bun from the table and looked about their rooms in awe. She came to the window where a scene of blinding white snow greeted her. Below lay the ruins of the old castle, remains of the high walls poking through the snow. But within those same half-standing walls, the snow had been cleared, revealing the dark, muddy earth beneath. In the centre of the clearing stood an unassuming platform of pale blue rock. Five spires topped with sparkling crystals ringed the circular platform, and in the centre, a contraption of gold winked up at her, its details obscured by the distance.

"The amplifier," Sigimar answered before she asked the question. "We built the original keep around it when it surfaced after..." he trailed off. After Dag had died and Sigimar had destroyed the artefact that had captivated his brother during the draugr attack. Hypatia reached out and squeezed his hand. Sigimar's smile was tight. "Drest knows more about how it works. You can ask him about it later. Now that you're here, who knows? Maybe we can push the boundaries of the healing light further."

"You think so?"

"You are the most powerful wielder of the healing light in recorded history, Hypatia. The territory kept safe from the taint of the miasma has been accomplished using the magic of those with barely a fraction of your talent."

She may be far from home in a land she never could have dreamed up in her wildest flights of fancy, but it was here she could finally make her mark. Hypatia would be more than the daughter of a traitor twice over. More than just a mousy woman trying and failing to be a respectable scholar. Here, in Ashla, she could be everything she ever dreamed of. A true scholar. A respected member of her community. A beloved wife. She touched her belly. No—it was too soon for that, wasn't it? They had years yet to add to their family. For now, ensuring that future was free of the miasma was the more pressing issue. In only a few months, Erlendr's plan would be set in motion.

"Do you think there are more towers like this out there?"

"Yes."

He seemed so certain. She hoped he was right.

"Would they have libraries too?"

Sigimar grinned.

"I guess we'll have to find out."

Hypatia couldn't wait to step onto that platform.

CHAPTER 27

Not even the wonders of the ancient tower could distract Sigimar from his anxieties. The moment he'd returned, dread nipped at his heels, stalked him from dark corners and whispered poison in his ears. What if he wasn't enough—enough of a leader for the people who depended on him, or a good enough husband to his wife, or strong enough to protect her? What if no one wanted him to lead, or even considered him more than a miserable, titled bastard throwing his weight around? It was a miracle he'd slept at all, and what little he'd had ended too soon. He'd spent much of the night tormented by his demons, or holding the red cloth Erlendr had bestowed, wondering how best to present it to Hypatia. He must have slept eventually, because panicked whispers woke Sigimar from his troubled dozing.

Remnants of half-forgotten horrors were washed away in the dim pre-dawn light. The frantic murmurs became an incoherent panic. He managed to pull the covers up over Hypatia before Drest and Ingi barrelled into the room.

"Jarls, it's gone!" Eyes wide, complexion ashen, Drest was barely dressed, his long hair tangled and unbound.

"What?" Hypatia bolted upright, brows pinched and sleep-dazed.

"Not gone, stolen," Ingi corrected. Only his twitching hare's ears gave away his distress.

"What's gone?" Sigimar asked, dread creeping up his spine. How many wondrous things had they seen yesterday? The tower held endless storerooms full of treasures. That someone had gotten a little greedy was disappointing but not surprising. Except not just any trinket would have his huskarl so shaken.

"The amplifier." Drest's voice wavered. "We'll have to evacuate. Thank the gods we have the portal. We have a week before the last of the magic wears off."

Hypatia froze beside him. Her hands trembled as they clutched the blankets of their bed. Sigimar put an arm around her, drawing her close. He would keep her safe, no matter where on Oblivion the damned miasma drove them. Perhaps it would be better this way. Elmheim would be a safer home for her than Ashla, safer for everyone. Still, in the wrong hands, and with the wrong spell, that amplifier could do great harm.

"How was it stolen?" Sigimar asked.

"What does that matter?! It's gone! The miasma will reclaim Ashla!" Drest moaned.

Ingi clicked his tongue.

"Guards at both the amplifier and the portal were knocked unconscious by either spell or physical force. I've already contacted King Erlendr with the news that Ashla's portal has been compromised."

Damn portal. He'd known it was going to be more trouble than it was worth. Now it had cost them their stronghold in Ashla. So much for Erlendr's grand plan. It seemed the gods had ignored their pleas. But first things first.

"Transfer the portal to somewhere more defensible. We can't risk an army marching through in the middle of the tower."

Hypatia needed to be sent somewhere safe as soon as possible. Where to send her? Ashla was compromised, as was Erlendr's castle. Did he know any nobles furthest from the miasma who might be willing to take them in for the winter? Suddenly he regretted his decade of reclusiveness.

"King Alfric is marshalling warriors as we speak. Please get dressed, and we'll have you both escorted to the crystal so that you may speak with the kings yourselves." Ingi bowed, shot a dark look at Drest and left with the distraught dragon in tow.

"Sigimar, we'll have to leave, won't we?" Hypatia asked, crestfallen.

"Yes. But all is not lost. I imagine much of what was found inside the tower will come with us back to Elmheim. Maybe, if we're lucky, another amplifier will be hidden among the other relics."

She opened her mouth to speak but shut it, rushing through her morning routine as he pulled on suitable clothes and ran a brush through his hair. Sigimar placed the red cloth in his tunic. Whatever came next would be frantic, no doubt, and he could not afford to misplace such a valuable item. Today might be a sad one, but tomorrow would be better. When the shock of the day had passed, he would tell her about how they could share their lives, no matter what the future held.

Hypatia fidgeted as she stared out the window, a dark cloud over her, coalescing like a physical presence at his back. He went to her side, a hand on her shoulder, breaking whatever anxious trance she found herself in.

"Please say what's on your mind. You know I won't be upset."

She gripped the fabric of her dress.

"What about the people, Sigimar?"

"They will come with us. No one is going to be left behind." He squeezed her shoulder.

"No, that's not—our being here is a symbol of hope for everyone in Elmheim. If we leave, if Ashla is covered again..."

Sigimar fought against a tide of guilt and grief. She was right, of course, much as he hated to admit it. To the people who served them, to the people of Elmheim, they were not simply a man and a woman, but symbols. He hated it. He'd suffered enough heartbreak striving to be a hero to others. He pushed down the guilt of all he'd been given as a result of his supposed heroism, from the things he despised—his title, his ties to the pact—to the things he could no longer live without—the love and support of others, Hypatia herself. Torn by the anger of not wanting to owe anyone else anything more, and the burden of knowing what it would mean if he washed his hands of the situation, Sigimar took a deep breath. He replied with more level-headedness than he felt.

"Then it will be as it was, and Erlendr will send well-provisioned parties out into Ashla to look for other wellsprings."

He was not the only person capable of finding a wellspring. If Erlendr wanted Ashla to be free of the miasma, he would take action. This was no longer just Sigimar's fight. He had Hypatia's happiness and safety to see to now—nothing and no one was more important than that.

In fact, he knew Erlendr would do just that. The king was desperate to put an end to the curse and thus the ancient pact. It was his only means of keeping Alfric by his side for the rest of his long life.

She seemed displeased by his answer, but the time for her to elaborate further was cut short. Ingi was at the door, asking them to follow.

Once inside the sparsely decorated room, Ingi and Drest left them to treat with the kings in private.

"Well, this isn't the homecoming I had hoped for you, Jarls." Erlendr's smile was as grim as his humour, seated beside an equally grim King Alfric, gazing at them through the half-globe of the dragon's eye.

Sigimar patted the spot next to him, waiting for Hypatia to sit, and faced his kings.

"We'll send everyone back to Askr and carry as many of the artefacts and books as we can before the miasma returns. Will there be space?" Sigimar asked.

But instead of discussing the logistics of the enormous move, the kings were silent, engaged in warring glares at each other. Alfric tsked.

"*You* tell them. Just know I'm against it."

That boded ill.

"I'm sending warriors and light-wielders to you. We cannot afford to lose what we've gained in Ashla," Erlendr began. It was what Sigimar had expected, except this was far sooner than he'd thought. Then Erlendr's gaze shifted from him to Hypatia, and a chill stole down Sigimar's spine. "As your king, I am ordering you, Jarl Hypatia, to take part in the mission."

Air escaped his lungs in a hiss, his breath stolen by every ugly feeling—white-hot rage, consuming panic, dizzying confusion, screaming denial.

"No," he growled, a protective arm around her shoulders as Hypatia stilled. He could feel her heart battering her chest as she curled into him.

Erlendr refused to meet his eyes as he spoke to Hypatia.

"You are the strongest wielder of the healing light we've ever seen, Jarl Hypatia. In the past decade, every half-cocked idiot has run headlong into the miasma, trying to replicate Jarl Sigimar's feat. None have succeeded. If we allow the miasma to retake Ashla, my people will become desperate, hopeless—reckless. Elmheim cannot afford to feed the miasma more fools than it already does. Nor can we afford unrest. We have a blood-sworn duty, not just to Elmheim, but to the whole of the Riverlands and the realms beyond to hold the miasma at bay. You are as much a part of the ancient pact as I am, as Sigimar is—you have been since you signed the marriage contract in blood."

How dare he? How *dare* he?

"You swore she would live safely, Erlendr!" Sigimar howled.

"And *you* were supposed to protect the treasures of Ashla, Jarl Sigimar!" Erlendr retorted, unmoved.

If Erlendr were here now, Sigimar would have choked the life from that miserable bastard.

"Without that fucking portal, that would've been possible! This is your damn problem, Erlendr! I will not lose my wife to this fucking curse!"

Not her. Gods below, not her, too. Was his brother's death not enough?

"And I will not lose the whole of Elmheim to it!" Erlendr roared. A tense, short silence reigned before he sighed and continued, "So protect her. As your king, I am ordering you, Jarl Sigimar, to lead the mission. You are the only person who has ever successfully located a wellspring. Do so again, and pray there is another amplifier. In the meantime, I suggest you guard the remaining treasures as well as you can."

No. He would not do this. He would not march out into that death fog, his wife in tow, hoping against hope that it would spare her—spare them.

"Fuck you! We refuse."

"Don't make me enforce the pact, Sigimar," Erlendr warned, weary but resolute.

It was easier to give into reckless anger than face the terrified scream trapped in his chest. He let the anger consume him, poison him, push him onwards.

"I dare you. If you're worried about unrest, wait until the other jarls find out what you've done," Sigimar growled.

He would give Erlendr the freedom he sought. If he wished to be free of his crown, no doubt the outrage of his fellow jarls would prod them into disavowing the king en masse. He would turn the hero-worship of the people into his sword, and he would strike Erlendr down.

"If we succeed, then it won't matter." Erlendr shook his head. "So be it."

"Sigimar?" Hypatia whispered, eyes wide with fear.

"He won't."

But Erlendr made him a liar. The king grabbed a roll of parchment, took a knife and cut his arm, blood dripping from a fast-healing wound. As his blood hit the contract binding Sigimar to his titles, his land, the ancient pact, and Erlendr's will, runes carved themselves into Sigimar's wrists.

"By the ancient pact, I command you, Jarl Sigimar Ashla, to lead the mission to find and purify the wellspring."

Sigimar cursed as the pact branded him to his marrow, crimson ink tattooing his wrists. He was bound, body and soul, to do as Erlendr commanded. He looked at Hypatia, stricken. How could he protect her now? Gods, could he do nothing right?

As Erlendr made to grab another parchment—Hypatia's—he broke.

Not her, too!

Anything but that.

He would sell his very soul to free her from the compulsion to walk into that certain death. Pride and anger forgotten, he went to his knees, voice cracking as fear choked him.

"Please, not her too. I'll lead your gods damned mission. Just, please, let her be safe. I beg of you. I'll wear these marks for the rest of my days! I'll find every wellspring in Ashla! I'll fight until my dying breath! Just please spare her. *Please!*"

Hypatia gasped in horror, going to her knees as well. She placed a hand on Sigimar, the other outstretched towards the crystal, as if that simple gesture could ward off the worst.

"No! No! I'll go! I'll go of my own free will." Tears rolled down her cheeks, her hands lifted in supplication. "Please, don't ask more of him. I'll go. I swear."

"Hypatia, no," Sigimar choked.

He couldn't let her do this. Not for him. Never for him.

"Sigimar, I won't let you go alone."

He shook his head, words of denial caught in his throat, tangled by panic. He wouldn't survive her loss.

"If I don't, who will go in my stead? Whose death will I be responsible for? And if not us, then who? Will we doom our children to this fight, when we have the power to end it?"

But despite her brave words, she was shaking, her fingers trembling as she gripped his arm, her eyes full of terror. What was the death of some stranger when Hypatia's life was on the line? He didn't care what kind of a man that made him. If Hypatia were safe—alive—everything and everyone else could rot.

"Better someone else than you. Better you're alive to have children at all than to risk your life like this."

But his pleading fell on deaf ears—twice over.

"Thank you, Jarl Hypatia, for your willingness to serve. I will send my people through to you. Prepare, provision yourselves, and may the forgotten gods bless your journey."

With that, the connection between their orbs was severed, along with any hope Sigimar had of sparing Hypatia the horrors lurking in the miasma.

"Ingi," Sigimar called.

Ingi entered the room, ears twitching and face dark. He'd heard. Good.

"If we send her far away, what would happen if he activates the pact then?"

"Sigimar, I won't—"

He put a finger to her lips and shook his head, turning back to Ingi.

"She would be overcome by the compulsion to return, in constant pain until she fulfilled his commands."

"You can't possibly be—"

"Yes, I can. Is there any way to dull the pain and the compulsion?"

"No, Jarl, I'm afraid not," Ingi replied, grim-faced.

His last defiant hope was snuffed out. Bitterness reigned supreme.

"Have that fucking portal guarded day and night, shifts ending at odd intervals, the changing of the guard known to you alone. Do what you can to find out who stole our amplifier. And tell every bastard Erlendr sends that if anything happens to my wife, compulsion or no, I'll kill them myself."

As Ingi left to carry out his orders, Sigimar picked up the half orb and hurled it from the room, slamming the doors shut. He paced, mind and heart racing as bile crept up the back of his throat. In his waking nightmare, it was Hypatia who stood over the stave, staring up as the jaws of a monster snapped shut around her neck. It was her body that fell into the mud, spurting blood and twitching as he screamed, helpless and broken, wishing he too would flake away as the daylight returned to this cursed land.

"You would prefer I live as a coward? To let you go alone and risk your life while I sit around and do nothing?" Hypatia asked, breaking the panicked spell that had taken hold of him.

How could she ask that? How could she doubt it? It was not cowardice to be safe, to act as any rational person would when presented with the miasma.

"Yes! Your life is more precious to me than anything in this world. Honour? Titles? Kings? Pacts? Fuck them all! You're my heart, my light. I'd do anything to keep you safe."

She rushed him then, pounding on his chest with her small fists, red-faced as tears streamed down her cheeks.

"How dare you! How *dare* you! You're *my* heart! You're precious *to me!* Do you think I want to contemplate my life without you? Do you think my heart wouldn't shatter into a hundred thousand pieces? Don't you *ever* plead to throw your life away! I'll never forgive you! I won't!"

Sigimar's heart ached. He hated to see her so upset, her tears poison. And yet he could not take back his words. It was the only thing that made him a man worthy of her. He took hold of her fists in one hand and pulled her close with the other.

"I'm supposed to protect you. I love you."

"Damnit, no! Don't you understand?! If you love me, *don't leave me.* Don't die for me, *live for me! That* is how you can protect me. *That* is how I need you to love me, Sigimar. I cannot...I cannot be a widow again. Please, please don't do that to me."

Her anguished sobs broke him as nothing else could. What a fool he'd been. What good was a dead husband to a woman who needed both her life and her heart protected? No matter how much the future terrified him, no matter the nightmares to come, they were bound—by kings, pacts, fate, and by their own hearts.

Wherever she went, he would follow.

That the reverse was both true *and* shredded his soul with dread was as expected as it was unavoidable. But as he'd long known, courage was not formed in the absence of fear, but in its midst—surrounded, bloodied and drowned by it. She needed him to have the courage to love her as she'd asked. He needed to be that man for her, needed to love her exactly thus. It would not be easy. He might even fail. But he was compelled to try.

"If that's what you need, then I'll give it to you. If we're forced to walk into the deepest of hells, we'll go together," he said, wiping tears from her face as she stared up at him, her lip trembling.

"Together." She nodded.

"Always," he vowed.

Sigimar pulled the swath of red fabric from his tunic. Erlendr might have stolen her safety, forced him to drag her out into the gloom, but he could still give Hypatia a longer life. He could offer this token of hope for them both.

She needed him not to sacrifice his life for her, but to live for her.

He found he needed the same.

"Hypatia, I meant to tell you about this today, before...everything. With this, I can share my years of life with you. It would give you half of my remaining years, so that we can be together all the rest of our days. Will you have them—have me?"

She stepped away, eyes wary.

"This...this isn't meant to be some farewell gesture, is it?" she asked anxiously.

"No! No. This was—is—meant to be a good thing," he reassured her, drawing her close.

Her expression softened, and she stepped back into his embrace, her hands curled into his tunic as she gazed up at him.

"You won't regret it?"

"I could never regret a life with you in it, Hypatia. I want all the years with you that fate allows."

She wiped tears from her eyes.

"Then, yes. Let this be a promise, Sigimar. A promise that we will live facing everything together. You and I, we will be brave for each other, face our fears with each other at our sides. We will walk into that curse, and we will come out of it hand in hand. It won't take us from each other. Swear it."

She asked so much of him, to face his greatest fear, risking the life of the person he loved most all the while. And yet she had the courage to face her own dread, to march in there by his side. They could not walk in there expecting death. That would be no different from giving up. They had to have hope that they would live, that they would succeed. He had to have the courage to hope, no matter how terrifying.

"I vow it to you," he said.

As he was about to wrap the cloth around their wrists, Hypatia stopped him.

"No. Not today."

"But—"

She held a finger to his lips and shook her head.

"When this is over, when our task is done, then I will accept your years."

"But if something happens to me, I want—"

"To sacrifice yourself in some small way," she interrupted, quiet but fierce. "To rest secure in the knowledge that even if you are gone, I will go on. I fear that I cannot risk giving you that peace."

It took the wind from his sails. She was right. Even now, when she'd told him what kind of man she needed him to be, he was trapped by fear, unable to reach for hope.

"Live for me, my love. Fight for *our* future, not just mine."

He kissed her then—a vow to love her as she needed, a promise to have courage when it mattered, and a pact to face whatever came—together, for the rest of their shared lives. And yet as her tongue sought his, panic nipped at his heels, a dread that could not be outrun.

"Sigimar, stay with me. Here. Now. That's all we have."

"Don't say that," he whispered.

Her smile was rueful. She reached up to cup his face in her hands.

"Here and now is all anyone ever has, no matter how many years they expect to live. The past is gone, though not forgotten, and the future is unknowable."

"Has my scholarly wife become a philosopher?"

Hypatia ignored his humourless smile and pulled him down to meet her.

"Kiss me, husband," she said with a look that told him it would not end with a simple kiss.

Sigimar hesitated. Inside, he was nothing more than a tangled mess. The idea of losing himself inside her embrace, even if only for a moment, was too tempting to ignore. But the last thing he wanted was to bruise her with the desperation in his wild heart.

"I don't think I can be as gentle as you deserve."

"I don't want just your gentleness, my love, I want you every way I can have you. And these days, I always come prepared." She took a small jar from within her skirts and presented it to him, a sly grin despite her earlier tears.

It was all the assurance he needed. He swept her up in a harsh kiss and crushed her close. Tongue dominating hers, she wrapped her arms around his neck, her grip on his hair a pleasant sting. And then the little minx fondled both his ears, heedless of the danger, bringing him crashing to his knees. Taking fistfuls of the neckline of her dress, he tore it in two in one swift motion.

"Sig—"

He silenced her squeak of protest with his lips on hers as he peeled off the tatters. They snatched kisses between her fumbling with his belt. He pulled off his tunic and stepped from his leggings and boots.

Except she was still wearing a slip.

One rending later, and she was bare before him. Like a man starved, he lost himself in her heavy, lush breasts, her generous curves, licking and kissing every soft inch. When her own clever tongue found the shell of his ear, he held her thighs in a punishing grip as pleasure arced down his spine and pooled in his groin. Breathing harshly, his eyes found hers. Her full lips quirked up, not the least bit repentant for nearly making him spend.

"I've always wanted to do that."

"Then turn-about is fair play," he ground out.

He stood to his full height, a feral grin on his face as his wife, his love, swayed close, pressing her breasts into his abdomen, eyes never leaving his as she gripped his erection and licked her lips. To her confusion, he pulled away, and in a motion too quick for her to react to, he lifted her up in his arms and hooked her legs on his shoulders, backing her against the wall. As her hands scrabbled for purchase, he lifted her thighs and pressed his lips to her sex. It was her turn to be overcome. When he saw her fingers latch onto the latticework décor, he began his assault. Tonguing her folds, torturing her sensitive little clit, he refused to give her satisfaction until she begged sweetly, promising him every carnal delight in return. Only then did he deliver the release she needed with the barest nip. He slid her down his body as hers trembled. Grabbing the nearest soft pelt, slung over the back of the couch, he tossed it on the ground.

"On your hands and knees."

Breath heaving, Hypatia nodded, sinking down, heavy-lidded eyes looking back to him. He snatched the bottle from what remained of her dress and coated his cock before taking her hips in his hands and sliding home. Her little mewls of pleasure drove him on until he lost himself in her heat, in the sight of her fingers clenching the furs, in her grey eyes sneaking loving glances back at him. Being surrounded by her, and surrounding her, eased his tortured soul. But he needed her closer, pressed to every naked inch of him. He slid out, and coaxed her into his lap, hooking her legs around him. Wrapping her arm around his neck, Hypatia gazed at him with eyes full of everything he'd always wanted.

"I love you, Sigimar."

He rewarded her with another kiss, pouring his heart and soul into every flick of his tongue. Hypatia slid him inside, pressing herself onto him as he gripped a breast in one hand and let his other trail lower. Her little nails scored his wrist as he began rocking into her, refusing to free her from his kiss as his fingertips found her clit. Finally, with the contact he craved, he let himself go, grinding himself into her as deep as she could take him. She was bliss, and he would never have enough of her. Every moment with her, inside her, loved by her, would make him starved for more.

She broke from their kiss, gasping, crying for relief, struggling to either grind herself against his fingers or escape his maddening touch.

"Together," he growled in her ear.

Setting his teeth against the juncture of her neck and shoulder, he sent a shiver down her spine. Hypatia tightened around him and cried out as he gave her what she sought, sending him over the same blissful edge.

As they tumbled down onto the furs, her arms around his neck, she peppered his chest with kisses. He held her close.

Sigimar kissed the top of her head as dark determination flooded him. If he couldn't protect her by keeping her somewhere safe, then he would become a man even those damned creatures feared, as starved for her loving embrace as they were for flesh and blood. And when this was over, he would find a way to free them from Elmheim—forever. As she smiled up at him, he vowed to himself to protect that smile for an eternity, even if he had to do the impossible.

No one thought the miasma could be beaten back... until he'd proven them wrong.

"I love you too, Hypatia."

No one thought a jarl, once bound by the ancient pact, could be free of Elmheim. Sigimar would prove them wrong once more.

Whatever it took.

CHAPTER 28

Dark grey fog trapped them on all sides, an endless sea of death. What snow they trudged through was similarly fouled—until the healing light of many staves carved a path. Corruption seethed and hissed as it dissipated. The ghostly stalks of trees melted away as they passed. They were in the belly of a beast, where there was no sun or stars to guide them. Here, there was no East or West, no North or South, simply forward. No one dared utter a word. They were loud enough as they were, a small army fifty-strong marching through the gloom. Hypatia gripped her stave and swallowed, her heart beating wildly.

Sigimar led the way, surrounded by blades and magic. Hypatia walked in the middle, protected on every side, Kosta nearby ready to whisk her back to safety.

Sigimar's head flicked to the side. Several of the other elven warriors did the same. Everyone came to a halt, holding a collective breath. They waited. Hypatia strained her ears, praying.

Her prayers were in vain.

Clicking echoed out across the cursed plain. Once. Then twice.

Then too many to count.

"Shield wall!" Sigimar cried out.

Shields covered them on all sides, polished bronze so reflective they might as well have been mirrors. Shrieks rent the air, calling out on all sides for blood. Kosta held her round her waist, waiting for his orders.

"First wave!" Sigimar commanded.

Several light wielders poked the tips of their staves through small openings in the fortress of shields, pouring magic into them. The shrieks became angrier, more frantic. The draugar were flaking away, dying a final time. But not even death was enough of a deterrent.

The shrieks were closer now. Draugar flung themselves against the shields, clawed hands grasping through the gaps between them, desperate—starving. The further they'd travelled, the more desperate the creatures had become. Lunging at their ranks despite her magic and that of many others, they preferred the agony of dissolving—and the possibility of a mouthful of flesh—over their unending hunger.

"Second wave!" Sigimar called out.

Hypatia pushed her magic into the stave. It multiplied her magic, radiating inside the shield wall, dissolving the draugar before they could tear or maim. Everyone else similarly equipped did the same. Slowly, she raised her stave, slotting it through the small opening above her head.

"Steady!"

Hypatia braced herself. She knew what was to come, but it didn't make it any easier to hold down the bile surging up her throat. In an instant, the draugar attacked from all sides, throwing themselves on the shields, grasping for the cracks, desperate to pry them open. Others reached for the staves even as they flaked away, ripping them out from the fortress as their last act.

"Burn bright!"

Hypatia pushed her magic into her stave and closed her eyes. As every light wielder did the same, they burned as bright as the sun. The shrieks died in an instant, the clicking silenced, and only the hiss of evaporating corruption remained. Only when that, too, had gone quiet did Sigimar give the order to let down their guard.

A tear snaked down Hypatia's cheek as the wall of grey greeted her eyes once more. A shaky exhale was all she could afford her ruined nerves before they marched on once more. But raised voices in the rear held them up.

"You were going to let it take my eye, you damned coward!" one of the elven warriors yelled at a light-wielding fae.

"*You* were sloppy! If you had held like you were supposed to instead of stepping on my feet, I never would have lost my stave!" the fae shrieked back.

"Enough!" Sigimar rounded on the two. "Go collect your stave. And you? Up front, with me. If you have energy to fight each other, you have energy to lead the march."

Sigimar spared her a fleeting smile before he took up the lead. And on they marched as sick dread curled in her gut.

Hypatia had no one but herself to blame for her fear. She'd fought hard not to be left behind, to march with Sigimar out into the miasma, her magic there to protect him. It had taken two full days to equip and provision the fighting force. Two precious days fewer that they had to purify the nearest wellspring and hopefully bring back another amplifier—if there was one to be found. If not, they would be forced to make a hasty retreat through the barren, grey wastelands choked by the miasma, the cold earth turning to sucking, squelching mud under the boots of so many.

Only Sigimar and Kosta were familiar among the faces for this dire mission and only they ever had a kind word or smile for her or anyone else. For the past two nights they'd retreated to the safety of a pocket realm, a longhouse with a connecting room for every warrior, and each morning, she woke from a half-sleep to choke down a bite of breakfast among the hostility and squabbling of the warriors. The first day, Sigimar had been able to defuse the fights, even had them singing a bawdy song before the day was out. But now? There was no camaraderie here. Only sharp looks and sharper words. Why in the gods' unknowable names

Erlendr had chosen such men and women for this mission was a mystery to her.

At first, she'd assumed that the looming miasma and constant attacks had driven the warriors to the edge of their tolerance. But if even she remained brave-faced for it all, what had gotten into the warriors?

Still, she would not let their snappish moods and ill manners deter her. Despite her wariness of both monsters and allies, despite the bone-deep exhaustion creeping up on her, she would see this through.

But every click in the gloom sent her pulse pounding. She'd barely slept, even when Sigimar pulled her against him, even within the supposed safety of a pocket realm. Unlike the rest of her fellows, Hypatia had not been trained for a journey like this. She was weaving on her aching feet, constant, dreaded anticipation draining her to the marrow. Even her lightly packed satchel, with a few rations, water and her journal weighed her down, making her shoulders ache. The only thing she feared more than the threat of the creatures was being too insensate to respond to an attack when it came.

Because it *would* come.

It *always* came.

Sigimar never failed to defend her. She couldn't fail him. She couldn't lose him.

Sigimar fell back in their little formation and walked by her side, nestled in the middle, protected by spell and sword on every side. He picked her up in his arms in one fluid movement.

"Sigimar, wait! My boots are filthy and—"

"You're exhausted. Let me carry you for a few hours."

No one else needed to be carried on this horrid march. Not even Kosta had complained about his lot as her designated ride back to the tower if things got too dangerous. With the hostility of the warriors already at a fever pitch, would another nuisance set them off?

"But—"

"You can't help if you're too tired to stay on your feet. Everyone else here is a seasoned warrior—you're not. Sleep. We'll be making camp soon anyway."

Humiliation burned her cheeks. She looked around at the warriors still marching in formation, but their eyes were trained outward, watchful, never slowing their pace.

"I'm sorry," she whispered, tears stinging her eyes as she clutched her stave.

"Shhh, no. Don't apologise. Just sleep." He pressed his lips to her forehead.

She couldn't. Not for some time. But eventually have drifted off. Hypatia woke to an impossibly soft bed, thick covers and the muted conversations of soldiers at rest. The pocket realm. Sigimar lay beside her, deep in sleep. Their refuge had been tethered to a stave radiating the healing light, making it unlikely the creatures would gain entry, though if they did, warriors also took shifts guarding the entrance. Hypatia closed her eyes, hoping to get a few more hours of sleep, when the tone of the conversation outside their room shifted.

"Who will be named jarl when this is over?"

"Focus on surviving first."

"I am. I just want to know what happens when we succeed. If Jarl Sigimar and his brother could do it with two men, why wouldn't we be able to do it with fifty? We haven't lost anyone yet."

"King Erlendr will decide."

"How? Everyone here will have done their part. Do we all become jarls, or is it just the person who purifies the wellspring who gets the title?"

"This is foolish. I'm going to sleep."

"Fine, but when the light wielders hiding behind our swords and shields get titles, and we don't, you'll admit I was right to question it."

"Go to sleep or I'll choke you out."

Hypatia curled into Sigimar's warm embrace and squeezed her eyes shut, desperate to forget the warrior's words. Sleep was elusive as anxiety held her in its grasp. Had she been foolish to believe in the goodness of the people on this mission? As the night dragged on, she worried if she should wake Sigimar and tell him. But what could he do? One man against dozens? If she spoke of her fears, would he demand they turn back, dooming Ashla and Elmheim? Would he even be able to physically stop the mission, with those dreadful marks on his wrists? Would he get distracted in the middle of an attack, questioning if he could truly trust the people at his back?

When the camp roused, she decided to hold her tongue. She couldn't risk adding to the friction already present.

"Did you sleep?" Sigimar asked, his finger tipping her chin up.

"A little." She smiled, a small, brittle thing.

He frowned but said nothing, kissing her brow and helping her into her attire. They ate with the rest of the soldiers and light-wielders. Whatever tension had begun in the night had intensified this morning. The laughter around the fire was hollow. Glances between friends the day before were sharper, distrustful, watchful. Gone was any semblance of trust or unity. Sigimar sat closer to her, his arm slung around her shoulder.

When they began their march, Sigimar stayed nearer than he usually did. He still led the charge, but they'd tightened their formation, keeping her protected by several rows of soldiers. She cursed herself for keeping quiet all night. What if Sigimar had gone out there and calmed them all down before the distrust had infected the rest of the camp? What if they'd needed him to face the squabbling head-on, to speak to them one warrior to another? How could he lead if she withheld such things from him?

"I heard them last night, bitching about protecting us," a wizard closest to her whispered to his companion.

"They'd be worm food without us. Or worse," the fae man hissed.

"I'll watch your back if you watch mine. No telling what happens once we purify the wellspring."

The fae man nodded.

"Maybe those without our magic go mad with jealousy. How do we know the jarl didn't kill his brother to have the glory all for himself?"

When they caught sight of Hypatia staring, her mouth agape, they turned their backs on her, whispering so quietly she couldn't catch what they said next.

She kept her eyes averted, so as not to draw the attention of others. Gods, what was happening to them? Had greed poisoned their minds? She'd seen it often enough in Lethe. Good men became animals in the face of wealth and power. Weak men became monsters. Just like her father. Hypatia looked to Kosta, praying to the forgotten gods that he hadn't lost his senses to whatever madness scratched at the minds of the men. Kosta sidled closer, a worried look in his dark eyes. Had he heard the whispers too? She reached out and took his hand. He squeezed, asking her a question with his eyes. Hypatia shook her head. Not now. The second she said the word, they would get out of here. Sigimar dropped back to march at her side, gripping his axe warily. Had the whispers reached his ears?

That was when she heard it.

Not clicking.

Not shrieking.

Not whispers.

A melody so haunting tears streamed down her cheeks. It was calling her, begging her to come closer, to free it. Melody and voice blended, plaintive notes carving misery and awe in equal measures into her heart. Her throat ached, and it was all she could do to contain a sob, terrified of making a sound.

Nothing mattered but the sound.

"Tia?" Kosta whispered.

Danger forgotten, she cried out. It had burrowed into her flesh, her marrow, her very soul. The song was agony and ecstasy. It held her heart in its fierce grasp, consuming her.

"I have to find it!"

"Do you hear it?" Sigimar bent down, hand on her back.

"It's close. Please!" She grabbed his cloak in her hands, pleading, her will no longer hers alone. Dimly, she was aware that she was not entirely in control of her own body, her own mind. The melody coursed through her veins, as necessary as blood.

His posture stiffened.

"The wellspring is at hand. Be on your guard!"

Shivers ran down her spine, fever and chills wracking her body every second she failed to comply with the song's demand. Someone would have to hold her back soon, before she broke into a run, desperate to find the source. Sense eroded between ragged breaths. Only the barest tether of her will held on. The others who wielded the light looked about in awe, as distressed as she, threatening to break rank, pushing against the backs of the warriors, frantic to escape their armour-clad prison.

She had to free it.

"Do you hear it?" they whispered amongst themselves.

"Why is it getting harder to breathe?" Kosta asked, wheezing.

The calls came from the front of their marching party first. Pressure crushed her chest as the miasma cleared. Whatever Sigimar, Kosta or the warriors said was lost to her as her last shred of control snapped. Hypatia broke into a run, slipping past the defences to reach a glowing blue stave, her own forgotten. Others who wielded the light jostled for space beside her. As one, they grabbed the stave and pulled it from a pool of muck. It wanted her light, and like a mother with a hungry babe, she fed it, marvelling as she felt its gratitude. Hypatia wept. The longer her light shone upon it, the sweeter the melody became. Agony, despair, terror—banished. Hearts and minds touched hers, flashes of lives lived: a first kiss, sewing the final stitch of a masterpiece, a warrior's battle cry: the taste of perfectly brewed tea, basking in the heat of the summer sun, a lover's embrace.

When the last note was silenced, the spell broke. Hypatia gasped for breath, the weight on her chest easing with every inhalation. Mind muddy, she looked around, confused, as did the others with their white-knuckle grips on the stave. Releasing it, she stumbled back. The madness had gone. Her will was her own again. Hypatia shook. How had the stave taken her mind from her? Her will?

What had come over her? She knew the dangers of the miasma, and yet she'd cried out and charged ahead, heedless of the risk. She could have brought death down upon them all. What had she done?

"S-Sigimar?"

"I'm here. I haven't left your side." His smile didn't reach his anxious eyes.

"What was that?" Her hands trembled as he took them in his.

"The wellspring. It's been purified. Look." He jutted his chin skyward.

She craned her neck and gasped. Blue replaced the grim, sooty grey of the miasma. It was the first true sky she'd seen in days.

"Then...we did it?"

"Not yet," he murmured. "Everyone, stand back," he called out, pulling Hypatia away from where she'd knelt in the muck.

The ground rumbled beneath her feet. Warriors and light wielders scrambled back as the ground in the centre rose up. Black, crumbling earth formed a mound until it was taller than Sigimar. The ground stilled and the mound stopped growing, soil and rock falling away to reveal the tips of five small spires. A warrior moved in first, pulling soil and spindly roots away from the mound.

"It's..." The warrior gasped.

"An amplifier," Sigimar sighed, the tension draining from him.

Tears welled in Hypatia's eyes. It was going to be alright. They would be safe now. She wrapped her arms around Sigimar's neck and laughed as a triumphant cry went up amongst the soldiers.

Sigimar violently shoved her away.

Knocked back several paces, she landed flat on her back, head hitting the frozen ground hard enough to make her feel ill. Dazed, she stared at the sky, revealed through the dissipating miasma, as she caught her breath. Confusion slowed her thoughts as she struggled to turn onto her side. Dizziness prevented her from getting to her feet.

Why would he hurt her?

When she looked up at Sigimar, he had the oddest expression twisting his rugged features—pain, shock, fear. Then he coughed. A river of blood poured from his mouth. Her eyes trailed down, alighting on the glint of metal. A longsword was lodged in his midsection, nearly cleaving him in half.

That was when the screaming began.

CHAPTER 29

"King Otmar sends his congratulations," the fae warrior hissed in his ear as he placed a boot on Sigimar's back and wrenched his sword free. "And thanks you for the soul stave and the second amplifier."

Sigimar staggered forward, choking on blood. For an elvish man suffering from a potentially fatal wound, his mind was remarkably clear. Perhaps that was the effect of being so near to death.

He peered down at his side. So much blood and gore. And yet the other was as pristine as when he'd woken that morning. The bastard's first swing would have cut him in two but for the extra armour Sigimar had on to protect his spine. Would it be enough?

Sigimar looked up. Hypatia was on her side some few paces from him. He'd shoved her away in time, thank the gods. Now if her brother would collect his wits and teleport her to safety, he would be eternally grateful.

Hypatia screamed, desperate denial in her horror-struck visage as she reached for him from her prone position. If only he'd had one more chance to tell her he loved her. To tell her she deserved to be happy, safe and cherished. He had truly wanted to love her as she needed. He had wanted to have children with her, explore with her, learn with her, grow old together.

Chaos broke out around him. Spells and swords flew in earnest then. Had they unknowingly brought Otmar's malefactors with them on this expedition?

Sigimar fell to his knees. It'd been centuries since he'd suffered these kinds of injuries. His training had been dedicated to fighting creatures, not armed attackers. But he was certain the next swing would take his head if he didn't do something.

To never be able to hold Hypatia again. Never feel her lips on his. Never experience her smiles or laughter again. He could not die this way. Not like this.

Summoning a strength he didn't know he possessed, he vowed to survive, no matter the cost. No matter the pain.

He kicked out one of his legs, his torn side protesting mightily as it knit back together. The crunching of a kneecap had him grinning with feral pride. Sigimar turned to face his attacker.

What met his eyes was a scene of slaughter.

His attacker fled. Warriors ran each other through with blades while vicious spells mutilated the fallen. There was no obvious one side or another. In the chaos, every person pitted themselves against every other living being. In the middle of the melee, some way off, a strange artefact pulsed malevolent energies throughout the clearing. He felt it slide over his skin and skitter away. A spell? He patted his chest and thanked the forgotten gods for his piercing.

Sigimar couldn't protect Hypatia forever, not against the warriors they'd brought, not when the lot of them were frenzied. For now, the battle was concentrated away from her, but that could quickly change. That artefact needed to be destroyed if anyone was to survive. Thankfully, he wasn't the only one whose duty was to protect Hypatia. His eyes met Kosta's in the distance. The mage had teleported out of range of the battle.

"Kosta! Take Hypatia and get out of here!" Sigimar roared as he dove into the madness.

A wizard with horrendous burns crawled through the muck to the spires of the amplifier, away from the melee.

"It's *mine!*" the wizard shrieked, reaching for it as he was decapitated by an axe-wielding elf.

"*I* will be the jarl!" the elf roared before a spell tore a hole through his chest, carving out his heart.

Dodging both spell and blade, Sigimar grabbed the nearest axe and swung it at the malevolent artefact—only to embed it in the chest of a shapeshifter as he reformed from smoke. Another dodge and he caught sight of his foe.

The fae man who had nearly cut Sigimar in two limped away, dragging a leg twisted at an odd angle. So be it. Revenge could wait. He advanced through the melee once more.

Hypatia's scream tore his attention from his task. Ah gods, hadn't Kosta taken her away? Sigimar turned, sprinting for her, heedless of the swords and magic that stood in his way. The world slowed as he pumped his legs.

Arms raised to protect her head, Hypatia closed her eyes as a witch aimed a spell at her. Heart in his throat, he lunged to protect her as a ball of molten rock raced towards her. Too late. He wouldn't make it. Hypatia flew from the force of the spell, knocked into the dark mound. Earth from the mound rolled off, burying her.

Gods, no!

Whatever had possessed the warriors here had turned them into a pack of bloodthirsty berserkers. He should have taken her and let them kill each other to the last. The only thing that mattered was her safety.

"Kosta!" Sigimar roared as he grabbed a smaller axe from his belt and hurled it into the witch's head.

"Here!" he called, appearing atop the mound and quickly destabilizing it. Dirt, mud and rocks rolled off, revealing more of the amplifier's blue crystal spires.

Kosta still had his sanity. Good.

"Get her out of here! Now!" he called back, fighting his way to her, praying she was whole enough for the healers to fix.

When he next laid eyes on where Hypatia had been thrown, she was gone. The heap of dirt covering her? Gone. Part of his heart eased. Kosta had taken her from this bloodbath. More dirt fell from the mound.

"Hypatia!" Kosta screamed.

A mound Kosta was still standing atop, his eyes searching the battlefield.

Dread set in anew.

As Sigimar neared, his world shattered.

He fell to his knees, a scream trapped in his throat. The earth had opened up. The light of day revealed a pit that must have gone to hell itself, a pitch-black wound. Kosta was beside him in an instant.

"No, no, no!" Kosta cried.

"Hypatia!" Sigimar screamed into the void.

His world, his light, his love—gone.

Wherever she goes, I follow.

A shield flew through the air, concussing Kosta. The mage tumbled into the void as Sigimar reached for him, overbalancing. Together they fell, Sigimar cradling him as they were swallowed by the pitch black. Whatever the damage, Sigimar was likely to recover, whereas his brother-in-law would perish.

Whereas Hypatia might have already perished.

The fall beat thought from his mind. There was no direction, only pain. He hit object after object, slowing his fall. Bone after bone broke and broke anew in his dark descent. Agony burst through him as something sharp sheared a foot clean off. He landed on his back, nearly bashing his own skull open. Kosta was out cold, spared the worst of it by the shield of Sigimar's body.

He must have blacked out, because when he opened his eyes, everything hurt but he was able to move. Kosta was atop him, his steady breathing assured Sigimar that his brother-in-law lived. He looked around, eyes adjusting to the dark.

Beside him, Hypatia lay still.

"Hypatia," he whispered, voiced cracking like his breaking heart.

A sob choked him.

It was his fault. If he hadn't given into anger when he'd taunted Otmar, boasted of his wealth, Hypatia might still be with him. Otmar would never have known that Ashla was full of treasures. But it had always been easier to be enraged than to admit hurt, pain, vulnerability. He'd been angry for so long, a jumbled mess of sharp edges, begging for a reason to cut someone. In his pain he'd reached for poison. Now they suffered the consequences—Hypatia suffered them. Gods, he'd been such a pig-headed fool. If only he'd learned to hurt without lashing out, Hypatia might still be alive.

There was no way in the hells she'd survived the fall, when only his elvish blood had saved him—was saving him—from certain death. He pushed Kosta aside and crawled over to her, tears blurring his vision as his bones righted and mended, deep lacerations closed and the parts he'd lost regrew. She lay face down, her hand visible from underneath the long cloak she'd worn.

He would never forgive himself for allowing her to come with him, for not finding some way to send her to safety. They'd vowed to be together always, but what good was such a vow when she left for somewhere he could not follow? When it had been his fault that they'd been parted? He'd known how important it had been to her that they faced their fears, that they chose to be brave, and it had been as important for him to face the miasma with her at his side, proof that he could protect her, that it wouldn't take everything from him. But he would rather have lived as a despicable coward if it meant she would be alive now. What good was it for them to face their fears, to save a cursed land, if it cost them everything?

He reached to touch her, terrified of what he would find broken and bloody, knowing that it would break him—heart, mind and soul. And yet when he dared lift her cloak, his mind could not comprehend what he saw.

She was whole, unharmed and breathing.

The harsh sob that escaped him echoed in the darkness. He gathered her close and wept tears of relief. In the silence, he could hear her soft breathing, and the clink of her charms beneath her dress. He thanked the gods for her life, for giving him another undeserved chance to be the man she needed, for sparing his heart. Thanking the gods for such mercies, he buried his face in her hair and simply breathed her in.

Yet such mercies were short-lived.

In the vast darkness of the cavern, the sounds of clicks echoed. He grabbed Hypatia, cradling her with one arm and swung Kosta over his other shoulder. As his eyes adjusted, he realised all was not covered in complete inky blackness. A band of soft lights stood at his shoulder's height and trailed off into the distance, the faint outline of ancient ruins visible. Were there people down here? Was this path illuminated by the healing light? Should he follow them, and potentially go deeper into the maze, or to attempt to climb back up and out into the melee above? A series of thudding noises echoed down from above. He moved out of the way just in time. Another body fell from above, splattering at his feet.

The clicks were closer.

The creatures would be drawn by the blood, smell it, and would chase it down. There was enough spattering the walls on the way down that he prayed they would be drawn into the light above rather than coming after him in his blood-soaked pelts and armour. Climbing up with two limp bodies and no rope to tie them to him would be impossible. Decision made, he raced down the lighted path, hoping against hope the illuminated orbs contained the healing light.

But the faster he ran, the more clicks and screeches rang out. He hoped the echoes were playing tricks on his senses—that they feasted on the corpse of the warrior who had fallen rather than chase after him. Following the lights, the path had widened, becoming smoother. He came around a bend in the trail and nearly jumped out of his skin as something—someone—blocked the path. Light hair, pale skin, a woman's curves. He reached for a weapon he no longer possessed.

"Gods below! Who in the hells are you?" the woman squeaked, hand going to her chest. "How did you find this place?"

His answer was cut off by a screech. One that was close enough not to echo.

"You've roused them, you damn fool!" she hissed, turned, and ran.

Sigimar followed. The scrabbling skitter of claws nipped at his heels. She made a hair-pin turn and disappeared into another tunnel. He nearly slipped as he mirrored her lightning-fast retreat. When he caught up to her again, she was standing still, the room ringed with the dim, winking lights. On a pedestal stood a lintel and post structure. She raised a blade to her finger and pressed it into the stone.

"Oh gods," Sigimar breathed, relieved and horrified as a shimmering blue surface cascaded between the posts.

A portal. Hopefully one that lead anywhere but here.

"And why do you sound so relieved? I'm not taking you with me. You're probably corrupted."

"Please, none of us have been touched by the draugar, and she wields the healing light!" Sigimar gestured to Hypatia as the clicks sounded just outside the room.

"Does she now? And what of that one?"

The draugr stuck its head into the room and screeched, clawed hand stretched into the room, snatching it back whenever it began to sizzle, snapping its sharp-toothed maw at empty air. Sigimar turned, keeping his eyes on it, backing away as it grew bolder, more inured to the pain of its own purification.

"Teleportation," Sigimar answered.

A pause as she turned Kosta's face to look at him, humming appreciatively over Sigimar's shoulder.

"Very well, but if you've lied, you'll be bait the next time I come through here."

They rushed through the portal as the creature leapt into the room proper. Sigimar landed in a heap in the bright sun, smashing his knees on icy rock rather than falling on Hypatia. The glow of the portal disappeared.

In a small clearing surrounded by evergreens, a cold gust blew flakes of snow. The hum of life—the creaking of branches, occasional birdsong, the whistling of the wind—brought him the first sense of peace since they'd begun their march into the miasma.

He had his first good look at the woman who had grudgingly saved him.

Average height with white skin pinkened only at her cheeks and lips, she skewered him with a green gaze as she pushed strawberry blonde strands from her eyes. She appeared as any witch might, but for her eyes. A wiser man might have looked away from her glare, for in their depths he sensed terrible, ancient power. The look in them made even the eyes of elves nearing the ends of their three thousand years of life appear young. Was she a sorceress?

"Come along. The pretty wizard has a head wound and tending it will give me a chance to get a better look at him."

"Where is this?"

"Isro."

"How? There shouldn't be a portal in Isro," Sigimar said, getting to his feet and adjusting his precious cargo.

There shouldn't be a sorceress in Isro either. Any sorceress worth her salt could easily topple a reigning witch queen and rule for eternity. It was why they were almost universally driven out of positions of power and forced to wander or hide.

"There isn't, my elvish friend. And if you would like to keep being my friend, you will keep that in mind." Her gaze pierced him then, a trickle of sweat rolling down his spine as he felt the immense pressure of her magic surround him. Definitely a sorceress. She smiled in a way that gave him chills. "What a useful charm you bear. What useful charms you all have. But did you know that a charm is only as powerful as the one who enchants it?" Her green eyes flashed with destructive promise.

This was not a woman to be questioned or trifled with. He should have known as much when he found her deep in Ashla, walking around in draugar-infested tunnels.

"Understood." Sigimar swallowed.

The pressure disappeared and a real smile lit her face.

"Excellent. I've always loved a quick study. This way. My home isn't far."

When he looked back, the portal had vanished from sight. Invisibility? Another shiver skittered down his spine and crept into his limbs. Gods, that had been close. He'd almost lost everything dear to him. Sigimar released a shaky breath and tightened his hold on the mages, adjusting Hypatia so that he could bury his face in her hair. *Breathe. She's alive.* A few moments more, and he quelled the tremors wracking him. His heart felt tattered, his limbs like they were weighted down by a thousand boulders. If they survived the next few hours, he might sleep for days. Sigimar turned to follow the sorceress home, hoping for all their sakes that he hadn't just traded one grisly end for another.

CHAPTER 30

The scent of stew brought Hypatia out from the heavy darkness. Thick wooden beams illuminated by flickering firelight greeted her as she cracked open her eyes. Bundles of drying herbs hung along the walls like decorations. Over-stuffed shelves groaned under the weight of books and jars in haphazard arrangements. Had the journey to Ashla, the maddened frenzy of their supposed allies, all been a nightmare? Was this some pocket realm? Whatever it was, she was simply grateful the fear and terror was behind her. Hypatia closed her eyes, resolving to drift back to sleep as heavy footfalls on creaking floorboards drew closer.

"Thank the gods, you're awake." Sigimar rushed to her side and cupped her face in his large hands, fingers caressing her cheeks and brow.

"Sigimar?" Her heart lurched at the worry in his eyes.

She tried to rise but couldn't. A strangled note of panic escaped her lips.

"It's alright. The magic inside your charms was strained and used yours as a stoppage to keep you alive. You'll be fine soon."

He helped her sit up in the unfamiliar bed. Now that she thought on it, who would create such a cramped, chaotic space on purpose? This couldn't possibly be a pocket realm like the one she'd been sleeping in the past few days. On that note, she had more pressing questions.

"Where are we? What happened?"

Sigimar's grip on her tightened, his brows pinched as his eyes stared out at some horror she could not see.

"We were attacked. You fell into the ruins under the amplifier. We...we got lucky, and help was close at hand. We're recovering in Isro," he replied, halting.

How did one fall into a set of ruins? She looked about her. Only she and Sigimar were present.

"Kosta?"

"Safe."

Hypatia sagged with relief. Pulling Sigimar's arms tighter, she burrowed into his warmth. She closed her eyes, battling the image of Sigimar nearly cut in two, the blood pouring from his mouth and side. He was here, beside her, whole and unharmed. They'd survived. But how? The last she remembered, a blast of fiery rock had hit her. She touched her face, hand shaking. Would her skin be scarred? There should be burns at the least, pain most certainly. But she was unharmed, her skin smooth, not a twinge of discomfort. Who had healed her? Hypatia shivered, pushing the memories away. They could haunt her later. Not now. She focused on breathing, on the feel of Sigimar's pulse against her, of her own heartbeat. They were alive. That was what mattered.

"Isro? That's not possible."

"I'm afraid it is. I'm sorry."

"Why are you sorry? None of this was your fault. And we're alive and well!"

Sigimar couldn't meet her eyes, his hands balled tight. How could he berate himself after all this?

"But it *is* my fault. Otmar was the one who set our people against us. It was his man who struck the first blow, who likely turned everyone against each other, probably from the very first night. I let my temper get the better of me when I first met him, insulted his pride, and threatened him. The Riverlands turned on him. I placed you in danger—hells, everyone in danger. If not for my outburst, he might never have tried to hurt us. I don't even know if anyone else survived what happened in Ashla."

"Sigimar, no." She reached out, a hand to his cheek, the other atop his fist, "You are not responsible for the evils perpetrated by others. I am not guilty of my father's crimes, just as you are not guilty for Otmar's. Remember? Put the blame where it belongs."

"You could have died, Hypatia," he whispered, tortured, eyes shining with unshed tears. "I can't lose you."

"You didn't lose me. And you didn't cause this. You didn't invite Otmar's agent on our journey. And no one forced Otmar to incite a slaughter. No one forced him to be cruel or greedy."

"But—"

"No, Sigimar. This is not your burden. We're alive. We kept our vow to each other. Together, in all things." She took his hand and placed it on her heart as she placed hers on his.

He stared at his hand, no doubt letting his senses calm him when his mind was set on self-inflicted torturing. After all, it was what she needed too. By some strange twist of luck or fate or the blessings of the gods, their hearts still beat. She needed to let that fact ground her as much as he, else her mind would insist on showing her horror after horror.

"I thought I'd lost you," he whispered.

"And I you," she answered, holding back her own tears.

The door to the small, cramped room swung open.

"Oh? Has your lady-love awakened?"

"Tia? You're awake!"

Their moment was interrupted by two intruders. One, a woman with a piercing green gaze, strawberry blonde hair and skin as pale as cream. A witch? The other was Kosta, and yet not.

"Kosta? How?"

Gone were his sharp, underfed edges, the hollows in his cheeks, the brittle dullness of his dark hair. He'd filled out, muscled arms and soft belly, cheeks rosy with health, his hair full and glossy, a twinkle in his dark grey eyes. Here was the brother she remembered, built sturdy and solid.

His smile was infectious.

"Agnetha made me a health tonic. Isn't she wonderful?"

"Potion, dearest, and yes, I believe I am." Agnetha preened at the compliment.

"A pleasure to meet you. I'm Hypatia." Hypatia nodded, attempting to stand.

"No, no, rest. The magic of your charms ran out and then drained you nearly dry just to keep you unharmed." Agnetha put a hand on her shoulder and handed her a bowl of savoury stew. "I understand it was desperate times and all that rot, but when next you purchase a slew of protection charms, best go with higher calibre. Less likely for them to use up your magical energies when theirs fail."

"You saved us then?" Hypatia asked.

"After a fashion."

"Thank you."

"Oh, you'll pay me back. Never fear. Eat up and join us when you're ready." She winked, hooked her arm in Kosta's and strolled from the room with him.

The way Kosta looked at Agnetha...she'd never seen him look at another that way. Had he fallen for their pretty rescuer? She turned to Sigimar, brow raised in question.

"Yes, they've been making eyes at each other since he woke up. It's a little sickening. I'm glad to be out of their company. Not that they cared or noticed I was there." He rolled his eyes.

She moved as far over on the narrow bed as she could, making room for Sigimar to lie beside her. He released her from his arms and folded himself onto the bed, head on her lap as he caressed her legs through the sheets. Setting her stew aside, she ran fingers through his burgundy hair, soothing him.

"Tell me what happened."

He released a shuddering breath, her soft-hearted, brave giant. At times like these, she wished she were big enough to fully hold him, strong enough to fight the battles in his stead, brave enough to face the dangers alone so he wouldn't have to. But that was not to be. Nor was it what either of them needed. Instead, they faced their nightmares together.

He recounted the harrowing battle, the madness above, the terror below, and the race through the underground.

"I didn't know it at the time, but your charms protected you from the fireball. Just not from the force of it. Not entirely. When you fell below I thought..." His grip on her thigh shook. She pulled her fingers through his hair and rubbed his back. He swallowed. "I thought you were dead, but your charms had saved you again. We were lucky to meet Agnetha. Any longer and...I don't know. The battle was still raging above. Some malicious magic had turned everyone against each other. I've never seen anything like it. But I know it was Otmar's doing. It was one of his men who nearly cleaved me in two and who was unaffected by the spell."

"But how did we not succumb?"

"We all wore charms against magical attack."

She remembered Sigimar's piercing then. But Kosta wasn't wearing any charms that she knew of.

"Even Kosta?"

Sigimar snorted, daring to look at her with a grin that didn't quite reach his eyes.

"Crazy bastard has it tattooed on his backside. Something about 'covering his ass.'"

Hypatia giggled, covering her mouth when her laughter turned into guffaws at the thought. Once she began, she could barely stop. True mirth wove itself into the ragged ends of her panic. When at last she could catch her breath, some of the burden had lifted from her heart.

"Gods below, I shall never allow him to forget it. Though I suppose it is only fair he should suffer such pains in his behind when he spent our childhood being a proper pain in mine! Tell me you've made at least one joke at his expense since you discovered it."

"I might have, but our host has spent so much time admiring it." Sigimar smirked up at her.

"Oh gods, yes, well, hopefully they don't start anything while we're here. I'm not sure I want such things burned into my psyche."

"You're such a hypocrite."

"I fail to see how." She arched her brow at the accusation.

"One word, my love—*aphrodisiac*," he enunciated the word slowly, drawing out her shame with a twinkle in his eye. Finally his smile reached the amber depths.

Hypatia gasped and slapped his shoulder.

"You evil man! How dare you bring that up," she cursed him, her cheeks heating. Perhaps that did make her a hypocrite of sorts. Poor Kosta had looked positively ill the next time she'd seen him.

Sigimar chuckled, sitting up and handing her the steaming bowl of stew.

"Eat up. I fear our host requires something of us—of you—before we're allowed to return. She knows everything...unfortunately," he grumbled.

Yes, she'd not forgotten what Agnetha had said. As she ate, Hypatia hoped her rescuer was not as treacherous as Otmar had been. But as she finished her stew, strength and energy returned to her, as if she'd finally slept well for several nights. She'd not felt so well in years.

"Gods, I feel—"

"I know. She assured me that was for free. But Hypatia, be warned, she's an enchantress. She can drag truths out of you with a single command."

A shiver rolled down her spine. Just what the day needed.

"Ah. Well, perhaps we should face our mercantile host."

Sigimar ushered her into the next room where Agnetha and Kosta were seated before a fire, chatting animatedly, eyes sparkling. Agnetha turned a smile their way and waved them over to a couch opposite theirs.

"Your charming brother and your doting husband have already told me all about your little adventures into Ashla. Given the dangers of what lies beneath the miasma, I've been trying to convince them to leave it be, but the kings of Elmheim and Gortos have made that impossible. If you wouldn't mind placing your hand upon this orb, Hypatia?"

Hypatia looked to Sigimar who grunted but nodded.

A blinding light emanated the moment her skin touched the cool crystal. Hypatia snatched it away. It took a moment for everyone's flash-blindness to abate.

"Gods below, that really is something." Agnetha laughed, wiping her eyes before she snared Hypatia in her bright green gaze. Her mind felt sluggish, pliant. No, not again. Just as before with that horrible song, her will was not her own. Oh gods, was this what Sigimar had meant by the power of an enchantress? *"Speak only the truth, Hypatia of Lethe. What will you do with the treasures of Ashla?"*

"Study them," she replied, compelled by her voice.

"And then?"

"I don't know. Perhaps they can help people."

The witch sighed, sitting back in her chair, cozying up to Kosta. Whatever spell she'd wrought had dissipated. Hypatia sat ramrod straight, heart galloping in her chest. The witch had the power of a silver-tongue!

"I apologise for that. You seem to be the one in charge of these two, so I had to be certain of your motives. I heard you want to dispel the miasma. With your talent, that might even be possible. But you may change your mind after you've heard what I have to say."

But it was not a matter of wanting to dispel the miasma or not. Erlendr had magically compelled Sigimar, had threatened to do the same to her. She reached out to grab Sigimar's arm, sighing in relief to see the marks on his wrists had gone. Thank the gods for small mercies. She supposed that he'd done exactly as Erlendr had demanded, and now he was a free man once more.

"It was not by choice that we went into Ashla. We were forced," Hypatia clarified. "And may very well be forced once more."

She found it hard to believe Erlendr would be satisfied with just one expedition, and as Agnetha had just made clear, Hypatia's magic would be the linchpin in any wild scheme to dispel the curse. With the fate of that expedition in doubt, as well as the safety of the amplifier they'd just unearthed, she was certain she would be forced to face the miasma and the draugar once more. Probably as soon as Erlendr discovered her whereabouts. A shiver rolled down her spine.

"That is far from ideal." Agnetha grimaced.

"Will you help us find another wellspring? Secure another amplifier?" Sigimar asked.

The blonde witch gave him the most curious stare.

"Wellspring? Amplifier? Gods, what ridiculous names. This is what happens when everyone forgets their history." Agnetha rolled her eyes and sighed before returning her attention to Hypatia. "I will try to be concise. When the Wild Hunt came to Oblivion, Ashla took in a great many refugees."

"The Wild Hunt?" Hypatia asked.

"You don't...gods below. The Wild Hunt is how the fae built Faerie—sacrificing the souls they captured on their hunt to create, sustain and grow their world. A world that rewards them with lands and powers over them. It's the same principle as how they create their pocket realms, writ large. Every self-important fae lacking in conscience got in on the hunt. A world without iron, one that could be bent to their will, was too much temptation for some. Using those staves you saw, they gathered up their victims' souls in order to feed them to Faerie. There is no afterlife for one violated in that manner, no reincarnation, nothing. They are gone. Everything they were, are, or could be, swallowed up by a world that shouldn't exist. That is the Wild Hunt."

"Oh…"

What could she say? Now the voices crying out made sense, the snatches of lives lived, the experiences that weren't hers that had flooded her mind and heart. There had been so many, pleading for relief, for freedom. Their pain had nearly driven her mad with the need to assuage it. How long had they been trapped? Suddenly, the stew wasn't sitting so well in her stomach.

"As I was saying, Ashla took in refugees aplenty. They could afford to, given their access to the Frey-devices, your 'amplifiers.' They were created by the people of Ashla in ancient times to help them grow great surpluses of crops, keep the people healthy, ward off bad weather, etcetera. Each could only amplify a single spell, but their powers could stretch that spell over the whole of Ashla."

"Really?" Hypatia perked up.

"Yes."

"Aha! Told you so!" Hypatia poked Sigimar in the side.

Sigimar grunted, putting a finger to her lips to shush her.

"Ahem. Are you done interrupting me?"

Hypatia kept her own counsel. If Agnetha could be believed, Hypatia had been right all along. Maybe that also meant she could stretch her healing light across the whole of Ashla? But how? Sigimar's lost amplifier—Frey-device—had only been able to spread a spell across a small part of Ashla. A question for another time. Agnetha continued her tale.

"As I was saying. The powers of just one Frey-device could stretch a single spell over the whole of Ashla—and when the threat of The Wild Hunt arose, they used these devices to protect the kingdom with defensive magic. The nine rulers of Ashla refused to believe The Wild Hunt would come to their doorstep, or breach their defences. Theirs were the wealthiest, healthiest, most powerful lands on the whole of Oblivion, a shining beacon in the dark, where all were welcome so long as they came in peace. You can see how well that worked out for them, no? Such arrogance," Agnetha scoffed, as if the outcome of history were a foregone conclusion. In Hypatia's experience, few who lived through extraordinary times believed the outcome of such upheaval was certain. "In any case, The Wild Hunt did come, and the invaders used several Frey-devices to catastrophic effect. They broke through the defensive spells, planting their staves in them so that their soul-sucking powers could be amplified instead. Six of the nine islands fell in the span of a day, every living thing collapsing in an instant, their souls ripped from their flesh and dragged to imprisonment within those amplified staves."

Hypatia felt ill. So many had suffered a fate worse than death. Even though she'd had her magic and soul stolen, she'd not been in pain. But the souls within the staves remained in agony all that time. Throat tight with emotion, she fought back tears. Did the greed of the hunters know no limits?

"Ah, but the dragon ruling over Ashla's central island was harder to fell than the others. When the fae invaders failed to control his Frey-device, he used it and his dying breath to lay a curse. One that would spread across the whole of Ashla and stop the Wild Hunt in its tracks."

"Corruption?" Hypatia asked.

"Yes. While the dragon king could not reclaim control of the lost Frey-devices, he could create a corruption curse—the miasma—to prevent The Wild Hunt from reclaiming those staves and the souls within to sacrifice to Faerie. And it worked. Few could fend off the taint of the curse, and as for those who did... well, perhaps they fled. But I suspect they never got the chance. Do you know what happens to a soulless body when the corruption latches onto it? Nothing, to about half. They simply collapse and eventually perish. The rest? Exactly what happens to those who are tainted yet live—except their transformation into draugar is instantaneous. A fitting end for the fae hunters, but a tragic one for the surviving people of Ashla."

Hypatia shivered. How had any survived such a tragedy? Even the trained warriors of Elmheim succumbed to draugar when outnumbered.

But Agnetha was not finished.

"And make no mistake, the Frey-devices are only one of the powerful, terrible things buried under the miasma. I admire your noble heart, Hypatia, but do you trust that everyone else on Oblivion will always put the good of others first? That they wouldn't use the power of the Frey-devices and other treasures for their own greedy ends, or worse? The dragon king thought he was saving his kingdom, and yet he sold his soul for a plague that has tormented Oblivion for ages, its only cure the same spell that can free the trapped souls within the staves. King Otmar seems to believe himself in the right, as his use of that Frey-device he stole from you means that Gortos is now protected by a spell that has ejected all his enemies from his realm.

Hypatia gasped, her wide-eyed gaze meeting Sigimar's. He ran a hand down his ashen face. What horrors would that monstrous man unleash on the Riverlands? What wasn't he capable of? Never mind Ashla, he could plunge the whole region into war. One that could allow the corruption and draugar to spread.

"Are you certain?" Hypatia asked, swallowing down bile.

"Yes." Agnetha grimaced.

"How did Otmar steal the amplifier from my keep?" Sigimar asked.

"The question you should be asking is *why*. A second Frey-device could be on its way to him as we speak, if our fears are correct and one of his surviving agents claimed the one you just uncovered. Gods only know what he plans on doing with them, but make no mistake, it will not be long before the rest of the Riverlands discovers what mighty force is protecting his kingdom. What do you suppose they'll do then?"

It was a fair question, and one to which she feared she knew the answer. Otmar had already proved that what lay beneath the soil of Ashla was a temptation some would happily kill to possess.

"I cannot in good conscience leave those souls trapped in the staves... but wisdom suggests we should leave it all buried." Much as Hypatia hated to admit it, she couldn't deny Agnetha's logic.

She'd been soulless herself once, and she would not wish it upon her worst enemy. Even in that state she'd been lucky. There was no corruption in Lethe. Her soul had not been in agony. At least, not that she recalled.

That aside, Hypatia burned with curiosity. So much good could be done with a single one of those Frey-devices. No more sickness. No more famine. Unprecedented prosperity was within the grasp of so many.

Yet so much harm had already been wrought. Countless generations had been lost to the struggle against the curse, beating it back. And now with one in the possession of a greedy king, inciting the envy of his neighbours, what fresh harm would come to pass?

Agnetha seemed pleased by her answer. Regrettably, Hypatia would have to disappoint her.

"Unfortunately, I fear it is already too late for wisdom to prevail. Though the souls are free of the stave we discovered, the Frey-device still rose from the ground. If Otmar's accomplices survived the battle and took that second device, it could very well be on its way to him already. With two devices, he could remain protected with the first and begin a war with the second."

CHAPTER 31

"And how do we know that any of what you say is true?" Sigimar asked. It wasn't as though any of them possessed the power of an enchantress, able to drag truths from someone with only a few words. A power she had used on all three of her guests. "I spent five hundred years pouring over every last ancient text and testimony in Elmheim about the history of Ashla, and never once did I find a tale as spectacular as yours."

It was inconceivable that such a history could be lost to time like that, not one as dramatic as she'd described. There were tales of the Wild Hunt plaguing much of Oblivion eons ago, but none had any connection to Ashla's curse. The long-lived elves had been in Elmheim since the miasma first arose and were often some of the most renowned chroniclers, their works copied and recopied over the ages to ensure their survival. If the enchantress were lying, what was her true aim?

Agnetha was not to be trusted.

"Whether you believe me or not is beside the point. With the south-eastern island fully uncovered, even a few days spent near where we bumped into each other could mean dangerous items falling into unworthy hands. With one Frey-device already in Otmar's hands and another potentially on its way to him, ensuring the miasma retakes Ashla is of paramount importance. We are simply lucky that the Frey-devices have a one-spell fail-safe. No doubt that, now Otmar has protected his realm, he will use the second for less savoury purposes."

Tall tales or not, at least that he could believe. But she was sorely mistaken if she thought things could remain as they'd always been.

Sigimar shook his head.

"There's no going back now. King Erlendr is desperate to end the corruption curse. Now that he knows it's possible, now that everyone knows it's possible, it's only a matter of time before Ashla is fully uncovered.

Erlendr would allow for nothing less. He loved Alfric in the same all-consuming way that Sigimar loved Hypatia. What wouldn't a man so stricken do to keep the one who held his heart by his side?

"Desperate?" Hypatia asked. "But why?"

"King Alfric. His vow as Elmheim's king prevents Erlendr from sharing his remaining years with him. Until the miasma is gone, he is not free to live or love as he chooses," Sigimar replied.

Hypatia placed her hand atop his and squeezed. She knew that desperation as well as Sigimar.

"Agnetha, do you know how the Frey-devices work?" Hypatia asked.

"Why do you ask?" She raised a pale brow.

"Maybe we don't need the miasma to protect the artefacts of Ashla. Could you use the Frey-devices to weave a spell? One that prevents misuse of the artefacts and staves? Or even prevents them from being found at all by those with ill intentions?"

"Perhaps. The idea has merit, but to do so would be exceedingly dangerous." She frowned.

"Dangerous is waiting to see what Otmar does with a second of those devices," Sigimar grunted.

That was the immediate danger. The staves and the souls within them were still deep in Ashla's interior. The second amplifier could be in Otmar's hands already. Given the tensions already brewing in the Riverlands, war could spark at any moment.

"Yes, Otmar has always been a right bastard. Understandable, given his history. All his children were lost to senseless war. No wonder he refused to cede the last of his line, his daughter, to Elmheim. But he has never been the most creative thinker. Crafty, certainly. That you sit here rather than Farohildis is proof of that." She nodded at Hypatia. "But how did he manage to get his fingers into Ashla?"

A curious thing that. It seemed Erlendr had spies in his court. Spies so highly placed that they could ensure one of Otmar's warriors made it onto a secret mission into the heart of Ashla. Sigimar should have buried the portal the moment he'd arrived. Alfric was right. The damned things would cause greater problems than they solved.

"Someone let him in," Kosta groaned. "Just like Father."

"Just so, dearest." Agnetha smiled at Kosta. "Luckily, the forgotten gods have smiled upon you. For I am rather skilled at gaining information." Agnetha turned to Sigimar then. "Now, Jarl Sigimar, perhaps you would be so kind as to invite your saviour to your home?"

No doubt her powers would be useful to him. But what use were the lot of them to her? Agnetha could walk into any realm, any castle, with a few words. She'd survived in tunnels below draugar-infested Ashla without anyone's help. Strictly speaking, she didn't need anyone else's help.

"Not until you tell us what you want," Sigimar replied warily.

"Only what belongs to me, my elvish friend. You interrupted me before I could retrieve it last time. With your magic," she nodded at Hypatia, "your strength," she nodded at Sigimar, "and your stunningly useful skill," she purred at Kosta, "that should be no problem."

"You think I'm useful?" Kosta asked, a smile of delight on his face.

"The only way you could be more useful, dearest, is if you possessed portalling magic, but even then, I wouldn't want to risk your precious life draining you of the blood to do it. Teleportation is much safer."

Sigimar sighed as Kosta puffed up with pride, fairly preening with the woman's praise. There was no doubt in his mind that this enchantress, and possible sorceress, had the power to stymy their return if she so pleased. If they failed to return to Ashla, there was no telling what the news of their disappearance would do to the people of Elmheim, or to Erlendr's growing desperation. If they didn't find Otmar's second thief, another precious amplifier would be lost, if it weren't already. He shuddered to think what the rapacious fae king would do with a second device, or any of the other treasures of Ashla. As much as he hesitated to trust Agnetha, and as little as he believed her motives, her smile told him she knew as well as he that they had little choice.

"So be it. Swear you will do us no harm, and I will agree to take you to Ashla. Or Kosta will, given he will transport us."

"*I so swear*," she replied, eyes flashing.

Sigimar smiled at Hypatia, one he knew would not reach his eyes. "Shall we face the nightmares again?"

Hypatia took his hand in hers, nodding, resolute.

Pride and panic in equal measure gripped him. Sigimar fought to keep his composure. He couldn't lose her. Some dark, inescapable abyss waited for him, threatening to swallow him whole in her absence. If it were up to him, he would spend the next year simply holding her, assuring the frightened child inside him that she was here, alive, whole and unharmed.

But such needs could not be attended to in times like these. He had to settle for holding her hand as they left the warmth of the enchantress' cottage for the whipping winter winds of the world outside. All three passengers held onto a part of Kosta and braced for the ride. Teleportation would cause less of a scene than coming through the portal and prevent questions about how they'd accessed it.

Between one breath and the next, he was surrounded by white walls veined in gold and silver, all of it spinning along with his senses. But this was no serene or happily bustling place. Chaos reigned. Once he had his footing, Sigimar found his home turned upside down.

Beyond the one spot in the tower forbidden to any but Kosta for the sake of his teleportation, a panicked cacophony drowned out the sound of their arrival. Harried personnel loaded crates onto platforms to be magically lifted, managers and guards yelled orders, artefacts clashed and clanged as they were strewn across the floors. Others openly wept.

They'd not arrived ahead of the news of their failure. But the moment the people buzzing about saw him and Hypatia, they rushed forward with tears in their eyes, a cry going up.

He and Hypatia did their best to calm the crowd. They had pressing matters to see to.

"Where are Ingi and Drest?" Sigimar asked in a booming voice.

"Here, Jarls!" Drest cut through the crowd, shoulders sagging with relief. "We thought you'd died! The only survivor to make it back said you'd perished along with the others, and that the amplifier couldn't be found."

Lies. But it was possible the survivor was innocent of Otmar's treachery. Both he and Hypatia had fallen into a hole, and, if the spy had managed to recover from his injuries and steal the amplifier during the chaos, then the survivor could have been telling what they assumed to be the truth. Though at this point, coincidences were not to be trusted.

"Where is the survivor now?" he asked, hoping they'd not yet escaped his grasp.

"He left for Elmheim not long ago."

Of course he had. Sigimar cursed.

"Jarl Sigimar! Jarl Hypatia! Thank the gods you're both safe!" Ingi pushed through the crowd, his eyes red-rimmed. "We're evacuating as quickly as we can. One of the nymphs warned us a storm is coming that might test what little remains of the magic protecting us. If you'll come this way, we'll send you through immediately. You can tell the kings what's happened when you arrive."

Sigimar shook his head.

"We have to do something first. Drest, Ingi, come with me. The rest of you, keep evacuating. Bring as much as you can, but don't risk your lives for anything here."

Sigimar pulled the shapeshifters into the room he'd come from, shutting out the curious, awe-struck others. Agnetha seemed lost in thought, running her fingers over the intricate designs on the walls of their small room. In order to ensure everyone's safety, it was kept permanently empty, not a single soul allowed inside, so that if Kosta had to teleport, there would be no danger to him or whoever he brought with him.

"And who are you?" Ingi asked of the enchantress.

"Oh, no one in particular. You may call me Agnetha." She sized up the two newcomers, her penetrating gaze falling on Drest. "A dragon?"

"How perceptive of you." Drest bowed.

"*Did you allow Otmar's people into Ashla?*"

Drest bared his teeth, grunting and growling, fighting to keep his mouth shut.

"Just answer her, Drest," Sigimar sighed. Later he would offer the man a tankard and tell him how impressed he was that the dragon could defy the enchantress at all. Then again, dragons were naturally immune to the magic of others, so long as their hearts weren't wounded. "No one believes you're working with Otmar. We're just being thorough."

"*Answer me.*" Agnetha's eyes flashed, a sudden pressure catching Sigimar by surprise and sending everyone to their knees.

"Yes," Drest hissed.

Sigimar's chest hollowed out, every heartbeat laced with pain. After all their years together, all the trust he'd placed in him, the moments of weakness he'd shared, all of it lies! All the suffering, the death, the danger Hypatia had been subjected to! Only luck had saved them from death.

"You WHAT?!" Sigimar roared.

"Be still."

He strained to be free of the enchantress' hold, letting rage take him. Dragon or no, Sigimar would kill the bastard. Agnetha's pitying gaze only goaded him on. He fought with all his might, and yet he remained immobile, glaring at the traitor who'd dared call himself friend.

As his heart hammered in his ears, he swallowed down his rage. Agnetha wouldn't free him in his current state. Nor should she. His anger had done enough harm already. He could not become a better man if he only ever reached for that poison. And yet he could not stop the accusations that flew from his lips.

"I trusted you! *We* trusted you! With our lives! Only luck saved us, you bastard! This is your fucking fault!"

Ingi palmed a hidden dagger, ready to sink it into Drest's heart.

"Stop."

The command froze everyone, but it didn't stop the pain pumping through his veins. Sigimar's eyes bored into Drest's, bile rising up. He'd never been so thoroughly betrayed. Had everything been a lie? Had he never once been the true friend Sigimar had thought him? Had the dragon looked at him with disgust rather than compassion all this time? Agnetha put a hand on his shoulder, guiding and then sitting him down some distance away, a puppet to her will.

"If you cannot play nicely, then you'll be asked to sit in the corner. There is much left to uncover, my elvish friend, and I'm confident I can keep our traitorous dragon well and truly contained. Now, shall we settle in for a nice, long chat?"

Lips freed, Sigimar grit his teeth. Damn it all, the enchantress was right.

"Fine."

"Very good." She twirled a finger, summoning a plush couch. "Come now, no one said interrogation need be uncomfortable."

All but Drest and Ingi stumbled, freed from the weight of Agnetha's power. Hypatia ran up to Sigimar, throwing her arms around him, eyes full of understanding. If only his heart could be mended as easily as cuts and bruises.

"Sigimar..." She cupped his face, eyes asking the question she dared not utter in front of their audience. He was grateful for that. There would be time for grief later.

He kissed her hand, not trusting his words quite yet. She led him to the couch and settled beside him.

Agnetha turned Ingi's frozen form to face her and repeated the same question. Sigimar only prayed Ingi proved to be who he'd always assumed.

"*Did you allow Otmar's people into Ashla?*"

"No."

"*Did you send any artefacts to Otmar?*"

"No."

"*Are you beholden to Otmar in any way?*"

"No."

"Is this sufficient for you?" Agnetha asked them.

Sigimar nodded, as did Hypatia. Ingi was released from Agnetha's spell and proceeded to glare daggers at Drest.

"Now, my new dragon acquaintance, would you like to be forthright, or shall I drag truths from your lips?" Agnetha turned the dragon so that he stood upright, a prisoner of her magical restraints. By the grimace on his face, the feel of her direct magic was a great deal less pleasant than that of many witches.

"I will tell you all," Drest choked. "But please, whatever you do to me, please save Sara."

"What does Sara have to do with any of this?" Sigimar asked.

"What do you mean, save her? She was one of the first sent back to Elmheim. You ushered her through the portal yourself," Ingi added.

"I made a deal with Otmar for two dragon hearts right after you met with him. He was the only sovereign in the Riverlands who would take the risk, knowing otherwise he wouldn't get a single artefact of his own. You'd threatened him that he would get nothing, so he was receptive to my offer. It would only have been a few things, two of hundreds just collecting dust," Drest explained.

Sigimar clicked his tongue.

"If you'd told me any of this, I would have helped you, Drest! Why would you do such a thing? Especially when eating hearts is what got you banished to Elmheim in the first place!"

"How did you even speak with him?" Hypatia asked.

Drest seemed so small in that moment. No longer a dragon of frightening size. No longer a creature with scales, teeth and fiery breath. He was just a man before Sigimar, one consumed by panic, as powerless as any man in the face of a cruel twist of fate.

"The dragon's eye crystal. Otmar has one, too. To save Sara's life, and to save our child's, I need those hearts. No one knows if she'll be strong enough to survive the birth. Witches often have trouble birthing shapeshifter children, but Sara is human! She has none of a witch's innate magical strengths. And our child...they will inherit my illness. A dragon's heart would cure our child's illness and could save Sara's if the pregnancy endangers her life," Drest said.

Ah gods. Sigimar looked to Hypatia then. What wouldn't he do to protect her if she were with child? He understood now. Gods, did he ever. But it only dulled the sting of betrayal a fraction.

Agnetha sighed, a sad, sympathetic sound.

"Wing rot."

"Yes," Drest whispered. "It's a death sentence. Unless one can consume a dragon's heart. I offered Otmar cursed weapons first, sent them along with a small crew, but they never made it."

"Why would he want weapons tainted by the corruption curse?" Hypatia asked.

"Otmar possesses the healing light, much like you. He would have nothing to fear. But he didn't get them. He started demanding more, for the hearts and for his silence. But nothing I offered him would placate him, not until he learned of the amplifier."

"You gave him ours!" Hypatia gasped. "But you knew what would happen!"

"I know, damn it! But Sara is due any day now! They could both die! I couldn't let that happen."

"So you fed my wife and me to the miasma instead!" Sigimar shouted.

Sigimar ran a hand through his tangled mane. No, that wasn't fair. It was not Drest who had used the power of the ancient pact to force them into the gloom.

"How could I know Erlendr would send you off on some fucking death march?! I thought we would all relocate to Elmheim, and this nightmare would be over!" Drest yelled back.

Exactly the same as Sigimar had assumed. No one could have known what lengths Erlendr would drive them all to.

"So why did you let Otmar's assassin through the portal?" Hypatia asked. "You'd already given him what he wanted."

Thank the gods Hypatia was being more level-headed than he. Where he was swept away with the tide, she was his rock, a beacon in the storm.

"He found out about the stave. I don't know how. But he said he wanted it for the second heart. I thought I was sending a thief along, not a murderer, I swear!"

"He wants the souls, or failing that, the stave." Agnetha answered the next question before anyone could ask it, her tone dark and foreboding. She rose from her seat and stalked toward Drest, each step laced with the promise of pain. "Did he get them?"

"I don't know about the souls, but the stave had been fractured into three pieces When I sent his thief through with the amplifier and the stave, I expected to get the hearts in return."

"He wouldn't have, Agnetha. All the souls were freed before the people turned on each other," Hypatia said.

Their blood was on Drest's hands, on Otmar's, on Erlendr's. And, if Sigimar listened to the dark whispers in his head, his, too. All of them were driven to protect the ones they loved, no matter the flawed or twisted method—no matter the consequences. Gods below.

"How did you slip past my guard rotations?" Ingi grouched.

"I packed the artefacts in with some of the crates already waiting to be sent over. Our people delivered them to Elmheim, and one of Otmar's was supposed to take them from there," Drest answered. "But then one of his people took Sara. Otmar said if I didn't get him another stave, he would kill her. If she dies, so will I."

"You love her?" Agnetha asked.

"Yes."

"I'm sorry," the enchantress said, not without sympathy.

"I don't need your pity!"

"I understand you love her, but aren't you being a little melodramatic?" Kosta asked before thinking better of it. Several sets of eyes sent him censorious looks. "What?"

"No, dearest, he is being quite literal. To kill a dragon is no easy feat. Their scales repel magic, they grow to a frightful size, and when they change shape, they can overcome nearly any injury. To kill a dragon, you must break their heart," Agnetha explained.

"Gods below," Hypatia whispered.

Drest bowed his head as best he could while snared in Agnetha's restraints, tears coursing down his cheeks.

"I will take whatever punishment you see fit, but please save Sara. She doesn't know what I've done, and she's in terrible danger."

"I'm sorry, but I cannot allow you to give Otmar what he seeks," Agnetha replied.

"Sara and my child will die!" Drest protested, fighting his magical bonds.

"Two lives are not worth the souls of millions!" Agnetha shouted, her power shaking the very tower itself.

Nothing had so much as scratched the outer walls of the tower in all the time it lay buried beneath the ground, nor when it rose from the depths. To hold a desperate dragon still and shake a tower immune to damage required unthinkable powers. Sigimar readied himself to flee, securing an arm around Hypatia's midsection. He would haul her like a sack of grain if need be. There was no doubt in his mind. Enchantress most certainly. That she could command with a single word was proof of that, but Agnetha must also be a sorceress. No mere enchantress had such awe-inspiring magical might, or the self-assurance to face a dragon without hesitation. After all, no matter what kind of death faced her, a sorceress would be reborn from her own ashes.

With a remarkable lack of self-preservation, Kosta approached Agnetha, a hand on her shoulder and a placating smile on his face.

"We won't let him get what he wants. But maybe we can make him think he will?"

The tower settled as Agnetha let Kosta hold her, whispering endearments all the while. Had Kosta tamed a sorceress? Gods help them all.

"Otmar expected me to fly into the miasma to fetch him one. I only just managed to convince him to wait until everyone evacuates."

"Which will take how long?" Sigimar asked.

"A day, two at most," Ingi answered.

Two days to plan a rescue mission, or to leave Drest out to dry and sentence an innocent woman and the child she carried to death in the process.

Or, two days to plan another trip into the miasma and pray they all survived it.

Sigimar put his head in his hands.

"Fuck."

CHAPTER 32

The shouting was getting them no closer to a solution. The only thing it did was give Hypatia a headache.

Though Drest remained bound by Agnetha's power, that didn't mean he'd remained mute during the contentious debate still bouncing off the walls of the small antechamber. Sigimar was torn between giving Drest to the kings to punish, and simply banishing him from Ashla. Under no circumstances did Sigimar want to go marching back into the miasma after they'd so narrowly escaped death. Hypatia's cowardice tended to agree. Except she knew Drest would do anything to get Sara back safe, and, short of killing him, there was not much any of them could do to ultimately stop him. Dragons were some of the few beings who could fly into the miasma and survive the curse.

Ingi wanted to return to Elmheim and convince the kings to send out another mission come Spring. It was the most rational course of action but would only delay the inevitable—facing the miasma once more. Sara would almost certainly die, and there was no guarantee the people of Elmheim wouldn't lose all hope, or that Otmar or another sovereign wouldn't slip more spies and thieves into Ashla. With two amplifiers already stolen, it was only a matter of time before the other monarchs of the Riverlands set their sights on getting one, or more, of their own.

Agnetha wanted to save the souls within the staves, even if it meant ploughing unprepared into the heart of the miasma. Given the threat of

Otmar's greed, she was willing to risk it all—as soon as possible. But she cared naught for Sara, Drest, Elmheim or dispelling the curse.

Between the heated threats, insults and screaming matches, Hypatia was mostly unnoticed as she walked to the tall window and pressed her forehead to the cool glass. Kosta joined her, his dark grey eyes full of concern.

"Reminds you of home, right?"

Hypatia snorted.

"Mother and Father never argued over anything quite so grand in scale. The most serious thing they ever fought over was who should drive the Diamond chariots in the Hippodrome."

"Simpler days, those. I must admit, I'd assumed I'd spend my life stumbling from one sticky situation to another. I guess I wasn't wrong. Just thought those situations would be a touch less dire." He smiled wryly.

"We've always been rather good at that—getting into trouble."

"And getting out of it! We've both been rather good at that, too."

"You are, at least. You could always wish yourself somewhere better. I was always left to apologise in your stead, you big lout." She smacked his arm.

"Don't complain! If I hadn't left you holding the bag, you would never have learned how to turn invisible."

"Ass."

"Bookworm."

That surprised a smile out of her. It was short-lived. Kosta pressed a hand to the glass, all joviality gone.

"Do you think...if we go back in there, we'll make it out?" he asked, eyes on the horizon.

Dark despite the early hour, a blizzard howled outside. A storm that would blow the miasma back into their corner of Ashla, choking the life from everything that had managed to hold on in this unforgiving place.

"I don't know. I'm afraid of losing everyone I love if we do go."

"Mmm," Kosta agreed. "But I'm afraid if we don't, that nasty elf king is going to force you into it, the same as he did your husband. And unlike in Lethe, we can't just pretend you're dead to escape."

She feared he was quite correct. The love Erlendr had for Alfric would drive him towards the deed, whether it was next season, next year, or next decade. Even Agnetha had pronounced Hypatia's the strongest light she'd ever seen. Erlendr would be a foolish leader not to use Hypatia in every way possible.

"You could leave though, Kosta. I wouldn't be upset if you did. I would prefer it, actually."

"You don't want me here?" he asked, hurt.

"No, not that. I don't want you to die here."

Not if he didn't have to. She'd lost him once already, stood by as an empty urn had been placed in the mausoleum. She'd had no power to save him then, had been incapable of convincing him to go against their father. The thought of attending his funeral again was too much for her to bear. Kosta put a hand on her shoulder.

"All the more reason I should stay. I...I didn't stand up for you before. I didn't help you and I should've. I ran when you needed me and I'm sorry for that. I've always been a coward. Everyone knows it. But this time...this time I don't want to be. If you were brave, I can be too. I should have saved you before Father...you know. Or at least, I should've taken you to the emperor to ask for help. He was always nice to me. In any case, this time, I'm going with you, to be your ride to safety if you need it. I won't muck it up again."

She hadn't realised how much she'd needed to hear those words. He was the only family member to have ever apologised to her. And if he were committed to going back into the miasma, it gave her that much more courage to do so herself.

"Thank you, Kosta."

She touched a hand to her belly. If her suspicions were correct, she had another reason not to let the miasma linger. Hypatia sighed. She knew what she should do. She'd known it the moment she'd freed the souls from their prison. It was the right thing to do—the brave one. The most dangerous one, too.

"Agnetha?" Hypatia asked, as she inserted herself into the middle of the verbal melee.

"What?" the witch snapped.

"If we were to do what we discussed in your home, how many Frey-devices would you need uncovered for my magic to dispel all of the miasma?"

"With your power amplified by some of mine? One. Ashla's central tower was secretly made to be the master of them all. But it would leave the staves in danger of getting snatched—by Otmar or his lackey." She pointed accusingly at Drest.

"If the solution were so straightforward, why has it never been done before now?" Ingi asked.

Agnetha speared him with a withering look.

"Firstly, Hypatia is the only one I have ever encountered with healing light strong enough to pull this off. Second, the few who were left alive after the miasma first arose were busy fleeing for their lives, or defending against hordes of draugar. By the time the Riverlands had recovered enough to contemplate more than mere survival, thousands of years had passed, and the knowledge of the towers, the Frey-devices, and much besides, had been lost, replaced by the certainty that the miasma must have been a divine curse." Agnetha sighed, rolling her eyes. "Even if it worked, the staves would still be there, waiting for the next unscrupulous thief to snatch them and fill them with souls. It would also mean travelling into the heart of Ashla where the curse was first laid."

"How is that any different than what we've already done?" Hypatia asked.

"I told you, a dragon ruled in the heart of Ashla."

"And? What does that signify?" Hypatia quirked a brow.

"Must I spell it out?" she huffed. "It *means* that when the miasma first arose, there were a great number of dragons on the island, dragons who were made soulless and their bodies corrupted by the curse. They'll still be there, as big or bigger than they ever were in life. I've seen what becomes of the bodies of soulless sorcerers who were left to roam the miasma all these years—true horrors, absorbing the bodies of creatures they devoured, becoming more monstrous with every meal. The cursed dragons will be worse."

Hypatia hid her shaking hands in her skirts, back ramrod straight, lest she give into tremors. Gods below. Was she really asking to go back into those horrors? To face curse-riddled dragons that could swallow her whole? There would be no hiding behind a shield wall, no careful battle manoeuvres to keep her safe.

"I could help," Drest offered.

"You mean help yourself," Agnetha hissed.

"As if anyone here could trust you!" Sigimar shouted at Drest.

"This is all a moot point," Ingi cut in. "If you're speaking the truth, Drest, Otmar believes the jarls are dead. When he learns they're alive—and trust me, word will have already reached Askr by now—there's no telling what he'll do, especially if he suspects you've been compromised. If the jarls don't arrive in Askr with the rest, he'll get suspicious that you're plotting with them against him, and Sara will die. If the lot of you wish to dispel the curse and save the woman, you'll have to be more cunning than that."

Hypatia took a deep breath and willed her hands to still, her heart to slow. She needed to be logical about this. She couldn't lose her head to fear. There would be time for that later. If she were so lucky.

"Alright, so our problems are these: first, Sigimar and I must be in Askr long enough for word to reach Otmar of our safety, and that we don't intend on going back into Ashla anytime soon. The second issue is that we must get to the heart of Ashla."

"And survive the dragons," Sigimar added, fists clenched.

Hypatia placed a hand on his, providing a semblance of reassurance she herself did not feel.

"*And* that, in order to lift the curse. To do that, we must free the souls from the staves. Then, Agnetha must connect the remaining Frey-devices together, and send my magic to them to dispel the rest of the miasma. Once that's done, Agnetha must then work a spell to prevent the theft of the staves and other artefacts before Otmar or anyone else can get to them. We rescue Sara, and then destroy all the staves."

"A perfectly succinct list," Kosta replied, sidling up to Hypatia. "And I have an idea for the first problem. We ask two of your fae friends working here in the tower to glamour themselves into looking like you and Sigimar and go to Askr in your stead."

"They can do that?" Hypatia asked.

"No, not well enough to fool everyone." Sigimar shook his head.

"Well, anyone can if they use the right spell...and the right ingredients." Agnetha shrugged. "And if you mean to free the souls and destroy the staves thereafter, I can take you into the heart of Ashla, connect the Frey-devices, and then protect the land from thieves."

"If you swear to save Sara, then I will make a vow to protect you from the dragons, and not to touch a single stave until the souls are freed," Drest added.

"Then all that's left is to deal with Otmar, to make him come to us with Sara." Hypatia nodded.

Silence.

Hypatia frowned. What reason would he have for risking a journey, rather than staying safely ensconced in his keep and letting everyone else dance to his whims? The Riverlands were already riled up, provoking him for his treatment of Sigimar. A wise king would not come to them.

Indeed, he'd already secured himself the first amplifier, protecting his lands from his enemies. With a second on the way to him, why would he venture forth?

"Lure him out. He wants one of those staves? That's our bait," Sigimar began. "When we dispel the miasma, you contact him to trade—the stave for Sara and the hearts. He won't know that the souls have been freed and that the stave has been destroyed." Sigimar looked to Drest.

Ingi shook his head.

"These are all fine ideas, but they require everything to go flawlessly. What if the disguises are dispelled? What if Otmar sends a proxy or strings Drest along? One mishap and someone dies," Ingi replied. "Jarl Hypatia's magic is more powerful than any seen in recorded history. If what you say is true, Agnetha, then she is the only one who has ever had a chance of completely dispelling the miasma in thousands of years. If she dies in this endeavour, it will be chaos. When the kings thought you'd died, riots broke out across Askr, and the jarls threatened to convene a Thing to dethrone Erlendr. While some of you may not care about the political ramifications," Ingi eyed Agnetha tellingly, "that turmoil would allow Otmar or his people to slip into Elmheim and Ashla to do as they please—with anything they can steal from Ashla."

Ingi was right, of course. Any plan of this complexity was bound to run into trouble somewhere. Hypatia's stomach knotted.

"Then what do you suggest?" Hypatia asked.

Ingi began pacing, his ears twitching all the while.

"The decoys are a good idea. But even with bait, there's no guarantee Otmar will come, or that he will bring Sara for a fair trade. Light a fire under him. Once the people have been relocated, Drest should tell Otmar he's been discovered, but that he's also on his way to claim one of the staves. Tell him Erlendr knows what Otmar has done, that he knows how to deactivate the amplifier from afar, and that he plans to marshal the Riverlands against him for violating the ancient pact. The stave is a relic of the Wild Hunt, which he seems to know. His only recourse would be to use it to flee to Faerie where even one of them would ensure he continues to live as a king. For that reason, I doubt he'll come with his warriors. Whoever offers the souls to Faerie is the one who will be rewarded, and I doubt he'll risk letting anyone else get those rewards. In the meantime, someone will have to inform Erlendr, but only after the plan has been set in motion. If nothing else, his arrival could be a fail-safe against Otmar, the dragons, and everything else in Ashla."

"That can't happen before we've set out. And not before someone secures our contracts from Erlendr. We can't let him bind us in blood again and force us back if we're in the middle of a fight," Sigimar added.

"Then I will go to Askr," Ingi sighed.

"Why you?" Sigimar asked.

"I did not come to Elmheim willingly, Jarl. I was banished here for thievery. A great deal of it, in fact. I can also play your part in this deception, if Agnetha can do the spell work."

Hypatia blinked in surprise. The officious, meticulous Ingi, a thief? Though a shock, she supposed his experience would be of great assistance now.

"*If?*" Agnetha asked, affronted.

"But how will Erlendr, Otmar or anyone get to us once we reach our destination?" Hypatia asked.

Agnetha sighed, lips thinned in a grimace.

"A portal. For good or ill, there's one near our destination," Agnetha admitted. "I'll give you the coordinates once we leave. I trust your King Erlendr has someone who can navigate?"

"He does," Ingi replied.

"Otmar will have no difficulty getting to wherever we go. His wife, Asta, can use portalling magic if she must," Drest added. "But she'll still need us to give her the exact coordinates of Agnetha's portal in order to allow Asta to connect to it, lest she risk portalling directly into a draugr's stomach."

"When Otmar arrives, I can make short work of him. But what of the matter of timing?" Agnetha asked.

"Drest will have to carry the dragon's eye crystal with him. I can contact him once I've secured the contracts. After the souls have been freed and the miasma dealt with, Drest can contact both Otmar and Erlendr with his crystal," Ingi replied.

Agnetha laughed.

"You must have been quite the thief."

Ingi's ears twitched, but he kept his counsel.

Gods below, this was really happening. Another mad journey into the miasma, this one more dangerous than the last. So much could go wrong. Hypatia's heart thundered in her ears.

Hypatia took Sigimar's hand in her own. Grey eyes met amber. She knew he hated the idea of going back as much as she, but they'd be forced to eventually. Fate seemed to have dealt them this card. It was up to them to choose how to play it. He squeezed her hand, saying with his pained expression what he'd said many times before. Neither of them wanted to face a world without the other. Unfortunately, caution was not in the cards.

"Together?" she asked.

"Together."

Hypatia sat in front of a vanity as Agnetha brushed her hair. Ten to fifteen strands would do, she'd said, the ingredients for the spell. Brynja had volunteered to play pretend with Ingi in Askr long enough for him to steal their contracts—and inform the kings of their whereabouts at the right time should Drest fail. The healer was preoccupied opening crates trying to find one with a few of Hypatia's dresses to wear.

"Do you know?" Agnetha asked, her voice hushed.

"Know what?" Hypatia asked, heart thundering in her ears.

What ominous things could Agnetha have to tell her now?

"It's early stages yet. Very early." Agnetha nodded at her belly.

Oh gods, then her suspicions had been correct. Excitement warred with terror. A gift, and one given at the worst of times. The future she'd wanted with Sigimar was within her grasp, but only if she lived long enough to seize it.

"I suspected. Please, don't say anything."

"My lips are sealed. This early and there's no guarantees. But I thought you should know before we…"

"It's because I suspected that I'm going, if you must know."

"Oh?" Agnetha raised her pale brows.

"I cannot leave this curse for my…well, it wouldn't be right to pass on the burden, not when I can do something about it. Not when I can leave the world a better place. I know that makes me sound heroic, but I'm really not. I'm a coward. If I thought I could run, I probably would."

Ah, if only such a thing would save her from what was sure to come. If Sigimar knew, he would positively forbid her from venturing out. Maybe even Erlendr would relent. But that would just delay the inevitable, or ensure another generation would be forced to fight the miasma. Her child would no doubt be among them. As terrified as she was, she couldn't fathom asking it of a child.

Agnetha paused in her ministrations, catching and holding Hypatia's gaze in the mirror. She squeezed her shoulder, eyes fierce.

"That doesn't make you a coward. It makes you intelligent. You know what we call a supposed hero who dies before they do something heroic? A fool."

"I suppose we'll find out which we'll be soon enough."

Agnetha nodded.

"I noticed something earlier." She jerked her chin to one of the open crates. "There's a stave in there, one of ancient design. A fair sight more impressive than any you've used, I'd wager. It will be extremely useful to you when we go into the miasma. I suggest you take it. All I ask is that when this is over, you give it to me. Mine is in the tunnels where your husband first made my acquaintance."

If that was all the powerful woman wished of her, then it was a small thing to give.

"I think that's fair."

Agnetha resumed brushing her hair. It reminded Hypatia of days long gone, of kind-faced servants and simpler, smaller problems. How to avoid the next party? How to escape the next marriage proposal? How best to slink away to read her books? *That* Hypatia was such a distant memory now, it seemed like the life of a woman wholly unrelated to her. Her fears had been so laughable, her dreams so ordinary. And yet she could still smell the expensive perfume, feel the glide of silk along her skin, the tiny bird in her chest throwing itself against the gilded bars of her cage, begging for freedom. Lulled into another life, Agnetha's next words startled her.

"Oh, and Hypatia?"

"Yes?"

"Bring a sharp blade."

Hypatia frowned. If her last experience were any indication, she would be entirely useless with a blade in hand, no matter how diligently Sigimar had attempted to train her.

"I'm not sure I'd know how to wield one."

"Not for the creatures. For yourself. Better to die by your own hand than to be devoured."

"Oh..."

Hypatia's gut sank. She gripped the skirts at her navel.

Please, gods, let me keep this child. Let us all live.

"And with that, I think we have enough for the spell. Brynja, was it? Let's get to work."

CHAPTER 33

"We do *not* act like that," Hypatia pronounced.

"Brynja is going to ruin this entire plan," Sigimar grumbled.

Sigimar looked on with increasing concern as both Ingi and Brynja had been transformed by Agnetha's spell. They'd donned whatever spare clothes had remained strewn about the ancient tower and made their way through the portal with all due fanfare—and a giant heaping dose of overacting. His ears heated watching the two of them fall over each other, fawning and sighing and touching. It was obvious Ingi and Brynja were having a laugh at his expense. Sigimar *was* openly affectionate, but the pair of them acted like they were only a heartbeat away from running into the nearest room to pounce on each other. Clearly, his subordinates didn't know him *that* well.

If they kept it up, they would endanger the whole plan with their comically obscene display.

Kosta scoffed, a hand on both Hypatia's shoulder and Sigimar's before he teleported them away. The bright, sparkling hues of the ancient tower vanished, replaced by the dim, cramped cottage Agnetha called home.

"What in the gods unknowable names are you talking about? That was tame. Some of us attended your *wedding*," Kosta piped up.

"We will never speak of it," Hypatia retorted.

Sigimar did his best to cover the bubble of laughter that threatened to escape at her pique. Now *that* was a day to remember. He supposed, as they marched to certain doom yet again, that they'd had that at least.

Standing in the main room of Agnetha's cottage, the enchantress rummaged about in the other room for the supplies she believed they would need. Any offer of help was quickly shooed away, lest any one of them misplace something in her disorganised heap.

Without something to keep himself busy, anxieties worried at Sigimar. The future was not guaranteed. He'd begged the gods for another chance to tell this woman he loved her, that she was his world. Wasting it would be a sin.

"Hypatia."

"Yes?"

He took her hands in his, rubbing his thumbs over her knuckles, drinking in the sight of her. She was a gift.

"I want you to know, before we do this, that meeting you, being with you, has made me the happiest I've ever been. I love you."

"Oh, Sigimar."

Her eyes misted with tears.

"That! *That!* For the love of the gods, do that where I don't have to watch it!"

"Kosta?" Hypatia raised a brow.

"Yes?"

"Shut up." She scowled at her brother as he wandered off to help Agnetha with their supplies. Sigimar noticed Kosta wasn't shooed away. "And Sigimar?" He turned back to Hypatia. "I love you too. I wouldn't trade my time with you for anything in the whole of Oblivion."

"Not even a way out of this mess?"

"No, not even that." She bit her lip, as if there was more she wished to say. He waited. He would always wait. "And when this is over, there is something I want to discuss with you."

"And you can't say it now?"

"No, I...no. But it is a good thing. So consider it something to look forward to."

Sigimar nodded.

"And what is that stave you brought along? A decoy?"

"Oh, no. Though I suppose it can serve in a pinch. Agnetha said it will magnify my light and use less of my magic at the same time. More powerful than those we first brought into Ashla. Given the size of what we're fighting..." She trailed off. Hypatia picked it up from where it had leaned against the wall, her grip on the gleaming gold and pearl stave white-knuckle.

Sometimes he forgot he wasn't the only one doing his best not to panic.

"I will be there. I won't leave your side."

Hypatia nodded.

"And you're not the only one who's bringing a shiny new toy." He flashed her the blade of his new axe. Another piece of treasure Agnetha had spotted lying about in one of the tower's hoards. He was more convinced than ever that she was no simple witch, not even just an enchantress. "As for our overly knowledgeable companion," he nodded at the woman, "be wary. I don't think she is what she seems."

"Oh, you think so too? It seems very strange to me that she was there when we needed her most and that she knows everything we need to know. I could swear I recognise her from somewhere, too. But so far, she seems to be an ally."

"That could change," Sigimar warned her.

Hypatia nodded, leaning in.

"Do you think...she was there? When the miasma first arose?" she whispered.

"Either that, or she knew someone who was."

Or Agnetha was the most well-informed woman in the whole of Oblivion. She'd known with a single glance what every artefact lying about the tower was capable of. But if she'd been alive since the miasma first arose, that would make her as old as some demi-gods. The thought sent a shot of unease through him. He didn't know what he should fear more: Agnetha, or this scheme to dispel the miasma for good.

"I would love to question her about it. When else does one get a view directly into such an ancient past?"

The sparkle in her eyes brought a smile to his lips. She adjusted her small satchel, as if she wished to reach for the book inside, itching for a chance to write down her theories. Always, she brought light wherever she went.

"My scholar wife returns."

"I never left." Hypatia smiled. Her grip on her stave had loosened. "What do you suppose her true motives are?"

"Aside from fucking Kosta?" he asked, wry grin tugging at his lips.

Hypatia snorted.

"Besides that."

He sighed, eyes trailing back to the woman in question.

"I don't know. All I know is that she knows too much about things no one else on Oblivion does. We can only hope she doesn't betray us in the end."

"Are the two love birds ready?" Kosta called.

Hypatia took Sigimar's hand. He pressed a kiss to her palm and returned her determined look. So small, and yet such a mighty heart. It was time to conquer his own fear.

"We are," he answered.

"Then follow me. I must warn you, I've not been to the place we're to travel to in some time. Best get your light ready, Hypatia, and hope for the best," Agnetha advised as she led the way to the portal, her boots sinking through the deep snow.

A bitter cold had settled in the Riverlands, every breath freezing his throat and shocking his lungs. The squeak and crunch of the snow was like treading on ground glass. Winter was fully upon them.

As Agnetha dispelled the magic hiding the portal from view, Sigimar squeezed Hypatia's hand in his. They faced the rippling surface and stepped through together.

Greeted by a blast of swampy heat and pitch black, save for the weak light of the portal's surface dancing off the rubble at their feet, Sigimar strained his senses for threats. The stench of old rot pervaded the muggy air. Their steps echoed in the room, an odd, soft, swishing noise creating a background hum. A cavern? As Agnetha and Kosta came in behind them, Hypatia held her stave high, infusing it with a pure white light. No one said a word as they took in their surroundings.

Wherever they were, the room was massive in a way that boggled Sigimar's mind. Not even Hypatia's light reached the edges of the place. Massive columns lay tumbled and broken across the floors, steaming, hissing pools and limestone stalagmites interspersed bits of rubble and rock. The ceiling was shrouded in utter darkness.

"This way," Agnetha whispered.

Sigimar stuck close to Hypatia, his great axe raised and ready. Memories of Dag's last moments nipped at his heels. He pushed them away, doing his best to breathe through the fear, to focus on what lay before him, on ensuring his footfalls were silent. As they wound around debris and steered clear of whatever fetid liquid filled the pools and puddles, Kosta tripped. He landed partially in one of the pools, the scraping of rocks and the splash deafening in the relative quiet of the cave. Sigimar hauled him to his feet without a word. But as they stood, the dampness of Kosta's coat disappeared, hissing and bubbling away in Hypatia's light. The very liquid in this place had been corrupted.

Hypatia froze, turning around, eyes wide, her gloved hands gripping the stave like a lifeline.

"The hum stopped."

Terror cut Sigimar to the marrow.

The great misconception they'd laboured under was that the cavern they'd entered had been in its normal state the moment they'd stepped through. Hypatia had assumed that the odd hum had been the natural background noise of air flowing through the cavern. She had assumed that the pools of liquid had always been bubbling with steam. Most importantly, she'd assumed that they had been alone.

Hypatia's magic flooded the stave as her hear heart skipped several beats. The cavern had gone quiet, save the hissing of the liquid in the pools. The corruption-laced liquid. As she looked up at Sigimar, something much higher up caught her eye.

She gasped.

A great, eyeless, horned skull stared back.

A dragon.

Animal instincts demanded she keep her gaze on the thing. Eyes trailing along the body of the creature, her mind would not—could not—comprehend the horror. Shapes fused into other shapes and yet her mind refused to see what was in front of her, sparing the terrified animal inside her. Fused to the ceiling, whatever it was had sprouted millions of little stalactites from its long, serpentine body.

Words impossible to form, only a harsh exhale escaped her lips. Then everyone else turned, sharing in her waking nightmare.

"Fuck," Agnetha cursed. "Burn brightly, Hypatia!"

The moment her words echoed in the pitch dark, the stalactites moved, wriggling along the serpentine form of the creature, producing the distinct hum once again. Panic gripped her once more, and she poured her magic into the stave. The pools beside them hissed as if boiling, and the sightless skull of the dragon moved. It opened a maw of endless teeth, roaring as it dropped from the ceiling.

A shockwave of debris accompanied the ear-splitting landing of the creature as it turned columns and stalagmites into powder. Sigimar stepped in front of her, shielding her from the worst of the flying rocks. As it reared its terrible head, coiling up like a snake about to strike, Hypatia's heart thundered in her ringing ears. The thing was covered with grasping arms and flailing legs, skeletal and grey. It released another shriek as its innumerable appendages flaked away in her light, enraging it further.

One moment it was rearing above them, the next its unhinged jaw surrounded them, sword-like teeth poised to sink into them all, its gut-roiling breath enough to make her gag. Another screech rang out as it flailed its body, nearly deafening her. It widened its jaw before snapping it against the air above them, its thrashing, snake-like body destroying both stalagmites and the remains of ruins. And yet it wasn't flaking away in her light. Nor was it able to close its jaws around them.

"I've put up a barrier! Nothing in, nothing out!" Agnetha shouted, teeth gritting as she raised trembling arms and hands high. "But if we want to end this thing, I'm going to have to make it more like a net. It won't be nearly as strong, so when I tell you to, Hypatia, burn bright!"

Hands bloodless, Hypatia nearly dropped her stave, nearly passed out from fear as the creature's jaws enveloped them. Part of her wanted to slide away, go somewhere safe and quiet in her mind, protect her from certain death. The light in her stave flickered. Yes, that would be better, to hide. To go away. But Sigimar took her hands in his and helped her hold the stave high. He was at her back, one arm wrapped around her waist, bracketing her body as her bones turned to jelly.

"Hypatia! You can do this!" he shouted above the unholy din of the dragon's furious thrashing.

"Now!" Agnetha shrieked.

Too many teeth lurched closer, sinking through the holes of a shimmering net as another wave of putrid stench wafted from the mouth of the beast. Hypatia closed her eyes and screamed, pouring every bit of terror into the stave clenched in her hands.

"It's working!" Kosta shouted.

But Hypatia didn't dare look as she shook in Sigimar's arms, tears streaming down her cheeks, letting that primal scream ground her, prevent her from escaping into her mind. She screamed and screamed until her breath hitched, closing up her throat.

The stench of rotted breath cleared from the air as Hypatia sobbed.

"You did it, love. You did it," Sigimar murmured in her ringing ears.

Breath shaky, she dared open her eyes once the crashing and cracking of rock subsided in the cavern. The horrid hum of a million limbs thrashing against each other silenced. The head of the creature had disappeared, and the rest of its body was flaking away in her light.

"I-is it dead?" Kosta stuttered.

Agnetha patted his arm, a small smile on her ashen face.

"Technically, it's undead. We'll need to walk the length of it to completely dissolve it, but—"

In another movement too fast for her mind to comprehend, the headless beast coiled itself around them. Rubble and grasping limbs poured through the holes in the net-like barrier. Grasping hands with blackened nails and sucker-like mouths on their palms thrust towards them, hungry and desperate despite her light. Heart galloping and teeth clenched, Hypatia kept shining until the thrashing coil of the dragon's mutated body dissolved into nothing.

Once every last nightmare-inducing inch of the dragon was gone, whatever held her together collapsed. Kosta wobbled over to a boulder and threw up. Agnetha rubbed his back and handed him a skin of liquid. Hypatia shuddered in Sigimar's arms, unable to hold herself up any longer, a soft, keening sob emanating from a throat raw from screaming. Sigimar held her through it all, the wild beat of his heart hammering in her ear.

Chapter 34

Hypatia's light served the dual purpose of illumination and dispelling whatever small pockets of miasma lingered in the underground tunnels. The winding paths stretched out great distances and soared overhead, as if carved by the cursed dragon itself. Hypatia shivered. Perhaps they had been. Eyes swollen from sobbing, throat sore from screaming, and every nerve alight, she waited for the next horror to burst out of some dark shadow. Every so often her light would hit on some strange formation amongst the rock—glimpses of the decorative and architectural flourishes of Ashla's ancient past. Though she held the stave aloft, her hands wouldn't stop shaking. Sigimar and Kosta walked ahead, alert for danger, while Agnetha kept pace beside Hypatia.

"You're braver than you give yourself credit for. You all are."

Hypatia whipped her head to Agnetha, eyes wide with horror. They were supposed to remain as quiet as possible. Even now, more of those creatures could be hiding somewhere.

"Never fear, I've dampened the sounds we make as a precaution. And anyway, the dragon's presence alone would have ensured no other creature dared get close, lest they too become a meal."

Her heart slowed down, but still the dread gnawed at her. If this were bravery, then she wished to be a coward for the rest of her days. Heroism was greatly overrated, and Hypatia swore she'd have nothing to do with it ever again. If she lived long enough for such a future.

"Not one of you shamed yourselves. I'm a little upset by that. First time I saw one of those monstrosities, I made quite the mess," Agnetha chuckled.

"O-oh."

Hypatia supposed there was that to be grateful for. At least she'd not loosed her bowels in the thick of things.

"Here. Take a sip. It'll help with the nerves."

Agnetha handed her a skin of liquid. Hypatia took a sip, nearly choking as fire coursed down her throat.

"Gods," she croaked.

"Don't be shy. The second sip is always easier."

Hypatia braced herself for more pain, but it never came. Liquid warmth slid down her throat instead, easing her hurts and releasing the stiffness in her neck. The sharpest edge of her terror dulled. Whether it would settle well in her stomach was another matter entirely.

"Good gods," Hypatia muttered.

"Are you self-taught in your studies?"

"Um, yes, I suppose so. I had tutors for the basics, but higher education in more esoteric studies is not usually the purview of women in Lethe. Neither is the study of magic at all, really," Hypatia sighed, handing the skin back to the witch.

Agnetha's impressive scowl at that ugly pronouncement nearly had Hypatia snorting in amusement. No doubt a woman of Isro saw such limitations for what they were—nonsense.

"I had the opportunity to thumb through that book in your satchel," Agnetha began. Dread and shame roiled in Hypatia's gut. Gods, she should have burned that thrice-damned journal when she'd had the chance. "Marvelous artefacts you found in Lethe. And your translation of the old co-operative magic circle was quite good. I haven't seen one like it outside of the ancient records. Modern circles are much simpler, to prevent what I imagine would have plagued your circle had you used it, but there is something to be said for the beautiful complexity of bygone magics."

"I...what?"

"Why, your seventeenth symbol around the outer circle, of course, and the central logogram. As I said, you were quite close, but with those logograms even one wrong stroke changes the spell quite a bit. The symbol for 'give' was improperly drawn into the symbol for 'take' and 'magic of the soul' became 'magic with the soul.' Very technical, but significant in effect."

"A-ah. I see," Hypatia muttered as her world tilted on its axis.

Had all the suffering she'd caused, all the death and misery, been because of a simple translation error? Hysteria bubbled up. It took an effort of sheer will to hold herself together. But then Sigimar's deep voice echoed in her mind. She was not to blame for the actions of monsters. She hadn't forced a single person to perform the magic she'd recreated. She'd made a tool, but it could have helped people instead of being used to kill. With a deep breath, she calmed herself.

"I added my notes in the margins. I hope you don't mind. You should be quite proud of your academic accomplishments. So few people have what it takes to make such a robust study of the past," Agnetha sighed. "You should try the corrected circle sometime. This way, all different kinds of magical energies can be shared. I think it would be rather beautiful to see. The old magics usually are..." Her look was faraway. Was now the time to see what she could glean of Agnetha's past?

"And where did you study?" Hypatia asked.

"The university I first attended was wiped out of existence. The rest was self-study." Agnetha's tight smile invited no further queries.

Damn.

"In any case, thank you for the distraction."

"Yes, well, we should be near the exit to the surface soon enough. Once we arrive, I doubt there will be any time for chit-chat."

No, they'd be too busy fighting for their lives. Against more of those monstrous, corrupted dragons. Gods help her. She prayed King Erlendr brought warriors in great numbers.

"Um, how exactly will King Erlendr's men, or Otmar, know to take the same route through the underground that we have?"

"I've been marking the trail." Agnetha tilted her head to the side, drawing Hypatia's gaze. All along the path they'd walked, four sets of footsteps glowed faintly in the dark. It was rather ingenious.

"You know a great number of spells."

She'd never considered how impressive it would be to do so many varied things with magic. After all, mages didn't possess such breadth of talent. How quaint Lethe would seem to someone like Agnetha with all her might. Hypatia supposed her fellow mages were lucky no one she'd outside Lethe met seemed to know of the empire's existence at all.

"Most witches do. The truly remarkable thing is that mages only seem to be able to do one. Stranger still, your magic is like nothing else on Oblivion, you and your brother both. No taste, sensation, scent or sound to accompany it. Very curious."

Hypatia was spared from her overly curious stare by walking straight into Sigimar's stationary back.

"This is the end of the path," he cursed.

"Are you certain this is the way, Agnetha?" Kosta asked.

The witch hemmed and hawed over the collapsed rubble blocking the tunnel.

"This was not here last time."

"When were you here last? A flow of limestone is covering most of this rubble!" Sigimar hissed.

He was right. If Agnetha were telling the truth, it must have been hundreds, if not thousands of years since the cave-in. If she were lying, was she simply too proud to admit it, or were they about to discover her ulterior motives? Were any of them powerful enough to stop her if she proved to be an enemy?

"Don't you already have an inkling, young man?" Agnetha asked, her grin sharp-toothed.

"Sorceress," he growled, gripping his axe.

"So you've dared to speak it aloud after all. Very brave of you, Jarl Sigimar. And you should be so lucky. Because this," she motioned at the impenetrable rock that blocked path, "isn't a problem."

The witch—sorceress—opened the path with a flick of her wrist, carving a perfect, even path and pushing the precisely cut rock away into the tunnel behind them.

"Well? Go on then. The conclusion of our heroic quest awaits us." She raised one pale eyebrow as she jutted her chin.

Sigimar took Hypatia's hand and pulled her to his side, a wary eye on Agnetha as they took the lead. Hypatia tried to catch Sigimar's gaze, but he refused to meet her eyes, his grim focus on the path ahead. Thankfully, Kosta asked the burning question on her mind.

"What's a sorceress?"

"A very powerful witch. Much maligned throughout history," Agnetha sniffed.

"With the power and immortality of demi-gods, and often sharing in their lack of concern over the lives of us mere mortals," Sigimar added.

Hypatia gasped. But why did someone so powerful need people like them to see this through? Wasn't she powerful enough to end the miasma herself?

"And yet this one has come to your rescue—repeatedly. I even tried to speak to you when you landed in Isro, but you rebuffed me."

"I thought I recognised you from somewhere!" Hypatia gasped.

But what had she wanted back then, when no one knew of Hypatia's power and Otmar hadn't had a chance to blackmail Drest?

"Yes, and how was it that you appeared exactly where and when we needed you?" Sigimar asked, his tone casual, though his hand gripped Hypatia's.

If she'd been following them all this time, what was her true aim? Was she not truly interested in protecting the staves, but in stealing one? Or was there some other dreadful thing she wished to get her hands on?

Kosta snapped his fingers and smiled.

"Oh, I've got it! You must have the power to see the future. I've heard of such people. Though they all sound so miserable about it. I can't fathom why."

Oh sweet, silly Kosta. Would he never learn to read the room?

Agnetha chuckled instead of bristling, giggling instead of lobbing threats or curses they would be powerless to defend against. She wiped a mirthful tear from the corner of her eye.

"You're a delight, Kosta. No, I've no such power. And stop looking at me with such naked suspicion, Jarls. I've simply been trying to warn you against uncovering and misusing Ashla's hidden treasures, and I have a personal interest in—"

The rock above their heads split, a deep, grating crack echoing in the dark. Then the ground beneath their feet began to rumble, nearly sending Hypatia to her knees. Only her already tight grip on the stave prevented her from dropping it.

"Run!" Sigimar called, hauling Hypatia along at speeds she'd never have been able to reach under her own power.

They raced through the tunnel as jagged rock splintered from the ceiling, crashing down. Sigimar ducked, dodged and leapt over the deadly obstacles with precision, hauling her up and over his shoulder. Breath was knocked from her lungs as his shoulder pounded against her ribs with every step. All the while, Kosta and Agnetha were left farther behind. At least the sorceress shielded them with her magic, pushing debris from their path as they tried to keep pace with Sigimar's frightful speed.

But from her position on his shoulder, watching her brother struggle to reach her, she witnessed something that stopped her blood cold.

The whole tunnel was caving in.

A veritable avalanche of rock spilled out not a few paces behind Kosta and Agnetha, dogging their steps and threatening to overtake them. Hypatia's cries begging them to move faster were lost in the deafening roar. A flash of light streaked from Agnetha's hand and into the tunnel. A blink later, and a giant glowing insect with too many legs to count was racing down the tunnel, Kosta and the sorceress on its back. It quickly closed the distance to Hypatia and Sigimar, its segmented body easily flying over the obstacles and twisting out of the way of falling rock. Without a moment's hesitation, Sigimar swung atop it near its head, adjusting Hypatia so that his body shielded hers.

Wind and debris whipped past, tearing her skirt and fur cloak, ripping her hair from the confines of her braids. A rock snagged her satchel, nearly yanking her off the beast. Sigimar pulled her back against him, a hard correction. She didn't trust her hold on the summoned creature's hard, smooth carapace as it outpaced the cave-in. Ahead, the tunnel opened up—to a dead end.

Sigimar must have seen it too. He curled around her, as if his body alone could prevent them dashing themselves against the wall, or protect her from being crushed by the cave in. Hypatia closed her eyes and tensed, anticipating her demise.

Then they were flying through the air, weightless projectiles careening towards their deaths. And yet they were slowing until they stopped. Were they already dead? Even the roar of cracking, tumbling rock was dimming, though a terrible pressure made her gasp. Had she died so quickly she'd avoided pain entirely?

Hypatia dared to open her eyes.

Their summoned beast was no more, and Agnetha stood near the tunnel's exit, hands outstretched and shaking, as if she held the whole of the underground world at bay. Perhaps she did. Hypatia's light illuminated fissures in the rock as they knit back together. Rubble turned liquid, coagulated and reformed, sealing the tunnel completely—perfectly. Debris ceased raining down, and the rumbling of the earth quieted, stilling, until only the occasional plink and clattering of tiny stones echoed in their smooth-walled chamber.

Agnetha's arms dropped to her side and she swayed, breathing hard. Kosta took her elbow, acting as her support. The pressure dissipated instantly.

"Gods below," Sigimar whispered.

She'd commanded Oblivion itself. Hypatia was dumbstruck. She'd never seen such power in all her life. No earth mage had ever accomplished such a feat, not even in myths.

"Structural engineering," Agnetha huffed, hands on her knees as she caught her breath, "is not my strong suit." She wiped her brow, slick with sweat and raised her chin at the wall behind Hypatia and Sigimar. "So we'd best get inside the tower. Then we get to the top. Our soul-filled stave and the Frey-device should be on the surface, if memory serves."

Hypatia's light didn't reach the ceiling in this part of the underground. The narrow clearing they found themselves in was littered with rubble covered in limestone flows. When she turned, Hypatia gasped. Elaborate, interlocking designs peaked out from beneath a layer of limestone, unweathered and pristine despite their ancient origin. It looked precisely like those from the tower she'd briefly called home. Hopefully its internal structures were built similarly.

With another flick of her wrist, Agnetha cracked the stone fused to the doorway. It came off in perfect sheets, shattering as they hit the floor.

"Now, why don't we—"

Several terrible things happened at once.

A sheet of rock as big as a horse fell from the ceiling, decapitating the sorceress.

The stave dropped from Hypatia's bloodless hands as dark blood splattered across the hem of her dress. More slabs of rock fell as Sigimar hauled Hypatia into the safety of the tower, her last view that of Kosta's wide, dark eyes.

Agony exploded in her chest.

When at last the dust settled, she ran towards the rubble spilling into the entrance of the tower, frantically clawing through it. Kosta could still be alive. He *had* to be alive. She would not lose him like this. Not again.

"Hypatia! Stop! Stop. He probably teleported away. If not...either way, he's gone."

But her heart told her he was still there, trapped in the rubble. He'd been shocked by Agnetha's death. He hadn't disappeared, even as the ceiling came down around him. She couldn't bear the thought of him trapped, hurt, terrified.

"No! No! Kosta! KOSTA!" Hypatia shrieked, blinded by tears.

"Tia!" his muffled voice came through the rubble.

"Kosta! Oh gods! Why are you still there? Teleport away!" Hypatia called back, stilling so she wouldn't miss a word.

"My arm got clipped. I think it's broken."

Was he too injured to flee? Gods, no. He had to get out of there, before he was well and truly killed by the collapsing rock. Who knew when it would next shift and crush him?

"We'll try to get to you!" Hypatia began tearing more rocks from the pile.

"There's blood everywhere. Her blood. Gods, her head is gone. Gods below," he croaked.

Sigimar stopped her with a hand on hers, hauling her away. Hypatia fought his hold.

"Kosta, you must teleport! Now!" Sigimar called as he frantically scanned the room.

"But I'm hurt, and I can't just leave her here."

"Sorceresses are immortal! They rise from the ashes of their combusting corpses, but her blood is flammable! Teleport yourselves outside her cottage and then take cover! Now! Or we'll all die in the explosion!"

Kosta screamed in agony before the sound abruptly ended. Gods, she hoped he'd made it. Sigimar hauled Hypatia away from the door and towards the staircase.

"Why are we running?"

"Because her head is still out there, and it's going to set itself alight!"

And the door to the tower was wedged open with debris. Hypatia doubled her pace. Up and up they ran, no thought but that they must flee and quickly.

The explosion chased them up the stairs, a blast of heat, dust and rock enveloping them just as Sigimar covered her bodily. When her ears finally stopped ringing, they dared to move. Panting, sweating, their eyes wide, Hypatia and Sigimar slumped against the steps, her trembling hand secure in his savage grip.

They'd survived.

Barely.

CHAPTER 35

"I've lost the stave!" Hypatia gasped. "Gods, I held it all through the tunnels, and now it's gone!"

Would her power be enough to fell one of those horrid creatures again? Without Agnetha and Kosta, Sigimar's life would depend on how brightly she shone. Her eyes met his. Only now did she realise the interior of the tower was dimly lit, even without her magic—and that she could see the quiet, resigned acceptance in his eyes.

"You don't need it." He shook his head.

"You can't know that. What if...what if I'm not strong enough and one of those things eats us because I lost the stave and—"

Sigimar pressed a finger to her lips, leaning in close.

"It's gone, Hypatia. We will be enough as we are."

"But what if we're not?"

Sigimar was silent, but his eyes told her what his words could not. There was no recrimination in his sad, small grin, in the softening corners of his amber eyes, in the caress of his fingers against her cheek. If they perished because of her foolish error, then that was that, and he loved her anyway. But she didn't want this to be the end. She wanted to live, to spend lifetimes by his side, in his arms, their lives as intertwined as their bodies in the middle of the night. She would do anything to ensure that future.

Anything.

Her heart skipped. She felt for the strap of her satchel, following it to the opening flap. She looked down at it. It was worse for wear, scuffed, a chunk of the corner sheared off. And yet her journal, the one containing the ritual was still somehow inside. The one Agnetha had fixed. She tore it out and flipped the bumped, torn and folded pages to the one she needed. At the top, Agnetha's notes in an unfamiliar language but with the corrected inner logogram clearly denoted. And then her heart sunk. The notes for the outer, crucial logogram were missing, torn off by whatever had cleaved her satchel.

"No..."

"I'm sorry, Hypatia. I know how much it meant to you."

"It's not...I thought we could...that this could save us, that it would *finally* do some good, but it's useless! Another thing that could have saved us, and I've ruined it!" She threw the book in her impotent rage. "I'm sorry. I'm so sorry." Tears blurred her vision.

Sigimar dried the salty tracks on her cheeks and took her hands in his.

"You're worried you need more magic than you've got?"

"Yes."

"And you were willing to revisit the worst moment of your life to do it?"

"I would do anything if it meant we could...that we would get to live."

"Come with me then." He urged her to follow, snagging the book and tucking it into a pocket before he ascended the few steps up to the next floor of the tower. He looked about and unhooked his cloak, laying it down.

"What are you doing?"

"Giving you more magic."

"How? I couldn't possibly figure out the ritual in the time we have lef—why are you removing your clothes?"

His grin was wry as he stripped out of his tunic.

"Do you remember how the warmth charms were created when we first met?"

"I...no?"

"Old magic, Hypatia. Specifically, sex magic."

"Gods below, you can't be serious!"

"I'm deadly serious. Now, strip."

A shiver ran down her spine. She began divesting herself of her clothes. The chill of the tower had her wishing for those very same warmth charms. Her hands shook at the thought of another ritual. Old fears clawed at her heart. What if the ritual went wrong? What if it hurt Sigimar in the process?

"H-how does this work exactly?"

"You're the vessel in this ritual, so you need to yield yourself to me." He pointed at his cloak as he pulled off his boots. "My job is to give you release and draw the symbol on your belly."

"Symbol?" she swallowed, forcing herself to take off the last of her clothes. Sigimar would never suggest anything that would cause her harm.

"A triangle."

"Using what?"

"My tongue."

At least it sounded rather simple. Though she wasn't certain it would be so easy for him this time. Hypatia was hardly in an amorous state of mind. She started to unlatch the necklace of charms but he touched his fingers to hers to stop her.

"No, keep it on. It'll serve as the symbol of my trust in you."

He must have felt her tremors then. Sigimar brought her hands to his lips and kissed them.

"Breathe. This ritual cannot harm either of us. I would never have suggested it otherwise."

Hypatia released a shaky breath, girding herself for what was to come. Whatever this ritual entailed, Sigimar would be with her.

"What about you? What serves as my symbol of trust in you?"

He stopped disrobing. Only his tight leggings remained. He scanned the room and their belongings.

"My journal, perhaps?" Hypatia suggested.

Sigimar shook his head.

"No, it would need to be something I expected to keep."

Her chest hollowed out. Gods, would even this not go right?

"And it needs to be an object?"

What could she give him that would serve? She'd come only with a few supplies and her journal, nothing more. Gods, why hadn't she thought to give him something tangible before now?

"No, it could be a secret, something you value, to give me as a symbol of your trust."

Her heart leapt. Their child. But was now the time to speak of it? Did she have another choice? Did she really want to face the possibility of death without telling him, now that she knew?

"A-and when do you need to hear this secret?"

"As I lay you down," his voice gentled as he closed the distance between them.

She stepped into his embrace, the heat of his skin warming hers. As he lowered her down onto the fur of his cloak, Hypatia whispered the words to him—her very last secret.

"I'm pregnant."

"Gods below!" he gasped, eyes wide as they flicked from hers to her belly. *"How?!"*

"How *else*?! You've not allowed me to sleep a full night in weeks!"

His grin was irrepressible, a beacon in the dark.

"We're going to be parents?" he asked, hands cupping her cheeks.

She nodded, tears coming to her eyes.

"I love you," he whispered, fervent and fierce.

Her reply was swallowed by a kiss she would never forget. Achingly tender, his hands reverential against every inch of her skin, his ferocity leashed in every tight, coiling muscle she scored her nails along. Her heart bloomed with warmth.

Sigimar broke their kiss first, his eyes shining with heated purpose. He kissed his way down her body as his hands kneaded her breasts, glided over her belly and remained there. He pressed a kiss there, touching with his forehead and whispering too quietly for her to hear. Before she could ask him what he'd said, his hands moved to her thighs, spreading them as he kissed his way to her neediest point.

"Together, Hypatia. Always. I swear it to you."

"I love you so much," she whispered back.

His tongue delved inside her before he licked his way up, stealing her breath. He traced the first line on her belly, hot and wet, his eyes flicking back to her as she shivered. Some strange sensation pooled inside her, her hands gripping the cloak beneath her.

"Breathe," he whispered as he kissed the inside of her thighs, waiting for her to relax.

His tongue continued its erotic assault until she was too breathless and aching to notice whatever was coiling through her aside from her need for release. She cried out with every tortuous flick of his tongue, trying desperately to grind herself against him as he held her pinned.

He painted the second line.

She gasped. Every hair stood on end, gooseflesh prickling her skin as if sensuous electricity danced along every nerve. Something brushed along senses she never knew she possessed, power and promise curling around her, almost tangible. When at last Sigimar gave her what she sought, he drew the last line.

Release, more intense than any she'd experienced, overwhelmed her. She screamed as every nerve in her body was set alight, her mind going blank with ecstasy. Sigimar soothed her through the wave upon wave that struck until at last she could open her eyes and unclench her fists. She trembled with the force of whatever the magic had done. Every limb felt light, every scrape and bruise had healed, every ache assuaged—even her mind was calm. Truly, a feat. She reached a hand up to Sigimar's face above her, tracing the line of his beard. Hypatia was wholly unlike herself.

Not least because her skin radiated.

Literally.

"Am I...glowing?"

"You're always glowing to me." He smiled as he crouched over her, covering her body with his.

She flicked his nose.

"You know what I mean."

Sigimar chuckled.

"You've got more power now than ever before."

"How much time until..."

"Until you use it."

She released a shaky breath as his hard length prodded her.

"What about you?" she asked, rolling her hips. Hypatia could think of worse ways to meet her potential demise.

He shook his head as he hissed a breath through clenched teeth.

"No time."

He helped her to her feet. She pushed away any lingering disappointment.

"Then, when this is over?" Hypatia asked, pulling on her dress and boots.

"My reward for surviving?" He grinned as he laced up his leggings.

Her heart skipped a beat. No longer was he talking about dying for her, about noble sacrifice or honourable deaths. He wanted to live a full life with her.

"For wanting a future with me." Hypatia smiled as she buckled the clasp of her cloak. "For wanting to be a family with me."

He paused, his hand on the clasp of his cloak.

"You pulled me from the deepest of hells. You still do. You saved me. Of course I want that."

Hypatia shook her head.

"I didn't save you, Sigimar. I, and many others, reached out to you, but in the end, it was you who took our hands, you who took those first few steps, and then the next, and then the next. You saved yourself, Sigimar. Every day you wake up and choose to take another step, you save yourself."

He secured his cloak without a word, took her hand in his and kissed her knuckles. Lacing their fingers together, he smiled.

"Then the gods have blessed me with the perfect travelling companion."

"As I have been." She squeezed his hand as they made their way to the central shaft of the tower.

In their tower, it had allowed them to ascend the staggering, full height of the building without effort. She only prayed it worked as theirs did. An ascent on foot would be gruelling. Sigimar pressed his palm to the doors. They opened to a platform with nary a protest, ready and waiting. Together, Hypatia and Sigimar stepped on, rising the moment the doors closed.

"I can hear it," Hypatia whispered.

Ancient souls called out to her, gaining volume and strength the higher they rose, consuming rational thought. She braced herself, knowing her will would soon be undone by cries of help she could not deny.

Their eyes met, solemn and decided.

"I'll protect you," he promised. "I'll protect our family."

CHAPTER 36

Some strange calm had overtaken Sigimar after the explosion, as if the blast had crystalised his mind, his purpose. Their plan had gone to the deepest of hells. Erlendr would never reach them in time if he used the portal, nor would he make it before Otmar arrived to steal the stave if he took to the skies on summoned beasts. Kosta and Agnetha wouldn't be able to teleport in, not until after Agnetha revived, which could take anywhere from hours to days. Drest was their last remaining hope of aid. The path laid before him became clear. Give Hypatia as much magic as her small body could hold, and get her to the top of this cursed tower. After that, they would be forced to wait until help arrived. Hopefully it would do so before Otmar's patience ran out and Sara's life was lost.

The higher they rose, the more unfocused and desperate Hypatia became. By the time they reached the top, she was writhing in his arms. Stepping out of the lift, he was grateful they were aboveground, natural light filtering through a nearby window. There would be no effort needed to dig themselves out to reach the top of the tower.

He swept into the nearest room. A gemstone bigger than a sleigh glowed blue, pulsating as it rested in a nook that seemed carved for the purpose of cradling it. Countless smaller gems, some as large as his head, others as small as a child's fist, sat in stands and nooks of their own. Whatever they were, it didn't concern him.

Sigimar turned to the soaring glass doors. Black earth came up to his waist beyond the glass, the first post of a buried balustrade visible outside. He surveyed the land. Bleak grey reflected back at him from beyond the small clearing, a thin layer of black and grey streaked snow covering the lifeless dirt.

No dragons in sight.

Yet.

"Sigimar," Hypatia whined piteously as she dug he nails into the arm of his tunic. "They're screaming."

He held her close, soothing her as she whimpered against his chest, fairly vibrating against him. They had to wait for Drest. Even a skilled warrior was unlikely to be able to take down a dragon if one appeared, enchanted axe or not. He fingered it in the holster at his hip. Though it was the size of a small hand axe now, a single drop of his blood would transform it into a giant battle axe, the blade so sharp even dragon scales didn't stand a chance.

"Sigimar."

The sound of Drest's voice reached him, as though it were coming from a great distance. Sigimar didn't have the magic to reply. Luckily, Drest didn't need him to.

"There are dragons circling everywhere. Hundreds of hearts are calling. The tower must be filled with them."

He eyed the gem at his side, cursing. A dragon's heart, its song audible only to one of their kind. Beacons guiding dragons to rest—or to feast. Just as Hypatia's magic drew her to the souls within the stave, the hearts would drag every mindless, starving dragon to this exact spot. If the towers hadn't been built to withstand everything, its contents would have been devoured long ago.

He supposed at least this solved Drest's problem. Even if Otmar came without payment, as long as Sara was unharmed, she could be saved.

A distant roar rattled the doors.

"I'll draw them to me. Go. Now!"

Sigimar touched his hand to the doors. As soon as they slid into the walls, black earth tumbled into the room. He scrabbled up the embankment, pulling Hypatia up after him. The moment they left the confines of the tower, the lung-crushing pressure of the place hit him full force. Hypatia staggered to the tower wall, leaning against it as she shook. Wincing, gasping, he scanned the fog and stepped back from the tower. There were no steps up to the top where the amplifier stood, and above it, the stave, hovering and weightless. Only someone who could fly or shapeshift would be able to reach it. A swirl of ivy-like decorations spiralled to the top. Would he be able to climb them? Would Hypatia?

A chorus of bellowing shrieks rent the air, reverberating in his very bones.

Decision made, he raced back to the tower where Hypatia stood, clutching her head in her hands.

"Get on my back." He knelt, tearing off his cloak and urging her on.

Hands shaking, she grasped his shoulders. He pulled her arms across his throat. Better he choke a bit than have her fall off. Her thighs trembled around his waist. He hooked her ankles and began climbing as swiftly as he could. A crack reverberated in his chest before a dark form plummeted through the grey, a rain of black soaking the filthy snow. The impact of a fallen dragon corpse nearly tossed them from the tower wall.

As the severed head followed the body, it slid across the ground, churning up dirt and rock as it came to rest only a few paces from the tower. Out of the corner of his eye, he saw the desiccated tongue of the dragon snake out, sprouting several more many-toothed suckers of their own, seeking out flesh.

"Hypatia! I need your light!"

He turned as best he could while still gripping the decorations. Hypatia raised her hand, light spilling forth, dissolving the hissing nightmares before they could reach Sigimar's ankles. Thank the gods she was not too far gone for that.

As the horrors turned to ash, Sigimar continued his ascent, pausing every time another corrupted dragon corpse fell from the sky. Five more fell, each impact nearly dislodging them both from the icy, slick walls of the tower. Just as they neared the top, the crack of thunder and flashes of lightning lit the gloom. Oblivion's most horrifying shadow play flashed in the sky as Drest's dragon form shot lightning from his open maw. A whale-like monstrosity with nine sets of wings gripped a flailing Drest in thousands of snaking tentacles. Wings pinned, Drest was dragged forward to what Sigimar could only surmise was its mouth.

In the next blast of lightning, Drest's form disappeared, only to reappear with another flash and crack, above the beast, driving it to the ground with lightning, tooth and claw. Sigimar redoubled his efforts, desperate to reach the top before the beast hit the ground. When it did, they would be thrown.

"Brace yourself!" Sigimar roared above the din as the beast tumbled from the sky at speed.

She'd barely tightened her hold on him before it hit the ground in a bone-jarring collision. For a moment, they were weightless, untethered by any grip or foot-hold on the outer walls of the tower. Then they fell. He scrambled for purchase, hooking a few fingers and toes into the décor before the momentum had him swinging wildly. He took the brunt of the impact with an elbow. In the split second when his elbow, fingers and toes broke, radiating pain up and down his spine, Hypatia lost her grip.

Her hand slipped past his frantic, slick fingers. Below, the dead dragon's horn stood out in stark relief against the corrupted grey of the beast's skull, poised to gore her. Leaping from his position on the wall, he pulled his axe from his holster, cutting his finger along the blade as he reached out to Hypatia, his arm mending in mid-fall. In an instant the axe grew in length and size, longer than his arm, its blade as big as his head.

Sigimar reached out, snagged Hypatia from the air, crushed her to him and struck out with his axe, trying to gain purchase on the glittering ivy decorations. The friction slowed their fall until at last the tip of the blade hooked on a pointed leaf, jerking them to a stop just above the sharpest barb of the dragon's horn.

They caught their breaths, frenzied grey meeting panicked amber. Hypatia latched herself to him, her arms around his neck, head pressed into his collarbone, her heart beating madly against his. He took a calming breath, dragging in whatever air his lungs could, running a hand along her back, as much for her sake as his.

On the field of battle, Drest valiantly fought the bloated beast, spewing lightning at every tentacle, the flashing and shadows portraying an epic brawl of claws gouging flesh and wing-claws ripping joints. There was no way to be heard above the unholy clash.

Sigimar redoubled his efforts, sweat beading his brow. Now that dragon corpses weren't falling from the cursed heavens, he made it to the top with relative ease. Though his ears rang from the piercing shrieks, neither he nor Hypatia needed instruction once they finally reached the top of the tower.

The stave hung suspended above the amplifier platform, glowing a piercing, cold, malevolent blue. All of Hypatia's focus was on the object. He took her by her hips and raised her high above his head. She struggled to reach it. The battle between titans drew dangerously close, Drest and beast wresting and rolling. Adjusting his grip to her knees, he gave her the extra boost she needed to seize the tip of the damned thing. Once in her grasp, it gave up its unnatural position. Hypatia bathed it in light, unaware of the dragons drawing close—so close he could see the gleam of Drest's scales on the edges of the clearing.

"Hypatia!" he called, unable even to hear the sound of his own voice, readying to take her in his arms and leap over the opposite side of the tower, whatever good it might do them.

Just as the dragons breached the wall of miasma and entered the clearing, sunlight broke through the grey shroud and the pressure of the place disappeared.

But would it be enough? Even as the clearing widened, the beast was too big to dissolve before it reached them at this rate. Hypatia looked up at him, eyes wide and wild as the stave fell from her grasp. He pulled her to the centre of the amplifier, pressing her palms to the device.

"Burn bright!" he yelled.

Hypatia nodded, flooding the device with her magic. He shielded his eyes against her brilliance, covering her with his body. Eyes as large as horses came right up to the edge of the tower. In an instant, the miasma disappeared, as if it had been an illusion all along.

Drest won the upper hand against the beast, pinning it as it came apart at the seams, cracking open, corrupted innards hissing against their magical antithesis. A few moments more, and the only sounds left on the wide, open plain in the heart of Ashla were the whistling wind, and Drest's heaving, draconic breaths.

As far as the eye could see, a light dusting of snow regained some of its original hue, mixed in with a dark slurry where battles had just moments ago been fought and won, gouges and craters the only telltale signs. Above, a sky as blue as sapphires, clear of clouds.

His heart stuttered in his chest. They were alive. Thank the gods.

"You did it," Sigimar whispered.

CHAPTER 37

"*We* did it." Hypatia took Sigimar's hand, threading her fingers through his. "And it's not done yet," she said with a calm she hadn't earned.

It would likely shatter when the shock wore off. Once again, the song of the souls had muddied her mind, dimming and altering her recollections of all the time she'd spent in proximity. Sigimar had no doubt considered it a harrowing climb. Aside from their brief fall, Hypatia's mind had been consumed by voices pleading, screaming, claws of grief dug deep in her head. She hadn't been herself. There had only been enough room inside her for a tiny sliver of herself, and its only task had been to hold on until she could do as those voices begged. It was so much worse this time. Her legs were already threatening to turn to jelly at the thought. Thank the gods she wouldn't need to do that again, once Agnetha returned to connect the towers to her magic. There were many staves yet to feel her light.

"*No, it's not.*" Drest's voice came from nowhere and everywhere at once.

Hypatia jumped, squeaking in surprise as an enormous amber eye stared down at them, nestled in a head larger than the uncovered tip of the tower. Gold horns curled up from his head, and scales of gold and obsidian covered a body that was truly as big as a palace, his wings a sparkling silver, big enough to blot out the newly uncovered sky.

"*That's* Drest?!" Hypatia gasped.

"Yes, of course," Sigimar replied.

Hypatia could feel the blood draining from her face. That was the man Sigimar sparred with, cursed at, the one Otmar thoughtlessly, cruelly drove into a corner? It boggled her mind. He could crush them all with a careless step.

She blinked, and he was gone.

"Where did he go?"

"Likely to take a few of the hearts inside the tower."

"And then he tells Otmar how to get here?"

Sigimar nodded.

"Once our reinforcements arrive."

Now that the greatest danger was past, they would have a moment to breathe. All that remained was waiting for Agnetha and Kosta to return, Erlendr's forces to arrive, and then luring Otmar into their trap. Except, just as Ingi had surmised, not everything had gone according to plan. Kosta was gone and hadn't returned, Agnetha had been killed, temporarily, according to Sigimar, and the tunnel leading to the tower had collapsed in on itself.

"But how soon can anyone reach us, now that the path to the tower has collapsed?"

A thick curl of smoke shot up and out of the tower, landing beside her and reforming as Drest. His panicked eyes met hers as he gripped her shoulders.

"What do you mean *it's collapsed?*! And where is Agnetha? Kosta?"

"There was a cave-in," she replied, dread growing. "Kosta had to take Agnetha away."

"But that means no one here has magic that can protect Sara from Otmar! And the only one who might bring us aid will be delayed! Erlendr will have to summon beasts to fly here. And he'll be bringing an army, so he'll be even slower!"

"And so will Otmar." Sigimar removed Drest's hands from her shoulders, his voice calm and measured. "Breathe. You have the hearts you need now. It may take a day or so, but Otmar will come, and he'll bring Sara. You brought the dragon's eye to communicate with him, did you not? Simply wait until reinforcements arrive to speak with him."

"You don't understand! Otmar doesn't need to travel by fixed portal! His wife has portalling magic!"

"E-even if that's the case, they don't know you've secured the stave for them yet, and they don't know precisely where we are. Would they really risk it?" Hypatia asked, a cold sweat trickling down the small of her back.

Agnetha had mentioned that portalling magic required vast quantities of blood. Surely a king who went to such lengths to protect his family wouldn't risk their lives in that way. Not when waiting a single extra day would do.

"After you left and I told Otmar I was getting his stave as well as that Erlendr could negate the magic in his amplifier, he placed a tracking spell on me. Now, thanks to our lies, he thinks the whole of the Riverlands is about to turn on him." Drest replied, voice hollow. "What wouldn't he risk?"

A terrible rending sound, like fabric splitting on a grand scale, signalled the arrival of their doom. What would Otmar do when he realised the stave no longer held the souls he sought? If Sara's death meant Drest would follow her, were she and Sigimar enough to stop a man with Otmar's magic and wrath?

"Hide! Now!" Drest urged them as he grabbed the stave, flitted between forms to cover the distance in the blink of an eye, and stood before a tear in the very air.

As if the world itself had been cut, it bled like a wound, dark red seeping from its growing edges, spilling onto snow and ice. As it grew, great cracks formed in the earth, radiating out behind it.

Having nowhere to go, Hypatia grabbed hold of Sigimar's arm and wrapped them both in her magic, erasing them from sight. A slight gasp was all Sigimar uttered before he went as silent as she. Once the tear was as tall as a person, Otmar stepped out, followed by Farohildis and her mother, Asta, breathing heavily and leaning against her daughter, looking much worse for wear. From the queen's slit arms ran rivers of blood.

"Where is the miasma? What have you done?" Otmar asked, his anger a barely banked thunder in his voice.

"Used my wings to push it away. Where is Sara? Or have you decided to die?" Drest growled back, looming over the fae king.

"Drest? Drest!" Sara's voice called out.

Within the tear, an image of Sara flickered, bound and lying on a fur pelt, a tapestry in the distance. Was she all the way back in Gortos? Inside Otmar's castle?

"Give me the stave, and you may pass through. Any trickery, and I summon her and end her life." Otmar sneered, producing a summoning token between his fingers.

Drest nodded, holding out the stave. Otmar put his hand on it and pulled, but Drest refused to relinquish it.

"Break the token once I enter. If Sara disappears, my dying breath will be a curse upon your daughter."

The air positively crackled around Otmar, lightning dancing between strands of his silver hair.

"Father, Mother is—" Farohildis began as Asta slid further to the ground in her daughter's arms.

A sharp glance from Otmar's dark eyes, his blue lips pursed, and Farohildis kept quiet, doing her best to shore up her mother's limp body.

"You have a deal," Otmar replied.

Drest relinquished the stave and leapt through the portal. He set to untying Sara, and glared at Otmar until he reluctantly crushed the token in his palm. Then the portal vanished as if it had never existed at all. The moment it did, Otmar rushed to Asta's side, kissing her head, auroras dancing around her until she opened her eyes and smiled.

Hypatia held her breath, dreading the moment to come. There was nowhere for them to go on this barren plain. Could they slip back into the tower proper and hide amongst the treasures within? How long until the spell drained her of her reserves, and they were visible once more?

"Something's wrong. Why didn't he ask for the hearts?" Farohildis gripped her father's arm.

Their eyes shot down to the stave in Otmar's hand.

"The stave... are there souls within it?" Asta asked, her thin voice carrying on the breeze.

Otmar held the stave in one hand, his other hovering above. Aurora-like tendrils of magic streamed from his fingers, wrapping around the stave as Hypatia's heart hammered. What would he do when he discovered the souls had been freed? Would he take the stave they'd failed to destroy and wreak bloody vengeance on the Riverlands? Would he find her and Sigimar and rip their souls from their flesh? If only there was a place to hide, but the land was flat, the only landmark the tip of the spire. There was nowhere to go.

Otmar's dark eyes flashed, and he threw the stave away, cursing bitterly.

Hypatia prayed he would accept his losses and leave.

"I'm sorry, my loves, I'm so sorry. At least take this and recover your strength." Otmar produced a jagged gem the size of his fist from a pocket in his cloak. Then he raised it high and plunged it into Asta's chest.

Hypatia gasped.

Gods below, he'd promised her life and then murdered her! Had he gone mad? Wasn't the dragon's heart supposed to heal instead of harm?

She didn't think he'd heard her.

But with that small noise, she'd sealed their fates.

Otmar's eyes flashed once more, scanning the surroundings until they lit on her. But he couldn't see her. It wasn't possible. With a flick of his wrist, her necklace was torn away and flung into the distance, taking any magical protection with it.

He must have sensed the spells within.

"This is your fault, you mangy bitch!" he raged.

Sigimar moved, grabbing hold of her waist, turning his back and diving as a malevolent bolt of crimson magic streaked towards them. Agony ripped through her shoulder, setting every nerve alight with pain. Her illusion shattered, they crashed onto the hard surface of the tower's apex, Sigimar's heavy body crushing hers beneath. Breath rushed from her lungs in a silent scream.

Then they were aloft once more, gripped in the claws of another spell as it dragged them from the top of the tower and tossed them onto the ground at Otmar's feet. Dazed, her eyes sought Sigimar.

He wasn't moving.

She righted herself, her shoulder ablaze with pain.

Something was wrong. An image was laid out before her, one her mind refused to translate into meaning, into sense. One her eyes refused to see. Sigimar wasn't groaning or shifting—he wasn't breathing.

Her love—her life—had a hole in his chest where his heart should be.

"No!" She choked on her denial.

Ignoring the fury of the fae royals, she crawled to his side, screaming and sobbing as her world crashed and burned around her. Again. Her love was gone. Again. Her future had turned to ashes. Again. Everything she'd fought for was pointless without him. She howled her denials into the freezing, whipping winds as the snow beneath her husband was stained crimson. She begged him to stay, to open his eyes.

"Together. You promised me we'd be together," she whispered into his blood-soaked tunic.

But he could not answer.

Sigimar was dead.

"Cut off his head to make sure the elvish mongrel can't regenerate, and be done with it. We'll strip the tower of its treasures and go to Faerie. The ancient pact will be dissolved soon enough, and the Riverlands will turn on us in earnest. There's nothing for us here," Asta sighed as she stood, the picture of health.

Asta had been on death's door but a moment before. But gone were the open, gaping wounds on her arms, gone were the founts of blood, her weak, reedy voice and her trembling limbs.

Hypatia's heart stuttered in her chest. Sigimar's heart was gone, but he still had his head. *There was still hope.*

Drest said he'd needed the hearts to save Sara if the birth threatened her life.

But he hadn't asked for the hearts during their exchange. Drest hadn't needed them. He'd taken some from the tower.

Hearts.

Plural.

If Otmar had plunged one into Asta's chest, that left one within her grasp. She had to have it, no matter what. She would not go on without Sigimar. Her child would not grow up never knowing his love, his warmth, and neither would she. Hypatia refused to grow old without him by her side.

Sweating from pain and heart racing, Hypatia grabbed hold of the dagger at her waist and made it invisible, straining to keep hold of the spell in her state.

"It would be my pleasure," Otmar replied, setting his sights on her as more malevolent magic swirled around his fingers. "But for all the misery you've caused me, you'll die slowly. I think a disembowelling is in order."

As he stood over her, a sneer on his blue lips, the ground rumbled. It nearly knocked Otmar off balance. It was all the distraction she needed. She lunged, sinking the blade deep into Otmar's leg, slicing through the tough leather of his boots, embedding it in bone. Crying out, he fell over.

Hypatia pounced on top of him, wrestling as she fought back tears of pain, desperate to find the second heart. Frenzy made her clumsy, but at last her fingers closed around a hard object in his cloak pocket. When he finally threw her off, she refused to let it go, rolling through the mud and snow a few paces from Sigimar.

The ground shook again, this time widening the fissures that had formed with Asta's portal.

"Mother, we need to leave—now!" Farohildis screamed.

Otmar cried out as he pulled the blade from his ankle, limping towards his wife with Farohildis' aid. Asta took a knife from her hip and slit her flesh, her blood pouring from the wounds. She formed a blade of blood and stabbed into the air, arms trembling, struggling as she tore through worlds once more. Horrible rending sounds competed with the ominous rumbles of the earth.

Hypatia crawled to Sigimar, desperate for one last chance to save him.

A pair of pink, embroidered leather boots stood in her path. Hypatia looked up. Farohildis stared down at her with a wrath that transformed her face from pretty to bone-chilling. In her hand, she held the stave.

"We're not leaving empty-handed," she hissed as the stave began to glow blue.

She was going to rip out Hypatia's soul.

The rumble intensified, turning into a deafening roar. More fissures formed. The ground exploded in a geyser of rock and dirt. As dark earth was thrown up like a plume, Farohildis was distracted.

Hypatia grabbed Farohildis' ankle and pulled her off balance, scrabbling over her to reach Sigimar as a corruption-cursed dragon's head burst through the ground. Without daring to pause, Hypatia stabbed the jagged, crystalline heart into the hole in Sigimar's chest.

Out of the corner of her eye, the monster reared up, a mess of barbed tentacles, bone and thousands of snapping jaws. Its ear-piercing shriek carried across the plain as it began flaking away in the daylight.

Otmar's light burned bright, painting the scene in front of her in vivid, horrifying detail. Farohildis' scream pierced Hypatia's ears as she crawled away from her family in her panic. Hypatia flinched as the beast's barbed tentacle snagged Farohildis first, dragging her towards its largest mouth. Otmar's howl of rage brought Hypatia's attention back to him, his magic dissolving the beast's tentacle, freeing Farohildis. The princess limped to her mother as the beast turned its attention to Otmar. Dread and hope mingled in her chest as its horns and the jaws along its spine dissipated in the sun. Would it be enough to destroy the beast, to save them from its ferocious hunger? Would fighting it be enough to drain Otmar of his reserves, to give Sigimar a chance to recover so they could run? But that nascent hope died a swift death when the monster plunged its open maw down on Otmar, swallowing him whole.

Hypatia gasped. All wasn't lost yet. Asta's portal! Maybe she could drag Sigimar through it.

But it was not to be.

Asta dragged herself and Farohildis through her portal, sealing it a moment later.

There was nowhere left for them to run.

In spite of the sun, in spite of Otmar's magic, the beast wasn't dead yet. Tentacles sloughed off, jaws open in feral screams melted away—and still it hunted. Not even certain death was enough to overcome its driving hunger.

Sigimar gasped, eyes flicking wildly. Her heart leapt. Then sank. She'd brought him back, just to die again. Tears fell anew as she flung herself across his body, pressing her face into his neck and shone her light, using every last reserve of magic and strength she possessed.

"I love you," she cried in his ear.

"Wherever you go, I follow," he called back, arms gripping her tight.

The beast dove, oozing, flaking maw wide open, row upon row of serrated teeth poised to skewer them. A hollow roar deafened her.

Hypatia closed her eyes for the end.

One that did not come.

When she dared open her eyes, what remained of the dragon collapsed on its side and rolled back into the dark depths from which it had sprung. The crashing of its giant body down the fissure echoed out onto the plain.

In the silence that followed, Hypatia simply listened to the sound of Sigimar breathing, heart breaking and mending anew with every beat of his pulse against her cheek. She didn't know how long they lay like that, just listening to the sound of each other's breath.

"We're alive," she marvelled.

"We are." He sounded just as astonished.

"How?"

"Your magic...it dissolved the dragon."

She wept tears of joy, clutching him tighter.

"Let's never do this again," she whispered into his chest with a choked sob.

Sigimar's howl of laughter healed the broken, jagged edges of her battered heart.

"Never again," he agreed, pulling her close and kissing her hair.

"Tia!" At Kosta's voice, she pulled herself up. He stood atop the tower, rumpled and wild-eyed, waving with Agnetha at his side, her skin streaked with soot. "Are you alright? What did we miss?" he asked.

Only two harrowing battles, several feats of epic bravery and the threat of death many times over. But as she looked into Sigimar's eyes, the horrors receded until he was the whole of her heart, banishing the darkness. An answering love shone in the amber depths as he cupped her cheek. They had a future now, a child on the way, a kingdom's worth of artefacts to uncover, and a bond that not even death had defeated. She knew now that no matter what happened next, they would have each other.

"Should we finish this?" Sigimar asked, a twinkle in his eye.

"As long as we're together."

"Always," he vowed.

A vow he sealed with a kiss.

Epilogue

Sigimar wished Dag were there to see it as he crushed the last of the foul staves into a hundred splintered fragments. He closed his eyes and raised his face skyward, letting the splinters fall from his palms. Today, the sun shone on the whole of Ashla for the first time in millennia. The curse was fully lifted. Every relic of the Wild Hunt was gone. The impossible had been accomplished in less than a month.

Hypatia slipped her hand into his.

"Is it truly over?" she asked.

"Yes," he sighed. No more curses. No more dangerous adventures. No more risking the life of the person most precious to him. Would Dag have been pleased? Sigimar hoped so.

Agnetha was already commandeering the last of the uncovered Frey-devices, weaving a complex spell to prevent the discovery and use of the artefacts by anyone she deemed unworthy. All that remained was to return to their home and live the lives they'd earned. A life of peace, filled with discovery and family.

"Sigimar, you don't think... Erlendr will demand we partake in another celebration, do you?" Hypatia asked, a certain dread creeping into her words.

Sigimar fought a smile.

"Once he's done yelling at us like misbehaving children? I don't think it would be possible to avoid it."

"Oh..." Her cheeks heated.

"Never fear. If you cannot contain your need for me this time, I'll be sure to find some private corner to satisfy you *before* you tear our clothes off."

"Oh! You're a beastly man!" Hypatia scowled.

"As long as I'm *your* beastly man, that's all I need." He raised her hand to his lips.

"Always," she whispered.

He'd been so foolish, thinking that the greatest thing he could achieve was glory and, later, that the best thing he could do with his life was to sacrifice it. There was no greater joy, no greater adventure, no greater wonder than the woman at his side, in knowing her love, and loving her in turn. He didn't need titles or fame, just Hypatia and the life they now, finally, had all the time to live. It was a life he desired more fiercely than anything in all his days. Sigimar wanted every day to be filled with her, with laughter, with promises for more. He didn't want to surrender his life as a noble sacrifice to ensure her happiness; he wanted to live it and be the one putting a smile on her face, the one she could lean on, the one she could depend on to be there—forever.

"Hypatia?"

"Yes?"

Sigimar reached into his pocket where, miraculously, the red cloth gifted by Erlendr still rested. He pulled it out and presented it to her, wrinkled and battered though it was.

"I asked you before to allow me to share my years with you. Back then, you rightly refused. I wanted to be the kind of man you needed, whose first instinct was not to die for you but to live for you, except I was still convinced that only by sacrificing myself would I be truly worthy of you—that it was all I had to offer. I didn't truly understand what you needed then. But I think I do now." Sigimar knelt before her and cupped her cheeks in his hands, searching her beautiful grey eyes as they misted with tears. "I need you more than my next breath. You are my light, my warmth, my heart. There is nothing in this world that can compare to the thought of waking every morning to you, and spending our lives buried in ancient texts while we watch our family grow. I love you, and I will fight with all that I am to protect our future together. Hypatia, will you share my life with me?"

She nodded her head, tears streaming down her face as she smiled. Her fingers interlaced with his own.

"Yes, Sigimar."

His heart felt like it might burst from his chest. Sigimar tied the strip of red cloth, binding their wrists. He felt as if some string leading directly to the very centre of him was pulled tight. Magic tugged at him. At the same moment, Hypatia gasped, her free hand pressing against her chest. Magic completed, the cloth disintegrated.

Their lives were now forever bound.

They would have the chance to grow old together.

But before all that, there was something he was looking forward to.

"I believe you promised me something in that tower full of dragon hearts," he purred.

She batted her lashes at him, playing the innocent.

"Whatever could you mean?" she asked, sliding her hands down his chest.

"Ahem!" Kosta folded his arms, glaring with every ounce of displeasure he possessed. "Could you *please* not—"

Agnetha interrupted Kosta, a hand on his shoulder as she pulled him close to whisper in his ear. Whatever she said didn't carry, but made the mage's face flame and his eyes darken.

"Go on then. I'll be waiting." The sorceress smiled in a way that left no doubt as to her intent.

"Right." Kosta cleared his throat. "I'll take you two lovebirds home."

"Kosta, must you always inter—" Hypatia began. Before she could finish, he'd teleported them to their tower and was gone just as quickly. She sighed. "He didn't even let me chastise him."

"I suspect he has more pressing matters to attend to," Sigimar snickered.

"Yes, well, I suppose we do, too." She bit her bottom lip, her eyes hooded. "Take me to our room."

As much as Sigimar loved pleasing his wife, they didn't make it more than a few steps before they crashed into the nearest unoccupied chamber and clothes were being torn apart. The door slid shut just as they tumbled to the floor, bodies entwined. He tormented her as passionately as she did him, until neither had the strength to stand. Lying together, no longer certain where one ended and the other began, he turned to her as she drifted off in his arms.

There was no sweeter fate than being tied to her, now and forever. Let her heart and his be bound for eternity.

"You entangle my very soul," he whispered.

"And you are the home of my heart." She kissed his chest, her hand over his.

Just as she was the home his heart had long craved.

This might be the very best day of his life, he reflected as she dozed next to him. But then, who knew for certain what fate would bring? With Hypatia at his side, with a child on the way, he suspected an even brighter future awaited them.

It was a gift—a life—he planned on treasuring the rest of his days.

I hope you've enjoyed Hypatia and Sigimar's story. Want to find out where they're headed next? Sign up to my newsletter for a bonus epilogue featuring our intrepid couple as they visit Lethe and meet Empress Selene and Emperor Belisarius: https://twolaurelspress.eo.page/jpchy

If you're craving more epic fantasy romance, check out my other books here on my website: https://www.elysethomson.com/#books

If you'd like to dip your toe into a new world, check out my next series where an archaeologist turned chosen one is forced to battle against both a primordial monster and her feelings for a doomed, seductive king in *The Oracle of Dusk* here: https://books2read.com/ood

Thanks so much for reading, and don't forget to leave a review! https://linktr.ee/elysethomson

Afterword

This was probably the most difficult book I've ever written. When I began, I decided to delve deep into my own experiences with grief to write my characters' struggles as authentically as possible, but this came with an unexpected toll. I hope that in writing this, I have let others dealing with grief and mental health issues know that you are seen, that you are the heroes of your own stories, and that even in the darkest of places, there is hope. To all my readers, I ask that whenever you can, be that beacon of hope for those around you.

As you may or may not know, reviews are really important to authors, especially those just beginning their careers. If you would be so kind as to leave a review for Isles of Corruption on Goodreads and your book retailer like Amazon, I would be extremely grateful!

If you haven't already, check out my other books. https://www.ely-sethomson.com/#books

If you've read all that and you're hungry for more, you're in luck! A bonus epilogue for *Isles of Corruption* is available for my newsletter subscribers. https://twolaurelspress.eo.page/jpchy

Book Links

Acknowledgements

No book is made without the love and support of a great many people. Isles of Corruption was no different. I have so many people to thank. Paulina and Sophia, for reading the roughest first draft. Alex, for being my rock through the whole whirlwind journey. My family; Mom, Dad, Sylvia, Ross, Kyle, Garrett and Jen for never doubting me. The best writing friends a girl could have (with a group name so lackluster, it doesn't bear repeating) Sophia, Rachel, Asha, Rebecca and Shirley. You kept me sane and gave me a place to belong. My life is richer for having known all of you. And finally, my friends in Pitch'n'Bitch, you always make me smile.

Special thanks to my amazing editors, Rachel Le Mesurier and Edie, my talented map maker Alec McKinley and my lovely cover designer, Maria Spada.

ABOUT THE AUTHOR

Elyse Thomson is the pen-name of author, bookbinder and self-proclaimed hermit residing in Canada's capital. She writes escapist fantasy with daring heroines, magical mayhem, swoon-worthy romance and court intrigue. Having graduated from University of Toronto with a Bachelors in History and Classics, she is delighted to bring her love of all things ancient to her work. When not writing, she's restoring antiquarian books for a select group of clients, gaming, or snuggling up with either her husband or her neurotic terrier, Freya.

If you would like to know about the author and the release of the next books, or be the first to get access to exclusive snippets and other goodies, visit the website or join the newsletter.

Also By

Mages of Oblivion Series
The Firetongue Heir
Poisoned Empire
Conspirators' Kingdom
Isles of Corruption

Cycle of Calamity Series
The Starlight Princess
The Oracle of Dusk
The Midnight King
...and more to come.

Book Links